SEDUCTION

"You have no choice in the matter, love," Helena said. "It is I who mean to seduce you. You cannot be so boorish as to refuse a lady's request, can you?"

He took his hand away. "I'm a rake, my dear. I promised not to ruin your reputation. I gave your brother-in-law my word on it. You are an innocent, Helena. Don't force me into taking advantage of your innocence."

She shoved his hand away when he attempted to refasten her bodice. "Reputation be damned, Waverley. I want you. Doesn't that count for anything? I thought you felt the same for me."

His mocking words cut like a knife. "I have feelings of lust for every pretty lass who comes my way. I have a reputation to uphold, you see."

"Is that all I am to you? Just another pretty lass? Don't you want me?"

"Want you? Don't tempt me any further, love, lest the consequences destroy us both. . . ."

Books by Pearl Wolf

TOO HOT FOR A SPY

TOO HOT FOR A RAKE

Published by Kensington Publishing Corporation

Too Hot For a Rake

Pearl Wolf

ZEBRA BOOKS
KENSINGTON PUBLISHING CORP.
http://www.kensingtonbooks.com

ZEBRA BOOKS are published by

Kensington Publishing Corp.
119 West 40th Street
New York, NY 10018

All Kensington titles, imprints, and distributed lines are avail-
able at special quantity discounts for bulk purchases for sales
promotion, premiums, fund-raising, educational, or institu-
tional use.

Special book excerpts or customized printings can also be created to fit specific needs. For details, write or phone the office
of the Kensington Special Sales Manager: Attn. Special Sales
Department. Kensington Publishing Corp., 119 West 40th
Street, New York, NY 10018. Phone: 1-800-221-2647.

Zebra and the Z logo Reg. U.S. Pat. & TM Off.

ISBN-13: 978-1-4201-0481-3
ISBN-10: 1-4201-0481-0

First Printing: April 2010

10 9 8 7 6 5 4 3 2 1

Printed in the United States of America

To Evan Marshall

ACKNOWLEDGMENTS

It has been my privilege to work with Kensington Editor-in-Chief John Scognamiglio, who guides my manuscripts so expertly through the publishing process. On the way, he's taught me to be a better writer and for this he earns my respect and my gratitude.

I also owe a great deal to my critique partner Shelley Freydont, for her insights and her unfailing support in a million ways.

Ohio surgeon Dr. Rick Nedelman gives freely of his time when I post my medical questions about injuries from duels and such. Bless the man!

I like to think I am meticulous in my research, particularly since this is a historical romance. Still, the best of us make mistakes. If you find any in this work, be sure to let me know and please accept my apologies.

—*Pearl Wolf*
Web: www.pearlwolf.com
Email: pwpearlwolf@gmail.com

Prologue

Paris: Sunday, the Twenty-second of March, 1818

A young Englishman stepped out of the hired chaise, his face at once assaulted by the icy March winds. He shuddered against the inhospitable cold that bit into him and raised his eyes to the formidable facade of Le Chabanais.

To keep his beaver hat from blowing away, he held it firmly in place as he climbed the steps of the building, an establishment that took its name from its location: 12 rue Chabanais. He raised the knocker on the door, let it fall and waited. One eye appeared through a small hole.

"I've come to see Lord Bannington. Is he at home?" He pressed his calling card to the hole.

The door opened a crack and a hand snaked out to snatch the card from him. "I shall inquire if monsieur is at home."

When the door clanked shut, the man had to content himself with stamping his feet to keep from freezing. He raised his fist to bang the knocker again, but the ponderous oaken door swung open.

"Entréz, s'il vous plait, monsieur." The man led him through a dimly lit hall that opened into a large room where

the visitor was at once blinded by the blaze of hundreds of candles.

He handed his coat, hat, muffler and gloves to a footman and surveyed the scene. The mirrored room was the size of a large London ballroom. Its walls were lined with red banquettes. Young ladies in various states of undress lounged on them, apparently awaiting the arrival of male clientele, a reasonable assumption considering the nature of the business conducted at 12 rue Chabanais. Someone behind him tapped a fan on his shoulder. He turned, startled by the astonishing sight of a tall, buxom woman of a certain age. She wore a low-cut black gown studded with crystals, long white gloves and a black lace mantilla attached to her hair, powdered in the French fashion.

"Monsieur? Welcome to Le Chabanais. I am Madame Z'evareau. How may I serve you? Our salon offers the finest young ladies in Paris. But you can see that for yourself. How many of our ladies would you like this evening? One, two, more?"

He took the hand she offered and bent to brush his lips over it, a gesture she appeared to expect. "No, madame. I am not here to be entertained this evening. I seek an audience with Lord Bannington. He resides here, does he not?"

"Ah, oui. Le roué Anglais. He is our guest. The dear boy may be occupied at the moment, however. Allow me to inquire." She turned and said to a young lady nearby, "Entertain the gentleman, Cecelie." She hurried off, Darlington's card in hand.

"What is your pleasure?" Cecelie asked him. In spite of her painted rouged cheeks, charcoaled eyelids and short red hair, she could not have been more than sixteen. She wore a sheer white chemise over long black stockings and red high-heeled shoes.

"I'm not here for your services, mademoiselle. I've come to see Lord Bannington." He resisted the urge to loosen his neck cloth.

The harlot giggled. "You are a friend of *le roué Anglais?* Then there shall be no charge, monsieur. He pays for all his friends." She reached up to kiss him on the lips, but Darlington restrained her.

"You do not like Cecelie? Perhaps you would prefer another . . . ?"

To his relief, Madame Z'evareau returned, saving him from further embarrassment.

"Lord Bannington will see you now. Follow me, if you please."

He tried to ignore the snickers he heard and the lascivious ogling that followed him as he made his way past the red banquettes, but he reddened just the same.

"Pay no attention to my girls, monsieur. Sunday evenings are always thin of visitors here at Le Chabanais. Our clientele prefer to remain at home with their families, you see. My little cocottes work hard all week. One must allow them the release of a bit of naughty mischief on Sundays." She led him up the red-carpeted grand staircase to the first chamber on the left and knocked on the door.

"Come," a deep male voice said as she opened the door. "Thank you, Madame Z. You may leave us. Come in Darlington. Have we met before? I can't recall, for I have an atrocious memory. Shocking, but there it is."

Desmond Bannington had dark hair streaked with hints of the sun and blue eyes the color of the sea. His lordship lounged on a large bed in the middle of the room. He wore nothing save loose black silk pantaloons, but the women in his bed wore nothing at all. His head reclined on the breasts of a young girl whose fingers played with his long curls. Another was trimming his nails while a third massaged his feet. Embarrassed, Darlington allowed his gaze to wander over his lordship's opulent surroundings, his eyes fixing everywhere but on the bed.

The chamber was large, its walls lined in red silk. The

floors were covered with a carpet of Turkish design. The ceiling revealed a scene filled with curvaceous women engaged in sensual couplings, and over the bed itself, a mirror the length and width of the bed was prominent. Opposite the headboard there stood a large desk and chair. Beyond that, a huge stone fireplace faced the footboard, two comfortable chairs on either side, a round table between them. A settee facing the fireplace completed the sitting area.

"What do you think of my home, Darlington?" asked Bannington, much amused by the scandalized expression on the face of his visitor. "I prefer to live here, you know. Meets all my needs most conveniently."

"Handsome surroundings, but as marquis—"

"Marquis? Why do you address me thus? I am Lord Bannington. I have had no other name for these past twelve years."

"So I have been informed, my lord."

"Why have you come? Who sent you?"

"I must insist upon speaking with you alone, your lordship."

"Pay no attention to my playmates. None of them understand the English tongue. What is it you want of me?"

"My mission is too sensitive. Privacy is essential, your lordship."

A condescending grin met Darlington's plea. "As bad as all that, eh?" He turned to his companions. "All right, my lovelies. Party's over." He kissed each one in turn. "Amelié. Babette. Colette. Be off with you, my delectable ABCs. I'll send for you later," he said, lightly patting each one on the derrière after each kissed him adieu.

When the giggling trio put on their robes and danced out the door, Waverley said, "You shall join me for dinner, old chap. The food's excellent, and I am starving." He rang and at once a small brown man appeared as if from nowhere. He wore a turban, a yellow satin coat, black tights and shoes with turned-up toes.

"Dinner for two, Rabu. Tell Madame Z we should like two bottles of her best wine and some French brandy."

"Yes, mastah!" As he bowed his head, he almost touched the tips of his shoes.

"You seem shocked, Darlington. This is my valet Rabu. I lived in India for years, you see. The little devil adopted me there and I cannot rid myself of him no matter how hard I try. One must be gracious in defeat, mustn't one?" He rose from his bed as he spoke, donned a dressing gown and slid his feet into slippers.

"Le Chabanais is the finest bordello in Paris, you know, which is why I choose to live here. It is well known for its cuisine, thanks to Madame Z's outstanding chef. Let us sit by the fire, sir. You can tell me your business after we finish our dinner." Waverley sprawled in a seat opposite Darlington and took some snuff from an ornate box resting on the small table beside his chair.

In spite of himself, Darlington enjoyed every bit of the French cuisine, the delicious food a rare treat for him. The first course was a delicate turtle soup. The second was a ragout of beef, which proved to be succulent. The meal ended with a chocolate soufflé that defied description. When Rabu cleared the last of the dirty dishes, he set the brandy on the table along with a bowl of nuts and some fruit.

"Leave us," said Bannington, dismissing his valet with a wave of his hand. He waited for Rabu to disappear through a side door. "We are alone now, sir. What brings you to Paris?"

"I have been searching for you for almost a year, your lordship. I am an envoy from the home office, sent to find you."

"Really? What can the home office possibly want with an expatriate like me?"

Ignoring this for the moment, Darlington said, a hint of frustration in his tone, "I made my way to India to seek you, but you had already left that country."

"Ah, India. I lived in Calcutta for ten years. It is where I made my fortune, more to luck than to business acumen, I might add."

"You led me a merry chase all over Europe, my lord. My search led me to Greece, Italy, and Spain, all to no avail."

His host's brow furrowed. "Come to the point, Darlington. Why were you sent to seek me out?"

"Prince George, our Regent, most urgently requests your return to England, my lord."

Waverley was amused by the young man's pompous turn of phrase, but he ignored it. "The Regent? How is this?"

"The Third Marquis of Waverley, your father, passed away a year ago. His Majesty is anxious for you to return to take his place."

Bannington's eyes widened. "Then I am the Fourth Marquis of Waverley?" He laughed, a sound tinged with resentment.

"Sir?"

"If my father knew I was being summoned home to England to take his place, he would rise from his grave to protest, for there was no love lost between us. This is the first communication I've had from him since he disowned me twelve years ago. Inform Prince George that I renounce my right to the marquisate. I have no reason to return, for I have fashioned a life in Paris that suits me well. I have many friends here, and none in England. Besides, there is no longer anyone alive at Waverley Castle now that my father is dead." *Now that my father is dead, there is no longer any opportunity for reconciliation, though God knows I tried more than once during my long exile.*

"You mistake, my lord. Your grandmother is alive. Her ladyship lives at Waverley Castle."

Thunderstruck by this news, Bannington turned pale. "My grandmother is still alive? You can't be serious. I thought she died years ago."

"No, my lord. Your grandmother is eighty years old and very much alive."

"Is she being well cared for?"

"I can't answer that question, my lord. Six months ago, distant cousins took up residence at Waverley, to care for your grandmother."

"Their names?"

"Mrs. Jennie Trasker and her son Harry."

"Never heard of them. How do you come by all this information, Darlington?"

"My information comes from the intelligence division of the home office. It is entirely reliable, though not public knowledge, my lord. I must urge you to reconsider and accept the marquisate, for the sake of England if not for your grandmother. If you do not, Harry Trasker is next in line. My information is that he is ill equipped to take your father's place."

Bannington stared into the embers in the fireplace as if they held the answer for him. *Grandmother alive? Does she still love the lad I once was or did my unforgiving father forbid her to communicate with me? All these years I thought I had no family. Now I have a grandmother and two cousins. I must return, if only for her sake. A gamble, to be sure, but no worse than the risks I've been forced to take all my life. Waverley Castle. I loved it well once.* Aloud he said, "If I decide to return, what then?"

Darlington relaxed for the first time, for this was his area of expertise. "When you return to London, you will find a warm welcome awaiting you. Viscount Sidmouth, the home secretary, is most anxious to welcome you. You may count on him to counsel you in light of this . . . delicate situation."

"Delicate? Have you been withholding something from me? Is my grandmother in any danger?"

"I have not been so informed, but I cannot say for a certainty."

Desmond again stared into the fire, struggling with his conscience. He recalled a gentle lady who loved him well. At last he spoke. "If my grandmother is alive, I have no choice but to return to England."

The envoy looked relieved. "It is my duty to escort you to London for your investiture by the Regent. How soon can you be ready to leave, your lordship?"

Bannington's brow cleared and he smiled. "How long have you been searching for me?"

"I've been away from my home for more than a year."

"Have you a wife? Family?"

"No, your lordship. But I am betrothed."

"I wish you happy, old chap. All right. I'll be ready as soon as may be."

"Appreciate it, sir."

"I need time to wind up my affairs here. Shouldn't take more than a few days at the most. Will that do?"

"Yes, of course. With your permission, I'll arrange for a carriage to take us to Calais, where I can book our passage to Dover."

"Order two carriages, one for Rabu and all my possessions and one for the two of us. Which reminds me. I haven't any place to stay. I have no idea whether my father's London domicile is habitable and hotels frown on my little Indian, which makes me uncomfortable. Any suggestions?"

"I would be honored if you were to accept my hospitality, your lordship. You may stay as long as you need to arrange your affairs. I live in Mayfair, an easy ride to Carlton House where you shall meet with the Prince Regent."

"You are an excellent fellow, Darlington. I accept your offer."

Chapter 1

Lady Helena Fairchild shivered in anticipation as she stole across the lawn. The night was misted in fog. Only the dim glow of the street lamps pierced the gloom. She paused in the shadows of the familiar oak tree and stopped to listen. When she heard no sounds from within or without the town house, she gathered her silk gown, tucked it into her pantalets, turned and climbed the tree.

With customary ease, she slithered along a sturdy branch that led to the balcony. Her hands and feet found purchase on the ornate grillwork and she let go of the tree limb. It snapped back with such a loud crack, she froze, waited a heart-stopping moment, and then eased herself over the balustrade. The door was ajar. She stepped into Darlington's chamber and waited for her eyes to adjust to the dark.

She followed the sound of gentle snores coming from the bed a few steps away. The drapes were not drawn, for the night was warm, one of those rare April nights that made the air feel as if it were already the middle of May. Her fingers trembled as she loosened the ribbons of her bodice. She pushed both sleeves off her shoulders and shifted her gown to undo the back buttons. It slipped from her hips and fell to the floor. She removed her chemise and her pantalets. A shock of cold air bruised her nude body. An irregular mountain of discarded clothing rested on the Aubusson rug.

There was no turning back now. She lifted the quilt and climbed into his bed. A small smile curved her lips when she noted that he favored the right side of the bed when he slept. That was a good sign, for she favored the left.

Though the erratic pounding of her heart seemed too loud to her ears, Chris didn't stir. She touched him. His arm was strong and warm and firm. How muscular he had become since she had seen him last. Was it only a year? His brawny body filled her with wonder. He turned, pulling the quilt with him. It slid to the floor on his side of the bed. Her eyes widened in astonishment, for he wore nothing. *Where is his nightshirt?*

She hesitated, trapped between panic and curiosity. Curiosity won. She dared to stroke his back with a feathery touch. Her hand trailed down to his buttocks and came to rest on one dimpled cheek. He sighed. She pulled her hand away, caught between fear of waking him and hope. She waited a few seconds and touched again, astonished at her own boldness.

She hadn't expected the spark of electricity that tore through her. When a beam of moonlight ran across his body, she raised herself on one elbow and rested her chin on her hand. She studied his body, unable to believe her good fortune. Once scrawny, the boy she fell in love with when she was still in the schoolroom had grown into a powerfully built man.

Darlington turned and flung an arm across her chest, sending her flat on her back. His hand came to rest on one breast, causing her nipples to pucker. When the rhythm of his breathing gentled and her heart ceased its knocking, she lifted his wrist and placed his arm by his side. The moon skittered behind a cloud, plunging the room into darkness.

Helena dared to spread her fingers through the curled hairs on his chest, her fingers trailing down to his navel. She steeled her resolve and explored further. Her hand wandered down to the mound of hair below his waist. She stopped when he threw one leg over her thighs and pinned her to the bed with one arm. His head settled on one breast as if he'd found his pillow. After allowing herself a moment of bliss, she moved his head away and resumed her exploration of his body.

She touched something soft and allowed herself a tiny smile. When his manhood began to engorge, she started to jerk her hand away, but his shot out and kept hers where it was. If he woke now, surely he would willingly seduce . . .

The door to the hallway flew open and a blinding light transformed the chamber into bright daylight. They had been discovered! Chris would be forced to marry her now. She had but a moment's regret. They hadn't had time to complete their lovemaking.

"Have I woken you? What's wrong, Waverley? I heard a noise."

Chris? But who's this in his bed? Helena hid her head under the pillow. A voice fogged in sleep said, "That you, Darlington?"

Darlington banged the door shut behind him and set the candelabra down. "Have you lost your senses, my lord? How dare you seduce one of my maids. I never expected a guest in my home to behave in such a fashion."

Desmond sat up and rubbed the sleep from his eyes. "Maid? What maid?"

"Get out of bed, lass, and return to your room at once."

She whimpered at the anger in his voice.

"Oh, for heaven's sake, don't cry. Do as I say. I promise not to sack you."

Christopher Darlington wore his dressing gown, having had no time for proper attire in the middle of the night. His blond hair was uncombed and lay limp, a few strands pasted to his forehead. Myopic gray eyes squinted at the bed's inhabitants.

Helena drew in her breath, lifted one corner of the pillow, and said meekly, "I'm not a maid, Chris. It's me."

Thundering silence met her words. Darlington's gray eyes squinted at her, for he was nearsighted and far too vain to use his spectacles except when absolutely necessary.

His hand shook as he fumbled in his pocket for his spectacles. When he jammed them on his nose, he found his voice and said, "Helena? What are you doing here? Cover yourself, for heaven's sake!"

The marquis felt as if he were a spectator at a melodrama. The leading lady enchanted him, for she had the body and the face of an angel. Her skin was bronze, her eyes shone like two obsidians, and her hair bounced in a crown of dark, burnished curls.

"Um. I can explain." Her head swiveled in her search for the quilt, but it was out of sight.

Waverley reached for the fallen cover and threw it over them both. His eyes met hers with a questioning intensity that made her turn red. "I await your explanation with interest, ma'am."

Helena sat up and clutched the quilt to her bosom. Distracted by the sight of his dark, sun-streaked hair and startling blue eyes, she managed to glare at him. "I thought that *he* was *you,* Chris. What's this . . . rake doing in your bed?"

The marquis managed to mask his laugh with a cough.

Chris ignored her question. "Collect your clothing and get dressed at once, Helena."

She swung her legs off the bed and attempted to yank the cover with her, but Waverley held his end in a firm grip. "Oh no you don't. Not before my host hands me my dressing gown."

Darlington glanced around him, found Waverley's robe on

the back of a chair, and launched it toward the bed as if it were the main sail of a ship.

The marquis let go of his end of the quilt when he rose, and Helena fell off the bed, quilt and all.

"Cur," she grumbled as she wrapped the quilt around her. She said, "Turn your heads!" She held the quilt with one hand, gathered her clothing with the other and sidled across the room toward the dressing screen.

When she emerged a few moments later, she turned her head from Chris to Waverley and back to Chris. She jutted her chin out. "How is it that this *rake* is occupying your bed chamber?"

"You chose the wrong chamber," growled Darlington. "This is the guest chamber. The Marquis of Waverley is my guest."

Oh dear! Was I in bed with a marquis? Her heart sank at the mortification.

"You owe me an apology, Darlington," Waverley drawled, examining his fingernails. "The young lady is most certainly not one of your maids. Indeed, she woke me from a deep sleep." He turned to Helena and added, "You needn't blush, ma'am. I merely supposed I was in the midst of a delightful dream." He stretched, yawned and ran his fingers through his hair.

"A nightmare, more like!" she said bitterly.

His eyes danced with amusement. "Allow me to assure you, ma'am, that nothing drastic occurred. You were not violated, ma'am. Not by me, in any event."

Nothing drastic occurred? What of your engorgement? What of the heat that seared my loins? You call that nothing, you cad? "Why is the marquis here, Chris?"

Waverley took a step toward her, picked up her hand and kissed it. "Darlington was kind enough to offer me his hospitality, ma'am."

"Don't touch me." She drew her hand away.

Darlington stepped between them. "How did you get in here, Helena?"

She glanced at the open door to the balcony.

"You climbed the oak tree? You're not a child anymore. You might have fallen and broken your neck."

"Would you care to make an introduction, Darlington?"

"Sorry, my lord. This is Lady Helena Fairchild, my betro . . . my next door neighbor."

"Pleasure, Lady Helena Fairchild." Waverley made an exaggerated leg.

Helena cast her eyes down. "How do you do, Lord Waverley," she murmured, appalled at what she'd done to this man, at the embarrassing places her hands had been, at how readily he had responded. At how much pleasure she'd felt.

"It isn't polite to stare," said the marquis, his eyes filled with amusement.

"My apologies, sir. For . . . for calling you a rake."

"Accepted, ma'am."

Chris interrupted. "I'm waiting for you to give me your explanation, Helena."

"Nothing happened, Darlington," repeated the marquis.

"He's right, Chris. I haven't been compromised."

"I beg to differ! The mere act of being in bed with a naked man is enough to be deemed a compromise."

"Is it indeed?" she challenged hotly. "The fault is yours, then, for having driven me to this desperate act." Her breath exploded in anguished bursts. "We need to talk, Chris. In private."

"Lord Waverley will excuse us, I'm sure."

Waverley held the door open for them. "Pleasure to meet you, ma'am."

Before Helena could make some biting retort, Darlington grabbed her by the elbow and attempted to push her toward the door, but she refused to budge.

"No, Chris. The servants . . ."

"They've all gone to bed. We'll finish this in the library."

Her heartbeat seemed to her loud enough for him to hear.

Finish this? What can he mean? Finish what? Her insides turned cold. They spoke not a word as he led her downstairs, but once inside the library, she broke the uneasy silence.

"Tonight was nothing more than a horrible mistake. I wanted to welcome you on the night of your return home, Chris. Besides, what difference can it make? Are we not to be married?"

Chris paced back and forth, hands clasped behind him. His eyes narrowed as he answered. "You don't know what you've done, do you? You don't even know who the marquis is, do you?"

"If he's a peer, he's a gentleman. He won't breathe a word of this."

"Oh, won't he? Waverley's bounced around Europe for years, ever since he left India. That's why it took me all year to find him. Do you know what they call him there? No. How could you?"

Helena recoiled at his fury. "You needn't shout at me. Well? What do they call him?"

"I found him at Madame Z's bordello, 12 rue Chabanais. A bordello! He chose to live there as a matter of convenience. When I asked for him, she laughed and said, '*Ah, oui. Le roué Anglais.*' I found him in bed with three young er . . . ladies. You can imagine my shock."

"Why had you sought him out?"

"I was sent to bring him home to England by order of the Regent."

"I see. And the marquis is known as the English rake in Europe? I've never heard of him. Perhaps his reputation isn't known here."

"If it isn't, it will be. Rumors travel like the waves across the English Channel. When it becomes known that you have been in bed with him, your reputation is ruined."

"Then we must marry at once. Make it right. You know I love you, Chris."

"Marry you? Ha! You've rendered that impossible! We're finished."

She turned ashen. "Finished? Am I to understand that you no longer wish to marry me?"

Chris forced a laugh. "How can I marry a woman who disgusts me? You destroyed all hope for our happiness when I saw you naked in bed with Waverley, like a common light skirt."

Helena searched his face. Was this the man she had loved since she was a child? Disillusionment assailed her. She said evenly, "Have you lost your desire to marry me? I cannot believe my ears."

"Believe that I'm done, Helena. You destroyed all hope for my marital happiness when you bedded the marquis. You know my ambition. I mean to become an ambassador for England one day. Your brash conduct has shown me that you can never be a proper wife for a man with a diplomatic career."

Had he battered her with a cudgel, he could not have wounded her more. Determined not to weep, she bit back her tears and said, "What a pretty speech, *My Lord Ambassador.* How noble of you to think of England before the woman who has loved you all these years."

He ignored her angry words and said, "In spite of what you may think at this moment, I'm a man of honor. I'll call on your father in the morning to inform him it is your decision to cry off. I don't intend to tell him why. Perhaps that will salvage your reputation. The duke is free to announce that it was you who broke it off. That way, you may still marry."

"No, Chris. I shan't ever marry. I won't put myself through the pain of loving and losing again, I promise you that." She whirled around and fled the library.

What a fool she'd made of herself. The man she loved no longer loved her. Her passion disgusted him, he'd said. What was wrong with wanting him that way? Wrong? Nothing, except she'd made love to the wrong man. *Why couldn't I make Chris understand that it wasn't lust? I did it for love. How ironic. What made me think I could be so bold? Livy's the adventurous sister. I'm not at all like her. All my hopes and dreams are gone. What is there left for me to live for?*

Helena hugged her arms as she flew across the lawn that separated their homes. The cold night air was chilly and damp. It cooled her flaming cheeks, yet nothing could ease the mortification of being discovered naked in bed with the wrong man. Tears formed in her eyes. Her soft-soled shoes skidded on the dew-covered grass and her arms flailed wildly before she regained her balance.

I wish I were dead! Tragically, she envisioned her funeral at the family crypt. The duke held her grieving mother close, his tears mingling with hers. Her brother Edward, grim faced, clasped his hands behind his back. Olivia leaned on her husband, Sebastian. Georgiana, Mary and Jane huddled together, sobbing for their sister's short life and her untimely death. Chris would receive the news and it would tear him apart. Hiccups of helpless rage welled up within her. *Serves him right!* She tried to think of something else, to rid herself of gloom.

The thought of Lord Waverley's warm body caused her to shiver, but the image faded only to be replaced by a disapproving Darlington, his eyes narrowed. He looked like the very devil.

Helena unlatched the gate and stepped onto her lawn. A single candle in her chamber held vigil in an upstairs window. A Great Dane loped out of the shadows, his tongue drooling as he panted. She bent and stuck out her hand to the pup. In it she held a bit of bacon she'd taken from her pocket. "Good boy. Come here, Prince."

The dog sniffed and snatched the bribe. She tiptoed across the lawn and stepped onto the terrace, her destination the

French doors leading into the library. The pup swallowed his treat and sped after her.

"Go away," she pleaded. Prince wagged his tail and waited for her to open the door. "I don't have any more treats, you traitor," she hissed. If she allowed him to enter the library, he would bound inside, bark in triumph, and rouse the whole household.

She made as if to throw a second treat in the opposite direction. "Go get it, Prince." The pup raced after it and the diversion gave her enough time to slip into the library. His ears perked up when he realized he'd been duped and he raced back toward her, but she managed to shut the door just before he could reach it. She tiptoed across the plush carpet and listened at the door, but all was quiet in the hallway.

When she reached her chamber, a lone candle on the mantel guttered. She drew in her breath at the sight of a familiar figure seated next to the fireplace, his forbidding eyes never wavering.

Helena's heart sank. "Father? What are you doing here?"

"It's past two in the morning, Helena. Where have you been?"

Chapter 2

Thursday, the Second of April, 1818

The Duke of Heatham intimidated lesser men, if not by his sheer size, then certainly by the power he inherited when his father died. At fifty-one years of age, the head of the House of Fairchild was often described as aristocratic. His grace had broad shoulders and slim hips. An athletic man, he stood six feet tall in stocking feet. His shock of black hair was beginning to gray at the temples and his penetrating brown eyes darkened when he was angry.

His grace had been prepared to issue a roaring scold to his daughter when she returned to her chamber, but he decided against it when she fell to her knees, buried her head in his lap and burst into tears. "Where have you been?" he repeated in a gentler tone.

"I'm so sorry, Father. I find this hard to tell you, but tell you I must. I'm such a failure."

"What do you mean, child?" The duke handed her a handkerchief. "Wipe your tears, Helena. You had better tell me the whole."

Helena did as she was told and drew in a deep breath. "Chris w . . . won't marry me. He's broken our betrothal."

His grace lifted her chin to meet her eyes. "Were you with him in his home without a chaperone?"

"Yes. Oh, what does it matter now? I'm ruined and it's my own fault. How could I have been so stupid? Help me, Father! What shall I do?"

Once again, the duke checked his desire to chastise his daughter, for her pain was all too evident. "What reason did he give, Helena?"

"He says I'm not proper enough to be the wife of a diplomat. He could not possibly marry me under the circumstances."

The duke frowned. "Circumstances? What were they?"

"He thought I behaved in an . . . unladylike fashion." She lifted her tear-stained eyes and said bitterly, "I can't tell you what passed between us. But I wouldn't have him as a husband now under any terms. Not after the terrible things he said to me tonight."

The duke stroked his chin. "You must explain this to me, Helena. I have no idea what you mean."

"Don't ask me to repeat this ugly tale, I beg of you. It will do you no good to hear it and only pain me the more. As it is, I haven't a shred of dignity left. I was full of joy at my beloved's homecoming just a few hours ago, when I knew who I was and what I was meant to be. My life is meaningless now. I feel so . . . empty. Help me, Father, for I've lost my way."

Having witnessed Lady Helena's departure from his window, Waverley made his way to the library. There he found Darlington draining a large glass of brandy. "Are you all right?"

"Allow me to apologize for Lady Helena's shocking behavior, Waverley."

"No need, Darlington. She thought she found you in my bed."

"And what did you think when you found a nude woman in your bed? Did you think I had provided you with the gift of a doxy to welcome you home to England? She had no right to do what she did, but neither did you."

"I won't deign to answer such a rude remark, Darlington. I had nothing to do with tonight's fiasco and you know it. Your anger is misplaced."

Waverley ignored the seething fury in his host's countenance and poured himself a brandy. *Perhaps I should have remained in Paris. Is this what I've come home to? Would a Frenchman rake me down like this? No, he'd be more likely to challenge me to a duel and join me for breakfast after the first harmless hit.*

He resisted the temptation to throttle his host. "The lady in question is in love with you, Darlington. Apparently, she appeared to be under the impression that you love her as well."

"Love her? Ha! Not anymore. A man needs a wife who comports herself respectably. Not some wanton hoyden filled with lust."

"You are mistaken. Lust is a part of love. That was clear, at least to me. Does that count for nothing to you?"

"If she really loved me, she would have remembered after all these years that I require a wife who behaves with decorum. Enough said, Waverley. I'm off to bed. I want some rest before I see his grace to tell him our betrothal has been terminated."

"What reason shall you give?"

"Oh, I'll tell him she's changed her mind. I'm too much of a gentleman to be the one to cry off."

Too much of a stiff-neck, I think. The lady's better off without your smug sense of morality. Let's hope she knows it.

"Goodnight, then," Waverley said and returned to his room. He climbed into bed, only to toss and turn. When it became clear to him that sleep was out of the question, he got up and began to dress. What was needed was a walk, he decided. It would take his mind off the trials ahead of him. He held his shoes in hand and stole quietly down the stairs.

The fog had lifted and the sun was beginning to light the treetops when he caught sight of a suspicious figure emerging from a side window of the mansion next door. The figure reached back inside the window and pulled out some sort of bundle. A thief. No doubt about it, he thought, as the culprit dropped the bundle to the ground and sprang nimbly after it.

Waverley stepped quietly behind a tree. With the patience born of years of caution, caution that had kept him alive through countless exploits, he slowed his breathing, readied his body, and waited. The thief peered from left to right, then hoisted the bag and lumbered toward the street. As soon as he passed the tree, Waverley grabbed him in a choke hold.

"What the . . . ?"

Stunned into surprise, Waverley pulled off the thief's cap. *A woman?* He let her go and she fell. "Lady Fairchild? I recognized you by the scent of your perfume. Verbena, isn't it? We meet again, it seems."

He yanked her to her feet so hard, she was forced to put her hands on his chest to keep from falling again. Instead of letting go, he let his arms drift to her waist, but she knocked them away. "I'll thank you to keep your hands to yourself, my lord. And stop sniffing my hair."

He put up his hands as if in surrender and backed away. "I meant no harm, but the odor is enticing, I confess."

She brushed off the leaves that clung to her clothing, pulled her tucked gown out from her pantalets and smoothed her skirt as best she could.

He picked a twig out of her hair and breathed in. "Sorry, ma'am. Your scent drives me to distraction."

"Stop that. Apparently, you are in the habit of seducing young ladies, sir."

Waverley swallowed a laugh. "Am I? In that case, perhaps I ought to live up to my . . . reputation."

"Take your hands off me, you rake! How ungentlemanly of you."

"How unladylike of you, ma'am, to have woken me in such a manner and with such feeling a mere few hours ago. You find me here because it was not possible to go back to sleep. Do you make a habit of climbing in and out of windows at the most unseemly hours?"

Helena wavered. "If you must know, I have . . . urgent business elsewhere. And there is no need to wake the whole household."

He was pleased to see a blush spread across her cheeks. The damp air had caused her hair to stick to her face and his fingers itched to push the strands away from her cheek. "The same business that brought you to my bed earlier?"

"Don't be ridiculous. It's none of your—it's a personal matter." She hoisted her portmanteau and turned to leave.

"Ah, a sick aunt, perhaps? How are you planning to get where you need to go to conduct this urgent business? Walk?" Her face had the look of an adorable child caught in a fib.

Helena ignored this remark and glanced both ways at the deserted street. "Where do you suppose one finds a hackney for hire?"

"Perhaps at the end of this row of town houses. But I can't allow my host's er . . . *neighbor* to seek a hackney without protection. London is far too dangerous a place for an unaccompanied gentlewoman. Allow me." Waverley offered his arm.

"No! I . . . I mean, thank you for offering to assist me, but I can manage very well on my own."

He raised one finger and tilted his head. "Or I could throw you over my shoulder, carry you to your door, ring the bell and return you to your family where you belong." He regretted his teasing words the moment they left his lips, for she turned pale.

"I was only quizzing you, ma'am. I promise you I'll do no such thing. Come," he added in a gentler voice, offering his arm for the second time. "Won't you honor my er . . . gentlemanly good intentions? We shall search for a hackney together."

She hesitated but finally rested her hand on his arm. He took charge of her portmanteau and led her down the street where he thought he might find a hackney for hire.

Persuaded that he meant her no harm, she relaxed and sought refuge in small talk. "You don't live in London, do you? If you did, I would have met you on more than one occasion, I'm sure."

"No, I don't. I was born in England, but I haven't lived here for years. I've lived in Paris since the end of the war. That's where Darlington found me. I'm to succeed to my father's title, you see. The ceremony will take place at Carlton House tomorrow morning."

"Accept my good wishes, then."

"Ah, here comes a hack. Let us hope there is no one in it and he is for hire." He raised his hand to hail the driver.

The carriage came to a stop in front of them. Waverley looked up and spoke to the driver. "Please take my lady to . . . where shall I tell him to take you?"

"It's . . . I'll tell him when we're under way."

He gave an indifferent shrug. "Suit yourself."

"Thank you, Lord Waverley, for your kind assistance."

"That's too formal for such an intimate acquaintance, don't you think? Call me Desmond."

"I barely know you, sir. It wouldn't be proper."

He bit back a laugh. "Barely know me? Let me remind you, ma'am, that a mere few hours ago, you attempted to seduce me. Does that not lessen the need for formality?"

She blushed. "All right. But I shan't call you by your given name. Waverley will do. I thank you for your assistance."

"Fare thee well, irresistible Helena." Without warning, he

pulled her into his arms and kissed her, his tongue teasing her lips open.

She struggled and managed to push him away. "How dare you, you . . . you rake!"

He grinned, the look on his face impish. "*Reformed* rake, if you please. Show some respect for my new title, ma'am."

Helena pursed her lips to conceal her amusement. "Quite a rapid reformation, sir. Just last week, all of Paris knew you as *le roué Anglais.*"

"You have me there, lovely lady. But I am determined to earn respectability now that I've come home again. Do you know, your lips taste like fine wine, fair Helena?"

"You shouldn't have kissed me, your lordship."

"Waverley. You shouldn't have kissed me, Waverley."

She suppressed the urge to giggle. "As you wish. You shouldn't have kissed me, Waverley."

"Think of it as payment for my assistance to you on this"— he glanced at the rising sun—"magnificent morning. While I must bid you a satisfactory resolution to your urgent business, I want you to know I shall always treasure the memory of a stolen kiss on my far from deserving lips." He handed her into the carriage and shut the door. "Drive on, my good man. The lady will tell you her destination once you are under way."

He watched until the carriage had turned the corner. Perhaps he should have convinced her not to run away, but far be it for him to interfere with someone else's life. He had enough to do to manage his own.

The sun rose as Waverley walked back to Darlington's town house. There was much to do this morning. He did not mind the pomp of a formal investiture with the Regent. It was his meeting at the home office he dreaded. He wished it were over and done with, but he tried to shake off such uneasy thoughts.

So long as his grandmother was alive, he'd do everything in his power to care for her. When he was a lad, she had loved him well. Of that at least, he had no doubt. Would she even know him now, or had she lost her memory? He didn't know what he would face when he reached Waverley Castle, truth be known.

He shrugged off these depressing thoughts when his stomach growled, forcing the demons of the past out of his mind. Instead he obeyed the message of his stomach and returned to Darlington's home, wondering what treats his host's excellent cook had prepared for his breakfast.

"My sister's asleep at last," said Olivia, her blond hair in disarray. She removed her robe and joined her husband in their bed. Unlike many matrons of the *ton* who preferred sleeping in separate chambers, she insisted upon sharing their bed. In fact, they had never slept apart since their marriage two years earlier.

Sebastian drew his wife into his arms, for he loved the feel of her bare body against his. "What possessed Helena to come to you in the wee hours of the morning?" he asked when they were settled.

"Darlington's broken their betrothal."

"Good God! She's loved him for an age. Why would he do such an odious thing?"

Olivia shifted her head. "For heaven's sake, darling, don't plague me with your questions just now. Isn't it enough that my sister has worn me to the bone? Allow me to snatch a bit of sleep before our son wakes and demands my attention."

Chapter 3

Later That Morning . . .

The duke sat at the head of the table in the breakfast room, his eyes bloodshot from too little sleep. He held the morning paper at arm's length and pretended to read, instead steeling himself for the inevitable confrontation with Christopher Darlington, who was, at the moment, cooling his heels in the library. Things never seemed to work the way they ought with his children. Pity. Well, he had wanted a large family, hadn't he? Now he wondered what had ever made him entertain such a foolish notion. He reached for his coffee just as his butler appeared in the doorway.

"What is it, Dunston?"

The Heatham butler, a tall, thin gentleman in the employ of the family as far back in his own childhood as the duke could recall, said, "Mr. Darlington wishes to know if you are ready to receive him, your grace. He is most impatient."

"Bloody cheek," muttered the duke. He exchanged a look of exasperation with his butler. He put the newspaper down and drummed his fingers on the table. "Plague the man. I won't have him interrupt my breakfast. Tell him to wait. And send for Lady Helena. I want her here with me when I see him."

"Very good, your grace." Dunston attempted to bow out, but Darlington swept past him, ignoring the butler's disapproving hauteur. The duke's unwanted guest was groomed to meticulous perfection, yet the countenance he leveled at the duke was one of determination.

"Forgive the interruption, your grace. I am long overdue at the home office, you see. My business with you won't take long."

To convey displeasure for having entered without his permission, the duke cast him a withering glance. "This is a most unwelcome intrusion, Darlington. You might at least have allowed me to finish my breakfast." Hoping to annoy his guest, the duke added, "Summon Lady Helena, Dunston."

He was right, for Darlington said hastily, "No need, your grace. Your daughter knows why I have come."

"You're here far too early, Darlington. I never grant an audience before noon." The duke proceeded to sip his coffee, his eyes trained on his newspaper.

"Allow me to beg pardon again for interrupting your breakfast, your grace, but I am persuaded you will agree that it was necessary once you hear me out."

The duke sighed. "Well? What is it you wish to say?"

"Lady Helena wishes to cry off. We are no longer betrothed."

The duke made as if he knew nothing. "Is this some silly quarrel between you two? I'll ask her the same question, you know."

"By no means, your grace. We've already settled this between us. I have accepted her decision," Darlington said as if he were negotiating a treaty. "Now we must both get on with our lives."

Dunston reappeared and said, "Begging your pardon, your grace, but Lady Helena is not in her chamber."

"Find her, then. At once."

At this, the duchess swept past the butler.

"Good morning, ma'am," said the duke cheerfully.

She glanced at Darlington in puzzlement, ignoring his presence for the moment while she addressed her husband. "What is the meaning of all the shouting and banging of doors upstairs, your grace? You know it puts me out of humor to be woken thus." That said, she turned to greet their guest. "Welcome home, Christopher. Does Helena know you've come home?" She honored him with a smile. "Are you ready to set a date for the wedding? Helena will be so pleased."

"It appears our daughter is nowhere to be found," said the duke drily.

"Oh no. I'm sure that cannot be. She must be taking more time to look her best for you, dear boy. If you haven't eaten, do join us for breakfast. Believe me, your wedding will be the event of the Season. What day have you in mind?" The duchess kept to herself her determination to agree to a date only if it was not in conflict with her daughter Georgiana's debut ball in June, an event the duchess had been planning for months.

A footman entered with fresh coffee, the butler right behind him.

"Have you located my daughter?"

"No, your grace."

"Oh well," said the duchess. "No doubt she will appear soon. Now, young man, you must allow me to take care of everything. I shall see to the announcement of the wedding day in the papers. And I beg one more favor of you. Please do not deny me the privilege of arranging all the details of your wedding breakfast to our dear daughter."

Darlington fixed her with a grim stare. "Do not trouble yourself, your grace. Your daughter has cried off. She no longer wishes to marry me."

The duchess stared at him in disbelief. "Cried off? But how can that be? Helena has wanted to marry you since she was in the schoolroom. Why on earth would she cry off now?"

"Perhaps it is you who wishes to cry off, Darlington," said the duke, his shrewd eyes fixed on his unwelcome guest. Time froze except for the ticking of the clock on the mantel.

Darlington was the first to break the silence. "Lady Helena informed me of this last evening. She leaves me no choice but to accept her decision. If you'll excuse me, I'm obliged to take my leave. Good day." He bowed first to the duchess and then to the duke.

Her grace cast a worried glance at her husband. "Please, Christopher. Don't go without seeing our daughter. Helena sometimes takes a morning stroll before breakfast. I'll just have a look in the garden." She crossed to the French doors and threw them open.

"No!" cried the duke when he spied their pup, but it was too late. The Great Dane leapt into the room, skidded across the floor and caught the end of the table linen, causing several dishes to tumble to the floor.

"Prince!" the duchess screeched.

Dunston lunged for Prince but the dog bounded toward Darlington, rose on his hind legs, planted his muddy paws on Darlington's immaculate coat and licked his face.

"Get this beast off me," Darlington muttered through clenched teeth.

"He's just a pup, lad. You needn't be afraid," said the duke, stifling the urge to grin. He glanced at the hall door, where several staff members had gathered, drawn by the unaccustomed noise.

"Don't just stand there gawking, you lot. Somebody do something with the mutt, for heaven's sake!"

At their master's command, two under maids rushed into the room and began to clean up the mess of broken dishes on the floor while several footmen moved cautiously toward the Great Dane. One of them managed to pull Prince away from Darlington, but not before the pup tore the sleeve of his coat from its mooring.

"How dreadful. Let Dunston take your coat, Christopher. He'll have it repaired in no time," said the duchess, offering her apology. "We've only had Prince a few months. For the children, you see. I assure you, the dog meant no harm. He's just a puppy."

Darlington fought Dunston for possession of his coat with one hand while he mopped his face dry with the other. "Leave off," he growled, thrusting the butler's hands away from his lapels. "My man will see to it."

With unaccustomed restraint, the duke managed to suppress his urge to laugh. "Just the pup's way of being friendly, you know."

At this, Darlington lost control of his temper. He said acidly, "Apparently, your grace, you appear to have difficulty teaching proper manners to your dog as well as to your daughter!"

Before the duke could put Darlington in his place for daring to hurl such an insult, the entrance of three more of the duke's children enlivened the breakfast room. Georgiana, a debutante of seventeen years, was the acknowledged beauty of the family. Fifteen-year-old Mary was the shyest, spending as much time as she could playing the pianoforte.

Jane, at ten the youngest Fairchild, loved to eat and to pry. These habits irritated everyone in the household from the lowliest servant to her autocratic father. "Don't you dare hurt my Prince," she said to the two footmen struggling to control the frisky pup. She grabbed two biscuits from the table. "Here, Prince," she crooned in a singsong voice. "Look what your Jane has for you, love." The obedient pup drooled, his eyes on the treats and bounded out of the room after her.

"I'll take my leave now," muttered Darlington and withdrew, trying to maintain a shred of dignity in spite of his torn coat.

"What's happened to cause Chris to be in such a pelter?" asked Georgiana.

The duchess put a finger to her lips to silence her when it became clear to her that the duke was on the verge of exploding, for the duke had reached the limit of his patience. Assaulted by the din of servants disturbing his ordered routine—his grace hadn't even had time to finish his morning paper, for heaven's sake. "Clear the room, Dunston! Georgie! Mary! Find some useful occupation at once."

Alert to the menace in his grace's growl, Dunston shooed the servants out of the breakfast room, for they had dawdled in the hope of hearing more of the family gossip.

The butler followed discreetly in their wake, just as Sebastian Brooks strode into the breakfast room, his eyes wide as he took in the chaotic scene.

"What a mess! Was it the pup?" he asked, amused. "Morning, sir. How are you, ma'am?" He bent to kiss his mother-in-law's cheek.

The exasperated duke let out a sigh. "Morning, Sebastian. Prince made untidy love to Darlington when he came to tell us Helena had cried off their betrothal."

"I can't believe Helena has cried off. After all these years," said the duchess, shaking her head in sadness.

"You're right not to believe it, love. It's the other way around, I'm afraid."

"What can you mean? How is this? Where is my daughter?"

"Helena's safe at home with my wife, ma'am. She arrived there early this morning."

The duchess began to rise. "I must go to Helena at once, then."

"Stay a moment, my dear," said the duke. "Is Helena distraught?" He directed the question to his son-in-law.

"Olivia finally persuaded her to rest, but it wasn't easy. She cried for hours."

The duchess looked startled. "What is more important than my daughter's unhappiness? She needs her mother."

"In due time, ma'am. We must first put our heads together and determine what's to be done. The gossips in London will make Helena's life a misery when the news gets out," said the duke.

The duchess looked thoughtful. "Oh dear, the *ton*. I hadn't thought of that. You're right, of course. Of all times for this to happen! Just before Georgie's ball. What can we do?"

Sebastian raised a hand. "If I may speak?"

"Of course, son."

"Olivia and I think you ought to consider sending Helena out of London until the scandal plays itself out."

"I agree," said the duke, for that thought had also occurred to him. "But where? Can't be Bodmin, for we've lent the castle to relatives of my neighbor, old Tremayne, for the month. His grandson is to be married in the Heligan Gardens and he hasn't enough room to house all his guests."

"What about Heatham House in Brighton?" asked the duchess.

"Brighton is out of the question, my dear. There are many members of the *ton* living there year-round who would be only too happy to keep the London gossip alive." He turned to his son-in-law. "We'll all return to your home with you, Sebastian. We can't discuss this without Helena. She should have a say in this matter. Besides, his grandparents want to see their grandson."

Sebastian grinned. "He'll be delighted, I'm sure. Go on ahead without me, sir. I have an appointment at the home office. I'll join you as soon as I can."

"What shall I do with my life now, Livy?" asked Helena in a tragic voice for the fourth or possibly the fifth time. Her eyes were rimmed with red. "Don't ask me the how and the why of it. Suffice it to say I tried to be bold like you, but I failed miserably." She touched the back of her hand to her forehead. "My life is over."

"Nonsense, you goose. What you must do is leave London until the scandal dies down," said her sister. "And while you are gone, we Fairchilds will do everything in our power to right the wrongs Chris has so unwisely saddled you with when he cried off."

Helena gave her sister's words some serious thought. "You're right, Livy. I won't be able to bear facing up to the gossipmongers. Even the daughter of a duke can't escape their scorn when she doesn't behave properly. What must I do?"

"The question is not what you must do, but where you must go. Any thoughts as to where you might like to hibernate for a spell? Pick a country, if you like."

"Oh, I don't care. Just as long as it's far enough away so I never have to see Darlington's face again." Helena dabbed at her eyes.

"That's right, love. Dry your tears. But . . ."

"But what?"

"You're really going to have to develop a stiffer spine, dear. You've worn your heart on your sleeve for so long, it's almost become a part of you. It won't do if you're ever going to convince people it was you who cried off and not that cad." Olivia paused. "He never gave you any reason, you say? Extraordinary."

"No. He gave no reason," she lied, and changed the subject. "Develop a stiffer spine, you say? How can I? I'm not like you, Livy. Not in the least." She turned her face to the wall, too ashamed of her brazen act last night to confess the truth. "Why would I lie," she lied, piling one falsehood upon another. "Chris said I wasn't a proper wife for an aspiring diplomat."

Olivia raised her head at the sound of approaching horses. "A carriage is coming. Must be our parents. I've sent Sebastian to fetch them."

"Oh no. How could you, Livy? Must I see them? They're the last people on earth I want to face just now."

"Yes, of course you must, you ninny. They're not your enemies. They're on your side in this business. Besides, you'll need their help. Come. Dry your tears and we'll go down to greet them."

Olivia had to grip Helena's hand and drag her down the stairs.

"Where's my grandson?" the duke demanded.

"I'll send for him, Father, but you must play with him in the morning room where my busy little terror can't destroy anything. We've removed all breakable objects within his reach there." She took her father's arm and led the way into a sunlit room overlooking the garden.

As soon as the baby appeared with his nurse, the duke shed his waistcoat, neck cloth and silk vest. He sat on a blanket on the floor with his grandson, who giggled and gurgled while the otherwise dignified duke of the realm entertained his namesake by making a fool of himself.

"I wouldn't have had this happen to you for the world," said the duchess, clasping Helena's hand in sympathy. "But if it were meant to be, my darling, better by far for it to end before you wed Darlington."

"I think Helena would be better off if she left London for a while, Mother. Do you agree?"

"Yes, I do. If she doesn't, the *ton* will make her life a misery. Have you given any thought to where you might like to go, love?"

Helena wished she were anywhere but in this roomful of loving relatives, for their pity served only to make her spirits sink lower. Appealing visions of a dungeon without a door or a storm-tossed shack sinking into quicksand invaded her thoughts.

She tried to hide her resentment at their well-meaning concern. "India? America? A penal colony in Australia, perhaps?

I don't really care just as long as it's as far away from London as possible."

"Don't talk such nonsense, Helena. Land's End is far enough," said Olivia, annoyed.

"Or the Isle of Scilly," said Sebastian as he entered the morning room. He stopped to chuck his son Tony under his pudgy chin. "Unfortunately, both places may well prove to be a dead bore."

"Oh, what difference does it make? My life is over anyway," whined Helena between sniffs.

"Nonsense, my girl," put in her father. "You're only twenty. Eligible suitors will be hounding me for your hand once the news is out."

"I'll never marry," said Helena, her voice tinged with tragedy.

The duchess ignored this foolish remark, for her mind had been occupied with the more practical task of finding a solution. "You know, Livy, your mention of Land's End has given me an idea. My godmother lives there."

Helena heaved an exasperated sigh. "I know you're trying to help, Mother, but what has that to do with . . . with anything?"

Her mother went on as if Helena hadn't spoken. "I last saw her when I visited some twenty years ago with my dear mother, rest her soul, but we still exchange Christmas greetings. She lives alone in a castle overlooking the sea. She would no doubt welcome a visit from you."

"You can't be sure she'd have me, Mother. What of the marquis? He might well object."

"Her only son died last year, but her grandson has just returned from his travels to assume his father's duties," put in Sebastian.

"How do you know, darling?"

Sebastian looked at his wife and shook his head slightly as a warning to her to hold her tongue. "I made his acquaintance just this morning. The home secretary introduced us."

"You won't be in the way even if the new marquis is in residence, dear. It's a very large castle. Besides, his grandmother will act as your chaperone," persisted the duchess.

"As you wish, Mother." Helena showed little interest in the rest of the conversation.

The duchess pressed on. "You'll like it there, dearest. It's near Sennen Cove, a charming little village where the English Channel meets St. George's Channel."

Upon entering the drawing room, the duke heard this remark. "That area has a bad reputation. It's known as a hotbed of smuggling activities."

"Not anymore, sir. There may be an occasional shipwreck in bad weather, but by and large, smuggling appears to have died out," said Sebastian.

The duke appeared to be satisfied with this answer.

"If you crave anonymity, you couldn't find a more suitable place to hide. No Londoner would be caught dead in such an out-of-the-way place, especially during the Season. But the decision is entirely yours," said the duke.

"It doesn't matter to me where you send me, Father. One place is as good as another."

The duchess hastened to add, "I'll write to the marchioness at once."

"Good idea, Mother." Olivia rose to ring for the baby's nurse. "You'll have to give the lord of this manor to me, Father. It's time for Tony to feed and then to nap, two of his favorite pastimes. And while he does, we can dine in peace."

Clinging to his grandfather, little Tony babbled in a language only he understood. "You're welcome to the scamp, Livy. He's had the audacity to wet my shirt." But the duke didn't seem to mind in the least, for he hugged the child and covered his face with kisses.

* * *

Dinner was a somber affair, due to Helena's lingering melancholy. Afterward, the women withdrew so that the duke and his son-in-law might enjoy their brandy.

"What do you think of Land's End, Sebastian? Is it a good idea to send Helena so far from her family?"

"Assuming the dowager marchioness agrees to it, I believe it to be an ideal solution."

"I knew old Waverley," the duke said. "A dour man. He held a seat in Parliament, but rarely made any speeches. He had a terrible row with his only son and the young fool ran away at an early age, I recall. Gossip had it that the lad led a wild life abroad."

"Wild lads grow up and often mend their ways, sir."

The duke chuckled. "I was a bit wild as a young whelp, too. Can't fault a young 'un for that, can we? It's how he behaves now that counts."

"I met the marquis this morning, sir," Sebastian reminded his father-in-law.

"What did you think of him?"

"I liked him. He was reluctant to return to England, you know, but when he learned his grandmother was still alive, he was quick to agree. He's ready to assume his responsibilities, he told me. 'I'm determined to bury the past and start again. I have only myself to blame for the way I have lived since I left England, but now I crave a better life. One that will restore my reputation and make my grandmother proud of me,' he said. His sincerity impressed me, sir."

The duke sipped his brandy. "Let us hope he really has outgrown his wild ways then."

My Lord did not take the news of Waverley's return from exile well. *After all these years! No matter. Harry Trasker will be as disappointed as I am. So much the better, for his mother's all too eager for her son to become marquis. It may well work to my advantage.* He wrote a brief note and rang for his secretary.

"Sir?"

"See to it that this reaches Smith and Isley today."

The dowager marchioness readily extended the invitation to Helena to visit and stay as long as she liked. In spite of this warm invitation, Helena drifted through her final week in London as though in a fog as thick as the one that habitually blanketed the city. She answered questions put to her with either a brief nod or a single word. Her abigail Amy saw to the packing of her clothing, but no amount of cajoling would engage her interest in the process of getting ready to embark on her journey.

"I've arranged for an escort to accompany you, Helena," said her brother-in-law at dinner the night before her departure.

Helena acknowledged this with an indifferent nod.

"Sebastian went through a great deal of trouble for you, Helena," said the duke in exasperation. "You might at least show some gratitude."

"Thank you, Sebastian," said Helena, her voice dull.

"You'll come back for my debut ball, won't you?" pleaded Georgiana, in a vain attempt to lighten the dark mood. "Please say you will, Helena. I couldn't bear it if you didn't."

"I suppose I must, if it would please you, Georgie."

The duchess put an end to the funereal atmosphere when she rose and said, "Come, girls. We'll leave the gentlemen to their brandy. Don't be too long, you two."

"I'm bloody well damned if I know what to do for that ungrateful child," exploded the duke after the women took their leave.

Sebastian turned to the footman serving brandy. "Leave

us." He waited until they were alone before continuing. "It's best you say nothing to upset her, sir. She's in mourning for her lost love as it were, but that will pass. She needs time, but she'll come about."

"The silly chit! I never liked Darlington for her, you know. Thought he wasn't good enough for her. Turns out I was right. I only agreed to the match because she begged me for it. Women! Just wait till you have daughters of your own, Sebastian. When they grow up they're bound to become a sore trial."

Sebastian buried his grin in his brandy snifter. His wife Olivia was the duke's eldest daughter. If his future daughters were anything like his beautiful, spirited wife, then he'd never find the time to be bored, for they would certainly enrich his already lively life.

"Helena will bounce back, sir. Mark my word. You are doing the right thing by sending her away for a time. She shouldn't be subjected to the haughty stares and the cruel remarks of the London journals and the scandalmongers."

"I certainly hope it's the right thing. At any rate, she'll be back in time for Georgiana's ball."

"Time enough for her to face the world with dignity once again. By then, the gossip will have shifted to a different scandal."

"I suppose you're right." The duke hesitated.

"Something else on your mind, sir?"

"I'm concerned about Waverley's reputation. Am I putting my daughter in another kind of danger?"

"I can understand your worry, but the marquis assures me he has turned over a new leaf. He's pledged his word to me, sir. He'll see no harm comes to her. Word of a gentleman."

The duke drained his glass. "Word of a gentleman, eh? That's good enough for me. Shall we join the ladies?"

Chapter 4

The rain added to the lingering chill of the April winds when Helena's carriage arrived at the door. Her driver Casper nodded to milady from his perch while Dunston let down the steps and waited with an umbrella for her ladyship to enter, after she said good-bye to the family.

Olivia squeezed her sister's hand as if to instill some courage in her. She handed her a small package. "I've a gift for you."

"What is it?" asked Helena without a flicker of curiosity.

Olivia laughed. "Don't go overboard with your enthusiasm, you goose. It's a journal to help you while away the tedious hours of your long journey."

"Sorry." She hugged her sister. "Thanks, Livy. I'll miss you."

"No tears, mind. Time to say your good-byes to the rest of the family." She gripped her in a fierce hug and whispered in her ear, "Be strong."

"Make yourself useful to the marchioness," admonished the duchess. She hugged her and stepped back to allow the duke to escort his daughter to her carriage.

"Well, Helena," he began, but the words caught in his throat.

He withdrew his handkerchief, blew his nose and composed himself. "Safe journey, my dear. Write to us, won't you?"

"Of course, Father." She wrapped her arms around him and squeezed her eyes to prevent the tears from escaping. "You have been the kindest, most understanding of fathers. You never once scolded me for having made the wrong choice. If nothing else, know that I'm proud to be your daughter."

"See you at my ball," said Georgiana cheerfully. "Order a beautiful gown for it, won't you?" She kissed her and stepped back to make room for Mary.

"Bye, Helena. I'll miss you," said Mary.

"Me too," said Jane. "Write me a letter all for myself. No one ever thinks to write to me, you know."

Helena laughed at this. "I will if you promise not to eat so many scones."

When Jane reluctantly agreed, Helena took her father's arm and climbed the steps into the carriage. She fought back tears at being forced to separate from her family just when she needed them most.

She took the seat opposite Amy and wondered why they were not moving. At last, she rolled down her window. "What's wrong? Why aren't we under way?"

"We're waiting for your escort, dear. Be patient," said the duke. "You must have one, you know, to see to your safety."

Helena sat back in the coach and closed her eyes, trying to still her rapid heartbeat. It was harder than she'd supposed to leave the only life she'd ever known. At last, she heard the sound of a horse stopping beside her coach.

"Ah, here he is at last. Safe journey, Helena," said her brother-in-law.

She glanced out of her window and stiffened in shock. Her escort was the Marquis of Waverley.

"Morning, ma'am," he said affably.

Helena reddened when their eyes engaged. Mortified, she

nodded and turned her head away. Was there to be no end to her misery? She forced herself to meet his eyes. "Morning," she mumbled.

He swept his beaver off and bowed to her. "Pleasure to make your acquaintance, ma'am. Lord Waverley at your service."

Helena's heart played havoc as it knocked against her ribs. Of all the men in England, why oh why had *this* man—this *rake*—been chosen to be her escort? Didn't Sebastian know of his reputation? Her father could not have known, could he? If he had known, he would never have allowed it.

How was she to bear his company for such a long journey when she couldn't even bear the sight of him? When she longed to stop the carriage to wipe that idiotic grin off his face? When he was a painful reminder of the worst mistake of her life?

She was so engrossed in fury, her abigail had to touch her knee to gain her attention. "Are you all right, milady?"

"I'm fine," she snapped. "What is it?"

"Well, milady, I've asked you the same question three times and you haven't answered me," said Amy in a trembling voice.

"Sorry. My thoughts were elsewhere. What is it?"

"Do you not think our escort handsome?"

"I hadn't noticed. Beware handsome men, Amy, for they may be dangerous."

"Oh no. Really?"

"You must protect me, Amy. Make sure the marquis doesn't behave in an improper fashion."

"I will, your la'ship. Don't you worry about a thing. Your Amy will take good care of you."

Helena's smile was wan. "Thank you, dear. I'll just close my eyes and rest a bit."

But the luxury of sleep eluded her. She felt lost, cut off from everything she loved. Seeking some respite from her grim thoughts, she clutched the reticule holding her new journal.

Helena had always wanted to travel, but not like this. Not running away from the vicious tongues of the London gossips whose whispers could infect an already festering wound.

For what seemed like the hundredth time, the humiliating scene of Darlington's rejection flashed before her eyes. For what seemed like the thousandth time, she asked herself how she could have been so wrong about him. Had she forced herself upon him? She would never know the answer now. She knew only that he hadn't loved her as she had loved him. Had Chris merely wished to wed the daughter of a duke to advance his diplomatic career? Helena sighed, searching for easier thoughts before the dismals sank her into madness.

To ease her mind, she turned to her abigail and said, "Tell me about Land's End, Amy."

"What would you like to know, milady?"

"That's where you were raised, isn't it? Did you live by the sea?"

"Near enough, milady. Me mum and me, we lived in the village of Sennen Cove. Me da, he owned Ship Inn, with rooms to let for travelers and an alehouse as well. Now me mum runs it wi' her brother, me Uncle Tom."

"Your father's dead?"

Amy looked out the window and bit her lip.

"Forgive me, Amy. I didn't mean to pry." Helena reached across and patted her abigail's hand.

"Oh no, milady. It's just . . . well, I don't know for sure."

"Oh? How is that?"

"You see he was took up by the excise men near on ten years ago."

"Oh," said Helena. "That's terrible."

"Yes, milady. He was a good da and I loved him. Everyone in Sennen Cove loved him, no matter he was a free trader."

A free trader? Amy's chatter did indeed distract her. "I'm so sorry," said Helena. "You must miss him."

Tears welled up in Amy's eyes. She sniffed. "I know 'twas illegal what he done, but we loved him and we had such a fine life. Now me mum has to work hard just to make ends meet."

"Tell me what you know of smuggling."

Amy was much encouraged by the interest her mistress showed. "Free tradin', milady. Me da warn't no smuggler. That would be bad."

Helena suppressed a smile, for Amy's tongue was reverting to familiar Cornish dialect. "Go on."

"There's not much of free tradin' going on as was before. Mostly, free traders don't hurt nobody that leaves them alone and keeps their tongue between their teeth. But then there's the outsiders—them's the real smugglers, not us, milady. Mostly, they come from someplace else and they do bad things. Nobody likes them, but everyone's afraid of them."

"Doesn't anyone try to stop them?"

Amy thought for a moment. "I don't know about that, milady. We don't speak bad of our own and we don't speak bad of outsiders for fear. That scurvy lot might well murder us. Most of the time, when the excise men come round to ask questions, folk don't see nothin' and don't say nothin'."

Helena said, as much to herself as to Amy, "I'd always thought that smugglers and pirates were romantic."

Amy's eyes lit up as she warmed to her task. "Some, mayhap. When I was a wee mite, I saw Black Bart hisself. It was dark at night, and me da had gone out, 'cause the lantern on the bluff had blinked three times." Amy leaned closer. "That's the signal that a ship has hit the shoals in the cove. The alehouse cleared out and I was left alone. I couldn't even see out the window, it was that thick with fog.

"Anyways, the door banged open and a tall man appeared dressed all in black. His cape swirled about him and his hat covered his face. Even though I was a child, I knew who he was right off. I lowered my eyes like I was taught, but he jus' laughed and pinched my cheek. Right here." Amy pointed to a place on her left cheek. Her eyes gleamed with the thrill of hero worship.

Helena felt an excitement she lacked only moments before. She might put her journal to good use after all and try to write a tale about free traders. Perhaps she would become a famous author like Caroline Lamb. Her spirits rose.

"What happened then?"

Amy leaned forward until they were nose to nose. "And then . . ."

She was so engrossed in Amy's tale, she gave a start when their carriage drew to a halt at a small inn in Reading on the road to Bristol.

"Change of horses, ma'am," said Waverley when he opened her door. "We'll stop once more to change horses, this time in Swindon, before we reach Bristol, but there we shall remain for the night. I've ordered a light repast here to sustain us until then."

She had no choice but to take his outstretched hand. "Thank you, sir." She stepped down and followed him inside to the dining room of a rustic tavern, for the inn lacked a private parlor. "My servants?"

"They'll eat in the taproom. Be easy, ma'am. I won't do you harm."

He held out a chair for her and she took it, while a waiter served them wine, cold meats, cheese and fruit, but she could not find a word to say. Thus they ate in uncomfortable silence.

"I don't bite, you know," Waverley said in an attempt at humor.

"Forgive me, sir. I'm not the best of company, but it has nothing to do with you. I . . . I'm sorry I'm such a poor companion."

"You're forgiven, ma'am. Let us try for easier terms, shall we? It will make the journey less tiresome." He sipped his wine. "You have a lovely smile, Lady Helena. I recall seeing it once. Do try to exercise it more often lest you lose the knack."

She laughed at this, and relaxed. "You've scored a well-deserved hit, sir. I'll try, I promise."

Helena slept once they were under way again, the wine having calmed her ruffled nerves. She woke three hours later, when they reached Swindon to change horses again, but she didn't leave her carriage, for the ostlers did their work quickly and they were back on the road within ten minutes.

By the time they reached Bristol, it was dusk. The courtyard of Arnos Manor, where they were to put up for the night, was lit by a full moon. The twin turrets of the baroque manor hinted of a Gothic past. No such thing, Helena learned when Casper helped her down. To the right of the front door, a bronze plaque read: "Arnos Manor, former home of the Hon. William Reeve, Bristol Merchant. Erected 1760."

Waverley threw his bridle to the stable boy and dismounted. His boots landed hard on the cobblestones, sending pins and needles through his feet. Bloody hell, it would take at least a week before he would recover from the bruising jolts of the rutted road, one of the better ones in England.

The marquis observed Helena, already at the door of the inn. My lady's abigail, a pert little thing, had her hands on her hips and was surveying her surroundings.

That lass is full of self-importance, he noted with amusement as he watched her accost the landlord. "My mistress needs your best rooms and a private parlor as well, my good man."

The landlord gave her a sly once-over. "And who might your mistress be, may I ask?"

"Lady Fairchild, from London, she is."

The landlord nodded. "All's ready, then. Been expecting her la'ship." He bowed to Helena, noting with approval her elegant traveling costume, a cloak of rich, green velvet and a matching plumed hat. "Welcome, milady. His grace always stays here during hunting season. His grace sent word ahead and that's a fact. Your chambers are ready."

Waverley strode to Helena's side. "Evening, ma'am. I'll join you for dinner in one hour." Without waiting for an answer, he bowed and entered the inn, nodding to the innkeeper as he passed.

"Milady," asked the landlord, "shall I send a tub and hot water up for you?"

"Thank you, sir. Please do."

An hour later, after Amy helped her bathe and change, Helena sat by the fire in the private dining parlor, staring at the flames. "Go down to the taproom for your own dinner, Amy, and see to it that Casper is fed as well."

"I thought to remain here to serve you, milady."

"There are waiters for that task. I won't need you again until bedtime."

"Yes, milady." Amy walked to the door, but with reluctance.

Helena sighed, understanding that she had done something to upset the young woman. "What is it, Amy?"

"But who will watch over you? That man—Lord Waverley, I mean—told the innkeeper he would take his dinner with you."

"I shall be quite safe, I assure you. I'll send for you if I need your help."

Amy chewed on her lip.

"Off with you, Amy," said Helena gently but firmly.

Amy gave in at last, but she bowed herself out with the utmost reluctance.

She brushed past a maid who proceeded to lay the table. The waiter followed, carrying a tray heavily laden with covered dishes.

Helena's eyes widened at the sight. "There must be some

mistake. My abigail could not possibly have ordered all this food for me. There's enough here for an army."

The waiter looked up from his task in surprise. "Oh no, milady, 'twas milord done the ordering."

"I see." Panic washed over her at the thought of having to dine with Waverley. She glanced frantically around the room, looking for a way out, ready to bolt. Only the one door and a window too small for escape kept her glued to her seat.

When the door swung open, Lord Waverley entered the dining room and made an elegant leg. He wore gleaming Hessian boots, fawn buckskin breeches, the kind that most men favored when traveling, a white linen shirt with an elaborately tied neck cloth and a blue superfine jacket over a yellow silk vest.

"You look startled to see me, ma'am," he drawled. "Did you not expect me?"

"Of course I expected you. I had little choice in the matter. It's just . . . your elegance has taken me by surprise."

"My valet will be pleased at the compliment, ma'am." He turned to the waiter, who remained at the sideboard. "You may go. We'll help ourselves."

Helena felt trapped. She wanted the waiter to remain, but she dared not say so without looking foolish. "I wasn't aware that you had a valet."

Desmond looked amused. "I sent him on ahead in my coach this morning. He's not used to riding a horse, you see." He checked his grin, wondering what her reaction would be when she met his unusual valet.

She changed the subject. "How is it you offered to be my escort?"

"You wrong me, ma'am. I did no such thing."

"Indeed? Then what is the right of it, may I ask?"

"Did you believe it was my own choice? You seem to have forgotten you are the daughter of a powerful duke. Frankly, I thought it was you who had requested my services, especially after that night. . . ."

Her cheeks grew hot. "Don't you dare bring up that night. If you are the gentleman you appear to be, I beg you to put it out of your mind."

"I might have put it out of my mind. . . ." He paused to examine his nails. When he looked up, his eyes pierced hers. "If you had behaved like the lady you appear to be."

Stung by this, she glared at him, drawn to him at the same time. His sun-streaked hair was tied with a black ribbon. His deep blue eyes mesmerized her.

"You've scored another hit, Lord Waverley. One I clearly deserve. My apologies if I have wronged you. Allow me to rephrase my question, if I may. How is it you came to be my escort?"

"That's better, ma'am. Your manners are improving."

"Improving? What have I missed? Oh. Sorry. Won't you be seated?"

"Kind of you." Before he sat, he filled their plates. When he set them down, he poured wine in both goblets. Only then did he flip the tails of his coat and take the seat opposite her. "Shall we dine?" Without waiting for her answer, he attacked his plate as though he hadn't had a meal in ages.

She toyed with her food, for she had no appetite, but her mouth was as dry as dust. She raised the goblet to her lips and sipped her wine. Helena watched him with lowered eyes as he devoured his food. She couldn't help comparing him to Chris, whose table manners were almost effeminate. No dainty dilettante here, she thought, watching him attack his dinner with a lusty appetite. Without warning, her terrible faux pas that night in Darlington's guest chamber came to mind and she blushed.

Waverley caught the blush. "Do my manners offend you?"

He shrugged. "Sorry for it, but I haven't eaten since early this morning and I am as hungry as a bear."

"Go ahead. Enjoy your dinner." She finished her wine in one swallow.

He stopped long enough to refill her glass. When his plate was clean, he wiped his mouth and took a deep draught of wine. "Ah! That's better. I didn't want to embarrass you in front of the waiter, but I did mean to compliment you on how well you look tonight, ma'am. Yellow becomes you. You should wear it more often."

She ignored his attempt at flattery. "Now that you have finished your dinner, if it's not too much to ask, what is your explanation as to how you came to be my escort?"

"Viscount Sidmouth, the home secretary, issued the order, but it was his deputy who delivered it. I agreed since our destinations are the same. I am going home to Waverley Castle and you are going there to visit my grandmother. It was put in the form of a polite request, of course, yet I felt I had no choice but to agree."

"Had no choice? How is that possible?"

"What reason to decline their request would you have me give, ma'am? Under the circumstances, I couldn't very well reveal our first meeting, could I?"

Helena hung her head. "No, of course not. Thank you for that. Did the deputy home secretary tell you he is my brother-in-law?"

"He did indeed. He also extracted a promise from me to treat you well. I gave my word, in fact, that I would behave as a gentleman toward you." Waverley grinned. "He knows of my reputation as well, you see. Have no fear, ma'am. I shall be on my best behavior, especially since you are to be a guest in my home."

"Thank you." She hesitated as if she thought better of what she had been about to say.

"What is it?"

She lowered her eyes to her hands. "I don't suppose I'll ever live down my mortification at what I did to you that night in Darlington's home. I cannot imagine what you must think of me."

He softened as he examined her face. "Aside from thinking that you are an incredible beauty, you mean? I think you are the bravest, most giving of females to have done what you did for the man you loved. If you must know, ma'am, I wish I had truly been the object of your passion that night instead of Darlington."

"Darlington spurned me for it."

"The more fool he, then. He'll never find another woman to love him with such devotion, ready to give *him* her all. If it had been me, I would have been honored," he said, his voice as soft as a song.

Helena burst into tears. "You don't understand. No one does. My life is over! I'll never love another man. It's just too hard to face such devastating rejection." Her words were said between hiccupping sobs.

Desmond rose and knelt beside her. "There, there. Don't despair. You're wrong, you know. All is not lost. Broken hearts have been known to mend. Yours will, too, I promise you. You're far too lovely to be left to grieve for very long." He helped her to her feet and held her, allowing her head to rest on his shoulder. How well he knew the sting of rejection, he thought bitterly.

After her tears subsided, she disengaged, picked up a napkin, and dabbed at his waistcoat. "Sorry." Helena giggled. "I've cried all over your coat."

"That's better. You have a lovely giggle. Do it more often for me, won't you?"

Helena kept dabbing ineffectually at his coat. As if she hadn't heard him, she said, "You see, I've had no one to talk to about that horrid night. I couldn't tell my family the real reason for crying off, could I?"

"No, I suppose not." He caught her hand and took the cloth away. "If it will ease your heart, you may talk to me about what is troubling you anytime you please. I've suffered the pain of rejection myself, though that was a long time ago. But I haven't forgotten the pain. It hurt like the devil and left a wound that took a long time to heal." He led her to the small settee opposite the dining table and sat down next to her.

"I feel such a fool! I've loved Darlington since I was twelve years old, you see. I've never wanted anything more out of life than to be his wife and bear his children. Why did I never realize he was the wrong man for me? He doesn't even think me desirable. I disgust him, he said. I'm such a failure."

"No, you're not. What you did that night wasn't so horrible. Most men would have been flattered by your attentions. *I* would have been flattered if you had meant them for me." He lifted her chin. "For what it's worth, I think you're very desirable."

"Am I? Then prove you mean it, my lord. Kiss me." She leaned toward him, closed her eyes and parted her lips.

But he stopped her. "Open your eyes, my dear. I gave my word to your brother-in-law that I would never take advantage of your innocence. That takes precedence, you see. Especially now."

Helena's eyes flew open at the sudden vision of the marquis without his clothing. "Why especially now?"

"I've become Marquis of Waverley. I have a duty to repair my reputation."

She turned her face away to hide her flaming cheeks. He was right, of course, yet she couldn't help feeling rejected once more. What was wrong with her? Had she no appeal at all?

"You're blushing again, ma'am. Why?"

"I feel like an ugly old crone. Undesirable and unwanted."

Waverley laughed. "I suppose I shall be forced to kiss you just to prove you wrong, but I shan't do so without your permission." He touched her cheek, turned her face toward him, then raised her chin until they were eye to eye. He leaned closer until his mouth was inches from hers.

Helena ran her tongue over her dry lips and closed her eyes in anticipation. Nothing happened again. "Get on with it, if you don't mind," she said, trying to ignore the mixture of fear and desire that his closeness had unleashed.

"I cannot bring myself to break my promise. How odd, considering my past. I don't even want to do so."

"What harm is there in one kiss?"

"Just one, then. An antidote to relieve your mind of any doubt as to your appeal to men."

He took her in his arms in spite of his reluctance. She breathed him in, the linen of his cravat tickling her nose, the wine on his breath drowning her senses. He smelled like man. No perfume or pomade, just man.

Waverley began his redemptive kiss by brushing his lips across hers.

Heat rippled through her body. She felt his tongue tease her lips apart, inducing shock waves down to her toes.

"One kiss delivered as promised," he said, drawing away, but she pulled him closer, clutching the lapels of his coat as if she was afraid he would vanish.

He nuzzled her neck. "You may not want me to stop, but I must. Besides, there are consequences, you know."

"I don't want you to stop, consequences be damned." She lay back on the settee.

His body pressed down against hers. She could feel his hardness through the fabric of her skirts, branding her stomach. A sound escaped from deep inside her, like the cooing of a dove. She shuddered when his fingers began to trace the neckline of her gown, each touch igniting her, turning her limbs to jelly. He tugged at the sleeves of her gown until they slid off her shoulders. She felt a welcome whisper of air wafting across her breasts. His hand curved around one breast and her nipple puckered. His thighs pressed against hers. She wondered at the curling of her toes. How odd. How wicked. She loved it. Somewhere in the haze of her thoughts, she yearned to know what came next. She squirmed beneath him, wanting more, wanting . . . what? She had no idea.

He groaned and released her mouth, then lowered his own until his lips found a breast. He took the nipple between his teeth. His hand sought the treasure between her thighs.

They paid no heed to the squeak of the door. Nor did the gasp of outrage from Amy's lips reach their ears.

When the heavy pitcher filled with water came crashing down on Lord Waverley's head, it produced a loud *thunk*.

That claimed their full attention.

Chapter 5

"Good morning, ma'am," Waverley said cheerfully as he took a seat opposite Helena. He behaved as though nothing had happened the evening before in spite of the visible bump on his forehead.

Astonished, Helena took in the slight, dark-skinned man wearing a turban, a bright yellow coat that fell to his knees, pants, and shoes with curled-up toes. He followed his lordship into the dining parlor.

Amused at her reaction, Waverley introduced his valet. "This is Rabu, ma'am. In the firm belief that I am unable to care for myself, Rabu insisted upon accompanying me home from India to accomplish that task. Isn't that right, Rabu?"

Rabu giggled, his grin reaching from ear to ear. "Yes, mastah."

"How do you do, Rabu," said Helena, much amused.

The little man made a sweeping bow. "Allo, meestress." He giggled again.

Waverley's lips quirked. "Pay him no mind, ma'am. Rabu giggles all the time. Weddings, funerals, disasters. In spite of the giggle, he's working hard at learning our tongue. I'll have the eggs and some ham, Rabu." At once, the valet bustled about serving his master.

Helena took a sip of her tea. "He is quite an . . . original, my lord. How is your head this morning?"

"My head is fine, thank you, except for this colorful bump developing on my skull. Speaking of which, how is your abigail? Dear little Amy is also an original. Was it you who taught her that delightful trick with the pitcher? Next time, advise her to empty it of water first before she puts it to such practical use." He dug into his breakfast with his customary zeal.

"I most certainly did not teach her such a shabby trick. Amy thought it up all by herself."

"Clever little puss," he murmured between bites.

Helena was fascinated by the extraordinary amount of food her escort was consuming. "You seem excessively hungry this morning. As if you haven't eaten for a week."

"Oh no, ma'am. I eat like this all the time. Since I am an active man, I use food to fuel my body." He wiped his mouth with his napkin and waved to Rabu to remove his plate. "Coffee, Rabu."

"Yes, sah!" Rabu said with a hint of the military. And giggled.

"We leave in one hour, to take advantage of the light, ma'am. I've asked the innkeeper to provide a basket for a midday meal. When we change horses at Taunton, a decent drink may be had, he informs me, but the food is not what he calls 'good grub.'"

She rose. "You'll excuse me, then. I must supervise the packing if we are to be ready to leave so soon, sir."

His eyes twinkled as he saluted her with one finger. "Don't be late, ma'am."

His last remark smacked of insolence, Helena thought, but she didn't answer. She walked up the stairs and down the hall to her chamber, where she found Amy folding her clothes. "We leave in an hour, Amy. Be sure everything is packed and taken down to our carriage. Tell Casper that Lord Waverley's valet will accompany us. He may sit up beside him."

"Yes, your la'ship." Amy's eyes were swollen from the tears she had shed over the tongue-lashing her ladyship had administered following last evening's fiasco.

Helena reddened in recollection of the humiliating scene. Amy had hit him with the pitcher all the while scolding him like a fishmonger for daring to "have his way" with her precious ladyship. To Helena's dismay, Amy had yanked Helena's bodice up while she continued to rant at the marquis. Waverley had merely held his head in his hands and groaned.

When he was able to stagger to his feet, he'd barked, "Leave off, lass. No need for you to protect your mistress any longer. Thanks to the cold water *and* the pitcher, the mood has quite left me." He'd stumbled out and slammed the door behind him.

Helena reached for her hat, but Amy was quicker. "Allow me, milady." She tucked her mistress' hair under, leaving a few curls out to frame her face in a most becoming way, a task at which Amy was a master. "You look lovely," Amy said, as she placed the pelisse on Helena's shoulders. Without a word, Helena left the room and proceeded down the stairs, to be met by the innkeeper.

"Allow me to settle the bill with you, sir."

"No need, milady. His grace directed that all charges be sent to him. Was everything satisfactory?"

"Oh yes. Thank you for your hospitality." While she spoke to the landlord, Amy passed them, carrying her ladyship's portmanteau. Helena followed her out into the yard and entered her carriage, but before Casper could close the door, she held it open and said, "See to Lord Waverley's baggage. His valet will sit up with you, Casper. Have you met him?"

Casper grinned. "Bit of an oddball, ain't he?"

Helena nodded in agreement just as Waverley drew up on his horse. He tipped his hat to her and smiled.

She smiled back at him, but there was no light in her eyes. *Good heavens! How am I going to get through the rest of this journey without further mortification?*

"Your ladyship—?"

"Say no more, Amy. Spare me, please. Your lectures make my head ache."

"I'm sorry for what I done, but Lord Waverley's a rake, taking advantage of an innocent lady like yourself. Men like him—"

"Enough, for heaven's sake! Not another word out of you, do you hear?"

She reached for her diary, picked up her quill and began to write whatever thoughts popped into her head.

"Milady?" Amy twisted the handkerchief in her hands as she spoke.

Helena glared at her. "Don't interrupt again, do you hear?"

A light rain began to fall but soon turned into a downpour. Casper pulled to the side of the road and stopped long enough for Lord Waverley to tie his horse to the rear of the carriage and enter.

"Beg pardon," he said. He removed his coat, already drenched, and dropped it to the floor. "That's better. I trust my joining you isn't too much of an imposition? We stop for the night in Exeter, still hours away. My horse doesn't seem to mind the rain, but I most certainly do." He tapped the roof with the blunt end of his whip, a signal to Casper to move on.

"No imposition, I assure you. Make yourself comfortable, sir." Helena removed her handkerchief from her reticule and handed it across to him. "Take this to wipe your face."

"Thank you, ma'am. My valet will restore it before I return it." He wiped his face, ignoring Amy's stern glare in his direction, and closed his eyes to bar further conversation.

Helena returned her diary to her reticule, for the erratic motion of the carriage sloshing through rutted roads made writing impossible. While Waverley rested opposite her, she too rested.

When Casper pulled up to a small hostelry in Taunton, the only sign above the door read "Inn." The sun had reappeared but the ground remained sodden. Waverley stepped down first. When he offered his hand, Helena took it, expecting to have to wade through puddles to the door of the inn, but the marquis swept her into his arms and carried her inside.

"Th . . . thank you, sir," she managed. "How kind."

He set her down in the taproom and bowed. "Pleasure, ma'am."

While Rabu spread the picnic fare supplied by the innkeeper of Arnos Manor in Bristol on one of two tables, Amy fetched a draught for the marquis, and lemonade for her mistress. Casper joined Rabu and Amy at the other table in the corner of the room, though the room was so small every word Helena and Waverley said to one another could be heard.

"Try to get some sleep when you return to the carriage, ma'am. Exeter is more than five hours away."

"You may ride with me and continue to rest if you wish, sir," she said shyly.

"Thank you, but my horse might object. He needs his exercise."

Helena's infectious laughter caused Casper to grin, Rabu to giggle and Amy to frown.

Once under way, Helena leaned back and closed her eyes, but try as she might, she could not sleep, for Lord Waverley troubled her thoughts. He was such a contradiction. Tender at times, brusque just as often. He was seductive at times, behaving with propriety just as often. Who was the real man inside these contradictions?

* * *

By the time they reached the Turks Head Inn in Exeter, a fifteenth-century hostelry, Helena was too weary to eat dinner in the private dining room. She ordered a light supper sent to her chamber and fell asleep soon after. At dawn, the sound of voices coming from the courtyard woke her. Startled by the rude noise, she pushed the covers away, went to the window and peered over the sill. The light lit the face of the man on the ground. The marquis! With caution, she opened the window a crack and peered out in time to hear Waverley speak.

"I need my horse, if you please," he said to the landlord.

"It's too early, your lordship. The stable lads are asleep."

"I ride this early every morning for exercise, sir. I'll make it worth their while. Yours as well." The marquis reached into his trousers, pulled out some notes and pressed them into the landlord's hand. "Ten minutes."

Curious, Helena drew her head in, snatched her robe and went to the door. She tiptoed to the banister just as Waverley entered and started up the stairs. Helena tried to hurry back to her chamber, but she tripped on the hem of her robe and sprawled facedown.

"Ooof!" She raised her head only to greet a pair of large, shiny Hessian boots. "What are you doing up so early?" she asked the boots.

"I might ask the same of you, ma'am. Are you spying on me?"

Her eyes traveled slowly up past the boots to the tight buckskin trousers clinging to his thighs before she was rudely snatched to her feet. He steadied her as she fell against him. A tremor coursed through her body. It took all her strength to keep her knees from buckling.

"I'm waiting for your answer."

She cocked her head to one side and stuck out her chin. "I asked you first."

Waverley's eyes turned to flint even as the scent of verbena nagged at him. "Well? What have you to say for yourself, ma'am?"

She stepped back and clutched her gown closer. Why did he wreak such havoc on her senses?

Without warning, he thrust aside her hands. "What are you hiding? Let's have a look." His fingers played a silent tune on her breastbone. They slipped inside the edge of her gown. Moved lower.

Her breath caught when the heat of his body penetrated hers. She closed her eyes, pursed her lips in anticipation of his kiss and leaned toward him, her hands splayed against the wall behind her to steady herself.

The back of his hand brushed across her breast. Her lips parted as she drew closer until she felt every hard inch of him.

"Enough for the moment, milady." He let her go and sauntered down the hall toward his chamber.

She shivered as she watched him disappear into his chamber. *Does he think me a strumpet who is desperate for him? Someone he can use whenever he pleases? Someday, I'll teach him a lesson he'll never forget, if it's the last thing I do!*

What was wrong with her? Had she no allure? Was she not desirable? She had been spurned first by Darlington and now by Waverley, the most exasperating man she'd ever had the misfortune to encounter. He told her she was appealing, didn't he? Was he just being polite? There must be something wrong with her, else why would men spurn her?

She slept restlessly, but three hours later she woke at a knock on her door.

"I need to pack your things, milady. It's after nine. We're almost ready to leave. Carriage is waitin' on us," Amy said timidly as she crossed the room and opened the curtains to let in the light. She proceeded to set out Helena's clothing.

"Very well." Helena sighed and rose from the bed. After Amy had helped her dress, Helena opened her diary and began to write quickly, before she lost her thoughts. The words poured out of her soul like swift arrows piercing her heart. She wrote what she felt. The doubt. The wanting. The anguish. The rejection.

"The landlord's prepared your breakfast in the dining parlor, milady."

Helena nodded. She let Amy help her with her pelisse, but she would not relinquish the bag that held her journal, in order to make sure prying eyes could not read it.

She was alone in the private parlor when Casper knocked and entered. "What is it, Casper?"

"Lord Waverley's not back from his morning ride, milady. He left word with the landlord that we're to wait for him to return before we leave for Bodmin."

"Wait for his lordship? Indeed we will not. It isn't necessary. We're not far from Bodmin. We'll go on as planned and the marquis may meet us there. Tell his valet to join us."

"I asked him already, milady. Rabu says he won't budge without his master."

"He will when you tell him it is his master's wish. We can't leave him behind, you know. Tell him to be ready to leave in fifteen minutes."

"Safe journey, milady. Pleased to be at your service," said the landlord as he helped her into the carriage, his mind already on the bill he planned to send to her father. Casper cracked his whip and the chaise was under way.

Helena smiled to herself at the landlord's final words. She hadn't bothered to question his bill, which made the man effusive. She sighed, her thoughts on the family she had left behind. Would she be able to hold her head up at Georgiana's debut ball so as not to embarrass her family? She allowed herself a small smile at a thought that crossed her mind. She would have to hold her head up high at Georgie's debut ball whatever the cost. The Duke of Heatham's children were not allowed to fail.

Their carriage came to a screeching halt. Helena's quill flew out of her hand, for she had been writing in her journal. She and Amy were tossed every which way, the contents of their small bags spilling out in a jumble.

Amy recovered first. "Ouch! You all right, milady?" She rolled down the window and stuck her head out. "Casper, you lout. Why'd you stop so sudden like? My lady's all shook up."

Casper climbed down from his perch, his rifle in hand, and opened their door. "Hush, lass," he whispered. "Don't be making a fuss. Stay inside and protect milady. There's a robbery just ahead, mayhap. Two highwaymen are tryin' to murder a proper gentleman, by the look of him. Be quiet while Rabu and I see what the lay of the land is. We have to stop them or we'll be next." He tied the horses to a tree and crept forward, rifle at the ready. Rabu followed him resolutely, his fists clenched, poised for battle.

"Oooh, milady! We're done for!" Amy moaned.

"Stop that whimpering, you silly chit. Casper and Rabu will protect us. It's their duty. Quick! We must prepare ourselves. What can we use if they fail? No, no. Don't look so alarmed and don't you dare start wailing. Let's search the carriage. There must be something here we can . . ."

A loud shot reached their ears. Amy jumped closer to her mistress. "They . . . they've murdered Casper."

"Stop it this instant," said Helena, exasperated, yet frightened in spite of her admonition. She pushed her abigail to the floor. "Stay right there. Don't move unless you hear me scream. Then get out and run as fast as you can and find help."

Helena cracked the door open just enough to slide down to the ground. She crept quietly toward the direction of the rifle shot. Her eyes flew open at the sight of Casper struggling with one of the masked men while the other held his bleeding leg and groaned. Rabu stood frozen at the side of the road, all resolve to fight now lost. Casper's rifle lay on the ground near the figure of a third man lying face down, not moving at all.

She tore her eyes away from him and concentrated on the immediate danger. Rabu was no help and Casper appeared to be losing the struggle. The man with the bleeding leg was trying to inch his way toward the fallen rifle. She found a sturdy branch lying nearby, gripped it with both hands and rushed into the fray.

"Stop, thief! We'll have no more of this nonsense!" The startled thug let go of Casper and turned to see where the voice was coming from, giving Casper time to thrust him off.

"Smith! Watch yer back!" screamed his accomplice. He reached for the rifle just as Helena ran to him and kicked it out of reach. She dropped the branch, picked up the rifle and aimed it at the man called Smith, never taking her eyes off his wounded partner.

"Casper, can you find something to bind these two brutes with? Rabu and I will stand watch until you return." She turned to Smith and added, "I also have you in my sight. I'm an excellent shot, my man."

Rabu came to his senses and joined her, a look of fearlessness on his face despite his shaking knees.

"Right and tight, milady." Casper stood up and brushed himself off. "Can you two hold them until I return, milady?"

"Of course."

"Yes, sah!" said Rabu, recovered from fright.

The wounded man snorted. "Women don' know how to shoot and that little man is worthless."

"Shut up, Isley. Don't set 'em off. I don't fancy me death."

Helena let out a harsh laugh. "Try me, Isley. Move one muscle and I'll shoot the other leg. Lie down, Smith."

"All right, miss." The man lay flat on his back and crossed his arms over his chest as if already dead.

"You too, Isley. On your back next to your friend. No. Not that close. Just close enough so we can watch you both. That's right. Now fold your arms over your chest and don't move."

"Can ye let us go just this once, your la'ship? We never done this 'afore, but there's no honest work to be had and . . . and we have families to feed," Smith whined.

Helena didn't take her eyes off either highwayman. "You should have thought of that before you murdered that poor gentleman lying over there."

"He ain't dead, miss. Just stunned-like. Go see fer yerself."

"Not on your life, you glib-tongued thief. I'll see to him once you're both safely bound. If he's dead, heaven help you. You'll both hang for it."

Casper returned with Amy in tow. "Got the rope, milady. We're gonna tie 'em up. Give us a hand, Rabu."

"All right, but be quick about it," Helena said. "Tie them each to a separate tree. And be sure to tie them tight, so they can't run away. We'll ride ahead to Bodmin. We're staying at the Pig and Whistle, an inn I know well. The landlord will summon the constable to fetch these two. If that poor man lying over there is still alive, we'll have to take him with us. The innkeeper will send for a doctor."

Helena watched Casper and Rabu roll Isley over and tie his hands behind his back while Amy secured his feet. "Ow," cried Isley. "Watch me wounded leg."

"And whose fault is that, lad? You only got what you deserved. Be thankful you're still alive," lectured Amy as she helped Casper and Rabu. They dragged him to a tree, where they sat him up and bound him securely.

Smith made as if to move. "Ladies don't know how to shoot," he snarled.

Helena lifted the rifle. "Care to test my skill? As you wish, but be prepared. I may be a bit rusty. I might miss your leg and blow your head off instead. Go ahead, you cur. Make one move and we'll see if I can shoot." She raised the rifle higher and glued one eye to its sight once more.

"Don't bother to shoot him, milady. We're ready for him," said Casper cheerfully as he and Rabu rolled Smith over. "Tie his legs tight, Amy. Just like we did t'other one."

When Smith was securely tied to a tree, Helena handed Casper the rifle and raced to the poor gentleman lying on the side of the road. Face down, the victim was covered with clumps of leaves. She brushed aside some of the debris.

"Merciful heavens!" she cried. "It's Lord Waverley!"

The earth began to spin and she fainted.

Chapter 6

Helena woke in confusion early in the evening. "Where are we?"

"Casper followed your instructions, milady. We went on to Bodmin like you said. We're at the Pig and Whistle Inn. How are you feeling?"

A mere stone's throw from Bodmin Castle. With a pang of homesickness, she recalled that old Tremayne's relatives were occupying the family castle for the wedding of his grandson. She shook off her melancholy and rose up on her elbows. "I'm fine, Amy. Tell me what happened. I don't remember anything past discovering Lord Waverley lying in the ditch."

"You fainted, milady. Casper and me, we carried you back to the carriage. We left Rabu to watch over his lordship. I stayed with you while Casper went back and helped Rabu carry his lordship to our coach."

"Is he all right?"

"Casper's fine, milady."

"No, you ninny. I mean the marquis."

"His lordship's got a big bump on his head is all—not the one I give him, but a new one. Doctor says no bones are broke."

"And the highwaymen? Have they been arrested?"

"People came running when they heard that first shot. A farmer and some of his friends are seein' to them, milady. He took them to his barn. They'll keep till morning for the constable, he promised."

Helena attempted to rise, but Amy stopped her. "No, milady. Doctor said you need rest."

"All right, but only until I feel able to rise."

Amy clasped her hands and beamed at her with smug satisfaction.

"Why are you looking at me like that?"

"Imagine a lady like you knowin' how to shoot a rifle. Ready to kill those highwaymen if they so much as moved. I was that proud, I was. Where'd you learn to shoot, milady?"

Helena tried to laugh, but it made her head ache. "I've never fired a shot in my life. I feel much better, dear. Help me dress. I want to visit Lord Waverley."

The abigail, determined not to allow her mistress to enter a gentleman's chamber without a chaperone, insisted on accompanying her. They found his lordship sitting up, being fed soup by Rabu.

Waverley grinned when Helena entered. "Good morning, fearless heroine. My deepest thanks to you for saving my life. Casper informs me you are an excellent markswoman."

There wasn't a hint of sarcasm in his voice, which caused her to blush. "How are you feeling, my lord?"

"Lucky to be alive. Have you had your dinner?" When she shook her head, he turned to his valet. "Take this horrid gruel away and bring us a proper dinner. And don't forget the wine. Her ladyship and I are sorely in need of some." He dismissed Rabu with a flick of his hand.

"Rabu, the giggler," she remarked wryly."Have you ever heard him giggle when he is hysterical?"

"I haven't had that pleasure. What does a hysterical giggle sound like?"

She thought a moment. "It sounds something like a cross between threatening sobs of fright and frenzied laughter."

"I see. Only God knows why he giggles." His eyes searched hers. "Who taught you to handle a rifle so well?"

"I've never so much as held a rifle in my hands until yesterday morning. Truth be known, I was even more terrified than my victims. Thank heavens they didn't press me to demonstrate my skills."

He began to laugh but held his head from the pain it caused him. "Oh. Oh. Oh. It hurts to laugh, but that is capital. Capital! Common highwaymen thwarted by a hoax! When I tell . . ."

Helena placed her hands on her hips. "Don't you dare spread this about, you cad!" But his infectious grin captivated her and she grinned as well.

Waverley made a face when Amy poked her head into his chamber. "Go away, lass. I've already had my knock on the head for the day, thank you."

Helena added, "Do go away, Amy. Do as you're bid. You needn't guard me against Lord Waverley."

"Yes, milady. If you're sure, milady . . ."

"I give you my word I'll behave like a gentleman, lass," said the marquis, bestowing a winning smile upon her. "I have no intention of giving you cause to thump me again."

When Amy withdrew, he said, "Give me your hand, intrepid Helena. What a brave girl you are." He held her hand and stroked it.

"No nonsense, Waverley. You promised Amy."

He lay back on his pillow and closed his eyes. "Indeed I did, but if the wish were the deed . . ." His look was thoughtful. "Had you ever seen those two men before?"

"No, of course not. What made you ask?"

"I can't help but wonder what two footpads from London would be doing posing as highwaymen so far from home."

"Why do you think they're from London?"

"I recognized their accent at once. They're London footpads all right. No doubt about it."

Rabu entered with a tray, and conversation ceased while the valet set a small table before Helena.

"Set it in front of the fireplace, Rabu. I prefer to dine with her ladyship there. When you have done as I bid you, help me into my dressing gown."

"Are you sure you're well enough to rise from your bed, Desmond?"

The sound of his name on her lips gave him a stab of pleasure. "I give you my word, ma'am."

Helena didn't wait for Rabu to finish his task. Instead, she found Waverley's dressing gown lying at the foot of his bed. "I'll help you, sir."

"No, no, meestress!" shrieked Rabu. "I must do for mastah." The cutlery he held clattered on the table. He raced to her side and wrested the robe from her hand.

Amused, Waverley came to his valet's rescue at once. "Make my life easy, I beg of you, ma'am. Allow Rabu to have his way. If he is prevented from performing a task he considers his own, he makes my life difficult by sulking for weeks."

"I understand. Sorry, Rabu." She handed him the dressing gown and did her best to keep a straight face. She turned away and took a seat at the table.

"Serve us before you leave the room, Rabu."

The valet looked crestfallen as he filled their plates. "So sorry, mastah." He giggled, but his heart wasn't in it.

Waverley put down his fork after the first bite when he noticed Rabu lingering. "Out!" His valet nearly tripped in his haste to depart.

"He means well, poor fellow. I shan't vex him again, I promise you."

"My cross to bear." He filled their glasses with wine. "We're one day away from Waverley Castle."

"That should please you."

"Indeed. I'm pleased, but I'm also apprehensive. I haven't been home in twelve years. I was so pleased when I learned that my grandmother was still alive. Will she recognize me after all these years? The thought haunts me."

"Did you not communicate with her?"

"No. I wrote to her several times when I reached India, but she never acknowledged my letters. I wrote to my father as well, with the same result."

Which means he was convinced his family didn't care about him, poor man. "Are you the only child in your family?"

"Yes, as a matter of fact."

"How unfortunate. I miss my family, especially my sister Olivia. She is the wife of Sebastian Brooks."

"So he said. You're all close?"

"Oh, yes. We squabble amongst ourselves, but when it comes to trouble, we meet it as one. You met them all when we left London."

"I can't recall, for the meeting was all too brief. Perhaps another time."

"My sister Georgiana will celebrate her debut in June. Will you come?"

"I'd be happy to attend." His fork fell onto his plate and he closed his eyes. "Your company is most welcome, ma'am, but I fear I need rest far more than food."

Alarmed by his ashen pallor, Helena rose quickly. "You must do so by all means." She opened the door to call for Rabu only to find him standing outside. "Your master needs to rest. Look after him. I'll send someone to clear the remains of our dinner."

She waited while the valet helped Waverley to his bed and settled him in.

Before she left the room, she patted his hand. "Sleep well, Desmond."

She used my name again. A good sign. "We're on more comfortable terms, aren't we?" He covered her hand with his. "I need your friendship, Helena. Have I earned that right?"

Her heart gladdened for the kindness in his tone. "Yes, of course. I desire that as well. You ought to rest now. I'll see you in the morning."

"I am persuaded I shall be well enough to continue our journey tomorrow morning. Good night, sweet Helena." He closed his eyes before she could raise any objection to his use of her name.

She found Amy and directed her to send someone to remove the dinner tray from his lordship's chamber.

"Where are you going, milady?"

"Have you seen my journal? I can't find it."

"No, milady."

"Search the room while I'm gone." She went downstairs to the stable where her horses, her chaise and her driver were quartered. "Casper? I need to search the carriage for something."

"What is it, my lady? Perhaps I can help."

"Nothing of great value to anyone but me. It's my journal. It has a black leather cover and two ties that secure it. The contents of our bags flew all over the carriage when you were forced to stop so abruptly yesterday."

The two searched for it but the volume was nowhere to be found.

"Thank you, Casper. Never mind. His lordship wishes to leave in the morning, assuming he is well enough to continue the journey."

* * *

Waverley woke at dawn, but lay with his eyes closed until Rabu's snores assured him he would not wake. He turned up the wick, reached under his pillow, and found the journal he'd taken from the chaise when Helena and Amy thought he was still in a swoon.

He untied the ribbons and read the last page. To his astonishment, Helena's deepest thoughts were all about him.

> *I fear I am not desirable to him. Be that as it may, I cannot hide from myself the fact that I desire Waverley. I cannot stop thinking of that night when he made love to me in Darlington's bed. I responded with passion then, just as I responded to his kiss now. I can't help but wonder, how could I have mistaken him for Darlington? How foolish of me. I should have known it wasn't Chris, but I ignored the obvious signs. Waverley must think me wanton, merely another flirt ready to bed him whenever he wishes. Rakes are used to such women. Does he think me one of them? Am I one of them? Perhaps I am. No matter. I mean to convince him otherwise.*

Waverley closed the journal and retied it, feeling like a cad for invading her innermost thoughts. He'd have to put it back into the carriage before she missed it. He turned the wick down and dressed without waking his valet. He closed the chamber door after him and crept downstairs, boots in hand. No one was witness. Good. He pulled his boots on out of doors and made his way to the stable behind the inn.

He was in luck. The carriage window was open a crack. He dropped the diary into the cab. The door to the stall creaked when he led his horse out, but his good fortune held. No one stirred. He saddled his horse and led the handsome chestnut away from the inn, feeding him lumps of sugar to keep him from snorting. Once past the gate, he mounted, gripped the reins and rode off at his usual pace.

Helena crawled out from under the bed and sat back on her heels, her traveling gown covered with dust. She brushed at it impatiently. "I've searched everywhere. And I still can't find my journal."

"It must be here somewhere, my lady." Amy pulled her from the floor and took over brushing away the rest of the dirt. "If you ask me, they need to hire a better chambermaid."

"Indeed," said Helena, distracted. She searched the room one more time as she reviewed the events of the day before, trying to remember the last time she'd seen it. She began to pace as Amy returned to packing her clothes. She had been writing in it when they came across the highwaymen. She couldn't recall seeing it afterward. Of course, her memory was a bit sketchy since she had been terrified at the time. "Oh, well. Perhaps it fell out of the carriage in all the excitement."

"Mayhap," agreed Amy, her hands about to fold a green sprig muslin morning gown away. "You can always purchase a new one, milady." She shook out the dress and began to fold its skirt.

"Yes." Helena imagined her journal lying torn and horse-trodden in the road, possibly destroyed by a passing farm wagon. Exasperated, she felt like screaming.

"I'll search the carriage for it once more just as soon as I finish packing, milady." Amy folded another gown and placed it carefully into her mistress' valise.

"Take your time," said Helena. "I'll have a look in on Lord Waverley." She walked through her door into the hallway and broke into a more hurried step, slowing down only when she came across the chambermaid on her hands and knees scrubbing the floor. Holding her skirts off the muddied boards,

Helena squeezed past her. She dropped them again and hurried across toward Waverley's room.

The door was open and the bed made. Indignant, she turned and stomped downstairs only to confront the landlord headed for the breakfast room carrying a tray of covered dishes.

"Don't tell me Lord Waverley's already come down for his breakfast? Really, he doesn't show the least ounce of sense. He needs more time to recuperate."

"But milady . . ."

"Tell the marquis that I insist he return to his bed. Do as I say."

"But . . ."

"Now, Landlord. If you please."

"The gentleman's gone out riding, your la'ship."

"He left the inn and you didn't stop him? You knew Lord Waverley was not well."

The landlord shrugged uneasily. "I never saw him leave, your la'ship."

"Stubborn man! I don't suppose you could have stopped him even if you tried."

"No, milady."

"No matter. I shall depart after breakfast."

The landlord nodded, relieved that she was no longer angry with him. It wouldn't do to upset the Quality. He handed the tray to a waiter and hurried away to prepare his bill.

What two kinds of fool was she, Helena wondered, angry with herself. *What's Waverley up to? Doesn't matter. I can very well reach my destination without his help. I don't want his help. I don't need it.* Yet her heart told her otherwise.

She toyed with her food, feeling like a homeless waif abandoned on the streets of London, left to fend for herself. She looked up in surprise when the door opened to reveal Waverley.

"Morning, sweet Helena. How are you feeling?" He

removed his riding coat, his gloves and his whip and took a seat opposite her. "I could eat a horse this morning." He beckoned to the waiter at the sideboard. "Eggs, ham, toast and coffee, please."

"If your appetite's returned, it's a sign you are well again, I suppose," she said with considerable asperity.

He looked at her in surprise. "What have I done to put you out of sorts, fair Helena? I merely went for my customary morning ride."

"You shouldn't have done it. You aren't well enough," she said primly, as if she were his nurse.

His lips quivered, yet he managed not to laugh. "I thank you for your concern, but the truth is, I tend to recover quickly from ailments. Besides, my injury was nothing more than a bump on the head."

"Where's Rabu?"

"He's packing. We'll have good weather until we hit the fog on the moors."

"How fortunate."

He put his cup down and sat back. "Don't be angry with me, sweet Helena. Can you forgive me?"

"You might have had the courtesy of leaving word that you were merely off for a morning ride!"

He picked up his cup to hide his grin. *She worries over me, poor lass. No one's done that for years. How nice.* "My apologies, especially since you saved me from certain death. I should have left word for you, sweet—"

"Don't call me that!"

"Are you not sweet? You're wrong, you know."

"I must see to the packing, sir." She stormed out of the room.

She's magnificent when she's angry. I cannot imagine how she managed to hoax two seasoned London footpads into believing she knew how to handle a rifle. She has such a lively spirit. He cleaned his plate and rose, a happy grin creasing his face.

Once under way, Waverley rode beside the carriage with mixed thoughts of Helena on his mind. His fingers tingled at the recollection of his hands stroking her breasts. Or was he a fool ten times over to let himself be beguiled by a beautiful face and a luscious body? He couldn't answer that question. At the same time, he couldn't stop thinking about sweet Helena.

It was a fine April morning, warm and sun filled. The marquis was eager to reach Waverley Castle in Land's End. He rode slightly ahead of Helena's carriage and came upon a familiar boulder. It was shaped like a bald eagle's head poised for flight. At this juncture, the road narrowed. On the north side, a forest of trees, on the south, the English Channel. The sound of the sea pulsed inside his ear. In spite of all the years he'd spent on foreign soil, there was no sound quite like the surf pounding the rocks on the magnificent Cornish coast.

Helena leaned back against her seat while Amy squirmed, trying to find a comfortable spot. She reached behind her for the hard object jabbing into her and picked up the black leather-bound journal. "Look here. I've found it, milady." She held up the tooled volume. "It was here all the time. Just stuck way down in the folds of my seat, see?"

Helena seized the diary from Amy's fingers and began to leaf through it. All the pages were accounted for, to her relief. "Thank you, dear. I can be easy again."

They stopped in Truro for refreshments as well as for a final change of horses.

It was past three in the afternoon when they were ready to

leave Truro for Land's End. Rabu climbed up to sit next to
Casper after Helena and Amy were settled. The marquis led
the way along the narrow road that ran parallel to the sea.

Helena inhaled the sharp tang of the brisk sea air and
listened to the seagulls squawking. She was as eager for the
journey to end as the rest of their party. How nice it would
be not to have to be jounced in a carriage for hours on end,
she thought.

At Waverley's command, Casper turned the chaise in the
direction of the castle. They made their way along the main
road, one much frequented by mail coaches.

The view of the sea to the south and the moors to the north
enchanted Helena. She took out her quill and opened the journal to a clean page and began to describe the beauty of the
rugged coast of Cornwall that met her eyes.

London

The duchess entered the breakfast parlor clutching a letter
in her hand.

"Good morning, dear. Up early, I see," said the duke,
wiping his mouth.

She took the seat held for her by a footman while another
brought her tea and toast, her customary breakfast. "I need a
word, your grace." She glanced at the servants.

The duke nodded to the head footman, who understood the
silent command well. He cleared the room of servants and
followed the last one out of the swinging door that connected
the kitchen to the dining room.

"What is it, my dear?"

"I've had a letter from Helena. Posted at Turks Head Inn in
Exeter."

"How is she getting on?"

"She doesn't say, Tony. All she writes is she has been asked to tell you that the landlord wishes to be remembered to you."

The duke chuckled. "I don't doubt that I will meet with his humblest thanks in the enormous bill he'll send for his services." He took a sip of his coffee. "Have we done the right thing, Ellen? Sending her so far away from us?"

"What else could we do to protect her from the gossipmongers? Besides, it's only for a short time. She'll be back in June for Georgiana's ball. By then the scandal will be old news and the gossips will have gone on to another *on dit*."

"If Georgie doesn't break her foolish neck before then," the duke said with asperity.

The duchess sighed. "What has she done now to vex you so?"

"The stable master informs me that she rode out yesterday morning with my best racer and tore through Richmond Park hell for leather. She rides without heed to danger for herself as well as for my horses, Ellen. You must speak to her about her wild conduct."

Instead of laughing at the duke's attempt to fob off his parental responsibility on her—it was *his* racer after all—the duchess covered her face with her napkin, as if in the process of wiping her lips. "Certainly, dear, but I shall need the benefit of your wisdom to do it. What would you suggest I say to her?"

The duke pursed his lips. "I suppose you think it my place to give her a good talking to," he grumbled.

"Not at all. I'll talk to her. It's just that I look to you for . . . direction in such a delicate matter."

"No. You're right, Ellen. I ought to be the one to talk to her. No. No. Don't protest. My mind is made up. She needs a father's sternness rather than a mother's soft reprimand in this instance."

"Whatever you say, dear. You always know best." She paused. "There is something else."

"What? Has that brat done something else to plague us?"

"It's not Georgiana. It's Mary."

The duke's eyes flew open in surprise. "Mary? You can't mean our most obedient child? All she ever does is practice the pianoforte. What can she possibly have done to distress you?"

Chapter 7

"We're almost there, milady!" shrieked Amy, startling Helena out of her reveries. "Waverley Castle is just beyond that bend in the road."

Helena rolled her window down and leaned out. "Casper, stop a moment." She flew out of the coach before he could climb down from his perch. The fog lifted as if on some ethereal command and her heart skipped a beat. The scent of wild verbena filled the air, its lavender blossoms crowding the roadside and swaying in the slight breeze. But the short flower spikes did nothing to obstruct the magnificent view of the sea beyond.

Waverley came up behind her and rested his hands on her shoulders. "Takes my breath away. I'd almost forgotten the sound of the sea. There's something holy about its power."

"Indeed," she said, wishing the moment would last—especially the feelings he aroused with his touch. "Oh, yes. It overwhelms me."

Amy sidled up to them and said, "Just as I told you, milady."

"Yes, Amy. It fairly robs me of speech." Waverley and Helena exchanged glances of amusement at Amy's determined enforcement of proper behavior between them.

"Right pretty," agreed Casper, who had handed the reins to Rabu and climbed down to stretch his legs.

Helena smiled to herself, for Casper's eyes were trained not on the coastline but on her abigail.

Amy shook a warning finger in his face. "Don't be standin' there, you lout. Help milady up so's we can go on to the castle."

"I know me duty, lass. Don't be thinking you have the right to order me about."

"Why you, you . . ."

"Enough. It's late and Lady Fairchild is weary," said Waverley in a voice meant to brook no nonsense.

Casper handed Amy in first, unable to resist squeezing her waist. She pushed his hand away and rewarded him with an indignant glare, which pleased him no end.

"Allow me, ma'am," said Waverley, helping Helena into the coach. "Though our long journey ends shortly, a new chapter begins. As always, I remain your servant."

"I can take care of myself, sir," she murmured in embarrassment.

He leaned into the coach and ran the back of his hand across her cheek. "You've already taught me that, haven't you? I shan't forget how you saved my life. Thank you again."

"You're welcome, my lord."

"Why so formal?"

She smiled at him. "You're welcome, Desmond."

"That's better, sweet Helena." He mounted his horse and led the way to the home he had not seen in years. What would he find waiting for him there, he wondered.

Helena ignored the jolt on the road as the carriage rattled on, for her mind was on Waverley. It dawned on her that she was in danger of losing her heart to a rake. *Or is it that I need to feel loved once more? With Darlington, it was one-sided. I know that now, to my regret. Is it the same with Waverley? Am I reading too much into his attentions?*

When the coach turned the bend, Waverley castle came into Helena's view. Gun ports and musket slits facing the sea ran unevenly across its crown. Below them were mullioned windows. At one end she noted a round tower and at the other, a square structure where the original keep may have been. Behind the castle rose a taller structure. From its modern design, Helena correctly assumed it had been more recently added. The whole stood sentinel above the sea, as if meant to protect the land from marauders.

When they reached the entryway, its large open gate listed like a sinking ship sorely in need of rescue. The coach bumped and swayed down an uneven drive lined with trees and shrubs. These had been neglected, Helena noted. She wondered why.

The marquis was first to dismount. His eyes swept the facade, despair writ large on his face. He surveyed the visible damage to his beloved Waverley and swallowed bile.

Casper climbed down at the entrance and lowered the steps. He offered his hand to his mistress. When he did the same for Amy, she glared at him and brushed it aside.

The sound of the sea crashing against the wall of craggy rocks below the old castle offered Waverley momentary relief from his misery. "I haven't heard anything quite like that lovely sound since I was a boy."

Helena ignored the anguish he was trying to mask, unwilling to add to his grief. "It is lovely, isn't it?"

"Ring for the butler, Casper," the marquis said.

Amy proceeded to fuss over her mistress, straightening her bonnet, tucking a stray curl in, smoothing her skirt. Helena caught Amy's hand, knowing if she didn't stop her, the abigail would waste whatever daylight was left in the grooming process.

Waverley offered his arm and led Helena to the landing in

front of the huge oak door. Casper raised the knocker and banged it on the door. He was forced to repeat this several times more before the door creaked open.

"Whatcher want?" said a gruff voice. The slovenly dressed man at the door scowled at Casper.

"Where is the butler?" demanded Waverley.

"We ain't got any butler."

"And who might you be?"

"Who wants t'know?"

Desmond drew himself up and said with all the pomp he could summon, "I am the Marquis of Waverley. This is my home."

The information did not appear to faze the man. "You 'is wife?" he asked Helena.

Desmond raked his eyes over him as if he were confronting an ugly toad. "Lady Fairchild is the daughter of the Duke of Heatham. She is my guest, come to visit my grandmother, the dowager marchioness. I trust her ladyship is well?"

The man scratched the stubble on his chin and thought, a rare occurrence for a man of his intelligence. "Wait here." Before he could clank the door shut, Casper put his foot in it to prevent him from doing just that.

The marquis turned to Helena and muttered, "This doesn't bode well."

"No, indeed." She summoned a smile in spite of her uneasiness. "You shall sort it out, I'm sure."

He patted her hand, comforted by her sympathy. "Depend upon it."

The door swung open to reveal a white-haired woman dressed in a soiled gown, a large ring of keys hanging from a chain around her ample waist. She squinted at them with faded brown eyes keen enough to note the servants as well as the carriage filled to the brim with baggage. Her bulbous red nose bespoke a tippler of whiskey and ale. She was short and squat, as if carved from a block of rough wood. Her hands were on her hips in a belligerent stance while the man who had summoned her stood by her side as if ready to attack if only she would give the command.

The woman said, "I'm Mrs. Trasker. I don't know what faradiddle you're tryin' to fob off on my son Harry, but it won't work. Everyone knows that the marquis' son died at sea years ago."

Helena raised her hand to warn Waverley not to speak. She said in a soothing voice, "You were misinformed, ma'am. This is indeed the marquis, and I am Lady Fairchild. My mother, the Duchess of Heatham, is goddaughter to the marchioness. The dear lady was kind enough to invite me to visit her. And the marquis was kind enough to escort me here. You received my mother's letter informing you of my arrival, I'm sure."

Her words took the woman by surprise but she recovered at once and barked, "Never saw such. Got lost, mayhap."

Helena shook her head in mock disbelief. "Lost? But how can that be when it was delivered by special messenger and signed for?"

"Come in, then. But not this . . . imposter," she said, trying to maintain her advantage.

Waverley stepped forward and flashed his most winning smile at the odious woman. He held out his hand to her—his signet ring staring her in the face. "Beg pardon, ma'am," he began as if taking her into his confidence. "After my investiture by the Prince Regent, I set off for Waverley at once, for I was most anxious to meet my family. You and your son are Banningtons, I have been told. Therefore, ma'am, we are cousins. It should be obvious that rumors of my death were exaggerated. As you see, I am very much alive."

The ring glistened in the waning sunlight. "When news of my father's death reached me, I returned to England at once to take possession of my estate and care for my grandmother."

"Ring is a fake, mayhap. Any jeweler might make a copy from one o' them books."

"Good God! Do you think it a fake? The Regent will be distressed when he hears of this forgery."

Emboldened, Mrs. Trasker added, "That's right. So I'll need more proof you're the marquis."

Waverley pretended to think on this bizarre request. "I suppose I might apply to Magistrate Wyndham. He was a close friend of my father's. He's known me all my life." He reached into his vest pocket and drew out his watch. "At this time, the magistrate is likely to be enjoying his dinner with his family. I would hate to disturb him, especially since the result will be in my favor, I assure you."

The woman stuck out her chin in a final attempt at defiance, though her eyes signaled defeat. She glanced over the entire group. "Din't 'spect so many of you. Rooms ain't ready."

"We'll make do," said Waverley with more cheerfulness than he felt. In truth, his hands itched to strangle the woman. "Bring our baggage in, Rabu. Casper will assist you." He turned to Mrs. Trasker and added, "I shall occupy my father's quarters in the east wing, cousin. Would you be so kind as to escort Lady Fairchild to the chamber opposite my grandmother's?"

Amy cleared her throat to gain his lordship's attention.

"Yes? What is it, Amy?"

"The men are hungry, milord."

"Thank you for reminding me, lass." He turned to Casper and said, "The kitchen's below stairs, just opposite the stables. After you unload our baggage, stable the horses and inform Cook of our arrival."

Not to be left out, Amy added, "Ask for Cook Wells. She's my aunt and she knows we're expected, 'cause I wrote to my mum. She's told her, I'm sure. And don't forget to remind her to prepare some supper for the marquis and her ladyship."

"Yes, lass." Casper winked at her.

"Stubble it, Casper," Amy growled. She turned away to follow her mistress.

But Helena stopped her. "Go along with Casper and Rabu and tell your aunt not to fuss over dinner for us. Something simple will do."

"But milady . . ."

"Do as I say, dear," Helena ordered.

Upon entering the Great Hall, Waverley said at once, "I must make our arrival known to my grandmother. Will you excuse me?" Without waiting for answer, he took the stairs two at a time to the second floor where he knew he would find his grandmother's chamber.

Helena remained behind and took stock of her surroundings, astonished at what met her eyes. Dust motes floated in the air like soiled snowflakes. Her senses were assaulted by a stale odor so foul as to offend the heartiest soul. There were wiited flowers in the decorative bowl adorning a grimy table in the center of the hall. The floors felt like sand beneath her feet. It was obvious they hadn't been swept in some time.

She heard the voices of two under maids chatting idly to one another drifting from somewhere nearby. Had they nothing better to do than gossip to pass the time? A cold chill seeped into her bones and she shuddered, for there was no fire in the grate. Two armored statues white with dust stood sentinel on either side of the grand staircase, its banisters sadly in need of polish.

Helena turned to face the woman who had tried so hard to prevent their entry. "Mrs. Trasker? I would be most indebted to you if you would lead me to my chamber."

"How long you gonna stay?"

Helena ignored her belligerence. "I cannot say. A month? Two? Perhaps three." She spoke casually, knowing her words would irritate. "Inform my abigail to join me as soon as she may. She can unpack my things while I rest. I'll meet the dowager marchioness at dinner."

"Her ladyship doesn't come down to dinner. She eats in her chamber and sleeps a lot, her bein' sick and all."

Helena understood that she was engaged in battling a formidable enemy. Here was a challenge she was determined to win. "Then I have my work cut out for me, Mrs. Trasker. I mean to relieve you of the burden of caring for his lordship's grandmother. The Duchess of Heatham, my mother, charged me with the task of seeing to her ladyship's well-being. I hope that will relieve your mind."

"That chamber opposite her ladyship ain't been used for years. You might be more comfortable if you stayed in Ship Inn. It's in Sennen Cove, not far from here."

"That won't be necessary. I'll be fine here. There's no need to trouble your servants, Mrs. Trasker. My abigail will put the chamber to rights."

"How is it you got a Cornish lass for your maid? I heard her accent."

Another battle, Helena thought grimly. Taller than her adversary, she drew herself up and glanced down at the woman in haughty disdain. It took but a moment for the woman to lower her eyes. "For your information, Amy Wells grew up in Sennen Cove. Her mother and her uncle are the owners of Ship Inn. I would be most welcome if I wanted to stay there, for their hospitality is well known. But I am here and here is where I shall stay. Do I make myself clear?"

Trying for intelligence, Harry interrupted, "I knows the place. Been there a time or . . ." His mother's icy stare silenced him at once.

Helena stifled the wicked grin threatening to disarrange her lips. She ignored the son, turned to the mother and said, "Would you be so kind as to lead the way to my chamber, ma'am?"

In a desperate effort to regain the upper hand, Mrs. Trasker invented what she hoped was a further obstacle to the unwanted invasion of what she had come to think of as her castle. "Coachman has to sleep over the stable. Your maid and milord's valet sleep in the servants' quarters in the attic."

Helena smiled indulgently, though it cost her. "That will suit us very well. Allow me to thank you for your cooperation, Mrs. Trasker. You're too kind." Helena strode to the grand staircase and waited, astonished at her unaccustomed audacity. Had her sarcasm found its mark? She couldn't be sure.

"This chamber ain't fit for pigs!" exploded Amy when she joined her mistress.

Helena put a finger to her lips and whispered, "Hush, Amy. Someone might be listening at our door. We can't let on how we feel just yet. Let's explore our surroundings first. What's behind that door?"

Amy opened the door. "It's a sitting room, milady."

Helena opened another door on the opposite side of the room. "Here's another chamber. It's in worse condition than this room, but it's large and it does have a bed. Would it do for you, do you think? Mrs. Trasker is threatening to house you in the attic with her other maids."

Amy peeked over her mistress' shoulder. "Better here than in the attic with that lot! Seems like they don't do a lick of work." She began to open the large trunk.

"Don't unpack just yet. Help me get rid of the dust and the cobwebs first."

As they worked side by side, Helena chatted aloud, telling her how kind the Traskers were in their warm welcome to her. She whispered orders while Amy played along, delighted to be included in the game of deception.

"Where shall I put these, milady?" she said in as loud a

voice as she could manage. Then she added, "May I set your toiletries on this here er . . . dressing table?"

They worked first in the bedchamber wiping grime and dust away with the worn sheets they had stripped from the bed. Helena had brought her own linens, the ones she had used at the various inns whose chambers she'd occupied. Amy would use only these to make up the bed for her mistress. They put the stale water in the pitcher to good use, cleaning the windows and mopping the floor. Helena helped Amy replace the mattress after they had beaten the dust out of it on the small balcony, its doors flung open to the fresh air.

A knock on the door interrupted their work. Amy opened it to admit Lord Waverley, who put a finger to his lips. He entered the room, shut the door behind him and surveyed the scene.

"Appalling! My father's quarters are no better," he said in a whisper. In a louder voice he asked, "Care to join me for a stroll in the garden, ma'am? I expect you need a long walk after being confined in a coach for so long."

"I'd be delighted."

Amy shooed them out, her head bobbing in approval for once. They descended the grand staircase as if in no particular hurry. The marquis knew his way well. He led her into the library and through the doors that opened onto the terrace. They strolled down the steps into the garden, stopping only when they were well out of earshot.

"What a shock it must be to you to find Waverley Castle in such a poor state."

He grasped her arms, a look of despair on his face. "That's the least of my worries."

"What's wrong?"

"My grandmother is running a high fever. I fear for her life."

"It may well be influenza. Who is taking care of her? Does she have a nurse?"

"I saw no signs of one. She's living in squalor. My own

grandmother! Her gown is stained with food, her sheets are soiled and the chamber itself hasn't been cleaned in an age. I left Rabu to clean up and stand guard over her while I decide what's to be done."

Helena said, "That was wise. You must send Casper and Amy to Sennen Cove at once."

"What can they do?"

"Amy's mother and her uncle own Ship Inn. They will know of a reliable physician. You must write a note describing your grandmother's condition and add your calling card. A local doctor will come at once. Request a nurse as well. I'll fetch Amy and tell her what needs to be done. When you've written your letter, bring it round to the front door. By then, the coach will be waiting." Helena paused and whipped her head around.

"What is it?"

"I thought I heard a noise. Someone may be listening."

Waverley's eyes searched. "No one's here. May have been a rabbit or some other animal."

Hidden behind a clump of trees, Harry Trasker stood frozen in place until Helena and Waverley were well out of sight. Then he hurried to his mother's chambers. "Game's up, Ma. Better hightail it out o' here 'afore that swell puts the magistrate on us."

"Keep your tongue between your teeth, Harry. The marquis can't do a thing to us. We got rights. We're Banningtons, ain't we? 'Sides, he won't raise a fuss. Swells like him are always be worritin' about what other swells think of 'em. We ain't done yet, m'boy. Not by a long shot," said Mrs. Trasker. She took another swig of gin from the bottle in her hand. "Best you get word to My Lord. He'll tell us what we need do."

Her son beamed at her. "Yer a right one, Ma. Allus has an answer. What d'ya want me to tell My Lord?"

"Nothing. I'll write a letter for you to deliver to him."

* * *

The marquis led Helena into the kitchen once Casper and Amy had departed for Sennen Cove. Cook Wells looked up in annoyance at the interruption, but the look on her face turned to joy when she recognized the marquis. "Milord! Welcome home. Let me have a look at you. A mite taller, but still devilish handsome as ever." Cook Wells wiped her hands on her apron and curtseyed, her green eyes alive with gladness. "D'ye recollec' me, milord? Course, I was only a scullery maid when you was a lad."

Desmond lifted her flour-stained hand to his lips. "Of course I do. How could I forget the pretty lass who used to sneak warm cookies out of the pastry room for me? This is Lady Fairchild. She's visiting."

"Pleased to meet you, milady."

"She's come to visit my grandmother. I don't mind telling you that I'm worried about her. I've sent Amy to town for the doctor."

"That's good, milord! Mrs. Trasker wouldn't let me fetch him when I begged her. I've been in such a worry ever since them Traskers came here six months after the old marquis passed, may his soul rest in peace. Milady felt fine then, though a bit t'other side of memory, if you take my meaning. Here her la'ship took 'em in from the kindness of her heart and look how they repay her."

Waverley won Cook's heart when he said, "How good of you to remain in her service. She might have fared worse if you had left her." She blushed at the compliment.

While they spoke, Helena surveyed the large, immaculate kitchen, the only part of the castle she had seen that was in decent order. She was near to fainting from hunger, for it was late. "What smells so delicious, Cook?" she asked, interrupting them.

Waverley grinned, for he was famished as well. "Well, Cook? Will you take pity on two starving souls?"

Cook Wells grinned. "Seems like old times, milord. I recollec' you was always hungry as a lad. Still the same, eh?" She indicated the large table where the servants took their meals. "Wish I could serve you in the dining room, but it an't fit for a pig, thanks to the Traskers. Sit you both down at the servants' table and I'll fetch you some fresh-baked bread and home-churned butter. That'll set you to rights while I prepare you a proper dinner."

Cook proceeded to serve them a fragrant creamed mushroom soup, some cold meat, piping hot tea and warm apple pie topped with a slice of cheddar cheese. Waverley asked for second helpings, to Cook's delight. He was amused to see Helena, usually a picky eater, devouring her food with zest. When she had finished her last bit of pie, she groaned in contentment, to the delight of both Cook and the marquis.

"I've never seen you eat so much, ma'am," said Waverley, his eyes teasing.

"Does my heart good to see you both enjoy my vittles. Later, I'll serve you both some . . ."

Helena and the marquis laughed, for they were full to bursting. "No, no, Cook. Don't trouble yourself. I can't swallow another morsel tonight," Helena said kindly.

"Speak for yourself, ma'am. I, for one . . ."

"Now don't be scoldin' the lady, milord. I won't starve you whatever the time, to be sure."

Waverley's laughing face turned serious. "Where are all the servants? My father always kept a large staff."

"The Traskers sacked most of them and hired on the worst bunch of lazy scoundrels I ever did see. They like to eat well, so they agreed to keep my two nieces to help me in the kitchen when I threatened to give notice, which I assure you, but for my dear marchioness, I was sore tempted to do. Mrs. Trasker set herself up as housekeeper and that tub o' lard Harry as bailiff. There are just a few lazy new hires that are supposed to do all the work. They do nothin' at all. Won't take orders from anyone but them Traskers." She shook her head in disgust.

"What about my grandmother? Has she no say in the matter?"

"She's forgetful, poor soul. Mayhap they convinced her it was her own idea. If those two had their way, she'd be dead. I prepare food for her every day and sneak it up to her, 'cause they won't let Emma or Trudy serve her." She hesitated.

"Something else on your mind? You can speak freely, Cook," urged Waverley.

"They didn't expect your return, milord. They set it about that you was dead. Drowned at sea, they said. Truth be known, I thought so, too. That Mrs. Trasker's always braggin' how her son Harry's the next marquis. Where have you been all these years, if you don't mind my askin', milord?"

"Doesn't matter. I'm back now, and I shan't leave again, I promise you that."

Helena asked, "Are there no gardeners, Cook? The grounds have been terribly neglected."

"Them Traskers fired the lot of 'em. Saving the dowager money, they claim. Pocketing her blunt for themselves, more like. There's lots of grumbling from the tenants who farm your land, let me tell you. Trasker collects the rents, promises 'em repairs, then don't make 'em like he should. The stable's a mess too, milord. There are only two stable boys, the laziest, meanest do-nothings I ever did see."

"Rest assured I mean to set things right," Waverley said. He glanced at Helena, who was having trouble keeping her eyes open. "But for this evening, Lady Fairchild must have a hot bath and a decent night's sleep. We'll sort out what's to be done in the morning."

At once, Cook rang a bell and two young maids appeared, both dressed in immaculate uniforms. "Fetch some hot water and clean cloths for my lady's bath. She's in the chamber opposite her ladyship." She turned to Helena and Waverley and added, "This is Emma and this is Trudy, my sister's daughters."

"The Traskers may have some sense after all. They love your cooking as much as we do," Waverley said. The twinkle in his eyes brought an appreciative laugh from Cook.

"Stuff it, Casper! I've had enough of your smart mouth!"

"Come now, Amy lass. What's wrong with a fine lad like me escortin' a lovely miss into the village? They'll be talkin' for days about you havin' snared the handsomest London coachman they ever did see."

"You? Handsome? Don't make me laugh. Your ugly face couldn't catch an old blind woman."

"Don't want any old blind woman. Just you, lass. Just you."

Amy was keen on having the last word. "Without me you wouldn't find your way around these parts."

"I can find my way anywhere, my girl. Besides, you need a strong man like me to protect you. Wouldn't be proper to let you wander about alone."

"I'm not alone here. This is my home."

When they reached Ship Inn, Amy said, "I'll thank you to make yourself scarce while I'm visitin' me kin."

"Don't be forgettin' we need a doctor for the marchioness, lass. I'll wait in the taproom." Casper sauntered away, rendering Amy speechless, a rare event.

"Amy!" her mother shrieked as she emerged from the kitchen with a full plate in her hand. "Let me serve the gentleman over there and then give us a hug."

"Welcome home, Amy me darlin'." Her uncle Tom's beefy arms wrapped themselves around her.

"Hullo, Uncle Tom." She kissed his cheek just as her mother returned and snatched her from him.

"I need your help right quick, Mum. The old marchioness

is real sick. I've come with milady's driver Casper. We've been sent to fetch a doctor and bring him back as soon as may be. Can you help?"

"Don't you worry, lass. I'll rouse Doctor Fenwick and bring him right back here." Her mother removed her apron.

"Ask if he knows of a nurse willin' to come back with us tonight to take care of the poor old woman."

"Right. Mrs. Hubley lives a few doors away from the doctor. I'll fetch her as well."

Helena lounged in her hot bath and surveyed her chamber with appreciation. In her absence, Amy had performed a miracle, though the furnishings remained threadbare. She had scrubbed the room and made the bed with her mistress' clean linens.

Her thoughts turned to the marquis. She tried to examine the feelings he evoked whenever he touched her as he had done that first disastrous night when she'd mistaken him for Darlington. More to the point, why did her knees threaten to give way whenever he was near? Why did she melt at the sight of him? Why had no man come close to causing her heart to bump against her ribs as he did? Chris had never set her on fire. Not the way Waverley did. Was he indeed a rake? A rake would have seduced her by now. Wasn't that what rakes did to the women who succumbed to their charms?

The tantalizing thought made her breath hitch. She wondered if there was something wrong with her. Did other women ponder such illicit thoughts? She found no answers, but the questions swam around in her head like a school of fish.

Odd. There were so many sides to the marquis. Rake though he may be, he was also a loving grandson. He yearned to right the wrongs wrought by those odious Traskers. He had his work cut out for him. Of that, she had no doubt.

When exhaustion overcame her, she stepped out of the tub, dried herself, and donned her nightgown. One of Cook's nieces had lit the fire, which made the room comfortable. She climbed into bed, pleased to feel the heat of a hot brick at her feet. She fell asleep hugging her pillow as though she held the marquis in her arms.

Chapter 8

Monday, the Thirteenth of April, 1818

"A letter for you, my lord."

"My Lord" looked up from his desk and took the letter from the silver tray. He read the few sentences and frowned. "Pack my bags and order my carriage. I leave for the coast in one hour."

"Mornin', milady. Sleep well?" Amy drew the curtains aside to let sunlight into the room.

Helena stretched, feeling well rested indeed. "What time is it, dear?"

"It's past ten, milady. I've brought you your chocolate and a fresh scone." She plumped up the pillows behind Helena's head.

"Did you locate a doctor?" Helena asked anxiously, recalling the events of the previous night.

"Doctor Fenwick's been and gone, milady. He'll be back to look in on the marchioness later today. We've a fine nurse for her ladyship, too. Mrs. Hubley's her name."

Helena took a sip of chocolate. "What did the doctor say is wrong with the poor dear?"

"I don't know, milady, but his lordship knows. He spoke to him for a long time after the examination. His lordship has asked that you join him in the library. Wants to tell you what the doctor said."

"Then help me dress." She handed Amy her cup, threw off her covers and stepped off the bed. Twenty minutes later, she went down to the first floor, knocked on the door to the library and entered. She glanced around her at the book-lined walls, a long library table in the middle of the room and a decent fire lit in the enormous fireplace. The only dour note were the threadbare velvet curtains drawn open at the doors to the terrace.

The marquis looked up from his desk and smiled. "Morning, Helena. Not in the best of condition, is it? It will have to do for the time being. Did you sleep well?"

"Yes, thank you. What did the doctor have to report?"

"Shall we take a stroll in the garden?"

"Yes," she said, understanding at once the need for privacy.

"Those bloody fools have been making my grandmother ill. She has influenza, a serious condition in a woman her age," he said as soon as they had walked far enough away from the castle to speak without being heard.

"Good God!"

"Her fever's so high, she's become delirious. Doctor Fenwick says it is often the case with a high fever. He left instructions and medication with Nurse Hubley. Amy did well, ma'am. The doctor and the nurse are fine country practitioners."

"I'm relieved to hear it. Send the Traskers packing, Desmond. They're up to no good."

"I agree, but I won't send them off just yet. There's something smoky about them and the people they hired on. I mean to find out what their game is first." He stopped at a stone bench and brushed the dead leaves from it. "I'm in a quandary, I don't mind admitting. There's so much to do, I can't think how I may accomplish it all. I don't even know where to begin. I dare not leave the management of the castle in the hands of Mrs. Trasker. Nor can I allow her idiotish son to continue as bailiff. According to Cook, my tenants are at their wit's end." He leaned forward, one elbow resting on each thigh, his head held in his hands.

Helena's heart constricted, for she couldn't bear to see him suffer. "You're not alone in this, Desmond. You have a friend in me. Allow me to help."

"What do you suggest?"

"Leave the management of the castle to me. I had the greatest teacher in the world, you know. I've been learning her methods since I was a schoolroom miss. I'm speaking of my mother, the kind martinet of Fairchild House in London, the gracious admiral of Heatham House in Brighton and the even-tempered doyenne of Bodmin Castle in Cornwall. She directs all three with such easy competence, one would never guess that the Duchess of Heatham has a master plan. I hasten to add that every one of the servants in her employ deems it a privilege to serve her."

Waverley let out a bark of laughter. "Ought we to go to the source and engage your mother to accomplish this impossible task?"

"I wouldn't mind if you did, for I miss her terribly. But first, you would have to duel my father to the death. He would never agree to part with his precious treasure."

"Ugh! A horrid thought."

"While I lack the years of experience my mother possesses, I believe I can accomplish the task for you. Will you allow me to try?"

"What role must I play to help you in this daunting task?"

"Merely inform Mrs. Trasker that she is to take her orders

from me from this day forward. I warn you it will be costly, for I mean to hire an army of willing servants. Do you have sufficient funds?"

"More than ample. Spend what you like to achieve your purpose."

"Good! Then it's settled. You shall deal with estate matters while I deal with the staff." They rose as one. "Here's my hand on it."

A wicked gleam lit his eyes. "If we're to be partners in this endeavor, let us begin on an equal footing." He took her in his arms. "We shall seal our agreement with a kiss." His lips found hers, and when he deepened the kiss, she did nothing to stop him.

London

The duke looked up when his wife entered the library. "Afternoon, my dear." The look of concern in her eyes was enough to alarm him. "Something amiss?"

"It's Mary, dearest. Mrs. Trumball came to see me again this morning. She informs me our daughter plagues her with musical questions she is not capable of answering. She's taught her everything she can. She hasn't the talent that's needed for a student with Mary's extraordinary abilities, you see."

"Are you suggesting we need a new governess? Mrs. Trumball has been with us since Livy was an infant."

"No such thing, Tony. Mrs. Trumball is devoted to us. Our children adore her and she loves them as if they were her own. It's precisely why she urges us to find a better piano tutor for Mary. She says that Mary is too gifted musically, well beyond what she herself is able to provide in the way of instruction. You promised to seek a solution. Have you found one yet?"

The duke rose from his desk and led his wife to a window

seat. He put his arm around her. "I haven't forgotten, love. It has merely taken me longer than I supposed. My man ôf business has made inquiries at the Royal Philharmonic Society on Bond Street. They have assured him that they can provide excellent candidates for hire. I've given him leave to select someone appropriate for our musical genius and present him to Mary, but first you must approve his choice. He is planning to bring a prospective teacher for you to meet this afternoon."

Chapter 9

Tuesday, the Fourteenth of April, 1818

Helena woke to face the wretched task of repairing Waverley Castle with considerable trepidation. The Traskers would sabotage her, she knew, if they could manage it. Much needed to be done to set things right within the castle's walls, not to mention the gardens lying in ruin. She almost regretted having promised Waverley she could do so with such assuredness. She might have told him she would merely try, to save herself embarrassment later if she failed.

The thought stiffened her resolve. Fail? No. Fairchilds did not fail. The only question was how and where to begin. Could she do it? She wasn't sure, but she was determined to find a way.

She rose from her dressing table as soon as Amy had finished fussing over her hair. The marchioness had asked to meet with her this morning. She crossed the hallway and entered the dowager's bedchamber. The door stood open in invitation.

The marquis sat at his grandmother's bedside, her hand clasped in his. "There you are, ma'am. I was just telling Grandmother about you. Come over here where she can see you, Helena. She's impatient to meet her goddaughter's child."

Helena noted that the bedridden marchioness' rheumy eyes were lit with joy. Her thin hand held tight to Waverley's as she spoke. "How glad I am to meet you at last, my dear. My grandson informs me you have agreed to oversee the management of the castle and set things right again. What a mull I've made of it, eh?"

"Don't fret, Grandmother. You couldn't have known the Traskers would take such advantage of your generosity. I'll send them packing soon enough and you'll never have to deal with them again."

"Oh, no. You mustn't do that, Desmond. Jennie and her son are Banningtons. It wouldn't do to disown your own family," said the dowager.

Waverley frowned. "How has this come about? Refresh my memory, dearest. In what way are they related to us?"

"Jennie is the daughter of Lord Robert Bannington. He was the only child of Marcus Bannington, the youngest son of the First Marquis of Waverley, Lord Thomas. Robert died when he was two and twenty, poor boy."

"You took Mrs. Trasker's word for this?"

"I'm not such a goose as all that, my dear. I found Jennie's marriage and Harry's birth recorded in the Bannington family Bible. You may satisfy yourself, if you wish. It rests in Waverley Chapel."

He smiled at her. "No need for that, dearest. Your word suffices."

"There is something else I must confess to you. You won't find it written in our Bible, Desmond."

"What is it?"

His grandmother hesitated. "Jennie was born on the other side of the blanket, as they say."

"Her father never married her mother and she has the audacity to call herself a Bannington?"

"Be charitable, dearest. The sins of the father shall not be visited upon the child. Lord Robert might well have married Jennie's mother had he lived long enough. Besides, Jennie has overcome her unfortunate birth. She married in church and her son Harry is legitimate."

Waverley was unwilling to upset her further, for she was becoming agitated. "Be easy, Grandmother. Of course Banningtons are welcome here. I shan't turn them away if it pleases you."

"Thank you." The dowager closed her eyes.

Desmond rose and placed his grandmother's hand at her side. He bent his head to kiss her on the forehead and tucked the quilt around her. "Rest, love. I promise to visit again tomorrow."

"That's a good lad, my dear."

He waited by her side until her breathing deepened to indicate she was asleep, then backed away and nodded to Nurse Hubley. That good lady sat by the window occupied with her needlework. He offered Helena his arm and led her out of the room.

When he closed the door behind them, she said, "I have a lot of questions. Where can we talk?"

"Your chamber is just across the hall. It's as good a place as any." His eyes sparkled with mischief. "Or are you afraid I'll ravage you?" He looked down the hall in mock fear. "Is Amy nearby with her water pitcher, by any chance?"

She bit her bottom lip to keep from giggling. "I don't need Amy to chaperone me. I can take care of myself, but the servants . . ." He lifted an eyebrow. "Very well. We'll use the small sitting room next to my chamber. It's through that door."

His eyes fell on her four-poster, but she tugged his arm and led him past it to the sitting room, restored to cleanliness and some sense of order in spite of its threadbare appearance.

"Question," she began when they were seated. "What made you run away from home?"

"You want my life story?"

"That would be a good start."

"Merely a good start? Do you have plans for a suitable finish, then?"

"Be serious, Desmond. It would be a good idea to know something about you before I set about my work on your behalf. What if the Traskers question me? I don't want them to suspect we're perfect strangers. I'd much rather be prepared with answers."

"Oh? So it isn't mere curiosity, is it?" He raised his eyebrows to feign innocence.

She pursed her lips. "Don't be cheeky. If you prefer your past to remain a deep, dark secret, that's your own affair."

He looked mournful. "Now I have ruffled your feathers, haven't I?"

"How s . . . silly." She burst out laughing. "You are incorrigible."

"That's better! You have a charming laugh. Do it more often. You're far too serious much of the time." He sat back, buried his hands in his trouser pockets, stretched his legs out and crossed them.

"You want to know about my past? I was fourteen when my mother died. I suppose I added to my father's grief by running wild."

"What do you mean?"

"I bedded a willing country lass from Sennen Cove, the daughter of a farmer. She accused me of impregnating her. I wasn't the only one she bedded, mind you. I didn't deny it, for I foolishly expected the real culprit to step forward. Unfortunately, he didn't have the gumption. Instead, the coward allowed me to take the blame. Cost my father a fortune to buy the family off to avoid scandal. He was furious with me and wouldn't believe me when I confessed the truth. Took me to London until things at home cooled off. But there, I got into even more mischief. I had an affair with a married woman—

the wife of an earl. Mistaking a boy's natural lust for true love, I begged her to leave her husband and run away with me. The lady laughed in my face and recommended that I take myself off to the devil for all she cared. She had no intention of sacrificing her elegant life for a randy schoolboy, you see."

"How humiliating," she said, fresh from the sting of her own rejection.

"I know you felt that way when Darlington cried off, but you're wrong. Do you want an impartial observer's opinion?"

"What is that?"

"In the long run, you'll come to see that Darlington did you a kindness. He saves all his passion for his diplomatic career. Did it never occur to you that marriage to the daughter of a prominent duke was all he cared for?"

She hung her head. "That may be, but it hurts just the same."

"I felt the same when my paramour rejected me, but I can no longer recall her face. I thought my life was over then. I know now how fortunate I was she chose to spurn my suit. My father did not agree. He packed me off to India on the first merchant ship that would have me."

"Why did you never return to England?"

Grief creased his brow. "I had no reason to return. I wrote to him begging his forgiveness, but he never answered any of my letters. He wanted nothing more to do with me, so I stayed and stumbled onto my fortune instead. After a time, boredom with the life I was leading in Calcutta overcame me. I left for the continent and wandered from country to country. The life of an expatriate is not a pleasant one. I felt like a fish out of water."

"You needn't go on if it pains you," Helena said.

"There's not much more to tell. I was living in Paris when Darlington found me. He escorted me back to England to take up my duties as Marquis of Waverley. I was reluctant to return, for I had many friends and lived a life I enjoyed. It was the news that my beloved grandmother was still alive that changed my mind."

The candle guttered, casting the small sitting room into shadows. After a brief silence, Helena said softly, "How terrible for you not to be given the opportunity to make your peace with your father before he died."

A look of anguish crossed his face. "I'll have to live with that for the rest of my life, a bitter legacy indeed."

She reached out and soothed the creases on his brow. She allowed a moment to pass. Her eyes never wavering from his, she began to unbutton her bodice.

"No, Helena. I can't let you do this."

"It's not your choice, my lord. It's mine."

He covered her hands with his to stop her. "You mustn't tempt me. You already know what they called me in Paris: *le roué Anglais.* I fully lived up to that reputation, I assure you. Aside from that, I will not seduce you. I promised. . . ."

She put one finger on his lips to silence him, took his hand and pressed it to her bared breast. Heat coursed through her at the feel of his hot hand. "You have no choice in the matter, love. It is I who mean to seduce you. You cannot be so boorish as to refuse a lady's request, can you?"

He took his hand away and said in a voice tinged with bitterness, "I'm a rake, my dear. I promised not to ruin your reputation. I gave your brother-in-law my word on it. I mean what I say, for if it were known, you would be subject to further scorn from those in Polite Society. You are here because you were forced to run away from one scandal. Isn't that enough? You are an innocent, Helena. Don't force me into taking advantage of your innocence."

She shoved his hand away when he attempted to refasten her bodice. "Reputation be damned, Waverley. I want you. Doesn't that count for anything? I thought you felt the same for me."

His mocking words cut like a knife. "I have feelings of lust for every pretty lass who comes my way. I have a reputation to uphold, you see."

"Is that all I am to you? Just another pretty lass?"

"You're making this hard for me, Helena. I'm trying to assume the mantle of a gentleman, but it doesn't sit easy upon my shoulders. Earning a reputation as a rake was far easier, in fact. Don't you see? I cannot allow you to squander your virtue. What if you find yourself with child?"

Tears rolled down her cheeks. "Don't you want me?"

He barked a bitter laugh. "Want you? Don't tempt me any further, love, lest the consequences destroy us both. You have your reputation to protect, and I want to retain my resolve to reform."

In desperation, she wrapped her arms around his neck and attempted to kiss him.

"Damn you, wench!" He lifted her in his arms and strode through the door of the sitting room into her chamber. He threw her onto her bed and tore off everything she wore.

Her body was trapped under his. The heat within her grew stronger in spite of the pain, for he was by no means gentle. His tongue parted her lips and delved deep, demanding a response, one she could not help but give. His mouth turned to feast on one breast while his hand caressed the other, causing blood to course through her veins. One knee drove her legs apart.

She felt herself melting in a pool of lust. Why did her knees quake? Why was her breath so short? Her bare breasts heaved. She crossed her arms over them.

"No, no. Don't cover your breasts." He stripped off his shirt, revealing muscled arms and chest. He kicked off first one boot and then the other before he dropped his breeches.

She was unable to turn her eyes away. The sight of his engorged member sent shivers through her. She heard herself moan when he ran his tongue over her body.

His hand found the pulsing place between her legs. His

fingers curled around the hair and she arched her back. He touched her in places that brought short gasps of passion from her lips. The loud beating of her heart seemed to fill the room like thunder.

She gave a hoarse shout. "I love you, Desmond." But her cry had just the opposite effect.

He wrenched himself away and lay on his back gasping for breath. "Bloody hell, I've gone far enough!" Yet as he spoke, need addled his brain. The lust inside him raged still. He wanted her. He needed her. He was torn apart by indecision.

"Please," she begged in a whimper. She writhed beneath him, urging him with her body, slick with sweat.

Abruptly, his mind sabotaged all desire. *Good God! Is this a test to challenge my resolve? Am I so weak willed? I gave my word. I can't do this. I can't take her no matter how much I desire her.* He rolled away from her and reached for his trousers.

She sat up, panting for breath. "You . . . you're leaving me? At a time like this?"

Wild-eyed, Waverley stopped to stare at her as if he didn't know who she was. Without another word, he got up, wrenched the door open and fled the room.

"Desmond! You can't leave me like this."

The door slammed shut behind him.

Chapter 10

When dawn lit her chamber, Helena gave up the struggle for sleep, feeling as if she had been tossed about all night in a hurricane. *How dare he abandon me so cruelly? That makes two failures. First Darlington and now Waverley. Am I that unappealing?*

She rose and rang for Amy, nearly tearing the ancient bellpull out of the wall in the process.

"Yes, milady?" Amy's hair was in disarray, her gown not fully fastened in her haste to reach her mistress' chamber.

"Don't stand there gaping at me, you goose. Help me dress. There's work to be done today." She bounced out of bed to her washstand, glanced at the water, and aimed her anger on her abigail.

"Can you explain to me why you haven't changed the water this morning? Clearly, this abomination has been here since last night. Move, girl. At once!"

Tears began to flood Amy's face. "Ye-yes, milady."

"Why on earth are you crying? Stop it this instant. Are you not happy in your position as my abigail?"

Without answering, Amy curtseyed and disappeared before another onslaught of hateful words came raining down upon her.

"That's better," Helena muttered to herself. "High time someone cracked the whip around here."

"Here you are, milady." Amy set the fresh water down and reached for a towel. "Let me help—"

"I don't need your help to wash. Do you think I'm as helpless as the old marchioness? Set out a morning gown for me and leave me be."

Amy stood frozen in her tracks. Was this her kind, sweet lady? No. This was some monster. Someone she didn't know. Her mistress had never treated her with such haughty disdain before. What had set her so out of sorts? "Yes, milady. At once, milady."

"Don't you 'yes' me to death, you lazy—" Amy's quick sobs stopped her cold and Helena breathed a sigh of frustration. "Now what? Why are you blubbering?"

"You've never before . . ."

"I've never before what? Out with it. And stop that caterwauling, for heaven's sake. You're giving me a headache. I mean to accomplish the impossible, which is to turn this bloody castle into a decent, respectable, *clean* establishment. Exactly what it was meant to be. Wipe your tears and help if you've a mind to, for heaven's sake, and stop sniveling like a child."

"Yes, milady," Amy answered in a barely audible whisper. She began to pull the covers off the bed in order to remake it with clean linens.

"No. Leave that for later. Summon all the staff to the Great Hall. Ten minutes. I mean to set them to work at once." Amy flew out of the room.

Helena finished her toilette and dressed herself. Anger and guilt etched her face as she realized she'd been far too harsh on her abigail. Yet once begun, she had not been able to stop her diatribe. Lack of sleep and her humiliating encounter with Waverley last night had propelled her fury and turned her mood black. She felt ready for war with anyone who dared to step into her path.

Who did the marquis think he was, abandoning her like that? Why did he raise her expectations only to change his mind, something he managed to accomplish each time he made love to her? Yesterday he behaved more like an enemy and less like a lover. Was she so unattractive? Darlington thought her wanton. Did the marquis think so too?

"Just you wait, my lord marquis. I don't know what your game is and I don't care. But I'll eat you for dinner and spit you out again, and then, when you fall hopelessly in love with me, I'll abandon you just like that. What will you do when I leave you high and dry, my man? Women have their ways, you know."

Having heard her mistress' last sentence when she entered the room, Amy looked mystified. "What ways, milady?"

Helena looked up in surprise, unaware that she had spoken aloud. "Nothing. I was just talking to myself. Are the servants assembled?" Amy nodded. "Then let's get on with it. We'll take the back stairs. It's quicker."

She swept out of her room, head held high, determination writ large on her face. Amy had to hurry to keep up with her. The dust covered everything but the open bottles of spirits lying around, just the way she'd seen the place last. Cobwebs still hung from the ceilings and cornices. As before, visible stains clung to the carpets, and every room retained the odor of stale wine.

When she reached the front hall, Helena was astonished to see a mere ten servants facing her. Only ten? Fairchild House in London had a staff of seventy during the Season and Heatham in Brighton kept a hundred servants busy when the family was in residence. *What do these so-called servants do all day? Drink themselves into a stupor? Most likely, if the oaf asleep in that chair is any indication.*

Helena didn't believe for one moment that they were properly trained servants. It was obvious to her these disreputable associates had been hired by the Traskers. But for what purpose, she wondered. She yearned to send them all packing, but she knew the difference between reality and fiction. She needed to discover whether any of them could be relied upon.

The footmen scowled like the thugs who had attacked Waverley on the road to Land's End. Surly under maids lounging in various insolent poses, seemed impatient to be off to their own pursuits. With the exception of Amy, Trudy, and Emma, none of the others was dressed in proper livery.

Helena lifted her eyebrows in astonishment when one of the under maids, wearing a gown covered by a none too clean apron, sneered at her. "Watcher want? Make it quick, milady. T'day's my day off."

The others snickered, but Helena kept an even tone. "What's your name?"

"Belinda. Wot's it to ya?"

"By all means, take your day off. Be sure to pack your things as well. You needn't bother to return."

"You can't sack me. I was took on by Mrs. Trasker. I takes me orders from her." Belinda looked around at her cohorts as she nodded triumphantly, her eyes blazing with victory.

Helena turned to Amy. "Fetch Mrs. Trasker."

"She's busy," said one of the footmen. His red nose hinted that the only work he did was the work of hard drinking.

Helena glared at him but addressed herself to Amy. "Inform Mrs. Trasker that Lady Fairchild wishes to see her in the library at once." Her eyes swept the hall, taking in each rebellious servant in turn. "Where is the rest of the household staff?"

"Wot you see is wot you get," said Belinda.

Helena's hands itched to wipe the insolence off the maid's

face, but she didn't move a muscle. "If you value your positions, remain where you are until I return." She walked toward the library door but turned back to face them. "Should any one of you decide to disobey my orders, you may return to your room and gather all your things, since your services here will no longer be required." Her knees turned weak as she advanced into the library. Before she shut the door, she heard loud murmurs of indignation. She didn't have long to wait for Mrs. Trasker to appear.

"Wot's goin' on? Why're you shtirrin' up trouble wi' my help?" A slightly inebriated Mrs. Trasker slammed the library door behind her. "Wha'dya mean upshettin' the shervants? I'm in charge here, not you. And don't you forget it."

Helena drew herself up, an icy glare trained on Mrs. Trasker. "You are wrong, madam. You are no longer in charge. If the marquis has not so informed you, I will see to it he does before this day ends, I promise you. It wouldn't surprise me if he charges you with neglect of his grandmother and hauls you in front of the magistrate. Rest assured, he possesses the power to do so."

"I don' believe you." Yet clearly she did, for she sobered quickly enough for her speech to show marked improvement. "You jus' wait till my Harry comes back." She put her hands on her hips, in a vain attempt to maintain the upper hand, a familiar tactic. "My son won't let you sass his ma like that."

"Don't try my patience, Mrs. Trasker. You and your son have run this castle near to ruin. The marquis has asked me to restore order to Waverley Castle."

"You think you can manage this drafty old place better'n me and Harry?"

Helena held her head high, willing her knees to stay strong. She knew it was a gamble to speak out, yet she had no choice but to risk it. "Of course I do. I mean to see to it that my orders are carried out and I expect your cooperation." She paused to let her words sink in, then added, "You had better march out there with me and inform your staff that they are to obey me without the insolence I faced this morning. Inform them that if they don't follow my orders, they will be sacked without a reference."

In a flash of insight, it dawned on Helena that Mrs. Trasker well understood she had a great deal to lose. The housekeeper couldn't risk allowing the marquis to dismiss the servants she had hired. Once more Helena wondered why.

"Well, Mrs. Trasker? Do you mean to cooperate?"

In a final effort to save face, the housekeeper whined, "If I agree, you'll not sack the ones already here? You see, they's kin, sort of."

Helena savored her victory, but she kept her elation in check. She wondered how much swallowing her pride had cost the older woman. There was no need to humiliate her further. "You may retain their services if that is your wish, Mrs. Trasker. But in return I expect you to stand with me while I instruct them in their proper duties." In a flash of inspiration, she added, "I plan to hire more help, for Waverley is woefully under-staffed. You will be obliged to hand over all household accounts to me. I'll manage domestic affairs from now on. Agreed?"

The woman nodded, such a look of defeat etched in her brow, Helena sweetened her tone. She'd need to make friends of both mother and son no matter how odious a task.

"We are not enemies. You and your son are Banningtons, part of the family, Mrs. Trasker. We all have a duty to the mar-quisate, do we not? Let us present a unified face to the ser-vants, shall we? They will be more manageable that way."

The older woman nodded grimly. "Right. Let's have at it then."

"Put a smile on your face, Mrs. Trasker. That will go a long way toward convincing the staff we are working together for the good of this household."

Helena walked to the door, unlatched it and kept her smile checked when several of the eavesdropping servants nearly fell into the room.

"Why are you lot hangin' about? Lady Fairchild has somethin' to say to you. You'll answer to both of us from this moment on, or find another place to work."

"Thank you, Mrs. Trasker," Helena said.

The older woman curtseyed clumsily. In a respectful voice, she added, "You're welcome, milady." She folded her hands and rested them on her stomach.

"Clean livery tomorrow morning, if you please," Helena said in an authoritative tone. "We meet here promptly at six to discuss your responsibilities." She spied the intrepid Belinda, one leg crossed over the other, a hand on her hip, the other resting on the handle of a mop as though it were a lamppost. She walked up to her and knocked the mop out of her hand, nearly toppling the insolent chit. Helena picked up the mop and began to swab the floor.

Mrs. Trasker looked aghast. "Here now, milady. Not your place t'do such dirty work. Belinda, take that mop from milady and get to work."

"But it's m'day off," Belinda whined once again.

Mrs. Trasker threw her a threatening glance.

"Gimme that mop." The surly young maid grabbed it, adding a reluctant curtsey.

To Helena's relief, Belinda's capitulation led to a flurry of activity in the hall. Without a word, Mrs. Trasker had signaled to each servant in turn and they had begun to work feverishly, dusting, polishing, and mopping.

Helena had won this skirmish, but she knew the war was not over. Time would tell, but her heart eased somewhat and her mood changed. The distraction of setting the castle to rights was a welcome diversion from dwelling on the marquis.

Besides, she'd never had any opportunity to manage anything

more pressing than her own wardrobe. She had observed her mother as a matter of course, but she'd taken for granted the methods the duchess had used to manage three large estates, tasks she performed with accomplished ease.

Helena nodded to Mrs. Trasker before taking her leave, delighted to hear the sounds of purposeful activity as she headed for the kitchen.

"Good morning, Cook."

"Good mornin', milady. I'm preparin' breakfast for my marchioness. Have you a mind to join her? She'd be delighted for the company, I wager."

"Thank you, Cook. I would like that very much."

"Mayhap my lady would like a bit o' chocolate while you wait for me to finish?"

Helena grinned. "How did you guess? I'm famished. I'll have it here, if you don't mind. The dining room is a disaster, but your lovely kitchen is warm and spotless. Let me have a slice of the warm bread that smells so delicious, and some of your lovely jam, too."

Cook beamed at the compliment. She served Helena, bustling about the kitchen like a busy hen who knew just what was expected of her. "There's more'n enough for you to have another slice if you've a mind to, milady. You have to keep up your strength. Emma and Trudy told me what you did this morning. Mighty fine work, I'd say. That lot needed to be taken in hand."

"I agree. But I'm afraid there are far too few servants to manage the business."

"Used to be more, but the Traskers sacked 'em all."

"Do you think we can rehire some of them?"

"Most of them moved away searchin' for work elsewhere."

"Unfortunate. We'll just have to seek more good workers like your nieces. Will we be able to find such people, do you think?"

Cook beamed at her, pleased to be asked. "Yes, milady. I be livin' hereabouts all my life. I'll pass the word, if you like."

Helena swallowed a mouthful of chocolate. "Mmmm. Delicious. Yes, please. I would be indebted to you."

Cook hesitated a moment. "But . . ."

"What is it?"

"No one I know will work for the Traskers, an' that's a fact."

"You can tell them they'll report directly to me. I have agreed to the management of the castle and its grounds and the marquis shall see to the tenants who farm his land."

Cook chuckled. "News travels like the wind in these here parts, milady. Everyone knows why you've come. Mayhap 'twon't be hard to find willin' workers after all." She added, "Breakfast for her ladyship's ready."

"Good. I've had a letter from my mother. She's her goddaughter, but it's been many years since they've seen one another." She turned to the door and noticed a timid Amy pressed against the wall, as if wishing to remain invisible.

"Amy? I'm glad you're here. Will you carry the tray for Cook?"

Amy's eyes lit up at the friendly sound in her mistress' voice. She breathed a sigh of relief. She had been forgiven, never mind that she knew not what crime she had committed to earn such a tongue-lashing. "Of course, milady." She took the tray from the table and led the way up the back staircase.

Helena followed behind Cook slowly, for the older woman's labored breathing signaled her difficulty in climbing the steps. She weighed far more than she should.

When the three reached the chamber, Cook put her finger to her lips, opened the door quietly and stepped aside for Helena and Amy.

The dowager was awake.

"Good morning, Helena, my dear."

"How are you feeling this morning, ma'am?"

"Her fever's down," said Mrs. Hubley, plumping the pillows so the dowager could sit to eat her breakfast.

"That's a good sign," said Helena. "With Mrs. Hubley's help, you'll be up and about in no time."

"Have you seen my grandson? He promised to visit."

"I haven't seen him this morning, ma'am. Shall I send my abigail to fetch him for you?"

The old woman sighed. "No, dear. I'll wait for him to come to me. He always keeps his promises, you know."

Right! When pigs fly. Aloud she said, "I'm sure he does, ma'am."

"My Des is a good lad." The dowager waved the tray away when she'd had her fill.

Helena nodded to Amy, who took the tray and withdrew, followed by Cook. The nurse returned to her chair and picked up her needlework.

"Let me look at you, my child. How is your mother? Is she well? I was at her wedding in Bodmin, you know. Tell me all about your family."

"She and my father are well, ma'am. I've had a letter in which they send you their good wishes. I am one of their five daughters—the second oldest, in fact. Edward is our only brother and the spoiled darling of all his sisters."

The dowager managed a weak smile. "I used to spend time in London during the Season, where we visited one another often. But I'm no longer well enough to travel."

Helena noted a frown on the dowager's face and said in alarm, "What is it, my dear?"

"I felt so hopeless before you and Desmond came to my rescue. I should never have allowed the Traskers into my home, but a lonely old woman is sometimes eager for family to care for her in her dotage."

Helena vowed to nurture this dear old lady and make her

life worth living again. She took the old woman's hand in hers and stroked it.

"I know they're up to no good, those two. They've sacked so many of the old-timers. Now I hardly recognize any of the staff."

"No harm will come to you from now on, I promise." Helena noted that the marchioness looked as if she was about to nod off. "Rest, dearest. Shall I return this evening and read to you?"

The dowager made no answer, though a smile played on her lips as she turned her head and shut her eyes. Helena tucked her in and withdrew. Here was useful purpose for her at last, she thought as she returned to her chamber opposite the dowager. She hoped she was up to the challenge. Her sister Olivia's farewell words rang in her ears: "Remember, my love. You're a Fairchild, and Fairchilds do not fail." The thought heartened her resolve.

She returned to her chamber, intending to write in her journal, but exhaustion overtook her. She was weary not only from lack of sleep but also from the earlier confrontation with Mrs. Trasker and that lot of churlish servants. She removed her shoes and her gown, crawled into her bed and fell asleep at once.

Chapter 11

Waverley's quarters were now restored, thanks to Rabu. Had his father been responsible for the neglect of the original old castle? He doubted that was the case, for the third marquis was meticulous in his attention to detail. But he died a year ago, enough time for neglect and decay to mar what, if memory served, had once been in sterling condition.

Waverley Castle was prominently mentioned in the "Guide to Historic Landmarks." Built in the fifteenth century, the castle lay unoccupied for almost a century. In 1733, King George the First, known chiefly for his generosity to his closest friends, ceded it to Lord Thomas Bannington, the First Marquis of Waverley. The second marquis, Lord Neville Bannington, was an avid student of architecture. When his lordship died in 1779, the modern wings facing north opposite the sea had not yet been completed. The third marquis, Lord James, Desmond's father, finished both wings well before he banished his only son and sent him off to India.

The marquis' suite in the east wing overlooked the gardens. A balcony ran the length of the suite as well. His chamber was large, and a fireplace in the middle of the east wall faced his bed.

A modern bathing closet was situated inside his dressing room in the corner of the west wall. Beyond that, a small room housed his valet, Rabu. The third chamber, adjacent to his sleeping quarters, contained Waverley's private office. It was connected to a waiting room housing a desk for his secretary and seats for visitors.

He sat at his own desk and tried to concentrate on the sheaf of papers his man of business had delivered to him. But his mind was not on his work. The thought of Helena nagged at him. He'd hurt her badly. The look on her face when he'd stormed out of her bedchamber without a word of explanation was enough to unman him. Rake or no, he'd never been that cruel to any woman. Not until now.

Bloody hell! Much easier being a rake. Thank your willing bed partner, offer a kind word and pay her. Simple. No complications. What's more, the lady in your bed has no other expectations. Fool! Did you really think you could shake off your dissolute past? Easier said than done, isn't it, your lordship? Instead, you surrender to temptation at the first opportunity. And hurt the only woman you've ever truly loved. You'll have to mend it, you know. The question is how?

He rang for Rabu.

"Yes, your lor'sheep?"

"Ask Lady Fairchild to do me the kindness of a few moments of her time whenever it is convenient."

"Excuse, please. You wear dressing gown. I help you dress, first, your lor'sheep."

"No. I'll do it myself." He rose and retired to his dressing room. *Will she agree to see me? Serves me right if she refuses.* He concentrated on choosing an appropriate wardrobe: morning trousers, a starched white shirt and neck cloth, a plain linen vest, and a blue superfine coat. He was seated at his dressing table tying his neck cloth when Rabu reappeared.

"Well? Will she come?"

"Yes, your lor'sheep. Her la'sheep say soon." His valet

picked up a comb and proceeded to pull it through his master's unruly locks.

"All right. Disappear when you let her in, do you understand?"

"Yes, your lor'sheep."

"Stop your giggling. It's not what you think."

Ill at ease, Waverley felt the need for fresh air and went out to the balcony. Rabu's skilled hair combing quickly unraveled, a result of the wind, but the sight of the gardeners at work restoring the damage calmed his unease.

Doubt assailed him. *What should I say? I'm sorry? Forgive me? I beg your pardon?* He let out a harsh laugh at the lame phrases that came to his mind.

A knock on the door caused his stomach to churn. "Come in, please."

"You sent for me, my lord?"

Helena's icy formality did nothing to calm him. He stepped inside and closed the balcony doors. "Won't you sit here by the fire, ma'am?" He indicated a chair opposite the one he planned to use.

"I prefer to stand, if you don't mind, my lord."

"As you wish." He dismissed Rabu with a nod. When they were alone, he said, "I haven't the proper words to ask you to forgive my behavior, ma'am. It was most ill-bred of me."

"Limit our discussion to matters of business, sir."

"All right, if you prefer. Cook informed me of your confrontation with Trasker's people. Well done."

"Thank you, my lord. Is there anything else you wish to say to me?"

"Don't leave me like this, Helena. We were friends once. Have I lost that in addition to your esteem? At least hear me out."

She unbent a trifle. "Very well." She sat on the edge of the seat opposite his desk and folded her hands in her lap.

"When Darlington found me in Paris, I was content with my lot. When he told me my father had died and the Regent demanded my return, I was tempted to tell him he and the Regent might go to the devil for all I cared. But when Darlington informed me that my grandmother still lived, my choice was clear. It was no longer possible to relinquish the marquisate. My grandmother was the only woman in my life who ever loved me. Until you came into my life. I wanted to tell you I felt the same way, but the words stuck in my throat. I'm not the same man I once was, Helena.

"*Le roué Anglais* is no more. It was a cowardly action to leave you in the lurch, and I apologize for the pain I caused you. I know now that I must change my ways, you see. For four reasons."

She showed a glimmer of interest. "And they are?"

He ticked them off on his fingers as he spoke. "The people of Waverley Park depend on their marquis. I owe it to them. I owe it to my grandmother. I owe it to myself, worthless though I may be in my own eyes. And last, I owe it to you."

"Admirable. I wish you success, but you owe me nothing. When I said I loved you, it was in the heat of passion, but it vanished in the cold light of day. While I remain under your roof, I shall keep my word to you to set things right within these walls. I plan to return home no later than the first of June for my sister's debut."

"Can we not be civil to one another until then, Helena? I shall not molest you again. Here's my hand on it."

She shook it as if they had been strangers. "Good day, my lord." She left the room without a backward glance.

London

"Done," said the duke to his wife when she entered the library.

"Oh, good." She bent to peck him on the cheek, for they were quite alone. "What is it you've done?"

"My man of business has found a suitable instructor for Mary. I did mention the Royal Philharmonic Society, didn't I?"

"Yes, dear. What's he like?"

"You've already met my man of business."

She laughed. "No, dear. I meant Mary's new instructor."

"His name is Signore Giovanni Bartoli. He's come to England to study classical composition or some such thing."

"He's from Italy, I assume."

"Of course. He must teach or starve, for he is impoverished. If Mary likes him, I mean to offer him wages in addition to lodgings and meals in exchange for lessons for our talented daughter."

"Most generous, dear. Has he agreed to these terms?"

"So I'm told. I have yet to meet him."

"What of his own studies?"

"Oh, he'll have plenty of time to pursue them, I assure you."

"Have you told Mary?"

"No, love. I leave all such arrangements to you. Besides, I was sure you would wish to interview him first. He's waiting for you in the blue drawing room as we speak."

The duchess hurried upstairs to the blue drawing room to greet the new maestro. She allowed herself a small smile. Knowing the duke as well as she did, the instructor had already been engaged.

"Good afternoon, sir," she said with her customary hospitality. "I am Mary's mother." She hid her astonishment at the thin young man who could not have been more than twenty, standing near the fireplace. He wore a plain white shirt adorned at the neck with a thin black tie in the Italian manner and a black coat over black pantaloons. His shoes were scuffed, but these were not what caught her attention. His long curled hair fell casually around an oval face graced with classic Roman features: full lips, thick eyebrows, and intense dark eyes. The only flaw, hardly noticeable, was a slightly bent nose. He was one of the handsomest young men the duchess had ever seen. She wondered what effect on her daughter Mary, an impressionable innocent at fifteen, was likely to be.

"Good afternoon, your grace," he said, bowing. "Forgive, please. My English, she is not good. I only come here three month."

"It is fine, sir." The duchess rang the bell to send for Mary. "I'd like you to meet my daughter Lady Mary. She will be your pupil."

He drew himself up with dignity. "First, I hear her play. I teach, but only if she, the daughter, has the talent."

"In that case, sir, we shall join her in the music room. There you can listen to her play." She gave the servant her order and led the young man downstairs to the large music room, at the end of which was a pianoforte.

Bartoli strode to it and ran his fingers over the keys. "Excellent instrument."

"You sent for me, Mother?" asked Mary upon entering the room. At the sight of the stranger standing near the pianoforte, she froze.

"Yes, dear. I'd like you to meet Signore Bartoli. He—"

"Play for me," the young man demanded abruptly, interrupting the duchess with a wave of his hand.

Mary glanced at her mother, alarm written on her face.

"Go ahead, dear. Signore Bartoli wishes to determine your ability in order to instruct—"

"No!" said Bartoli. "I do not teach if she has not the talent."

Mary sat and began to play from memory. Her fingers flew over the keys as if they had a life of their own.

"Mozart," said Bartoli, his hands clasped behind his back. *Eine Kleine Nacht Musick.* Yes. I will teach."

"Th-thank you, Signore. . . ." Mary stuttered.

"No, no. You must call me *Maestro.*"

Mary bit her lip and said, "Yes, *Maestro.*"

He took both her hands in his and examined her fingers. "You will treat these like your jewels, no?"

"Yes, *Maestro.*"

He turned away abruptly and moved to the door. "I take residence here in the morning. Good day, your grace. Good day, Lady Mary. Practice chords today. We begin work tomorrow afternoon." He bowed to them, turned, and left the music room.

The duchess eyed her daughter with alarm, for the child's eyes were misted over. "What's wrong, Mary? If you don't like him, we'll find another teacher for you."

"Oh no, Mother. I like him very well indeed. The maestro understands music. He knew I was playing Mozart."

Waverley Castle

Waverley had given Helena much food for thought. Was friendship possible after all that had passed between them? Perhaps that would be best. She made her way to the library to search for a suitable book to read to the marchioness. The door was ajar, the voices of Mrs. Trasker and her son, Harry, clearly audible. She was about to enter when she heard her name mentioned and thought better of it. She pressed against the wall just outside the door to listen.

"I say we murder the marquis and that bitch."

"Don't be so addlepated, Harry. How do you expect to become the fifth marquis if you're charged with murder? No, me boy. We'll have to think of a clever way to get rid of them. And don't you be doin' anything rash, hear? Can't have you suspicioned for murder. We haven't come this far for nothing, have we? Once we get rid of them and the old lady dies—it can't be soon enough to my way o' thinking—you're the heir. No question."

"What d'ya want me to do, Ma?"

"Keep a sharp eye, that's what. Don't trouble yourself about Lady Fairchild. I got her thinkin' I'm on her side. You got to do the same. Try to be pleasant, respectful-like, hear? That should throw her off her stride. If she wants new hires, well then, let her hire them. Where's the harm? Which reminds me, I promised to give her your accountin' books."

"But, Mum, you can't give . . ." He paused, then chuckled. "I get it. Give her t'other set, you mean."

"Clever lad. I been thinkin' it over real careful. Better to gull the pair of them into believin' they've won, see? Then they'll be off their guard when we strike." She took a swig of her coffee, as usual laced with a large splash of gin.

Harry scratched his head in puzzlement. "How you fixin' to get rid of 'em?"

"Never you mind, me boy. Just trust in your ma. Haven't steered you wrong yet, have I? Let them think they've won out. That's the ticket."

"Got ter hand it to yer, Mum. Yer mind's as sharp as a knife. Ye'll do 'em in fer sure. No question." He kissed her on the cheek, a wet, sloppy buss.

Mrs. Trasker wiped her cheek with her soiled apron. "All part o' me master plan, me lad. All part o' me master plan."

So they think they can do us in. We're in the way of their plans. What are they? Never mind. Forewarned is forearmed. We'll have to watch them, but we'll win in the end because we're smarter than thickheaded Harry and his sot of a mother. I'll have to warn Waverley, I suppose.

Helena didn't stay to hear any more of the conversation. She'd heard enough.

The marquis watched Helena from his office window as she rode off with Casper. She rode like a graceful swan gliding across a smooth pond. He envied Casper this duty, for the mere sight of her tormented him. He turned to the pile of work on his desk.

The wind in Helena's face and the sound of the sea were a welcome relief from this day's perplexing events. They rode at a brisk pace along the moors. At the sound of a dog's bark, her horse shied and threw her into a bramble of bushes. Her horse would have bolted were it not for the quick thinking of Casper, who grabbed the reins.

"Heel, Horatio! Heel, I say!" shouted an unfamiliar voice. The stranger threw his reins to his groom and dismounted to come to Helena's aid. "Give me your hand, ma'am."

Startled, Helena looked up into the kindly gray eyes of a handsome, fair-haired young gentleman dressed in the fashion of a country squire—buckskins, Hessian boots, a smart brown coat worn over a white linen shirt and simple neck cloth and a beaver hat.

"Thank you, sir." She brushed the leaves from her riding dress.

"Are you hurt, ma'am?"

"Nothing serious, sir. With the exception of my dignity, that is. My father would be shocked to learn that one of his daughters could not control her horse."

He smiled. "I beg to differ, ma'am. The fault was not yours. My unruly dog is the villain in this melodrama. Allow me to make myself known to you. The Earl of Glynhaven at your service. My estate rides alongside of Waverley Park, you see. Will you accept my apology for this mishap?"

"Of course, sir. I am Lady Fairchild."

"We've met, but I'm sure you don't recall. It was at your betrothal ball. Chris Darlington was kind enough to invite me. He was a classmate of mine at Oxford. How is he, by the way?"

At the question, Helena turned an interesting shade of red. "He . . . I . . . we . . . are no longer, er . . ."

"I didn't know. Forgive me, ma'am. I didn't mean to cause you embarrassment." He changed the subject. "How fortunate we've met, albeit under unfortunate circumstances. I've just come from Waverley Castle. I left my card along with an invitation to dinner and a ball Friday next."

"Kind of you. I'm sure the marquis will be delighted. But how did you know I was his guest?"

He laughed. "We don't find it necessary to read London journals for our information, ma'am. Our servants do a fine job of spreading the news."

"I might have guessed," she said with mock ruefulness.

"How is the marquis? I haven't seen him since we were young lads."

"He is well, sir."

"The dowager?"

"On the mend. She is recovering from influenza."

"Good news. I do hope you'll join me on Friday."

"I'd like that very much. I'm sure the marquis will be delighted to renew acquaintance with old friends and neighbors."

Chapter 12

Helena burst into Waverley's office and said, "Waverley, you must do something at once."

He looked up in surprise at this unexpected interruption. "Why bother to knock, ma'am? I'm sure your visit indicates yet another crisis." His words were mocking, for it was the fourth time she had interrupted him that morning.

"Oh, sorry. Are you in the middle of something? Well, this cannot wait."

"Indeed. Is it a matter of life or death?"

"Don't be ridi— Oh. You're teasing me," she said. "Well, no matter," she went on. "I went out into the yard with Cook to inspect the delivery of chicken, game, and beef for our table. She is of the opinion, you see, that the man does not give us fair measure. He cheats us. Intolerable!"

"That *is* serious." It took willpower to keep from laughing, for he knew that farmers had to resort to bribery in order to sell their produce to a large estate. "Are you angry because the Traskers are profiting from this arrangement?"

"Of course they are, but that's not why I am here. You cannot believe what I discovered when I went out into the yard."

He set his quill down, leaned back and crossed his arms. "No, I cannot, but I'm sure you're about to inform me. Was someone abusing the poor cat again?"

"Worse, sir. Much worse. It's the poulterer. That vile man was beating his helper, a poor defenseless lad, with a switch!"

"And you intervened, I have no doubt."

"What else could I do?" she answered, her face flushed. "That odious man threatened to beat *me* instead. If it weren't for Casper coming to my rescue, I'm sure the bounder would have done so."

At this, the marquis could no longer control himself. He burst out laughing.

"Laugh all you will, Waverley. It wasn't *you* he threatened with a switch."

"No, no, love. I wasn't laughing at you. Just at the scene your words evoked. If Hogarth were alive, he'd no doubt want to capture it in one of his paintings." The urge to take her into his arms nearly undid him, but he managed to restrain himself.

"This is no time for levity."

"What would you have me do?"

She rolled her eyes. "*Will* you be serious, Waverley? I removed that poor lad from the man's clutches and now that scoundrel is demanding the boy back. Claims he bought him from the orphanage."

"No doubt he did. Give the boy back. The lad's his property."

"Never. I'll not have that poor child's death on my hands. If you don't do something about this, I wash my hands of you and I'll return to London first thing tomorrow." She folded her arms and glared at him.

"How much does he want for the lad?" *Well worth the price for her friendship.*

"Too much. He says he paid ten guineas. The man's a lying thief, I tell you."

A costly friendship, indeed. "What will you do with the lad if we manage to buy him from the fiend?"

"Casper says he can put the boy to work in the stables. Do come down to the yard and settle this."

"All right, if you promise to protect me from being thrashed to death."

She ignored this sally and stalked out of his office, the penitent marquis hard on her heels.

After a vigorous round of haggling with the outraged poulterer, Waverley bought the boy for half a guinea. When the man drove off, the marquis turned to Cook Wells and said, "Let that be the last I see of that scoundrel. Find another poulterer." He turned to Helena and added, "Well, ma'am, the lad is in your care now."

Chuckling to himself over Helena's uncharacteristic pugnacity, Waverley stopped to visit his grandmother.

"Desmond, you naughty boy. Where were you yesterday?" In spite of her attempt to scold him, the dowager's eyes lit up at the sight of him.

"Sorry, Grandmother." He nodded to Nurse Hubley, who came forward to help the dowager sit up. "I had some business to attend to in Sennen Cove. I've engaged a secretary, Vicar Cullum's son, Rupert. He's a bright young man who should, I trust, ease my life."

"What good news, dear. The vicar's wife will be so pleased. She's a good friend, you know."

"How are you feeling, dearest?"

She grinned. "I sat in a chair for two hours yesterday. I shall be up and about any day now, I promise you."

"That's good news, but you must allow Doctor Fenwick to make that decision. All right?"

"Oh dear. Must I wait like a child for his approval?"

"Yes, indeed," he said cheerfully. "I shall leave you now, but I'll be back tomorrow." He opened her door to find Helena facing him.

"I came to read to your grandmother, but if I've interrupted your visit, I can come back later."

His eyes spoke volumes, yet all he found to say was, "Do come in, ma'am. I was just leaving."

"Did you have a nice visit with your grandson, ma'am?"

"Oh yes. The naughty boy has grown into such a charming young man."

"I met a neighbor of yours when I was out riding this morning. The Earl of Glynhaven."

"Martin? He's a boyhood friend of Desmond's. I haven't seen him in an age."

"He's invited us to a dinner party followed by a ball next week. I hope Doctor Fenwick says you are well enough." Helena plumped up the dowager's pillows.

"Hear that, Nurse? You shall have to help me recover in time for the dinner party and the ball. I haven't been to either in years!"

Nurse Hubley nodded but did not offer an opinion, content to wait for the doctor's diagnosis before she would commit herself.

Helena changed the subject. "I've had a letter from home, ma'am. My mother sends her best wishes for a speedy recovery and thanks you for your hospitality to me." She kept the other news in Olivia's note to herself. Darlington was betrothed to an American heiress. *He didn't waste much time, did he?*

"Have you come to read to me?" Helena nodded. "Oh, good. I'm eager to hear more of Emma's exploits."

"'Chapter nine,'" Helena began, reading from *Emma,* a novel by the popular author Jane Austen.

"Mr. Knightley might quarrel with her, but Emma could not quarrel with herself. He was so much displeased, that it was longer than usual before he came to Hartfield again; and when they did meet, his grave looks shewed that she was not forgiven. She was sorry, but could not repent. On the contrary, her plans and proceedings were more and more justified, and endeared to her by the general appearances of the next few days."

Helena glanced at the dowager to find she had dozed off. She marked the page, put the book on the bedside table and tiptoed across the hall to her own bedchamber. She removed her riding dress and boots and lay down to rest, but sleep evaded her. Did she care that Darlington was betrothed to someone else? Not a whit. That surprised her.

Her thoughts turned to Waverley. She couldn't deny that seeing him was the brightest moment of each day. She was happy at Waverley Castle, Darlington be damned. The American heiress was welcome to him. She noted the time and rang for Amy. It was time for her bath.

"I've a mind to wear my blue gown with the lace trim tonight," she said as she climbed into her tub.

"Special occasion, milady?"

"No. Well, if you count sacking the poulterer, that's a good enough reason for celebration."

"You've done wonders in such a short time, milady. Everyone says so." She held the towel for her mistress. "If you're goin' to wear your prettiest gown this evenin', will you let me fix your hair special, the way I do in London?"

"Good idea," Helena said. The vision of Waverley's anticipated admiration suffused her with a warm glow. Once dressed, she was impatient to impress the marquis with a grand entrance into the drawing room, but he had not yet arrived. Disappointed, she chose to position herself near the mantel where the mirror over it would reflect her twice. She would dazzle him.

But she was wrong.

The marquis was livid. "What the devil is the meaning of this, madam?" He waved a crumpled card at her, taking no notice of her splendid attire.

"The meaning of what?"

"This . . . this *invitation,* written by that bloody scoundrel's own hand, informing me that he is looking forward—looking *forward*—to renewing our friendship. Friendship? Hah! How dare he! How *dare* you accept an invitation from my worst enemy." He came closer and thrust the card in her face. "You . . . you *traitor!*"

She backed away as if she expected him to hit her, but she managed to regain her poise. "Sit!" she ordered, as if she were training a pup. She took a seat and pointed to the chair opposite hers, observing him carefully. Waverley's disheveled state—eyes blazing, hair unkempt, shirt open at the collar, neck cloth untied, vest unbuttoned, dinner coat lacking—took her by surprise. She had never seen him so overwrought.

It took a moment before he moved to obey her command, though it seemed to her like an eternity. He threw himself into the nearest seat, thrust one leg straight out and bent the other knee. He gripped the arms of the chair until his knuckles turned white and stared at her with fury.

She gave him a few moments to collect his wits before she began to speak. "That's better, my lord. I met the Earl of Glynhaven yesterday on the riding trail that leads to Sennen Cove. I was enjoying a brisk trot with Casper when the earl's dog frightened my horse and I was thrown into the shrubbery. He came to my rescue and introduced himself as your friend. How could I possibly know otherwise since you never informed me you considered him an enemy? How many more enemies have you?"

"Only one," he muttered.

She added reasonably, "You see, when he extended the

invitation, he said that he was entertaining some of the local gentry and I thought . . ."

"Just like him, the sneaky sod! Dressed to the nines, no doubt. Always was a dandy."

"What did he do to vex you so, Desmond?"

The sound of his name on her lips brought him to his senses. He stared at her as if for the first time. "You look lovely tonight."

Helena laughed. "That's better! When you stormed in here clutching that invitation, I feared I was about to be locked up in the Tower of London only to be scheduled for execution in the morning." Her attempt at humor brought a thin smile to his lips.

"Dinner, milord," announced their new butler.

"Thank you, Paynter," Helena said. "Tell Cook the marquis needs a bit more time to make ready. He shall need . . . ?" She looked to Waverley for an answer.

"Fifteen minutes." He flung himself out of his chair and left the room without another word.

Oh dear. He's so angry. How could I have known how he felt about Glynhaven? What happened between them, I wonder?

The marquis returned to the drawing room half an hour later as if this were his first entrance. Every hair was in place; his neck cloth was tied in the latest London fashion; and his long-tailed dinner coat was worn over tights, ribbed silk stockings and velvet evening shoes. Indeed, he was dressed as if for a ball, clad all in black except for his white shirt and neck cloth.

Funereal black, Helena thought, not without amusement. "You look smashing, my lord."

A tiny smile lifted the corners of his mouth. "Can I help it if my valet insists on proper dress for dinner?"

The dining room table was set for three. Waverley frowned. "Are we expecting a guest, Paynter?"

"Yes, milord." He opened the door and, to their surprise, the dowager entered, supported by a footman holding one arm and Nurse Hubley holding the other.

"Grandmother!" Waverley said, astonished. "How is this? Are you well enough?"

"Certainly," she answered, feigning indignation. "I had hoped to be made to feel more welcome, Desmond."

Helena rushed to her side as the footman and her nurse helped her into her seat at the head of the table. "More than welcome, ma'am. I, for one"—Helena stopped to glare at Waverley, who seemed to have developed feet of clay—"am delighted you have joined us for dinner."

"I am, too, love." Her grandson came to his senses and went to her side. In a gesture of chivalry he raised her hand to his lips. "Forgive my shock at seeing you, dearest. How glad I am that you are at last well enough to dine with us."

"Bad boy," the dowager chided, with a twinkle in her eye. She examined the bowl set before her. "Turtle soup? My favorite."

Waverley and Helena sat on either side of her and picked up their spoons. At the end of the first course, the dowager said, "I read the note from Glynhaven this afternoon. Said he looked forward to welcoming us next week. I'm so glad Helena accepted his invitation."

"If you don't care for it, Grandmother," interrupted the marquis, "we can send regrets." He refrained from glancing at Helena.

"Nonsense, Desmond. I'm looking forward to it. I haven't been outside these walls for an age."

Helena shot Waverley a triumphant glance as if to say, "I told you so!" but he took no notice, preferring instead to drain the wine in his glass. The dowager, innocent of the tension between them, marveled at the improvements Helena had accomplished within the castle.

"You've done wonders, my dear. And in such a short time!

It does my heart good to see my home being restored to its former glory. Don't you agree, Desmond?"

"What? Oh, sorry, Grandmother. My mind was elsewhere."

The old woman folded her hands in her lap and sighed. "I've caused you both so much trouble, haven't I? Can you ever forgive me?"

"No need for forgiveness, love. I was happy to help." Helena turned to Waverley, one eyebrow lifted as she awaited his response, but none was forthcoming. Instead, he behaved as though he hadn't heard the dowager and downed another glass of wine.

At the end of dinner, Helena asked, "Shall we retire to the drawing room, ma'am? No doubt, the marquis will join us after he's had his brandy. I want your opinion on the fabric for new drapes. I've several samples, and I can't decide which are best suited."

The dowager's face lit up. "Yes, I'd love to help you." When Helena came to her side to help her up, she added, "There's a dear." Helena signaled to the footman, who took the dowager's other arm.

Still sulking, Waverley said not a word, nor did he deign to assist his grandmother, which infuriated Helena.

She went out of her way to pass him and knocked his wine goblet over, spilling the red wine on his trousers in the process. "Oh dear. How clumsy of me. Beg pardon, sir." She never looked back as they left the dining room.

Chapter 13

Monday, the Twenty-seventh of April, 1818

"Mr. Rupert Cullum, milord."

"Show him in, Paynter."

The young man entered and bowed to the marquis. "Good morning, my lord."

Waverley smiled at the nineteen-year-old lad he'd engaged as his secretary. Cullum was neatly dressed in a fawn-colored vest and buckskin trousers, a starched white shirt and neck cloth, and a dark blue coat. The young man's brown locks were under control, his eager blue eyes alert.

"I'll have no formality here, Rupert. Leave off 'milord' this or 'your lordship' that, and no scraping and bowing, if you please. I give you leave to address me as sir and I shall call you Rupert."

The young man grinned in approval. "Yes, sir. What have you in mind for me today?"

Waverley waved a hand over his cluttered desk. "As you can see, you have your work cut out for you, Rupert, for I've no tolerance for this. Your office is through that door. Spend your first day sorting this dreadful pile on my desk and make a list of questions I may or may not be able to answer." He rose from his seat. "As for me, I am taking the day off."

"Yes, sir. Thank you for giving me this opportunity to serve you."

Waverley nodded and wasted no time in leaving his unfinished business to the eager young man's care.

When he entered his chamber, he said to his valet, "Have you notified Casper?"

"Yes, your lor'sheep. Riding clothes ready, too."

"You are a prince, Rabu. Help me change."

"Mornin', milady."

Helena shaded her eyes from the sun pouring through her window. She rose from her bed and put on the dressing gown Amy held. "Thank you, dear."

Her eyes swept the chamber, such a disaster when first she saw it. She gazed at the washstand, noting with approval the clean towels awaiting her morning wash. Next to the stand, her riding dress and undergarments were laid carefully upon a chair, while her boots rested on the floor, all expertly prepared by her abigail. Peace reigned between them after that ill-advised scold she'd given Amy. Helena sat at the small table in front of the fire and sipped her chocolate. "When I return from my ride, I'll wear the yellow muslin."

"I'll have it ready for you, milady."

When she descended the grand staircase on her way to the stables, the first person she encountered was the under maid named Nell, who was polishing the banister. She wore a clean white apron over her gown and a starched white cap on her head.

Nell stopped to curtsey. "Mornin', milady."

"Morning, Nell." Helena bit her lip to keep from letting out a whoop of joy at this sign of improvement. At the bottom of the staircase, she turned toward the front door, where Paynter was waiting. Two footmen dressed in the Waverley colors held open the heavy oak doors.

She stepped outside expecting to find Casper holding the reins. In his stead, the marquis waited. "Morning, ma'am. Mind if I join you this morning?" Without waiting for an answer, he lifted her into her saddle.

"It appears I have no choice, my lord."

"If riding with me is not to your liking, I'll escort you to the stables and you may ride with Casper."

"No. I'll ride with you this morning, sir. It wouldn't do to make a fuss in front of the servants." She snapped her reins and bent to the wind.

They rode side by side until they reached the narrow lane at the end of the drive. Waverley gave way and allowed her to lead. When the road widened again, he pulled up to her and signaled her to stop.

"What is it, my lord?"

"Can we walk for a bit? I'd like to talk to you."

"I usually dismount when we reach the stream where the horses may drink. It's little more than a mile from here." She rode on ahead.

He followed, a sheepish grin on his face. *I suppose I deserved that set down. She's giving me back my own. Makes it hard for me to apologize. Makes it even harder for me to win her trust back. If I didn't know myself better, I'd wager my blunt on the feisty lady. But she doesn't know I have the advantage of more experience. Interesting. We'll see who wins this skirmish.*

Helena needed no help to dismount. She dismounted, threw her long train over one arm, and walked her horse to the stream. The marquis followed her.

"Casper and I ride to the beach after the horses rest, but if you are in a hurry to return . . ."

"We'll take your customary route."

"Are you sure?" she challenged. "That's where I first met the earl. Suppose we meet him again? What then, my lord?"

Waverley understood he was being tested. "I won't embarrass you with any untoward behavior, Helena. Nor will I disrupt your morning ride more than I already have. I want to apologize to you. You could not have known how I felt about Glynhaven. I cannot trust him, but that's another matter. In spite of my feelings, I do intend to escort you and Grandmother to his dinner. I'll behave like a gentleman. You have my word."

He dropped to one knee. "Though I don't deserve it, can you find it in your heart to forgive me?"

"You have a hot temper, my lord. You may rise, for I accept your apology. Perhaps some day you might tell me why you despise the earl."

He caught her hand in his. "My name is Desmond," he said softly. "Have I forfeited the right to hear it on your lips once more?"

"Let go of my hand, Desmond."

He laughed and let her go. "Friends again?"

"Friends," she agreed, smiling for the first time that morning. "Can you satisfy my curiosity?"

"Anything in my power, friend." He took his coat off and spread it on the ground. "Won't you sit?"

She settled herself and leaned against the tree behind her. "What caused such a rift between you and Glynhaven?"

He paused. "I told you that I bedded a country lass from Sennen Cove. When she found herself with child, she knew it could not have been me, for we had long since ceased our dalliance. She was seeing Glynhaven, but he denied it, pointing the finger at me instead. My father believed his story over mine and bought off the farmer to avoid scandal. It caused a rift between my father and me—one past healing now that he is dead."

"Unfortunate for you that it is beyond healing."

"That wound shall never heal, which is why I cannot let go of my anger toward Glynhaven."

She could not bear the pain she saw in his eyes and changed the subject. "I overheard something quite by accident. It concerns the Traskers."

"What has that odious pair done now?"

She launched into a brief description of the conversation she'd heard.

"I suspected they were up to no good. This merely confirms it. I can well defend myself, but I can't guarantee your safety. Perhaps you ought to return home to London."

"Not on your life! If you think those two can scare me off, you're wrong. Each day that I correct the work Mrs. Trasker has neglected is a victory for me. I'll return to London in time for my sister Georgiana's debut, by which time I shall have finished what I set out to do. We Fairchilds do not give up, sir."

He reached out and tucked a loose curl behind her ear. "All right, but you must be careful what you are about. Perhaps I should engage a bodyguard to watch over you."

"Don't you dare! I'm not a weakling."

"As you wish."

In the hope of finding some information that would lead to ridding himself of the Traskers, the next day the marquis stole away at dawn and rode into Sennen Cove. He threw the reins of his horse to the stable boy at the Ship Inn, strolled into the taproom and ordered breakfast. A good thing, too, as it turned out, for the men eating in the taproom were full of talk about the latest shipwreck.

Waverley's dress—buckskins, a woolen shirt any craftsman might wear, a warm country vest and scuffed boots—gave no clue to his identity, which made it easy to listen without raising suspicion.

"That warn't no natural shipwreck, I say. No survivors? Hah! Means smugglers from outside are back at it again doin' their dirty deeds so none are alive to point the finger at 'em."

"Right you are, Ned. No decent Cornishman would kill for cargo."

"Black Bart never did. He was a gennelman, he was."

"Had an eye for pretty lassies, too. Ask any Cornish maiden hereabouts."

The raucous guffaws this provoked gave Waverley time to pay his shot and slip out of the inn without notice. He began his trek toward the beach, his hobnailed boots clicking on the stones. He'd taken a pick and an ordinance map in his ruck-sack, though he fancied he remembered every cliff by heart. He'd instructed Rabu to say he was going to look for fossils.

In truth, he needed to get away for a time. He needed to sort out his feelings about Helena. He needed to think about the inescapable duties that stretched before him like a death sentence.

It was Helena who invaded his thoughts most. She had become a thorn in his side. What was she to him? His judge? His conscience? His love? He was angry with her for forcing him to meet Glynhaven, the man who had driven him into exile.

He reached the end of the lane where shops gave way to white cottages with thatched roofs. Yellow daffodils and lavender irises colored the paths inside white picket fences leading to red front doors. Beyond the cottages the lane wound its way toward a footpath down to the sea.

As he climbed down, he breathed in the sharp smell of salt air, sweet to his nostrils. When he reached the bottom, he stopped to examine a blowhole, one of the favorite haunts of his boyhood. When the tide rolled in, he and his friends would ride the water spouting up, pretending they rode on the back of a giant whale. The lads played until it was time for them to return home, where chores awaited his friends, while Waverley trudged home to his solitary dinner in the schoolroom. The tide was out today and the hole a gaping pit as empty as his troubled soul.

How could he have been such a fool? He had no cause to berate Helena for accepting Glynhaven's invitation, for she could not possibly have known of the bad blood between them.

Waverley took the blame for Glynhaven's misdeed as a matter of honor. Waverley's father had told often enough how necessary that trait was for a man who would one day be marquis. Yet his father chose to believe Glynhaven rather than his only son. Waverley had expected Glynhaven to come forward and admit he had impregnated the farmer's daughter. Apparently, the earl had no conscience then, perhaps not now as well.

He pushed these thoughts out of his mind and trained his eyes on the shoreline. Nothing seemed to have changed. The wind kicked up from the sea and turned the air frigid, but breathing in the salt air seemed to cleanse that dark place inside him. A seagull swooped down for its prey. Petrels dove into the water for their supper as well, then soared back into the air in a graceful ballet.

Waverley climbed up and began to edge along the narrow cliffs, his eyes searching the ground for signs of traffic beyond the ordinary, hoping to find a clue to the shipwreck he'd heard talk of at the inn. The marquis suspected the Traskers of having their hand in the nasty business. He would find the proof in these cliffs if he was right. He came to the yawning mouth of one of the caves where contraband had often been stored until it was safe to sell it free of taxation.

He and his mates knew where the smugglers hid the cargo after a shipwreck. His father knew also but had turned a blind eye to it, for he enjoyed as well as the next man the gift of wine and brandy from France and tea from India that somehow found its way into his cellars—in exchange for keeping his mouth shut. His grandfather had also enjoyed such gifts. Where was their honor?

He came upon a familiar cave whose mouth was narrow. He knew it led to an underground harbor deep enough for a rowboat when the tide was high. Contraband had been stored here when he was a lad. Perhaps it still was. Waverley removed a candle from his sack and lit it with his flint.

When he crawled in, he searched deep inside only to be disappointed. There was no evidence of hidden cargo. Unfortunate, but there were hundreds of caves hidden along the coast.

When Casper rode up to the front door with milady's horse, Helena's heart fell, for she had been expecting Waverley. She changed her mind and decided against riding at all that morning. "Looks like rain, Casper. Stable the horses, will you? I won't ride today after all."

She turned and smiled at the butler, who held the door open for her. "Rain," she apologized, feeling foolish. She would have ridden in a downpour if Waverley had ridden up instead of Casper.

"She handed Paynter her whip and her hat, threw her train over her arm, and made her way to the kitchen.

Cook looked up from trussing her chickens and wiped her hands on her apron. "Milady?"

"Morning, Cook. Looks like rain. I won't ride this morning after all."

"Would you like some hot chocolate, milady? I've fresh scones just out of the oven."

Helena laughed. "How did you guess? You know, I have a little sister who would adore you, ma'am. Jane loves to eat scones and you bake the best I've ever tasted. Yes to the chocolate, but no to the scones, dear. I shan't be able to fit into my gowns if you persist in feeding me too well."

"Sit yourself down, milady, whilst I run down to the cellar and get some more cocoa powder."

"Cellar? One of the few areas I haven't visited. I'll come with you."

"Are you sure, milady? It's terrible drafty down there, and full of dust. Haven't enough hands to give it a thorough cleaning, which it needs, heaven knows."

Helena smiled to herself. Cook's remark was a sly request for more kitchen help. "Then we must hire more help as soon as we can, Cook. Thank you for bringing it to my attention."

Cook took the cellar key from its hook, lit a candle, and beckoned Helena to follow. "Careful on the steps, milady. They're worn thin and cracked in places."

Helena made a mental note to have them repaired. When she reached the bottom step, she sneezed from the dust.

"P'raps you ought to return, milady. I'll get the cocoa and . . ."

"No. I'm fine." She took the candle from Cook and inspected the huge cellar. "Where does that door lead?" Helena pointed to a door on the left.

"That's the door to the wine cellar, milady. Mrs. Trasker keeps that key." Disapproval rang in Cook's voice.

"I see." Helena wondered what could possibly be left in the wine cellar, considering Jennie Trasker's love of spirits. "And that door opposite these steps?"

"That leads to the old cellar under the abbey."

"You mean under the ruins?"

"Yes, milady, but no one uses it anymore."

Helena noted an obvious arc on the earthen floor in front of the old door. Someone had opened it not too long ago. "Have you a key? I'd like to examine that cellar, if you don't mind."

"My guess is it's flooded by now, bein' so near the sea and all. Ah, here's my cocoa. I have to hide it."

"Hide it? Why?"

Cook grinned. "Harry has a sweet tooth. He eats it by the

handful if I don't put it out of his reach." She measured a small amount into a tin she'd brought with her and put the cocoa far back on the shelf, hidden behind other provisions.

Harry has a sweet tooth and his mother tipples. An odd pair indeed.

Harry saddled his horse and rode off on a matter of business. His destination was an abandoned boathouse on an inlet where he meant to leave his mother's letter. He reached for the door handle, but to his surprise, a masked man in a large cloak opened it.

"You're late. What took you so long, Harry?"

Harry knew the voice, but not the man. He held out the letter without answering, for the man's acid tongue had wounded him many times. The masked man read it once and tossed it into the flames. "Any survivors?"

"Don't believe so, My Lord."

"Fool! Didn't you make sure of it?"

Harry twisted his cap in his hands. "'Twere the cap'n, sir. We couldn't find the body. Washed out to sea, mayhap."

"No more shipwrecks until you hear from me. Understood?" The masked man picked up his whip and strode to the door.

"My Lord?"

"Now what?"

"Me ma said to ask what yer goin' to do 'bout the marquis."

The masked man turned the knob. "Nothing for the moment."

"You look troubled, Helena. What is it?" the marquis asked after dinner.

"How do you plan to survive the evening with Glynhaven on Friday?"

The question startled him, for he hadn't given it any

thought. "I suppose I can always ignore him and engage in conversation with my neighbors."

"That would be difficult, considering the fact that he is your host. I have another suggestion."

"And that is?"

She shifted to face him and grinned. "It comes from my mother."

"Does the duchess hold yet another ingenious secret for dealing with this dilemma? What would she recommend to your father if he was forced to spend an evening in his enemy's company?"

"Simple deception to confound the enemy."

"Go on."

"Behave as though the enemy is your long-lost friend. Ask after his estates, a topic always close to a man's heart. Ask his opinion of the Corn Laws. What does he think of Wilberforce and his opposition to the slave trade? If your mind wanders when he answers, let it. He'll be too enamored of the sound of his own voice to care."

Waverley's lips quirked. "Did his grace follow this prescription?"

Helena laughed until she cried.

"What?"

"The thing is, my mother always manages to convince him it was his own idea. She congratulates him on having confounded his enemies once again."

He rose and helped her to her feet. "I'll skip the brandy tonight. Don't expect miracles, but I'll do my best to follow your mother's advice. She's a wise woman and so are you." Waverley kissed her brow.

She leaned her head on his shoulder and yearned for more than a mere kiss on the brow, but it was not forthcoming. She was forced to settle for the comfort of his arm around her and his cheek pressed to her hair.

Chapter 14

On the eve of the Glynhaven ball, the marquis settled his grandmother into the family carriage and said, "You shall be the most sought-after woman at the ball tonight. I fear I may have to stand guard to make sure no man steals your heart from me, dearest."

His flirting made the dowager giggle like a young girl. She wore a gown she'd worn years ago, one she treasured. It was made of delicate ecru lace embroidered with seed pearls and featured a mandarin collar and sleeves short enough for white kid gloves. Her skirt ended in a short train, and she wore a tiara of filigree gold atop short gray curls.

Nurse Hubley was in attendance as well, but she planned to visit the Glynhaven housekeeper, an old friend, during the festivities. She would be near enough to the dowager should she be needed.

When Helena glided down the front steps, Waverley lost his voice. She wore a yellow sarcenet gown over pale satin molded to her figure. It fell to just below her ankles, revealing matching slippers. Silk ribbons cinched its high waist. Her dark hair had been swept high, its long curls falling, tendrils framing her face, yellow ribbons artfully visible. Long white gloves further accentuated her exotic color.

She wore no jewelry, he noted with approval. A classic beauty like Helena had no need for jewels. "I seem to have misplaced my wits, ma'am. You dazzle me."

"Why thank you, my lord." She eyed his dress. "Well done, my lord! Such sartorial splendor."

Indeed, he presented a dashing figure, appropriately dressed for the evening's festivities in black, except for the crisp white linen shirt and fashionably tied neck cloth.

As she stepped into the carriage, she said, "Don't forget your promise to me. Behave yourself."

His eyes were lit with mischief. "Since I am escorting the two most beautiful women in all of England tonight, how can I fail?"

They reached their destination in high spirits. When the earl's butler led them into the drawing room, their host hurried to greet them.

"Good evening, Lady Waverley." The earl kissed the dowager's hand. "I am honored that you are well enough to join us this evening. Let me help you to a seat by the fire."

Waverley said pleasantly, "Hello, Martin. You look well. I haven't seen you since we were exploring the caves for whiskey. Do you recall?"

Glynhaven laughed. "How could I forget? There hasn't been a single dram since that tasted as good to me as the stuff we cadged from the caves." To Helena he said, "You look a vision tonight, ma'am. May I beg the honor of your hand for the first waltz?"

Before she could answer, Waverley said, "Lady Fairchild has promised that honor to me, old man." He caught Helena's raised eyebrow, which prompted him to add, "But it shall be my pleasure to relinquish my place to my host."

"Most generous, Lord Waverley," Helena said in approval. She turned to Glynhaven and added, "I look forward to our waltz, my lord."

The earl made them known to the other guests he had invited to dinner: Vicar Elbert Cullum and his wife; Squire John Hawkes and his wife; Magistrate George Wyndham, a widower; and Baron Andrew Swively, his wife and his daughter Eliza. The plump young lady reminded Helena of Jane. She made a mental note to remind Waverley to stand a country set with her, for she suspected the poor girl would not be much in demand at the ball.

At dinner, Helena was seated between Vicar Cullum and Baron Swively. Waverley was seated on the opposite side of the table, between Eliza and the vicar's wife. His grandmother was having a grand time enjoying the attentions bestowed upon her by Glynhaven and Magistrate Wyndham, seated on either side of her.

"Lord Saltash and his guests plan to join us later this evening, Waverley. Are you acquainted with him?" the earl asked.

"We've never met, but I've heard of him," he answered. He masked his irritation by engaging Eliza in conversation. This turned out to be frustrating, for the child was so in awe of his exalted station, she was able only to stammer brief answers. Though the food was excellent, the wine impeccable, the service *à la russe,* the dinner lasted too long.

Squire Hawkes was a man of few words, while the vicar, seated on Helena's left, gave her a detailed account of last Sunday's sermon, rather one of his best, in his modest view. When she ventured to glance at Waverley, he rolled his eyes and she had all to do to keep from giggling. She did not look his way a second time.

By the time the dinner guests repaired to the ballroom, the musicians were tuning up their instruments for the evening's entertainment. Local bucks critically examined young ladies of marriageable age, who were escorted by their parents. The prettiest lasses filled their dance cards easily, but the lads took their time before requesting a dance from far less attractive girls lining the walls. Asking the girls to dance was something a gentleman was obligated to do at least once during the evening.

Glynhaven found Helena and said, "I've come to claim you for the first waltz, ma'am." He offered his arm and led her onto the dance floor.

As he watched them waltz, Waverley couldn't help but wonder why the earl had invited Saltash, considering his well-known reputation. Indeed, all of Paris knew of Saltash and his risqué entertainments. His guests, never of the first rank, would be the only ones accepting his invitation. London was still in Season this time of year and such people would not be welcome by the *ton*.

Waverley sought out Miss Eliza Cullum, the vicar's daughter, and begged the honor of her hand for the first waltz. He attended to his partner on the dance floor, but his eyes searched for Helena and Glynhaven at the same time. "Have you brothers and sisters, ma'am?"

"Only one brother," she answered shyly. "He is just down from Cambridge."

"My secretary Rupert?"

She blushed, searching for an answer. "My parents and I are pleased he is in your employ."

"You may be proud of him, my dear. He's a clever fellow."

"Oh yes, my lord. We all are. He received the highest honors, you know."

Glynhaven was an accomplished dancer, much appreciated by Helena, for she loved to dance as well.

"You look enchanting this evening, ma'am."

"Kind of you to say so, sir."

"I mean more than kindness, dear lady. Much more. I have thought of nothing else but you since we met."

A startled laugh escaped her lips. "A bold statement for such a short acquaintance. We've met only once before."

"That was enough for me to fall in love with you. Will you give me reason to believe you will accept my hand in marriage?"

The music stopped and he led her off the floor, which gave her a moment to collect her thoughts. "I'm sorry, sir. I cannot encourage your suit."

"I'll find a way to win your heart, ma'am. I promise you."

She struggled to maintain her dignity. "You take too much for granted, for such short acquaintance, sir. I must remind you again that we've met only once before."

"The first of many meetings, I've no doubt. May I call on you to further our courtship?"

"You presume too much, sir. We are not courting."

"We shall begin courting as of this moment, then. Women, I have heard, often say no the first time. Allow me to call on you so I may begin to persuade you of the advantages of marriage to me."

"The marquis would be delighted to receive you so you may renew your acquaintance with him."

"Don't toy with my affections, ma'am. Allow me to speak plainly. My request was meant for you, not for Waverley." He answered casually, yet his eyes turned cold.

"I am merely a guest at Waverley Castle, my lord. You must petition the marquis if you wish to visit his home."

"Then allow me to invite you to Glynhaven. Are you free for dinner tomorrow evening? I'll send my carriage for you. We won't be alone. Lord Saltash and his . . ."

Before he could finish his speech, a footman approached

and whispered into his ear. Glynhaven turned to her and said, "Will you excuse me, ma'am? Lord Saltash and his guests have arrived and I must greet them." He hurried off.

Feeling somehow violated by his presumption, Helena scanned the room for Waverley. She found him on the opposite side of the dance floor seated next to his grandmother. She circled round the dancers and made her way through the crush of guests to reach them.

A handsome woman, unfamiliar to her, wearing a beaded black gown and a powdered wig, reached his side first. Mystified, Helena stopped and hid behind a pillar, wondering who she was.

She observed Waverley rise and heard him stammer, "M-madame Z? What brings you to England?"

The woman rapped his hand with her fan. "For shame! No kiss on the hand? Are you not glad to see me, *mon roué Anglais?* Or have you forgotten your Paris friends so soon? I am sad for it, especially since I have brought your alphabets— Amelié, Babette, and Colette—all the way from Paris to entertain you." He stood frozen in place, while his former courtesans took turns kissing him on the lips.

Madame Z spoke in her native tongue, but Helena's French was excellent. She understood every word. She recalled Darlington's words. Hadn't he found Waverley at Madame Z's salon? Hadn't Chris said he'd found Waverley in bed with three courtesans? She wheeled away and stalked off, her cheeks burning, her soul sunk far below the depths of hell. Nothing would have made her happier than an opening in the middle of the dance floor that would obligingly swallow her up.

What a fool I am! How could I let myself fall in love with such an incorrigible rake? One whose mistresses follow him all the way from Paris? Waverley must be quite a lover! Once a rake, always a rake. Isn't that what they say? I seem to have a special talent for falling in love with the wrong man. What's wrong with me? Sorry to disappoint you, Father. I'm just not capable of success. I am doomed to failure when it comes to love.

She fancied all eyes were upon her, when in fact no one took any notice of her misery. To cool her fiery cheeks, she made her way to the terrace and strolled casually down the steps into the garden, trying hard not to attract attention. She sat down on a secluded bench and wrapped her arms around herself as if to embrace her wretchedness. It wasn't enough that the pain she felt shattered her heart. She dug her fingers into her arm to punish her body as well.

How long had she been a guest at Waverley Castle? Was it only weeks? A lifetime, more like. She took no notice of loud voices signaling the approach of a group of people until one of them spoke her name.

"Lady Fairshild? Fanshy meeting you here."

Helena looked up at an unfamiliar gentleman who wove unsteadily on his feet. Clearly, he was drunk. His male companion seemed poised to rescue him should he fall. They all wore evening clothes, but the women with them had painted faces.

"Do I know you, sir? I can't recall having met you before tonight."

He executed a bow that almost toppled him. "Lord Shaltash at your shervice, ma-am," he slurred.

The two women giggled, enjoying the spectacle, but Helena sat immobile, her insides roiling, yet outwardly calm. "Nice to meet you, sir. Do you care to introduce your friends to me?"

He jerked a thumb at the young man by his side. "Mr. Tavishtock, m'coushin."

"Pleasure, ma'am," the young man said uneasily. "Come, Saltash. Time to retire." He tried to take his cousin's arm.

"Hands off, boy! I'm having fun."

Helena smiled, trying to hide her uneasiness. "And these ladies are?"

Saltash burst out in wild laughter. "Ladies? Tha's a good

one. These tarts wouldn' know a lady if they tripped over one. Ladies is as ladies does and these light skirts ain't."

He eyed Helena and tried to wink, but he had difficulty focusing. "Don' be coy, milady. Everyone knowsh you're Darlington's jilt. He's consoling himself with an American heiress, I hear. Is she better in bed than you?"

Her face ashen, Helena said in an icy tone, "You've had your fun, sir. Now leave me alone."

His cousin forcibly turned Saltash toward the terrace, but the man twisted out of his arms and turned back. "Who do you think you're talking to, bitch? Lord Shaltash, tha's who. Let me bed you and teach you how to keep a . . ."

As if from nowhere, Waverley came flying at Saltash and hit him so hard, the man spun around once before he fell to the ground. He turned as if to strike the young man as well, but Helena cried out, "Waverley, stop! Don't you dare hit that boy. He did everything he could to stop Saltash, but the man's drunk."

Waverley reached into his waistcoat pocket, withdrew his card and flung it on the ground. "Present that to Saltash. My seconds will call on him in the morning."

News of the brawl swept the ballroom, thanks to the two young ladies who had witnessed the fiasco. They ran inside looking for Madame Z, screeching at the top of their lungs. This brought a large number of guests swarming about like frantic bees searching for their hives.

White with rage, the Earl of Glynhaven was the first to reach them. "What have you done, Waverley? Saltash is my guest!" He signaled to two footmen to carry his lordship to his chamber.

Waverley threw him a look of scorn and, without deigning to answer, took Helena by the arm and attempted to drag her away.

"Let me go, you . . . you wretched *rake!* You're hurting me. What do you think you're doing?"

He stared at her, wild-eyed.

"Let go of me, you fool! Everyone is watching us. Have the

decency to leave me at least a shred of dignity. I am well able
to walk to the carriage without your help."

"You must give me the opportunity to explain about
Madame . . ."

She grasped the limb of a tree and refused to budge. "I
don't give a bloody damn about your bloody Madame or your
bloody French *whores!*"

He halted, his eyes and ears at once alert to his surroundings.
"Stop ripping me apart, you shrew! Everyone's watching us!"

"Really? How kind." She twisted her head around and
smiled genially. "Hello there, everyone. Having a good time?
Allow me to present your neighbor, Lord Waverley. His lordship is well known in Paris, you know. They call him *le roué
Anglais.*" She laughed as if demented. "Mothers, a word of
warning. You had better safeguard your daughters from him
lest he charm them into his bed."

"That's enough!" he thundered. He wrenched her hands
from the tree limb, swept her into his arms and stalked off to
the accompaniment of raucous laughter.

"Put me down, you beast! I'll walk to your carriage. I can't
wait, in fact, to return to Waverley Castle, *for the last time!*"

He put her down, grasped her shoulders, and glared at her.
"What do you mean, 'for the last time'?"

"I'm going home to London. Tomorrow morning, sir."

His eyes softened and he let her go. "Don't go, my love. I . . .
I don't want to lose you."

"You've already lost me."

"At least let me explain. I buried my past in Paris when I
heard my father died. I had no idea it would be flung in my
face tonight, but that part of my life is over. No one knows
better than me how unworthy of you I am, my darling." He
fell to his knees. "Will you marry me?"

"No."

"I'll make you!"

"Oh no you won't!"

"Then stay. Don't go home."

Her hands itched to hold his head and comfort him, but she kept them at her sides. "I might consider remaining a little longer, on one condition."

"I'll do anything you want, my darling. Just say the word."

"Renounce this ridiculous duel."

His face turned pale. "Renounce . . . ? Too late for that. It is a matter of honor."

"Get off your knees, Waverley. Let us discuss this so-called matter of honor sensibly. Saltash was drunk when he said those awful things to me. If I can forgive him for it, you must do so as well."

"Will you promise to stay at Waverley if I call it off?"

She hugged her shoulders as if the chill in her heart had invaded her body as well. "Yes."

Waverley detected a flicker of hope in her voice. "Very well, my love. If Saltash offers his apologies for insulting you, I'll call it off."

"You must apologize to him as well, for hitting him."

"You drive a hard bargain, my love. Hitting him was the highlight of my wretched evening." He grinned a familiar boyish grin, one that she had grown to love so well.

She bit her lip to keep from giggling. "Those are my conditions, Waverley. Take them or leave them."

"A kiss to seal our bargain?"

"That's asking too much. A handshake will be quite enough, sir." She held one hand out.

Waverley took her hand in both of his. "A mere crumb, my dearest heart. No doubt all I deserve."

Chapter 15

Sunday, the Third of May, 1818

The marquis had chosen his seconds from among men he'd known since boyhood. One was Farmer John Hawkes, and the other was a yeoman named Robert Nelson.

He met with them at dawn. "Thank you, good friends. I'm deeply moved by your show of support, but Lady Fairchild begs me to call it off and I have agreed. I intend to apologize to Lord Saltash. In return, I expect the gentleman to make amends for his conduct toward my guest by begging her forgiveness for his offensive remarks. You may inform Saltash that Lady Fairchild stands ready to accept his lordship's act of contrition."

"Well said, my lord. A duel in this day and age is a barbarous affair. Mr. Nelson and I shall convey your message to Lord Saltash," said Hawkes.

"You will find Lord Saltash at Glynhaven. He is the earl's guest."

But Lord Saltash refused to apologize to Lady Fairchild, demanding satisfaction instead. The duel was set for ten o'clock the next morning.

Both sides had agreed upon the beach in Sennen Cove for the location. The sun was not yet high, the sky was clear and the wind was mild. A light rain the night before had tamped the sand into a hard surface, good ground for a duel.

Waverley had the advantage, for this was Cornwall and the Cornish were a close-knit lot. They stood firmly in support of their own as they lined the rise above the beach to witness the match. The beach itself was declared off limits.

Saltash chose pistols for the duel, for he knew himself to be an excellent shot. His seconds were Major Hobey, a friend, and John Tavistock, his cousin. The earl had prudently forbidden the raffish guests Saltash had brought to Glynhaven's ball to appear this morning lest they cause an uproar. He knew well enough that these disreputable followers would not ingratiate him with the local populace. They would only serve to earn disapproval.

"I will ask you one more time, my lord," said Farmer Hawkes. "Will you agree to call off the duel and apologize to Lady Fairchild for the insult?"

"No. Lady Fairchild well knows I spoke the truth. Lord Waverley had no right to knock me down for my honesty, however blunt."

"Then we shall proceed with the examination of the pistols, my lord." Hawkes opened the pistol case provided by Glynhaven and handed it to Tavistock. While Tavistock and Nelson examined the weapons, Hawkes and Hobey drew a line in the sand and marked off ten paces in each direction.

Rabu helped Waverley out of his coat, vest and his neck cloth. The valet laid them on a boulder. He bent to help his master take off his boots. A few yards away, Saltash removed his raiment.

Dr. Fenwick called the two men to him and said, "Murder isn't necessary for satisfaction, sirs. Aim for a limb if you must, but avoid the heart, for that leads to certain death for one of you. Shake hands and be damned to hell for your cursed quarrel!"

"Take your places back-to-back, my lords," said Glynhaven. "When I lower my hand, begin your ten paces. Stop and turn. At the count of one, stand ready. At the count of two, take aim. At the count of three, fire."

Glynhaven raised a white cloth. When he lowered it, the men began to walk. At ten paces, they stopped and turned.

"One," Glynhaven cried out and each took his stand, Waverley facing the sea and Saltash facing opposite, their heads turned toward one another, the roar of the sea the only sound to be heard.

"Two." The duelers took aim.

The astonished crowd gasped when Saltash aimed for his challenger's heart and pulled the trigger *before* the count of three. When the bullet pierced Waverley, the crowd's protests filled the air. Waverley stood frozen for a moment in time, then collapsed in a heap. It had been the marquis' intention to delope before he fell, but he wasn't given the opportunity.

Helena took a final look around her chamber, despair lining her face. "Is my carriage ready?"

"Yes, milady," said Amy. She helped her into her traveling coat and handed her gloves and reticule to her.

"Wait in the carriage, Amy. I won't be long." Helena squared her shoulders and left the room. She stopped across the hall and knocked on the dowager's door. When Nurse Hubley opened it, she said in a whisper, "The marchioness is awake, milady. She's been waiting for you."

Tears threatened, but Helena blinked them back. She knelt beside the dowager's chair and took her hand. "I'll miss you, ma'am. Stay well and I promise to write often."

"So you are leaving us after all. Is there nothing I can say to change your mind?"

Helena kissed the old woman's fingers. "No, dearest, but you will always remain in my heart." Her tears spilled over in spite of her efforts.

"There, there," said the dowager, patting her head. "There, there."

Helena held the old woman's hand to her cheek for a moment. Without another word, she rose, nodded farewell to Nurse Hubley and fled the room.

She took the back stairs but paused when she heard raised voices coming from Mrs. Trasker's chamber, its door slightly ajar.

It was Harry's voice. Helena flattened herself against the wall and listened, her heart racing.

"I come back 'ere from the beach fast as I could, Ma. The marquis got hit. Mayhap he's dead."

"Dead? Tell it me all, Harry. Tell it me at once!"

"Lord Saltash got off the first shot. He hit the marquis, but . . ."

Dear God! Helena felt faint.

"Bold as brass, the feller aimed for Waverley's heart and pulled the trigger."

"Then you're the next marquis, me boy. The dream's come true fer us! Now we can tell My Lord to leave us alone. We'll do no more smugglin' fer 'im!"

Helena gasped.

"What's that noise, Ma?"

"Someone's outside the door. Quick, Harry."

But Helena was quicker. She poked her head into the room as if she had just arrived. "Good day, Mrs. Trasker. Harry. I've come to say farewell. I am returning to London today."

The Traskers exchanged glances when Helena put forward

her hand. "Good luck with your continued excellent work for the marquis and the dowager."

After some hesitation, Mrs. Trasker wiped her hand on her apron and shook the offered hand. "When did you say you're leavin', milady?"

"I'll be off shortly. My carriage is waiting for me as we speak, ma'am."

"Shake hands wi' milady, Harry. Don't want to send her off thinkin' there's hard feelings, do we?"

Helena maintained her smile while Harry shook her hand. "There are no hard feelings on my part, Mrs. Trasker. We may have had our differences, but we managed to settle them after all, didn't we? I'm off to the kitchen to say good-bye to Cook." She nodded her head slightly, turned and left the room.

Helena let out a sigh of relief when she reached the back stairs landing. Only then could she be sure that the Traskers were no longer able to see her. She flew down the rest of the flight to the kitchen, flung her arms around Cook and began to sob. "He's dead, Cook. The marquis is dead. And it's all my fault!"

"Nonsense, milady. Who's been spreadin' such a terrible lie? The marquis ain't dead."

"Harry saw the whole thing. I heard him tell his mother."

"Drat that man! He's no more sense in his head than a dumb sheep! The marquis is in his bed, milady, only wounded. Doctor Fenwick's tending him as we speak."

Helena began to sway, but Cook caught her and placed her in a chair, forcing her head down. "You've no time for fainting just now. Nor you can't run away to London neither. You're needed here an' that's the size of it." Cook bustled to the sink, wet a cloth and filled a glass with water. "Sip a bit of this, slow-like." She pressed the cool cloth to Helena's head and held the glass to her lips.

"Thank you, Cook, I'm feeling better now." She took another sip and added, "You're right. I can't leave. It's out of the question under the circumstances. Will you tell Amy and Casper to put up the horses and unpack while I inquire after his lordship?"

"God help us if his lordship dies," Cook murmured.

Helena hurried through the dining room door and into the hallway, where servants had already congregated, abuzz with the news of the duel.

Astonished at the lack of discipline she'd worked so hard to correct, Helena paused and demanded in a voice filled with authority, "Why are you lot here? Go about your duties at once!" She waited long enough to see them scatter, lifted her skirts and flew up the steps of the grand staircase. She turned right at the landing toward Waverley's suite of rooms.

When she reached his bedchamber, she knocked and Rabu opened the door. "May I come in?" she whispered. Rabu turned to the doctor, who met her at the door and led her into Waverley's large office.

"He's asleep, ma'am. I've given him laudanum to ease the pain."

"Will the marquis survive, Doctor Fenwick?"

"No question. If he hadn't lifted his arm to delope, he'd be dead. The bullet grazed a rib and exited through his left side. I've applied a liniment to the wound. He'll need nursing to watch for infection. If all goes well, his lordship will be sore for a time, but he'll be up and about soon, for he's in good health." He saw no need to inform her ladyship that the craven Lord Saltash had pulled the trigger before the count of three.

"What must be done for Lord Waverley?"

The doctor eyed her carefully. "Aren't you returning to London today?"

"Not now, sir. He . . . he needs me," she said, almost pleading. "I'll be his nurse if you will instruct me. His valet can relieve me when I need sleep."

The doctor hesitated.

"Please, sir. I . . . I must do this."

"Does the sight of blood trouble you, ma'am?"

"I'm not fainthearted, sir. I have younger sisters and a brother, and I am frequently summoned to the sickroom to tend them when they are ill."

"All right. You must see to it that the liniment is applied every four hours. Encourage him to drink liquids. Give him sips of tea, lemonade, water and broth. No spirits, mind. Add a few drops of laudanum into his drink when he complains of pain. I've left some for him."

"Will he suffer much pain, sir?"

The doctor shook his head. "Discomfort, more like. The bruise may hurt at the smallest movement. His lordship may also be restless, unable to settle in a comfortable spot, but that too will pass."

"Shall I see to it that he lies still?"

"Not in the least. Have that peculiar fellow—his valet—sponge him when you apply new liniment and a new dressing. Pay no mind if blood seeps through the dressing. That's a good sign. If it becomes excessive, send for me." He picked up his bag and turned to leave, but Helena placed a restraining hand on his arm. "Yes?"

"When shall you visit again, doctor?"

"Tomorrow morning, first thing." He bowed to her and took his leave.

Helena closed the door and leaned against it as if that would give her strength for the ordeal ahead.

London: Fairchild House

"Father, come quickly. Georgie and Edward are having the devil of a row!" said Jane.

The duke raised his eyeglass to his nine-year-old daughter

in a gesture of annoyance, but she paid no heed. He loved Jane, yet he found it hard to like her. For one, she was over-weight, and for another, she meddled. "Haven't you been taught to knock before you enter?"

"But, Father, you don't understand. They're about to come to blows."

"Have you been eavesdropping again? You know you are not supposed to listen in on other people's conversations. How many times must I remind you it's bad manners to do so?"

A large tear formed on Jane's round face. "I . . . I thought you should know."

He sighed in exasperation. "Now don't start weeping. There's no need . . ."

Before the duke could continue, his son burst into the library. "Bloody hell, Father! You must do something about Georgie!"

The duke looked at Jane, a twinkle in his eyes, sharing the joke with her. "It appears your brother must also learn to knock before entering."

Thus mollified, Jane crossed her arms and threw her father a look of triumph, as if to say "I told you so!"

"Where did you learn such incivility, Edward? Not at my knee, I'm sure. Pray tell me what is the matter, but lower your voice. We needn't amuse all the servants."

To his daughter he added, "Thank you, Jane. You may leave us."

"And don't be hanging at the door trying to listen in, brat," said her brother.

"I was only trying to help," Jane muttered and stalked off.

Edward followed her to the door and shut it firmly. When he turned back to his father, he said bitterly, "Georgie stole my clothes and sneaked out last night. Not for the first time, either!"

The news did not appear to stun the duke. "And you came by this earthshaking news how?"

"My valet informed me of it. He heard a noise and entered

my chamber to investigate just as Georgie climbed back into my window early this morning. *Wearing my clothes!* She has ruined my new Hessians!"

"Your Hessians are of little consequence, but my daughter's behavior is of great consequence. Thank you for telling me, Edward. You may go."

"No, Father. I prefer to remain here. It's my right to see you chastise her properly."

The duke's eyes glinted. In a voice full of menace, he said softly, "Your what? Your . . . right? Tell me I didn't hear you correctly, my son."

Edward made the mistake of insisting, though in a much lower tone. "It's me she's wronged, Father, and I ought to see Georgiana gets the punishment she deserves."

"Do you not think it premature to bury me before my time, son? I beg to remind you that I am still very much alive. When I die, you shall succeed me and do as you wish. Squander the fortune I shall leave you, if that is your will. Beat your sisters. Throw your mother out into the streets. . . ."

The duke's acidic tongue gave his son and heir cause to regret his disrespectful outburst. "I beg your pardon, sir," he mumbled in contrition. Edward's face turned a deep shade of red.

The duke ignored his belated apology. "Come to think of it, Edward, you're halfway to ruin already, what with your betting wagers and your sports-mad pursuits, a poor example for your sisters, to say the least. You have only yourself to blame for your sister's wild antics. I shouldn't wonder if Georgie hasn't learned to ape your ways."

"I'm sorry for my outburst, Father, but Georgiana . . ."

The duke waved his hand in a gesture of dismissal. "You may go, Edward. On your way out, be sure to close the door gently instead of slamming it as you did on your poor sister

Jane. Oh, and one more thing, *my lord*. Be so good as to ask
Dunston to send Georgiana to me."

Waverley Castle

   Helena sat by Waverley's bed and watched his restless,
sleeping form. She wiped his brow with a cool cloth from
time to time, relieved to discover that he wasn't feverish.
Alone with her thoughts, she couldn't help but dwell on the
events leading up to the duel. She had such mixed feelings
concerning them. It was Waverley's foolhardy decision to try
to delope, but clearly, he meant it to please her. If he hadn't
raised his arm into the air, he would have died. He was alive,
but she blamed herself nevertheless.
   What of Glynhaven's role in this sorry affair? How could
he not have known that Saltash was bringing Madame Z and
her tarts to the ball? What made him think she would accept
his proposal of marriage? Maybe she should have heeded Waverley's anger at the invitation. The Earl of Glynhaven was no
friend to the Marquis of Waverley. Foolish of her to think otherwise, but how could she have known how much bad blood
ran between them?
   Mr. Cullum, Waverley's secretary, had brought her the
news that the dishonorable Lord Saltash had fled to France to
avoid arrest for having pulled the trigger before the count of
three. He had reported that Saltash had taken his French
friends with him.
   Waverley moaned. She glanced at the clock on the mantel.
It was almost midnight. She picked up the light sheet cover-
ing him. He'd bled through the dressing. She rose to summon
Rabu to help her, but he was already at her side. In silence,
they turned the marquis on his right side to allow her to
remove the bloodied dressing. Rabu washed the wound care-

fully, after which she applied fresh ointment and rewrapped the wound in clean dressing.

She prepared another dose of laudanum and held it to Waverley's lips while Rabu raised his head. He never woke, but in a few minutes, his labored breathing eased and he ceased his moans. Helena beckoned Rabu to follow her to the door, where the patient could not hear her words. "I shall leave you now, for I must rest, but there is a footman posted outside the door. Send for me if you find you need my help with his lordship."

"Yes, your la'sheep. Sleep well, your la'sheep." He giggled, but his heart wasn't in it.

Chapter 16

The marquis woke to find his secretary at his bedside. "If you're here, Rupert, it's clear that I'm still alive."

"You are, sir, I'm thankful to say. How do you feel?"

Waverley ignored his question. "Where is Saltash?"

"I'm told his lordship and his party left right after the duel."

"He took the lot of them home to Devon?"

"No, sir. His lordship escorted his French . . . er . . . guests back to Paris."

The marquis frowned. "How came you by this information, Rupert?"

His secretary grinned. "I make it my business to have such information ready when you inquire."

"Which means?"

"Which means your duel has become legend hereabouts. You're a hero to the Cornish, sir."

"So soon? Oh, well. I suppose I should be grateful that I am not the villain in this melodrama."

The young man's eyes danced. "Far from it, sir. The villain is an outsider from Devon. What could be worse?"

Waverley grinned. "Bless you, Rupert, for having such a wry sense of humor." He closed his eyes for a moment, then added, "Lady Fairchild must have reached London by now."

"No, sir. Her ladyship is here."

Waverley's brows knit. "I don't understand. I was under the impression that milady meant to return to London."

"She's changed her mind, sir. Her ladyship has been at your bedside changing your dressings and applying liniment to your wounds. Rabu relieves her at midnight."

"Indeed?" A smile broke from his lips, but it changed quickly into a scowl. *Then she's in danger and I cannot protect her. That scoundrel Glynhaven orchestrated this whole fiasco. I should have guessed that he was up to some mischief. He'd like nothing better than to destroy me. Old grudges die hard.* "I want you to write a letter for me, Rupert."

"I'll fetch my pad, sir. I'll only be a moment." He rose and hurried to his office through the connecting door.

Waverley dictated the brief message and stated its direction when Rupert returned. "I leave it to your good judgment to send it to London with the utmost speed."

"Private messenger is quickest, sir, but costly."

"Hang the cost, but be discreet, Rupert. Hire someone trustworthy to deliver it. No one else must know of this. Understood?"

"Of course, sir."

With a sigh of relief, Waverley lay back on his pillow. "What would I do without you, Rupert?"

Usually serious, the young man allowed himself a grin. "Works both ways, sir. What would I do had you not offered me such a fascinating position?"

"Morning, your lordship," said Dr. Fenwick cheerfully. "I've come to have a look at that wound of yours."

Waverley rubbed the sleep from his eyes. "Morning, sir."

"Sleep well?" The doctor spread his supplies on the bedside table.

"Like the dead, but I'm not fond of the drug-induced state."

"Don't blame you in the least." He cut the dressing off and examined the wound. "Bleeding's stopped. No sign of infection, either. All to the good." He cleaned the wound gently, applied fresh liniment, and bound it.

"When may I resume activities, sir?"

"If you feel up to it, you may leave your bed for a short time today. But remember that you must continue to be cautious until you recover your strength. Nothing too strenuous, mind. No horseback riding, mind you. I recommend short walks when the weather permits. Rest as much as you can. You'll be fine in a week or two."

Waverley frowned. "As bad as all that, eh?"

"Actually? Not bad at all." The doctor could not resist adding, "You have only to consider the alternative, sir."

Waverley laughed. "I'll keep that in mind." He watched the doctor pack his bag. "Thank you, sir. Will you inform Lady Waverley of your instructions?"

"No need for that." He nodded toward the door between the bedchamber and Waverley's office. "I'm sure her ladyship's heard my every word. Come in, ma'am. I'm finished for today."

"Thank you, Doctor Fenwick," Helena said, "for allowing me to listen to your instructions. I have only one question. What do you recommend for his lordship's diet?"

"No restrictions. He may eat what he likes, in small amounts. I'll be back in the morning. Good day to you both." He made a courtly bow, then departed.

"Well, Desmond." Helena sat by his bedside and smiled.

"Well, Helena." He grinned back at her.

"Have you had your breakfast?"

"Not yet. I want to enjoy it in the morning room. The doctor said I might get out of bed for a time."

Helena rang for Rabu. "His lordship will take his breakfast in the morning room. I'll send word to Cook while you help him up. His dressing gown will do." She turned to Waverley and added, "Mind if I join you?"

"Mind? I dare you to stay away!"

The sun-filled morning room on the second floor faced south, where an unobstructed view of the sea could be had from its windows. The dining chairs were covered in blue and yellow patterned silk matching the draperies. All in all, the room provided a cozy setting much more intimate than the huge formal dining room on the first floor.

Waverley entered on the arm of his valet. The marquis was dressed in casual pants and a shirt open at the neck.

Helena threw up her hands in mock despair. "What's this? No sooner do I turn my back, you disobey my instructions. I said dressing gown, not morning clothes, Rabu."

"Don't blame Rabu, my dear. I chose this, though I could not manage a jacket, as you see. What's that I smell? Bacon? I'll have some with my eggs and toast."

Rabu helped him to a chair and hurried to the sideboard to fix his master's plate, ignoring the annoyed footman who felt it his place to serve. "At once, your lor'sheep."

"I thought you went home to London," Waverley said to Helena, mischief in his voice.

"I decided to remain to see you well again, since I was the cause of your . . . er . . . infirmity. Of course, if you prefer, I'll leave today. Nurse Hubley can see to your recovery."

He adopted a pained expression and groaned. "No, no. Don't leave me to such a horrible fate. If you do, I'll die."

A quiver of pleasure ran through her, but she did not let on. Instead, she pursed her lips and said, "I was about to enter my carriage when news reached me that you had been wounded."

"Does that mean . . . ?"

"It means what it means," she snapped and changed the subject. "Eat small amounts, Waverley. Doctor's orders."

He grinned and pushed his plate away. "He's right. My eyes are bigger than my stomach, it seems. I cannot swallow.another bite." A vision of breakfasting every morning, his wife Helena fussing over him filled him with warmth.

Helena made as if to speak but checked the impulse.

"Something on your mind? What is it?"

"Why did you delope? I'm . . . *we* are all glad you did, for it saved your life. That vile man was intent on murdering you."

He reached for her hand. "I did it for your sake."

"For . . . for me? What do you mean?"

"You were so against the duel, I thought you'd despise me if I killed the man."

She rolled her eyes. "Good heavens, Waverley. And did you also believe it would please me if you had died?"

"Would you have mourned me?" His smiling eyes betrayed him.

"That's nonsense and you know it. At any rate, you're not dead and you're not badly wounded. Saltash inflicted only a flesh wound. As soon as you are well enough, I'm going home."

Reason enough to feign continued illness, my adorable minx. I'll not let you go home, my love, even if I have to tie you to your bedpost to keep you here. Aloud, he said, "Rupert informs me that Saltash has fled to France to escape arrest. He said Magistrate Wyndham threatened to prosecute him for attempted murder."

"He deserves it for his cowardly act," she said. "Saltash took your French friends back to Paris as well. Shall you miss them?"

"Don't be cheeky. I had nothing to do with their visit. Are you still angry with me for my wicked past, love?"

"How should I be? It's your life to do with what you will," she said, but there was disdain in her voice.

"I'm done with all that, I promise you. You've shown me a better way to enjoy life. One I never thought possible. Will you redeem me from my past sins and agree to be my wife?"

She smiled as if she were dealing with a silly child. "You're delirious, sir. Perhaps a few drops of laudanum in your coffee will bring you to your senses."

"I was never more serious. Marry me. I love you, my darling." He paused a moment. "When I faced death, I realized I had but one regret. I was afraid I would never have an opportunity to tell you how much I love you. I almost wished to die, for I thought I had ruined all chance of winning you."

Helena's heart sang at his words, but she was saved from the urge to reveal herself to him when Paynter announced a visitor.

"Good morning to you, Waverley," the Earl of Glynhaven said in a hearty tone. "And to you, ma'am. No, no. Don't get up from your seat, sir. How are you getting on?"

"The marquis is doing well," Helena said. She turned to Waverley and added, "The earl has already visited here twice for news of you."

"How kind," Waverley murmured in an unconvincing tone.

Glynhaven shook his head in sorrow. "Still weak, I see. I've already begged Lady Fairchild's pardon for the bad manners of my guests. Unforgivable. I had no idea that Saltash would bring with him such a disreputable group of rowdies."

Oh, didn't you? Aloud the marquis said, "That surprises me, Glynhaven. Lord Saltash has a reputation as a degenerate. He's known for his mischief in Paris. I thought it known all over England as well. Perhaps it never reached your ears." He had the satisfaction of seeing the earl's face color.

Helena hastened to intervene. "Thank you for your visit, my lord, but I must bring it to an end. The marquis needs rest. Doctor's orders, you know. May I show you out?"

London: Fairchild House

"Well, puss. What have you to say for yourself?" asked the duke when Georgiana entered the library. "You've set the whole household in an uproar in addition to disturbing my peace." He eyed his daughter with what he hoped was an unforgiving expression. Without much success, as it happened, for this child was most like him, if not in looks, then certainly in temperament.

Fast approaching her debut at the age of seventeen, Lady Georgiana Fairchild was, in a word, stunning. The acknowledged family beauty had perfect features, if her numerous paramours were to be believed. The young lads waxed poetic over her translucent ivory skin, her green eyes ablaze with mischief, her wide, sensuous lips, her dimpled chin, her figure, her walk, her . . . In short, she was a veritable goddess who overawed her admirers.

Her wild ways, however, were another matter. Disapproving mothers warned their sons to beware such a devil-may-care temptress. Not good wife material, they whispered of her, though by that they meant she would not be an obedient mate for their darling sons. "She will empty your pockets with her gambling ways," one said. "Just ask your sisters," another warned. Not the best advice, for their sisters were out of reason jealous of this peerless nymph.

Georgiana took the hand her father proffered and kissed it, but she did not let go. "Never say you're angry with me, Father." In one swift motion, she curled up in his lap, put her head on his chest and held his hand to her cheek.

The duke found his daughter's bewitching ways irresistible. None of his other daughters would dare to behave in such an impertinent manner. He resisted the urge to stroke her hair. "You're an incorrigible minx, young lady. It was too bad of you to ruin Edward's boots. Your brother would like nothing better than to rip you apart, you know."

She giggled. "Serves him right, Father. He's become a pompous boor. Haven't you noticed?"

The duke laughed in spite of his resolve to remain stern. "Never mind that. Get off my lap, you disobedient chit, and sit over there while I determine what's to be done about your imprudence."

"You can always lock me up in the tower and serve me bread and water for a month or so," she suggested, smoothing her wrinkled morning gown. She bit her bottom lip and shook her head. "No. That won't do. For one, we have no tower. And if we did have one, it might make my dear brother positively gloat with so much satisfaction, I couldn't bear it."

"Be serious, Georgie. Edward demands satisfaction and he deserves it, don't you think?"

"All because I ruined his bloody boots? I'll buy him a new pair."

The duke raised an eyebrow. "With whose money, may I ask?"

"Will you lend it to me?" The look on her father's face gave the answer. "Bad idea, hmm? What do you suggest?"

"An apology is due your brother. And you must promise never to repeat your crime again. You know perfectly well that it isn't proper for you to invade his room and steal his clothing. Can you apologize to him with sincerity?"

A dangerous gleam lit her eyes. "I might, but only if he apologizes to me for having become such an odious stuffed shirt."

"Then you leave me no choice." His stern tone brought her up short.

"No choice? What do you mean, Father?"

"First, Edward must report to me that he has received satisfaction from you in the form of a sincere apology. Second, I intend to send your favorite mount back to our stables in

Brighton. Third, all our stable hands are under strict orders not to saddle up for you without my permission. They will be sacked without a reference if they disobey. And last, no allowance for a month."

"Harsh punishment indeed. How long will it last, Father?"

"That's for me to decide. And don't attempt to borrow a horse from any of your friends. Until you apologize to your brother, you may not ride at all. Do I make myself clear?"

Waverley Castle

"It's such a beautiful day, ma'am," Glynhaven said as he and Helena descended the grand staircase. "Won't you join me for a stroll in your garden?"

She was caught off her guard, not having time to form a plausible excuse to refuse him. "If it pleases you, sir."

"It pleases me more than you know, ma'am. You could add to my pleasure if you would consent to call me Martin."

She raised an eyebrow. "That goes beyond mere friendship, sir. Will you settle for Glynhaven?"

"A mere bone, but yes. I will if you allow me to call you Helena."

Again, she felt trapped in a snare being carefully laid, "Of course. We are friends, are we not?"

When she led him to the terrace, she was comforted when she saw several gardeners at work nearby. They would not be alone—a good thing in her view, though what about the earl made her uneasy, she could not fathom.

"Waverley's gardens are enchanting." He smiled, but his eyes did not.

"They will be when the work is completed," Helena said. "Lord Waverley has hired an inspired head gardener."

"Lucky man. An inspired gardener is hard to come by these days. By the way, you have earned my sincerest admiration."

"How so?"

"You behaved most properly in the face of my unruly guests."

"How kind of you to say so." She took a deep breath and added, "I'm going home to London shortly. Just as soon as the doctor says Waverley is well enough to fend for himself."

He stopped near a stone bench. "Will you sit with me a moment?"

"If you wish," she answered, yet she was again made to feel uneasy by the intent look on his face.

He sat by her side, lost in thought. When at last he spoke, he said, "I shall come soon to London to ask his grace for permission to pay my addresses to his daughter Helena. Will you marry me, my dear?"

She drew in her breath. "Glynhaven, did you not hear me? The last time you offered for my hand I refused you. I haven't changed my mind."

"Perhaps your father can change it for you, then."

She stiffened. "My father, sir, is not in the habit of forcing his children into wedlock against their wishes."

"Then I suppose I shall have to win your love on my own, lovely Helena. And make no mistake—I love you and win you I will!" He pulled her to him with force and pressed his lips to hers in a bruising kiss.

She struggled to free herself, but he held her in a fierce grip, one hand on the back of her head and the other round her waist. Desperate, she swung her foot around and kicked him in his shin as hard as she could.

He yelped in pain and let her go, at which point Helena stood up and hovered over him, her arms hugging herself. "You . . . you brute! How dare you, sir! Didn't your mother teach you how to behave toward a lady?"

Glynhaven fell to his knees before her and clutched her gown. "I beg pardon, Helena dearest. I—"

"How dare you! I. Am. Not. Your. Dearest! Let go of my gown. At once, do you hear!" She put her hands on his shoulders and pushed as hard as she was able. Hard enough for the earl to fall back and hit his head on the stone bench.

"All right, Helena, but—"

"And don't call me Helena! You've lost that right by your unwanted assault."

He rose and reached for her, but she took a step back. "I warn you, I'll scream. There are enough gardeners within hearing who will come to my aid, sir!"

To her astonishment, a slow smile crept across his face. "Good God, Helena! You're a bloody spitfire. Who would have thought it? If you think to deter my quest for your hand, you are mistaken, my love. We shall have some lively tussles together once we are married."

"That, sir, will be never."

"Never say never, my love. My sincerest apologies for being so clumsy, but I have never been in love before, you see. Give me time and I shall prove to you that I am worthy to be your husband."

"You needn't bother. My answer will remain the same. There's no longer any need for us to pretend friendship either, for you have wounded me beyond repair."

Glynhaven's eyes narrowed. "It's Waverley you love, isn't it? Yes, I see it all now," he said bitterly. "That rake has bested me since the days of our boyhood. And for no other reason than to show the other lads he could humiliate me." Helena turned to leave, determined to hear no more of his vitriolic tongue, but he grasped her arm in a viselike grip. "No, don't leave. And don't scream for help. Stay and hear me out. That's the last thing I'll ask of you. I give you my word."

"Let go of my arm, then." She said it gently, for his tone was dangerous and she felt afraid.

"Won't you sit down?"

"No, thank you. I prefer to stand, but I will listen to what you wish to say."

"Waverley always had the edge here in Land's End. Always. When we were children, he'd steal my friends from me. When we were old enough to want the young girls to notice us, it was always him they noticed. Not me. The other lads followed him as if he were the Pied Piper. And now he's won the heart of the one woman in the world I want for a wife. Isn't that ironic?"

She ignored the anger in his eyes and said, "He hasn't won my heart, sir. Nor have you. I'll take my leave of you now, if you don't mind." She turned and strode away. His final words assaulted her ears.

"Why so particular, my lady? How many more offers do you think you can garner, especially after everyone knows that Darlington jilted you?"

Chapter 17

Tuesday, the Fifth of May, 1818

Glynhaven had terrified Helena. The recollection kept her tossing and turning until first light. She didn't dare tell Waverley about the earl's brutal assault, for fear he'd challenge the earl to yet another duel no matter the poor state of his health. When she woke, these unsettling events combined to cause her to suffer a violent headache and she groaned.

"What's wrong, milady?" asked Amy in alarm.

"Oooh," she wailed and held her head. "I have the worst headache. . . ."

"Never fear, milady. Cook knows how to make a special posset, the perfect remedy for headaches. I'll run down and have her prepare it for you."

Helena lay back down and tried not to move a muscle, to lessen the pain.

"Find something simple in my wardrobe, such as a loose shirt and a large waistcoat. No neck cloth, if you please. Comfortable buckskin trousers and soft boots, as well."

"But mastah . . ."

"No argument, my man. I'm determined to walk about a bit."

A large tear ran down Rabu's brown face.

"What is it?" Waverley asked in surprise.

"How have I failed you, mastah? You are still sick and . . ."

The marquis laughed at Rabu's touching concern. "All right, you tyrant. You may accompany me to make sure I don't die."

"Thanks to your special posset, my headache is cured, Cook. Any progress in new hires?" Helena said.

"I sent Amy and Casper to the mop fair yesterday to find good people willin' to work here. If anyone can, Amy will be able to convince 'em the wages are fair and the work is respectable and the Traskers are no longer in charge."

"Good. We need more willing workers. I want to set Waverley to rights before I return to London."

Cook bit her lip and cast her eyes down. "I been meanin' to tell you . . ."

"What is it?"

"They had nowhere to go and they're old, it be a pity to put 'em out to starve."

"What are you talking about?"

"Brindle's our tanner, though there be no work for him nowadays. He keeps a leather shop below stairs. Lives there, too."

"In the cellar?"

"No ma'am. It be too drafty for him. There's a small staircase at the end of the storage hall. His shop is below. Then there's old Bridey, former nurse to the dowager. She sneaks down from the attic to see her lady from time to time. She lives next to Willa, milady's seamstress. She can hardly see to sew a proper stitch, but she can mend. I give her torn sheets and aprons to repair and she does fine with 'em."

Cook examined her hands before looking directly into

Helena's eyes. "That's the lot, my lady. It's either here or the poorhouse. I didn't have the heart to send 'em there."

"Who pays them their wages? They're not listed in my account books."

"No, my lady, they're not. I pays 'em from me own wages and feeds 'em. The Traskers don't know 'bout 'em, else they'd be long gone like all the others."

"Who else knows about them?"

"Only me and me nieces."

"We'll keep them on, of course. You're kind to share your wages, but that will no longer be necessary. Keep an account of what you have already paid them and I will see you are repaid. Perhaps Willa can mend some of my things. Does the marchioness enjoy Bridey's company?"

"Oh yes, milady. The dowager misses her when she doesn't visit."

"Arrange for Bridey to visit, then. I will deal with the Traskers if it becomes necessary. But for the time being, continue to keep their presence a secret." Helena rose, signaling the end of the interview. "Come. Show me the way to the tanner's workshop."

Helena entered a tiny shop richly smelling of leather and glue. The tanner Brindle had gnarled fingers and a timeworn face reminding her of an elf. "Good morning, sir. I am Lady Helena."

"Hear tell." He kept on gluing the sole of a well-worn boot.

"Whose boots are these, sir?"

"Eh, miss?" The stooped old man in the leather apron turned to her with a puzzled look.

"Whose boots are these?" she shouted, for Cook hadn't told her the ancient tanner was almost completely deaf.

"The old marquis wore 'em fer huntin' I recollec'. 'Tis a wonder they's still here, what with things disappearin' from my shop. Trasker's been sellin' all me boots ter line his pockets.

Right fine these boots were in the master's day. Copied 'em from Weston's in Lunnon," he said. "I kep 'em fine, too. Wi' my special leather polish."

"Would you mind if I borrowed them?"

"No, milady. You'll find no sorrow in 'em."

Helena shouted the question again.

"Hep yerself, miss. Fixin' to walk a bit?"

She smiled. "Yes. I thought I'd explore the cliffs by the sea."

"Eh? It's stiff ye be? No wonder, with all that jigglin' and jogglin' on them nasty roads from Lunnon. Them's good boots fer walkin', miss. Stuff 'em wi' socks and they'll fit ye right and tight. Hep yerself to one o' the master's walkin' sticks, too." He hesitated. "Mayhap . . . ?"

"What is it?"

"I've hid away some bits o' leather. Good stock, too. I'll make ye a pair o' sturdy walkin' boots, if you like, milady. Be m'pleasure. Jus' sit a moment and let me draw both yer' feet, if'n it ain't too much bother."

His kindness nearly brought Helena to tears. She touched his grizzled cheek. "Thank you, Brindle. You're a good soul." The man blushed from ear to ear.

When Brindle finished outlining her bare feet on paper, Helena took the boots—three sizes too large—and stuffed them with socks before she trudged toward the cliffs. She couldn't wait to tell Waverley about Brindle. He might even remember him.

She felt a rush of pleasure when she reached the cliffs. The sounds of the sea crashing against the rocks and the heady smell of the salt air intoxicated her. She untied her hair and let the strong gusts of wind ruffle it. She'd brought her diary with her. It helped to record what was troubling her heart. She crawled into a small cave that would protect her from the salt spray, the rain beginning to fall and the fierce winds. It made her feel free for the moment. Free of those irritating Traskers.

Free of the problems their surly servants continued to cause. Free of the difficulty of restoring a neglected castle in need of repair.

Two marriage proposals. Well, perhaps only one, since the earl's was too ridiculous to be taken seriously. She pulled out her journal and began to write on a clean page.

> *I can't tell Waverley about Glynhaven's proposal. What an insult to me. Weak as Waverley is, he'd challenge him to a duel. Men! Seems they only know how to settle arguments with violence. It was all my fault. I should have had enough sense to ask Waverley if he wanted to attend Glynhaven's disastrous ball. We might never have gone if it weren't for me.*
>
> *Waverley's asked for my hand. Wonderful. Glynhaven is cruel. Is he vindictive enough to make sure my father hears of Madame Z and her ABCs? Amelié, Babette and Collete, indeed! Father might not allow me to marry my rake if he hears of Waverley's outrageous past. Do I want to marry my rake? Yes, of course, for I love him. And when I become the Marchioness of Waverley Park, I'll pleasure my marquis with much more enthusiasm than his wretched ABCs.*

Helena put her pen down and lay back in the cave, suddenly weary. She closed her eyes and thought of Waverley. His touch. His kisses. His hands. His thighs. Oh yes, especially the feel of his powerful thighs. *Is it a sin to lust after the man you love? Livy thinks passion is a joy with Sebastian.*

She curled up inside her cloak, breathed in the heady salt of the sea, and fell asleep to the sound of gulls and terns squawking their dissonant tunes.

* * *

The rain turned back into a drizzle, allowing Waverley to continue prowling along the coast. He'd sent the terrified Rabu home and climbed carefully down to the pathway below, his thoughts on Helena. In a more innocent time when he might have courted a beautiful lass like Helena without the burden of a disreputable past.

Waverley stopped short at the sight of a pair of well-worn boots poking out of a cave. He inched toward the opening, his back against the rough stone. The boots did not move. Was the man dead or asleep? He removed the knife sheathed in his right boot, took a deep breath when he was close enough, and shouted, "Wake up if you want to live. Throw your weapons out and crawl out. Slowly, mind. Hands in the air." The boots disappeared inside the cave.

"If you play hide-and-seek, I'll cut your throat first and find out who you are later."

Helena was terrified. The roar of the ocean distorted the man's voice, rendering it impossible for her to recognize. That ominous voice might belong to Harry Trasker or worse yet, Glynhaven. She looked around for something she might use as a weapon and grasped a jagged rock.

"Out!"

"D-don't harm me, sir. I'm coming."

Was it the voice of a young lad, he wondered? If it was, the boy had large feet. Waverley cupped his mouth and shouted against the wind. "I'll count to five. One. Two. Thr . . ."

Helena scrambled to her knees, turned and crawled out backward.

Waverley found himself eying the woman he loved. It took him a moment to recover from the shock. "Helena? What are you doing here?" He began to laugh.

"Are you laughing at me? Why?"

"If you could see yourself as I do . . . Where did you get those boots? Your clothes are filthy. How did you ever . . . ?" The look of fear on her face stopped him. "Did I frighten you, love?"

"I . . . I thought I was about to be murdered by . . . I thought you were someone else." Tears streaked her face. "I'm glad it's only you, Desmond." She rose as if to put her arms around him.

"Stay where you are, Helena dearest. If we fall off the cliff into the sea, we'll die. I'll come inside." He inched the few steps along the wall to the cave's small opening. "By the size of those boots, I thought you were a man. I might indeed have murdered you!"

She laughed like a schoolgirl. "But you didn't, did you?" *Now. Do it now. Seduce him.*

Her lips found his, but he stopped her. "Explain yourself, Helena. What are you doing here?" He tried to look stern, yet his grin gave him away.

Helena's words tumbled out in a rush. "What do you think of my boots? They're a tad too large, but I like them. I was taking a walk when the rain began. I found refuge in this cave, you see, and . . ."

Waverley couldn't control himself any longer. He burst into a shout of laughter.

"You're laughing at me again!" Helena tossed her head in irritation. "I find no humor in this situation. You might have murdered me." Helena tried to scurry out of his reach.

"And where do you think you're going, my girl?" He grabbed her rump with both hands, pulled her back and held her fast, still shaking with laughter. "If you could see yourself, my love, you would laugh with me. Your face is smudged. Your cloak is torn. Your hair is flying every which way and the hem of your gown is decorated with mud." He pulled her closer and whispered in her ear. "Yet you smell like verbena and . . ." His lips closed on hers. *And you're driving me mad.*

He slid his tongue into her mouth, tasting, craving, wanting. She stirred beneath him and moaned little moans that engorged him. He spread her muddied cloak wide and tugged at the strings of her bodice, freeing her breasts. He kissed first one breast and then the other. Abruptly, he stopped. He sat up and held his head in his hands.

"What's wrong? Why have you stopped? Are you in pain from your wound?"

"There's no pain from my wound. Only from wanting you." He glared at her. "Why the devil can't you support me in my resolve to remain a gentleman?" he asked savagely.

"Hang your resolve if we love one another."

"I won't do it. Can't you understand that I want you for my wife, not my mistress? I'd be much obliged if you didn't put temptation in my way, you beautiful, irresistible temptress!"

He hurt her. "I beg pardon, my lord marquis, for foolishly allowing my desire to overcome my good sense. Perhaps we don't suit after all, my lord. You needn't worry. I can't accept a marriage proposal that comes from mere gratitude, not love." A gusty wind swept the rain into the cave and soaked them both, though it did nothing to dampen her anger.

"Helena, please! Listen to me. I won't ruin you *because* I love you, don't you see? The risk of getting you with child is too great." He stopped, lifted his head and listened.

Loud shouts reached their ears. They seemed to come from above.

"Milady? Where are you? Can you hear me?"

"That's Amy." Helena began to rearrange her clothing.

Waverley frowned. "I'd best be gone, then."

"She'll see you leaving."

"No she won't. I know these cliffs better than the back of my hand." He grabbed his cloak, kissed her hard and disappeared.

Helena climbed out of the cave and shouted, "I'm down here, Amy. Stay where you are. I'm coming up."

"There you are, my lady! You gave me such a fright, me heart near stopped. Why didn't you tell me you had a mind to wander these dangerous cliffs? I would have come with you to keep you safe." Amy held her hand on her heart as if to emphasize the point. "I was afraid somethin' fierce might have happened to you.

"Thank the Lord that Casper has such good eyesight. He spotted your cape sticking out of this here cave. Else we never would've found you. You're soaked to the skin and it's gettin' powerful dark. How would you have made your way back?"

"I must have fallen asleep." Helena let Amy pull her up from the final step to the path. "Thank you both for coming to my rescue. Foolish of me not to have told you, but you were nowhere about."

Amy exchanged a significant glance with Casper. "We told you we was goin' into town."

"Indeed you did, but it slipped my mind. Did you have a nice day?"

Casper offered Helena his arm. "Here, let me help you, my lady. We have some news that will be to your likin'."

"But first, we'll get you safely back. I'll wager you haven't had a morsel to eat since breakfast. Well? Have you?"

Helena laughed. "You're right, Amy. I'm wet and I'm fair to starving. Thank you for fussing over me."

"Someone has to, 'cause you don't take care of yerself. First thing is to get you out of those wet clothes."

Harry shook his mother gently. "She's been found, Ma. By Amy and Casper. Ma? Wake up. Lady Helena's back."

"Hmph. What? Why'd you wake me? So she's been found. What do ye want me to do?" Jennie Trasker rubbed the sleep from her bleary eyes, but she couldn't rub away the effects of the gin.

"You said to tell you . . . you said you wanted to put on a show. You know, be kind so she won't suspect."

"Plenty of time, Harry, me boy. Plenty of time." The house-keeper reached for the near-empty bottle of gin. "Go away boy, and let yer ma finish her nap."

After Amy helped her mistress bathe and change into dry clothing, she said, "Casper's waitin' in the kitchen, milady. We've somethin' to tell you."

Helena checked her grin, for Amy's fidgets gave her away. "Lead the way, my dear. I can't wait to hear your news." Once in the kitchen, she sipped the hot chocolate Cook had made for her and said, "All right. What have you to tell me?"

"We found lots more people lookin' for work at the mop fair today," Amy began. "They're willin' to work for you, my lady. They'll come round in the mornin' to meet you."

Casper tore his eyes away from Amy and added, "They're good folk, milady." He put his arm around Amy, and for once, she did nothing to remove it.

Helena's and Cook's eyes met. Here was a new twist. By the look of things, Casper knew he was in love. Had Amy discovered her true feelings yet?

"Good work, both of you. I'll deal with Mrs. Trasker to make sure the new hires begin their work as soon as possible without any interference from her."

Chapter 18

That Night . . .

Waverley pleaded his case in the drawing room before dinner. "Don't be angry with me, my darling. I love you and I want you for my wife, but I won't bed you and ruin all chance for real happiness. If you become with child before we wed, think of the scandal. Haven't you had enough of that?"

"You hurt me today."

"Yes. I saw it in your eyes. I didn't mean to do it. Forgive me my clumsiness. Might we begin again? My new mantle doesn't sit easy, my darling—I have far too many irresponsible years to make up for. Can you not put your hurt aside and help me to learn to be respectable? I know I don't deserve it, but I'm asking you to let go of your anger and give me another chance to prove my love."

His words tore her in two, but she said nothing.

"Well, my sweet Helena?" He took her in his arms and held her head to his shoulder. When she did not object, he chided, "Is that a yes?"

Her giggles cleared the air. "You *are* a rake. Incorrigible as well."

He laughed, for her tone signaled forgiveness. "Shall we dine?"

The dowager joined them in the dining room, which gave Helena an opportunity to tell them the tale of Cook's wily ways in keeping any knowledge of Brindle, Willa, and Bridey from Mrs. Trasker.

"I remember Brindle. When I was a boy, he often scolded me whenever I scuffed my boots. I'll be sure to visit him now that I know he's still with us." Waverley grinned at the fond recollection.

"Beware," Helena warned. "He complained to me that Harry is stealing his leather. No doubt he'll ask you to buy him some more."

"He can order as much as he likes, the old curmudgeon. I'm just glad to know he's still alive."

"My dear Bridey will no longer have to sneak in to see me, will she? Perhaps we can dismiss Nurse Hubley now," said the dowager hopefully, for she chafed at the woman's way of ordering her about.

"I shan't dismiss Nurse Hubley, Grandmother. She's brought you back to health."

"She's a tyrant, nevertheless," grumbled the dowager.

"You'll have Bridey for comfort, but Nurse Hubley stays."

"If that's the best you can do," she said sourly. In truth, she despised the regimen recommended by Dr. Fenwick and slavishly enforced by Nurse Hubley. "You aren't forced to endure that vile-tasting medicine Fenwick prescribes."

"The medicine he prescribed has healed you, Grandmother. And the exercises the doctor recommended have helped you to walk again. You are much stronger as a result. Don't complain so, dearest. It's for your own good."

Helena gently touched the dowager's hand. "Bridey can assist Nurse Hubley, ma'am. Will that suit you?"

"Humph!" The dowager knew she'd lost this battle and

changed the subject. "Poor Willa! She can no longer see well enough to sew. What shall you do about her? You won't sack her, will you?"

"Of course not. I'll arrange to hire a seamstress to help Willa as well. Don't fret, Grandmother. I have some news that ought to cheer you. I have asked Helena for her hand in marriage, and although she hasn't given me her answer, she gives me reason to hope."

The dowager's eyes lit up like candles on an altar. "Bravo, Desmond. Helena is just the right woman for you. You mustn't wait too long to wed, my children. I'm not getting any younger and I want to be here for the wedding of my only grandchild to his lovely bride."

London: Fairchild House

"Better, Lady Mary, but not perfect," said her new piano instructor. He was a handsome man with a thin mustache, meant to mask his youthfulness, for he was not yet twenty. "There is more to be had from such a one as you. Your ear is blessed with perfect pitch, yes?"

"Thank you, Maestro," she answered, blushing. Her eyes shone with adoration.

He sat down next to her and began to play scales, his very nearness sending chills through her. Abruptly he stopped, put his right arm around her, and cupped his left hand over hers. "Place your fingers so. You must work to force the left hand to be strong, you see. Pretend you have only the one hand, yes? *Allegro. Andante. Staccato.* One hour each scale with only the left hand, Lady Mary. Tomorrow you will show me, eh?" He rose from his seat, bowed and departed.

* * *

Lady Mary could not sleep. She could not eat. She practiced one extra hour each day. She counted the seconds until the Maestro's arrival for her lesson. She told no one her secret for fear of having Signore Giovanni Bartoli banished from her life forever.

At fifteen, Lady Mary Fairchild was suffering the pangs of her first love.

Waverley Castle

Helena was reluctant to ride even with Casper as protection, for fear she would fall into Glynhaven's hands again. Instead she opted for a stroll in the garden, for it was indeed a beautiful morning. Unruly brambles tore at her hem and scratched her ankles as she made her way to the pond. The grounds had been neglected far too long, but that was changing day by day, since Waverley had by this time engaged a reputable head gardener.

Her thoughts turned to her home in Brighton. She had such fond memories of Heatham House, where as children, she, her brother, and her sisters had learned to ride and to cool their feet in a pond graced with mute swans. It had been such a happy time, a time when she had no cares, a time when the world was as it should be and her future was assured as the wife of Chris Darlington. She had believed him to be the handsomest of lads then. She frowned. What had changed Chris from a loving fiancé to a pompous boor who judged her ill for making a mistake? She continued to dread her return to London, especially after Saltash's and Glynhaven's ugly taunts. How long would it be before Polite Society would forget the scandal that imprisoned her, she wondered.

The gazebo overlooking the pond was in grave disrepair, but she found a section of bench sturdy enough to hold her and sat down to rest. Thanks to unruly branches and thorns grasping at her, she'd lost most of her hairpins. She brushed a few strands of hair away from her eyes, surveyed the pond critically and made some notes for the gardener on the pad she habitually carried with her.

"Repair the gazebo," she wrote. "Clear a path to the pond. It is choked with leaves and branches and debris and must be restored as soon as possible."

She smiled as she continued making notes. She couldn't fail the marquis in this, for she knew her way in matters of management. Pleased with herself, she took pride in knowing she was well on the way toward restoring Waverley Castle to its former grandeur.

I left London, intent on escaping the humiliation of a broken betrothal, with no thought for anything but the weight of my own mortification. I never gave a moment's thought to what lay before me when I arrived at Waverley Castle, yet I've come such a long way these past few weeks.

I'm not that silly chit anymore. I'm a woman. And I'm capable of managing an entire estate, thanks to my mother, bless her. I'm a woman in all ways but one, that is. I can't stop loving Desmond, though God knows I've tried. He knows that, doesn't he? He's wrong in putting me off with what he fancies is his newfound honor. If he won't seduce me, it's up to me to find a way to seduce him. And if I fail, what then? Does it matter what Polite Society thinks of me? Not a whit. I'll have gambled. And lost.

She was so engrossed in her thoughts, she never heard the sound of crackling leaves, but when she saw who it was, her eyes lit up. "That you, Waverley?"

"Good morning, my love."

"You startled me. Unkind of you to sneak up without any warning. Are you well enough to wander about without Rabu to hover over you?"

"The little devil doesn't think I am, but I managed to escape his clutches."

"Were you looking for me, or did you find me here by chance?"

He tapped his chin with one finger. "Actually, I thought I heard a wild beast crashing through the woods. I came to investigate," he said with a mischievous grin. "Apparently, you are that wild beast, lovely Helena. What a lot of noise you managed to make."

Strange. Her tongue was tied in knots. "You're . . . you're up early."

He ignored this remark. "Why aren't you out riding this morning? I looked for you in the stables."

She colored, unable to fashion a suitable answer.

"Are you afraid of another unpleasant encounter with Glynhaven's dog? I'd be happy to ride with you to protect you."

"Thank you, Waverley. I'll accept your offer just as soon as Doctor Fenwick says you are well enough to ride again."

"So be it." He shrugged. "It would please me no end if you could remember to call me Desmond."

"All right."

"Not good enough, fair Helena. I want to hear it from your lips."

"Desmond."

"Pretty music when you say it." He sat beside her and brushed wisps of unruly hair away from her face. "Your hair's come undone."

"The brambles conspired to comb it that way, I expect."

"I like it when it flows down your back that way." One finger trailed across the top of her gown and she shivered. "Cold?"

"N-no."

His lips brushed her cheek and found their way to her mouth, but she turned to stone.

"What's wrong? What have I done to offend you?"

Don't be a coward. It's now or never. "Are you planning to play your silly game of seduction only to run from me at the last minute?"

"You know my reasons."

"You needn't practice this new game of honor with me, you know."

He raised an eyebrow. "No? Why?" One hand toyed with her slender throat, sending chills through her.

"Take your hand away. Makes it hard to have a serious conversation."

"Are we having a serious conversation? I hadn't noticed." He leaned forward to kiss her, but she turned her head away. "What's wrong this time?"

"The truth?"

"Of course."

Her penetrating eyes bored into him. "I cannot possibly agree to marry you without knowing if we would suit as lovers. Frankly, your reluctance leads me to wonder whether you are . . . deficient in that way. Is that why you need three women to make love to you at the same time?"

"That's a lie," he roared, stunned. He raised his hands as if to shake her but thought better of it, forcing them to his sides and clenching them into fists instead.

She was disappointed, for a shake would at least have been something. She settled instead for a further taunt. "A lie you say? Methinks the gentleman doth protest too much."

"You are thinking of my French . . . er . . . friends, no doubt. I have Glynhaven to thank for that, I suppose. Let me assure you that I most certainly am not deficient when it comes to making love. What a crackbrained thing to say! I'll have you know I'm perfectly capable of . . ."

"But how should I know this? You'll have to prove it, my lord," she challenged, hugely enjoying the encounter.

"There are rules about innocent maidens and I am trying

my best to be a gentleman and play by them. I've told you more than once, I'm done with breaking the rules."

Though her knees trembled, she managed a scornful laugh. "You can't be serious. There are no such rules for the likes of you, are there? You're a rake."

He scowled, offended. "You wrong me, dear heart. I am a reformed rake. You'll have to wait until we are married." He took no notice of the wicked gleam in her eyes, for his own were fixed on her bodice.

She crossed her fingers behind her back to ward off the consequences of the barefaced lie she was about to utter. "I can't marry you until you prove yourself."

He tore his eyes away from her breasts and said, "I don't have anything to prove." Her meaning dawned on him. "What are you up to, adorable minx? You know I won't bed you before we are married, and that's final. You'll have to take my word for it. There's nothing wrong with my ability to . . . to consummate my marriage to you or to . . . to any woman. Besides, I gave my word to your brother-in-law and I don't mean to break it."

"Then marry my brother-in-law if you can persuade my sister Livy to agree to such an arrangement, which I strongly doubt."

"Be reasonable, Helena. If you were to become with child, it would only cement my cursed reputation in people's minds. I cannot do what you ask, my heart's delight. You'll have to wait for our wedding night."

"What a quaint notion. Your chivalry is touching, my lord. Very well. You force me to confess the truth." She paused for effect and added dramatically, "I am not a virgin."

Unconvinced, he added with a touch of sarcasm, "No? Then what was that passionate scene in Darlington's home all about, pray tell? You certainly convinced me that you meant to seduce him into marrying you."

She threw her head back and laughed. "How innocent you are for all your rakish airs. Chris and I were already lovers. He was furious with me merely because I mistook you for him. I embarrassed him in front of his distinguished guest, you see. That toadeater told me so when he raked me over the coals afterward. You couldn't know, of course. How could you? You've never remained locked in my embrace long enough to find out."

"I'll marry you anyway." He folded his arms and glared at her.

Her eyes flashed. "Will you now? Such . . . *condescension*. I'm overwhelmed by your generosity. You still want to bed me even though I'm not a virgin, *my lord rake*. Do I have that right?" She shifted from irony to anger. "I think you ought to hear my terms for our marriage before you commit yourself to the odious task of seducing me, my lord rake."

"Your . . . terms?" He barked an unpleasant laugh. "Where is my sweet lady, the one I love, in all this?"

"Before I agree to marry you, I cannot in good conscience take your word for it. I must first sample the pleasures you say you have to offer, my lord rake. Indeed, that might well prove to be the only new experience for me."

His brows knit. "The only new ex . . . ? How many lovers have you had, my girl?"

Warming to the game, Helena thought a minute. "Let me see. There was Chris, of course, but before him there was . . . Dear me, I've forgotten the lad's name, poor boy. And then there was that stranger at the Brighton Fair two years ago. No. There were two men at the fair that year, I recall. Oh, and before those two, there was that cute Irish boy who worked in Father's stables. . . ."

"You're lying."

"Am I? How many lovers have you had, my lord rake? Many more than me, I daresay. Never mind. This isn't a contest. There's only one way for me to prove to you that I'm not a virgin, isn't that so?"

His lips thinned. "You're right. There *is* only one way. Turn around so I can unbutton your gown."

"A wise beginning," she said in a brisk tone and did as he bid.

He stopped struggling with her buttons. "Are you sure you're not lying to me?"

"If you're asking me to beg, let's forget the whole thing!"

Having reached the last button, he ignored this remark, removed her gown entirely, and spread it on the floor of the gazebo. He eased her down upon its folds. "Last chance to change your mind and confess. There's no going back once you break this rule, Helena. If this becomes known, you'll be ruined beyond repair."

"Nonsense. I'm the daughter of a duke. We *make* the rules."

He steeled himself as if prepared for battle. "In that case, I shan't waste any more time. Especially now that I know you have had such vast . . . experience." He dropped his trousers and lay down beside her, one elbow bent, his head resting on his hand, his eyes feasting on her for a moment before his hands found their way down to her thighs. He spread her legs apart and bent to kiss her sensitive nub, but she pushed his head away.

He looked up. "You don't like that? All right, I'll stop." He rolled onto his back, placed his arms under his head and stared at the sky through the large hole in the gazebo roof.

"Oh, I didn't know. It's what rakes do, isn't it? It's just that it's a novel experience for me. Do that again." An approving smile lingered, one she hoped would gull him into believing her lie.

Instead, her words served only to cause him to question her sincerity. "Have none of your lovers pleased you thus? A woman of your . . . er . . . vast experience?"

Her lips quivered. She bit the bottom one to keep from laughing out loud. "They were all dull fellows without much imagination. How could I know? Marriage to you, my lord rake, may turn out to be fun. Now let me show you what I have learned. Come here."

Her hands played upon his muscled back, caressed his firm buttocks, felt his heat, felt the lust seeping out of every pore of his body. Her aggressive attentions brought a groan from his lips, which made her drunk with power.

"We must stop before it's too late, my darling." His voice was hoarse with passion.

"Not on your life," she panted.

He capitulated readily. "I won't, then." He stroked her thighs. Every pore in her body vibrated as his fingers found the ridges of pleasure she never dreamed existed. She arched her back, opening all of herself to him.

Heated by her moans, he reached for her hand and guided it to his manhood. She ran her hand the full length of his member, causing him to shudder.

She can't be a virgin, can she? No. A virgin would not know how to pleasure a man like that.

Helena cried out when the first throes of pleasure over-whelmed her. Her body shuddered, every pore vibrating with new sensations. She felt hot liquid seep from every pore. She vanished in the magic of him. His shattered groans barely registered.

He spread her legs wide, his throbbing sex pressed against her, his hot breath setting her on fire. He lifted her hips and entered her, paying heed to the resistance he met. His head shot up. "What's this?" He tried to pull away.

"It's nothing," she gasped. She wrapped her legs around him and held on, her hips rising and falling with his thrusts, her hands playing havoc on his body.

He was near to losing all restraint only to hear her cry out in pain. He froze. "What's wrong?"

"Don't . . . stop," she panted.

"Have I hurt you?"

"No. I . . . cry out like this . . . all the time," she stammered, in an effort to keep up the fiction. Her hands pressed him closer and she bucked to encourage him.

He was lost. His head fell back and he thrust in and out until his passion found release.

Helena held him close, tears induced by the excruciating pain she felt, yet glorying in the sheer pleasure of his glistening body, his fiery ardor, and the taste of his salt on her lips. "Well done, my lord! My apologies for doubting you."

"Apologies accepted." He wondered at the sticky substance he felt oozing from between her legs. He tried to roll away, but she held tight. "I'm too heavy for you, my love."

"Stay where you are a bit longer, my lord rake. I like the feel of you."

He grinned at her. "But you're out of breath from bearing my weight." He rolled to one side and searched her face. "Well? Was I as good as all your other lovers?"

She giggled. "You'll do."

"Is that so?" Suspicion dawned on him. Something was wrong. He felt it in his bones. He raised his head and swept his eyes over her body in search of . . . he knew not what, yet something nagged at him. He stopped at the place between her legs that had given him such pleasure only moments before. And found the answer. She was covered with blood.

The anger in his voice was palpable. "Why you little wretch! Damn you, Helena! You lied to me!"

Though quaking within, she sat up with outward calm and began to dress. "What difference does it make? You've been lusting after me, haven't you, my lord rake?"

"Are you using me? What game is this you're playing?" His eyes bore down on her like two hot coals. "I'm waiting for your answer."

With a dignity she did not entirely feel, she said, "Don't try to deny it. You got what you wanted and so did I."

"Your reasoning escapes me, ma'am." His angry words spelled danger. "What purpose had you in mind?"

"Why, to be rid of my virginity, of course." She was drunk with the power of seduction.

"Bloody hell, my girl!" he thundered, frustration writ large on his face. "Hand me my trousers."

A wicked gleam of defiance lit her face. In one swift motion, she grabbed his trousers and flung them toward the pond. "Good-bye, my lord rake. Thank you for a most pleasant morning."

"What the . . . ?" He watched in astonishment as the arc of his trousers caught the wind and sailed away. He grasped at her, but she evaded him and flew out of the gazebo.

"Why, you little . . . !" he shouted after her, unable to follow without trousers. His words fell on air, like the wind rushing through dead leaves.

Helena hobbled off with a slight limp, for she'd left one shoe behind. The uncomfortable soreness between her legs throbbed. Small price to pay for her triumph. She hummed a tune to herself.

Her happiness in victory might have been short-lived had she witnessed Harry Trasker watching her.

Chapter 19

Sunday, the Tenth of May, 1818

Waverley's mysterious disappearance from the castle filled Helena with dread. Where had he gone? Had her deception driven him away? His disappearance without a word meant he could not forgive her lie, she was sure. When she pressed his secretary Rupert, he claimed ignorance as to his lordship's destination.

"His lordship informed me he had urgent business to attend to, milady, but he did leave word for you to act in his place until he returned."

She was uneasy at being left in sole charge in his absence, but she didn't let on. "Thank you, Rupert," she said. The young man bowed and left her. She sat for some time wondering what to do, for there was nothing pressing that needed her attention. She recalled the door into the second basement. The arc left in the dirt was proof enough that the door had been in use. She had a mind to investigate, but first she would have to locate the key.

At a knock on her door, Helena glanced at the clock on the mantel. "Come in, Mrs. Trasker. You're right on time."

She greeted the housekeeper in a brisk, businesslike tone but lingered before closing the accounts book, making sure the woman knew what she had been studying. She locked the book in the safe, placed the key in her pocket and rose to join the older woman.

She kept her eyes down, for fear she might giggle at the sight that met her eyes. Mrs. Trasker wore a starched white cap and a spotless gray muslin gown trimmed with white fulcrum, her chain of keys encircling her middle where once her waist had been. She actually looked presentable for the first time in Helena's memory. What's more, she was sober. Helena wondered what mischief she was planning.

"When you told me you had an interest in the Banningtons, I had the old portrait gallery cleaned to a shine, Lady Helena. It's been an age since anyone's ever asked to see it."

"How thoughtful," she murmured.

"My pleasure." The housekeeper led Helena to the end of the Great Hall. She stopped in front of a door Helena had taken little notice of before. Mrs. Trasker fumbled with her large ring of keys until she found the right one. As she did so, Helena noted a key larger than the rest, rusted with age.

"What's that key for?" Helena asked casually.

"Key to the old cellar door under the abbey. Ought to throw it away, 'cause no one uses it anymore. I'm sure it no longer works." There was an odd look on her face.

She was lying, Helena guessed, but she said nothing.

Mrs. Trasker inserted the proper key into the gallery door and stepped aside to allow Helena to enter first. In the long room, one wall was lined with large portraits in ornate gilded frames. They faced a bank of mullioned windows flanking an enormous fireplace over which hung the largest of the portraits.

"We'll start over here by the fireplace, ma'am. This here's the first Marquis of Waverley, name of Thomas Bannington. Lost his leg during the war in the American colonies. King

George rewarded him for his bravery with Waverley Park. It ain't the biggest holdin' in the kingdom, it bein' so far from London and all, but folks hereabouts speak of it wi' respect."

Helena examined the portrait for a moment, then turned to the next one.

"And this here's his wife, Lady Martha Fox. Her father was a local squire."

Helena examined the portrait of an attractive woman surrounded by three children and a large Russian wolfhound seated at her feet. The dog caused a pang of homesickness for her own Prince. When would she see her frisky pup again, she wondered.

"Lord Neville became second marquis when Lord Thomas passed. This here's his portrait. He was husband to the dowager. Her portrait's right next to his."

"'Lady Dorothea, neé Hargrave, born 1736,'" Helena read aloud. The dowager was truly a beauty in her day.

"And this here's Lady Mary, younger sister to the second marquis, Lord Neville. She was me grandmother." The housekeeper added, "She wed Baron Marcus Weston. Next to him is their son, Sir Robert." Mrs. Trasker beamed at the portrait of a handsome young man. With a great deal of pride, she added, "This here's me father, Sir Robert Weston."

"Where is your mother's portrait?" Helena asked innocently, knowing full well her father had never married the young maid, for Cook had already told her so.

"He was a'goin' to marry me mum, but he took ill and died afore the weddin'."

"He was betrothed to your mother, you say? Poor man. He was only twenty, according to the plate under his portrait. What did he die of?" Helena's eyes were all innocence, though she already knew the answer. Lord Robert Weston had died of syphilis.

The housekeeper's tone turned belligerent. "Don't know zackly. Some bad disease, mayhap. He was gonna marry me mum, I tell ya. He took ill is why he din't. Me mum tol' me so. And anyways, I turned out respectable. I married proper to John Trasker, a fine man let me tell you. We posted the banns, we married in church and me Harry's no bastard." Her voice had reached a shrill pitch.

"Calm yourself, Mrs. Trasker. I have no cause to disbelieve you. In fact, I'm impressed by your knowledge of the Bannington family history." *Dream your dreams of glory for your son, my girl. Even if Waverley were to die without an heir, the Crown would never allow the likes of your Harry to become the next marquis.*

"It's writ down in the family Bible in the chapel for anyone to see," Mrs. Trasker said, but the starch had gone out of her.

They moved on to the next portrait. Helena stopped to admire it and said, "Ah, here's a face familiar to me. I knew him. William was the second marquis' brother. A kind man, I recall. And next to him is his wife, Jane. They were neighbors of ours in Brighton and became family friends."

"That right?" mumbled the housekeeper, made painfully aware of the difference in their stations by this remark.

"Is this next a portrait of Lord Waverley's father?" Helena examined it carefully, but she saw no resemblance. Lord George Bannington was not handsome by any measure. She saw cruelty in his unsmiling face, which only reinforced what Waverley had told her of his father's steadfast refusal to forgive his only son. She moved on to Waverley's mother and immediately saw the resemblance to Desmond, now the Fourth Marquis of Waverley.

"How beautiful she was. 'Marchioness Drucilla Browne, born 1760, died 1804,'" she read. "The likeness to Lord Waverley is astonishing, don't you think, Mrs. Trasker? His lordship has his mother's blue eyes as well as her dark hair."

"Mayhap," the older woman muttered. "That's the last of the lot. Shall we go?"

"Thank you for this rare treat, Mrs. Trasker," Helena said, but her mind was on that rusted skeleton key firmly fixed on the ring round Mrs. Trasker's ample waist. There had to be a way to wrest it from her.

The opportunity presented itself, but not without a great deal of trouble.

London

Waverley reached Mayfair late on the third day, having ridden hard, stopping only to change horses. But his eagerness to accomplish his mission had its price. The wound Lord Saltash had inflicted upon him caused considerable discomfort.

He put up at the Pultenay Hotel, one of the finest in London, and ordered dinner as soon as he was settled in his suite. It was excellent, for the Pultenay was known for its outstanding cuisine. He drank a full bottle of fine French Bordeaux, undressed and fell asleep at once.

He woke much refreshed, bathed and dressed with the help of a footman provided by the hotel, for he refused to permit Rabu to accompany him. The poor man's fear of horses would only have served to slow down his master. He breakfasted leisurely and ordered a carriage for eleven o'clock, when he planned to visit Heatham House. If it turned out that Helena was with child as soon as may be, there was no time to lose.

Waverley Castle

Helena could not put the second cellar out of her mind. Perhaps there was nothing there. So be it, but she was determined to see for herself.

It wasn't as difficult as she had supposed to steal the key

from Jennie Trasker. The door to her chamber was slightly ajar and she was dozing, an empty brandy bottle on the table at her side. The ring of household keys lay on the table next to her, kept company by an overturned whiskey glass. Helena unhooked the rusted key, the largest on the chain, but as she did so, the door creaked open. She thrust the key into the pocket of her morning gown and took two steps back.

"What're ye doin' in me ma's room?" Harry Trasker growled.

Helena drew herself up haughtily and said, "Nothing's amiss, Harry, I assure you. I sent for your mother, but when she didn't arrive, I came here to ask for the key to the portrait gallery. I wish to take measure for a frame I plan to have made for the new marquis' portrait."

"Whatcha wanna do that fer?" He moved closer, forcing her to back away.

"You have no business questioning my actions, sir. Do not come any closer." But Harry kept walking toward her until her back was pressed to the wall.

"Bein' in me ma's room *is* me business." He put his hands on her shoulders.

"Get. Your. Filthy. Hands. Off. Me!"

"Why? I know you been used 'afore. You let the marquis have his way. I saw you tuppin' in the gazebo by the pond." His hand moved to her breast, but she pushed it away.

"Have you lost your senses? Take your filthy hands off me. I could sack you for this!" She tried to duck under his arms, but he held fast with one hand and played with her breast with the other.

"Give us a kiss," he said and grabbed her chin.

She kept her voice even and said, "All right. One kiss, but that's all, Harry. Don't hold me so tight if you want a proper kiss."

Harry eased away in anticipation of his reward. When his mouth clamped down on hers, she brought her knee between his legs and thrust it upward as hard as she could.

He let go of her and howled with pain. "Ow! Bitch!"

Helena ran out of the room without looking back.

London

"This way, milord," said Dunston, leading Waverley into the duke's library.

"Morning, your grace," the marquis said, bowing.

"Sit, Waverley." The duke indicated a chair facing his own. "How is my daughter?"

"Her ladyship is well, your grace. I must thank you for allowing her to visit us. My grandmother adores her. Your daughter doesn't know about my business in London, however."

"And what is your business in London, may I ask?"

"I came to seek your permission to offer for Lady Helena's hand, your grace," he answered at once.

"Indeed? What, pray, are my daughter's feelings on this matter?"

"Your daughter has professed her willingness, your grace." *I'm being tested. So be it. I'll play by whatever rules he sets down for me, as long as I win my love's hand.*

"That so? I cannot take your word for this, you realize. Does she know you are here to petition me?"

"No, your grace. I mean to surprise her with happy news."

His grace did not hesitate. "The answer is no, Lord Waverley. I won't allow my daughter to wed a man with your well-known reputation."

Waverley was stunned. After a long moment, he recovered enough to say, "Will you hear me out, your grace? I beg a few more moments of your time."

The duke took a bit of snuff. "You won't change my mind, I assure you."

"I know I have much to answer for, your grace. If I were in

your shoes, I would refuse an incorrigible rake like myself if he dared to petition me for my daughter's hand. But I am no longer the rake of my reckless youth. I've put all that behind me. I love your daughter, sir, and she returns my affections."

"I knew your father, Waverley. He never forgave you for your reckless behavior. Why should I?"

Why indeed? "I begged for his forgiveness many times over, but he never would, not even when my grandmother implored him to do so. He would not even answer my many letters. It's no excuse, your grace. I know that now, but I could not feel welcome in England under those circumstances. When he died, the Regent summoned me and I came back to England to take up my responsibilities determined to change my ways and restore my reputation."

The duke stroked his brow. When he removed his hand, he raised his eyes and bore them down on Waverley. "I've had an anonymous letter from Cornwall. Can you deny entertaining your French mistresses at a neighbor's ball? One, I might add, at which my daughter was present? The fracas led to a duel, did it not? It astonishes me that you have the gall to think I would agree to my daughter's marriage to you under these circumstances."

"I won't deny it, your grace. All that you say is true, but give me an opportunity to explain."

"There is nothing you can say to change my mind, young man. Don't embarrass yourself by offering me more false coin. The facts speak for themselves. I've already sent a letter requesting my daughter to return home at once. There's no more to be said."

"Thank you for your time, your grace," Waverley murmured awkwardly. He rose and took his leave.

Chapter 20

Monday, the Eleventh of May, 1818

The stolen key to the second cellar had cost Helena, what with Harry pawing her so mercilessly. She shuddered at the thought of his coarse hands on her breast, his slobbering mouth on hers. At the same time, she couldn't help but chuckle to herself. She was rather pleased with her quick-witted response. It did the trick, all right. *I don't dare tell Waverley. He'd murder Harry. Where has the marquis gone? Is he still angry with me?*

She dressed herself, thankful that she'd given Amy leave to spend the night with her mother at the Ship Inn. Helena was prepared with an excuse should Cook ask why she was on her way to explore the cellar. To her relief, she didn't need to tell another lie, for Emma was alone in the kitchen shelling peas.

Helena picked up a scone and took a bite. "Mmmm. Delicious. Morning, Emma. Where's Cook?"

"She's in the henhouse with Trudy, milady. Would your la'ship care for some chocolate to go with your scone?"

Helena laughed. "How clever you are. How did you guess that a cup of chocolate with my *second* scone is just what I need. I'll have it here, if you don't mind."

"'Twould be an honor, milady."

Amused, Helena took a seat at the servants' table. "How is Lemuel, my dear? I hear he and Casper have become fast friends since he began to work in our stables."

Emma blushed to the roots of her hair, for Lemuel was her beau. "Lem's well enough, I suppose, milady."

"You . . . suppose? Are you two on the outs?"

Emma served the chocolate to Helena, then put her hands on her hips. She was a pretty round-faced miss with plump cheeks and a rather large bosom. "He's a stubborn one he is, your la'ship," she burst out.

Helena curbed the urge to laugh. "He makes no secret of his feelings for you. What has he done to displease you?"

She hung her head, remembering her station. "I . . . I shouldn't say to you."

"It's all right, dear. Go ahead. I won't tell anyone."

"I'm tired of just bein' promised to him these four years and he says he ain't ready to post the banns!"

Helena wondered if she ought to find a way to increase Lemuel's wages. "Well, my dear, he's probably frightened of taking on the responsibilities of marriage. I'd advise you to show more patience and less anger."

"It's true I've been powerful hard on him, milady. Mayhap you have the right answer for me."

"Kill him with kindness, Emma. That's what they say."

Emma brightened. "I'll try it, milady. Slap me silly, I'll try it this very night."

"Good girl." Helena finished her chocolate and rose. "I'm glad we had this chat, dear. Thank you for a delicious breakfast. I'm off to inspect the cellar. I want to check on the progress the carpenters have made in repairing the damage. Cook certainly needs more shelves for preserves, even though she never complains. I'll return shortly. Keep up the good work, Emma. I'm proud to have people like you and Trudy on staff."

She reached up for a lantern filled with oil resting on a shelf, turned the latch to the cellar door and proceeded down the steps, noting that the cellar had been well cleaned since the last time she'd been there. The rotted shelves had been replaced, just as she had ordered. It warmed her heart to see the cellar decently restored at last. Cook now had all the space she needed to store vegetables and fruits, jams and condiments. Indeed, shiny well-marked jars filled with provisions for future use had already been prepared.

She reached the door of the old cellar and inserted the rusted key. To her surprise, the lock appeared to have been well oiled, for the key turned without a bit of trouble. The heavy oak door was another matter. She had to pull with all her strength before it gave way. She wondered why the hinges had not been oiled as well. They squeaked so loudly, they startled her enough to quicken her breath.

Once inside, she faced a set of ancient steps. She was forced to brush away the cobwebs before she could proceed. She trod gingerly, using her foot to sweep the debris on each step as she descended. There was no railing and the steps were worn. Why, she wondered, did Mrs. Trasker have the only key to this cellar? It appeared to have no use at all, except for spiders' webs, and these served only to assault her mouth, her eyes and her hair. The lantern flickered and made her heart skip a beat.

Nothing to be afraid of here. Just some old cobwebs in this dust-filled cellar. Probably hasn't seen use since the days of the Goths. Spiders have taken up residence. There's air here somewhere. If there weren't, the lantern would be of no use. There must be an opening somewhere. Else how would air find its way in?

When she reached the bottom step, Helena exhaled in an effort to banish the fear in her heart. She swung the lantern slowly to the right and to the left and saw nothing but uneven piles of straw, mouse droppings and thick layers of dust everywhere. She stepped still farther into the heart of the old cellar, wondering how far she ought to proceed before turning back. Cook was right. There was nothing of any value down here.

She spied an opening—an entryway into some sort of room—in the far corner to her right. She had more than enough light left to explore it, thinking to discover where the air was coming from. As she approached, she wondered idly why there was a cleared narrow path on the floor making her way easier. Who had made it? Where did it lead? Torn between curiosity and unease, she continued on with caution. The door at the top of the stairs banged shut.

Helena froze.

London

Waverley departed for Land's End in low spirits. He'd already wasted enough time in coming to London, to no purpose, as it turned out. He might have known the duke would turn him down once he'd read of the fiasco at the Glynhaven ball. He had a good notion as to whom it was who wrote that anonymous letter to the duke.

It had to be Glynhaven, the sneaky sod. He's bent on destroying me. He arranged for Saltash to bring Madame Z'evareau and her women to the ball. Damn the man! He continues to be a thorn in my side. But to what purpose? Glynhaven's actions stem from nothing more than envy.

He took the road to Bristol, one of the better roads England had to offer, which wasn't saying much. Most English roads were rutted and sadly neglected, causing many a stagecoach to overturn with disastrous effect, not to mention unwary riders whose horses step into deep holes. Waverley kept a sharp eye out for these, for he had no wish to take a tumble. His side was still sore from the flesh wound Saltash had inflicted.

What could he say to Helena? How could he explain it to her when he hadn't even told her why he went to London? Should he confess that he was afraid she might be with child? What possessed her to dupe him? No matter, for the fault lay with himself. He should have been strong enough to resist temptation.

Would she accept her father's harsh edict? Her father was a powerful man. Dare she disobey him? What then? There was always Gretna Green, he supposed.

No. He couldn't deprive her of the joys of a family wedding. She'd already suffered enough over Darlington's rejection and the vicious tongues of London gossipmongers. He couldn't subject her to the shame of a runaway marriage. He couldn't do that to the woman he loved. It would be better by far to give her up for her own sake.

He'd begged the duke to believe his wild ways were all in the past. Who was he fooling? His infamous past ended a mere three months ago when Darlington found him at the most well-known house of ill repute in all of Paris. Though Waverley lived at 12 rue Chabanais, it was not the only bordello he visited, to be sure, but it was his favorite nevertheless.

To satisfy an insatiable lust had been the opium of choice, for he found nothing else to mask his despair. Try as he might, he could not eradicate the burden of sixteen unhappy years spent in exile; an expatriate without a home. And when she didn't answer his letters, he'd assumed his grandmother wanted nothing to do with him as well. It never occurred to him that his father would not allow his grandmother to receive his letters. How glad he was to find she still loved him. But his father was dead. Now the gulf between them would never heal.

He stopped at a stream to rest his overheated horse. Thank God his grandmother loved him. It was a solace but it wasn't enough to sustain him for the rest of his life. Without Helena he faced a bleak future indeed, for she was the first, the last, the only woman he'd ever loved. He could never love another.

Waverley Castle

"No!" Helena shrieked and raced to the top of the stairs. She tried to open the door, shoving as hard as she could, but her efforts were futile. Instead, she placed the lantern on the top step, fumbled with trembling fingers for the skeleton key in her pocket, and found the keyhole. As she tried the key, she again met resistance. Petrified, she pounded on the door and screamed as loud as she could, a futile gesture. The old door was far too thick for noise to penetrate. Besides, the first cellar was not likely to be occupied. When her arms grew tired and her voice grew hoarse, she sat on the top step, engulfed in despair.

Keep calm. Think. Someone is bound to notice I am missing. If Amy were here, she'd be sure to look for me. At the very least, Emma will report that I have not yet returned to the kitchen, and that I am still down here somewhere. When they don't find me in the new cellar, surely they will have sense enough to search for me here. Even without a key, strong men can break the door down. I'd better move away, so the door won't crush me when they do. Dear God, I hope it's soon. My wick is reaching bottom. This is no time to panic. Water! I hear the sound of water running. Yes! It's coming from that corner of the room. Maybe it will quench my thirst. Smells damp enough.

Helena rose and held the lantern high. She started back down the steps, but when she was halfway down, she lost her balance. She tried to reach for the wall on her right for support, twisted her body in that direction, but she fell to the bottom, her face buried in a pile of rancid straw filled with rodent droppings. The lantern flew out of her hand and all was dark. She groped for the lantern, almost grateful it went out before it set the straw on fire.

She tried to stand, but her right leg buckled. Delicate French heels were not meant to traverse rickety wooden steps, she thought, disgusted with herself for not having worn the sturdy walking boots old Brindle had made for her. She managed to hop to the wall and lean on it for support.

Helena removed the offending shoe. The heel was wrecked. Brindle would fix it—if she managed to get out of this place alive, that is. She sighed and removed the other shoe, aware that she would be unable to hobble on one delicate shoe. She placed both on the lowest step. Had she broken her ankle? She wasn't sure. Gently, she pressed her tender foot down, but the pain shot through her like a shaft of lightning. She raised it again, took deep breaths, and rested against the wall to gather her strength. She hoped she would reach the source of the water at the end of the wall, and quickly.

She slid against the wall, hopping on her left foot all the while. When she reached the opening, she heard a soft moan. Her heartbeat quickened. *Is that an animal? No. That sound is human.*

"Who's there?" Her croaking voice was one she did not recognize. "I . . . I have a gun!"

A keening moan, stronger this time, pierced the air. It was a groan of pain, she realized. "Who are you? Can you speak? Try. Please?"

"He . . . lp," a weak male voice quavered.

"Make more noise so I can follow your voice. I have no light." Her back to the wall, she found the opening. She sidled into what appeared to be a corridor and inched her way in the direction of the weak, but repeated sound.

"Help, hel, he . . ."

She heard a faint but continual tap. Water seeped down the wall behind her back, drenching her gown.

"Here. Over here," the weak voice whispered.

"Where? Keep tapping." Helena stumbled and nearly fell. She reached down and felt the head of a . . . a man? Yes. It was a man.

She slid down the wall and sat next to him. "Who are you? How did you get here?"

"Le Clair," he gasped. "Captain of *Le Coq d'Or.* Shipwrecked. All dead. Murdered. Hid myself. Found cave. Crawled in here. Who . . . who are you?"

The man spoke only French, a language in which Helena was proficient. She answered in kind. "I am Lady Helena Fairchild and we are in the cellar of Waverley Castle. The door blew shut, but someone is bound to find us when they find that I am missing, for I am a guest of the Marquis of Waverley. How long have you been here, sir?"

"Don't . . . know. Long time. Water drips down wall. Thank God."

"The water kept you alive?"

"Yes."

"But you've had no food? For how long?"

"Don't know. Days . . . weeks." His head fell forward, as if the effort to speak had taken all his strength.

"All right, Captain Le Clair. Try to rest while I see what I can find." She wondered what it was she'd be able to do for the poor man. Indeed, she wondered what she'd be able to do for herself as well. The thought that neither of them would ever get out alive brushed her mind like a fever, but she thrust it away. She would not give in to her fears. Not now. Not ever. Surely help would come soon.

Helena reached down to touch her ankle. It had swollen, yet it did not hurt as much. *Not broken. Just bruised, thank heaven.* She grabbed the damp lace hem of her petticoat and pulled it taut with both hands until it ripped. She tugged at the stitches in order to remove them so she could tear the hem into strands of cloth. The task kept her mind from the terror lurking at the edge of her soul. When she judged she had enough, she wrapped the strands tightly around her swollen ankle and knotted it.

"C-cold. So . . . cold," Le Clair whimpered in a whisper.

"I'll try to fix that, Monsieur Le Clair." Helena removed the shawl tied around her shoulders and covered him as best she could. She felt his thin bones as she did and wondered if indeed he would live long enough to survive this ordeal.

Le Clair's hand touched hers, a sign of gratitude at the little bit of comfort her shawl afforded him. "Re . . . René," he breathed.

She was moved to tears at his touch. "There, there, René," she said, feeling helpless all the same. "Close your eyes and rest, sir. I'm going to leave you for a bit, to search for food, but I'll be back. I promise."

She inched her way to a standing position, her eyes having become better accustomed to the dark. When she tested her foot on the ground, she could not set her heel down without wincing in pain, but she could use her toes and the ball of her foot to keep from falling. She turned to the wall and gathered a bit of water in her hand to ease her thirst. It was akin to swallowing one small teaspoon at a time, yet it tasted like rare wine.

Thus fortified, she began to explore her surroundings. She felt her way back to the larger part of the cellar and inched along the wall opposite the steps. One hand touched a crevasse and she drew it back in fright. Yet there was . . . something. Something curious, she thought, willing herself to return her hand and feel about. She ran her hand up and down first. And realized it was a set of shelves, some rotted and eaten away, yet the first one she touched was intact. Built long ago by the Goths, no doubt.

With great caution she reached back until her hand hit the wall of the shelf and touched something round, not smooth but full of grit. Helena grasped it and drew it toward her. It was the size of one of Cook's jam jars.

Did the Goths know how to make jam? Might it still be good to eat? Suppose it's turned poisonous after all these years? How would I know if it is? I wouldn't, would I? What a gruesome thought. No matter. We either die of poison or starve to death.

She felt the top of the jar. A metal ring held it firmly against a rubber seal, which made her again wonder at the similarity to Cook's jars. She reached under her wet gown and tugged the rest of her petticoat loose. There was enough left to fashion a sling around her neck into which she placed the jar. She slid up the wall and made her way back to Captain Le Clair.

She sat down next to him and tore yet another strip from her fast-disappearing petticoat. She used the wet cloth to wipe centuries of grime off the jar. *Clever, those Goths. They knew how to make glass, too.*

Helena tried to pull the metal ring in order to open it, but it refused to budge.

The weakened man raised his head. "What is that noise?"

"I found a glass jar. From its weight, there may be food in it, but I don't have enough strength to open it."

"Food?"

Helena heard his stomach grumble. "I don't even know if it's safe to eat, Captain."

"If it isn't safe, it would smell rancid. Can you . . . break the jar?"

"Let me try." She placed the sling around the jar, held it by the bottom and rapped the top against the wall. They both heard the crack.

"May I smell it?" Le Clair asked, inching his way into a sitting position. Without a word, she placed the jar in his outstretched hands. He removed the fabric and said, "The bottom of the jar is in one piece. No splinters of glass. Good sign."

It seemed to Helena that his voice grew stronger with anticipation. She hoped he would not be disappointed. "Does it smell rancid?"

"No. It smells sweet. I should like to try it, with your permission, Lady Fairchild."

"I give you leave to forgo all formality, René. My name is Helena. Go ahead and taste it, but be careful. You haven't eaten anything in days. Put just a drop on the tip of your finger."

He did as she suggested. "It's . . . it's jam. Sweet, sweet jam. Raspberry, I think. Would you like some, Lady Helena?"

She smiled at his gallantry, certain he'd been starved. "No. I had breakfast not long ago. Go ahead, Captain, but just a little. You'll have to wait a bit to see to its effects on you before you eat any more."

"A wise idea. I'll give you the jar for safekeeping."

He did so, but not before Helena heard the faint sound of slurping. The starving man was licking his fingers. "That's wise, sir. Why not lie down again and rest? Help will come just as soon as they discover I am missing, I promise you."

Chapter 21

Thursday, the Fourteenth of May, 1818

Waverley reached the castle just as the sun came up. "Rub my horse down well, Jess," he said to the stable boy. The orphan he had purchased from the poulterer turned out to have a way with horses. "I've ridden him too hard, Jess." He threw the lad his reins and strode toward the kitchen, the closest entry to the castle. The smell of fresh-baked bread and God only knew what other goodies wafted into his nostrils, reminding him he was famished. He had not stopped to dine in his haste to return home to Helena, preferring instead to buy bread and cheese he could eat on the way.

"Morning, Cook," he said cheerfully. "What's that I smell?"

Cook's bleak red eyes stared at him in surprise. "Is it really you, milord? Thank God you've come home at last."

"What's wrong? Is it my grandmother . . . ?"

"No, milord. The dear dowager is well. It's . . . it's . . ." She began to sob into her apron.

"For pity's sake, ma'am! Don't keep me in suspense. What is it?"

Trudy appeared in the doorway carrying an armful of wood. "It's Lady Helena, milord. She's gone missing."

His heart sank. "What do you mean? When was this? Did she leave no message? Tell me what you know, lass," he urged.

"Emma said her la'ship came down here on Monday. She et some scones wi' her chocolate. Told Emma she was agoin' to inspect the cellar. No one's seen her since, milord."

"She's been missing for three whole days? Has no attempt been made to find her direction?" He grabbed a hot scone, burning his hand. "Bloody hell!"

Cook took a handful of butter, smeared it on his hand, and wrapped it with a cloth. "Here is some water for you to drink, milord. I'll wrap some scones for you to take."

"Just one, thank you, and I'll be off." Waverley raced back to the stables, where the lad was still attending to the horse he had ridden. "Where's Casper?"

"He went to Sennen Cove to fetch Amy, your lordship."

"Put the brush down, Jess, and show me what steel you're made of. Saddle up a fresh horse for me at once." He ate his scone while he waited. When Jess brought forward a fine bay, the marquis mounted and said, "Now run up to my chambers as fast as you can. Tell my secretary to meet me at the front door."

He raced round to the front of the castle.

Rupert was waiting for him. "Bad news, I'm afraid. Lady Helena is missing. We've searched everywhere, but her ladyship is nowhere to be found, sir."

"Yes, I know. As soon as Casper comes back, tell him to organize a search party for her." He wheeled around and rode off in the direction of the cliffs at a punishing pace. His frantic mind began to envision all sorts of disasters befalling the woman he loved. The wind kicked up, sending a chill through his bones. He couldn't focus his mind on anything but Helena. How would he go on living without the woman who had stolen his heart? Why couldn't he breathe? Why did his hands tingle at the recollection of touching her? He urged his horse on. A seagull perched on the edge of the rock ledge that ran above him squawked as if to object to the noise of the horse's hooves. The gull screeched and soared away.

When he reached the road above the sea, Waverley tied his horse to a tree and climbed down to the beach over the slippery moss-covered stones. The marquis turned his head at an unfamiliar sound. At first, there was no one in sight, but soon he made out a small figure running toward him and shouting at the top of his lungs. When he reached his master, the lad fell to his knees, his frail chest heaving, his breath coming in short bursts. "I run all the way," Jess panted.

Waverley waited to give the lad time to catch his breath. "What is it, son?"

"I heered summat that'll help us find milady."

"Go on," said the marquis, ignoring the lad's effort to include himself in the search. "What did you hear?"

"That Trasker feller came to the stable to 'itch up 'orses to 'is carriage. 'Is ma was wif 'im. I hid cuz 'Arry allus cuffs me for no reason when 'e sees me."

"What did you hear him say, Jess? Tell me quick, lad."

"'E said summat 'bout lockin' 'er la'ship somewheres where it 'ud soon be so far under water, nobody 'uld ever find 'er. An' then 'is ma said 'e did good."

Waverley frowned, searching his mind in an effort to unlock the meaning of Trasker's cryptic words. "He cannot possibly mean she's under the ruins of the old abbey," he said aloud. He thought a moment, then shouted, "Of course he can! There's an old cellar under there!" He asked, "Can you ride my horse, Jess?"

"There an't a 'orse alive I can't ride. Casper says I wuz borned in the saddle."

Waverley smiled at the lad's fearless pride, slid off his horse and boosted Jess into the saddle. "You must listen carefully, for I have a notion I know just where milady is. Here is what you must do. I'm counting on you and I know you won't fail me." In a few words, he told the boy and took himself off on a run.

The terrain along the coast was treacherous. It slowed his progress. By the time he reached Monster Point, the familiar crest he was seeking, he was cut, scraped and shaken to the core. It didn't take him long to find the familiar opening underneath "the monster's" chin. He removed his coat and his boots and placed them high up on the bridge of the monster's nose. He recalled that the tide had never reached that high when he was a lad.

The boulder he and his mates thought of as "the monster" stood sentinel over the English Channel, its long mane facing the land. The monster's forbidding face had stirred their imaginations, he recalled. At high tide, he and his daredevil friends took turns climbing up on the monster's nose and diving into the sea.

He ducked under the neck of the jagged face that hung suspended over the sea. His luck held, for the tide was not yet high enough to hide the sliver of sand he needed for entry. He stepped gingerly across the sand to a gap in the wall, the only path that led to the old cellar under the abandoned abbey.

When he was a lad, free traders had used it to store smuggled goods until the excise men were no longer on their trail. That gave him and his boyhood friends the opportunity to break into their stores and drink themselves silly.

The sand slip held an inch of water, the sign of a rising tide. He waded in, running one hand along the wall for purchase. The cave was dark, forcing him to stop and wait until his eyes adjusted to it. He inched around the first bend of the cave and followed the ripple of the uneven rock wall. He was forced to endure the discomforts of frigid seawater. He barked his shins on rough stone and resisted the urge to howl in pain. He thrust one hand to the top of the wall, and discovered the ledge that ran around the back of the cave. He allowed himself an inner smile of victory, for he knew he'd found the beginnings of the old cellar walls, carved as it were, from the natural seawall.

Waverley hoisted himself up onto a ledge covered with slime, knelt there for a minute to let the water drain off his soggy trousers and shifted his feet. Using the wall as a guide, he moved along the granite until he felt the seam that told him he'd reached the ramp into the old cellar. He bent his knees and crept up the sloping rock to the ancient cellar entrance, slipping and sliding all the way.

Behind him, darkness descended, forcing him to rely on sheer instinct. Waverley found the door. It was just where he remembered, he thought in triumph. He pushed it, but it did not give. He threw his body weight against the door, felt the metal of the rusted latches snap, and heard the clink of iron when the door fell to the ground on the other side, its rusted hinges rasping as it landed.

Rancid water rushed at him. He brushed it away from his eyes with the back of his hand, took a deep breath, and proceeded into the darkness.

As he stepped inside, his nostrils wrinkled in protest against the fetid air. He fell to his knees and inched along until he found the stone stairs, worn thin with age, that led up to the old cellar. In spite of their condition, he knew they would still hold a man's weight. Slowly he rose and began traversing the floor, his wet feet slipping on the mossy stones. He heard an odd sound and stopped to listen.

His ears detected a faint rustling in one of the far corners. Rats no doubt. He shuddered but continued on cautiously. He heard another sound. Another rodent? Or was that a groan? His heart slammed against his chest, but he forced himself to keep inching along walls slick with water, thick with lichen. He stumbled over broken staves from ancient barrels and shreds of old sailcloth. He froze when his foot touched something soft, a bundle perhaps.

Waverley nudged it again. This time the bundle moved. He bent to examine it. He touched it. Sailcloth. What was underneath? Bloody hell! He ran his hands over it until he found a hole large enough for one of his fingers. He hoped to God it wasn't some strange sea monster ready to deprive him of his finger. He heard a whimper escape. He pulled the canvas up in one sweeping motion and saw the whites of not one but two pairs of frightened eyes staring up at him.

"Stay back! I have a gun," Helena said in a quavering voice.

Waverley burst out laughing. "Not that old trick again, my adored raven. We both know you can't shoot worth a bloody damn." Relief at having found her alive flooded his whole being. "Are you all right, my darling?"

"Desmond? I thought we were going to die here. How did you find us?"

"Never mind that. You're safe now. Who's this beside you?"

"Allow me to introduce you to a fine gentleman, my lord. This is Captain René Le Clair of the shipwrecked *Le Coq d'Or*. He sailed from Cherbourg with a full cargo of French wines and brandies. But his crew and his passengers were all murdered by smugglers." She turned to the captain, who was in a swoon. "Wake up, René. This is the Marquis of Waverley. He's come to rescue us." She turned her face to Waverley. "He speaks only French."

"How did you get here, Le Clair?" Waverley asked in the man's native tongue.

"Never mind that, for now," Helena interrupted. "Captain Le Clair is gravely ill. You must take him out of here and see to his recovery. He wants those murdering smugglers found so he can testify against them, a thing he is determined to do before he returns to France."

"I'll take you both out of here. We'll go up to the first cellar and . . ."

Helena touched his face with her hand. "Not possible, my darling," she said gently. "Someone slammed the door at the top of the stairs shut and jammed the lock. The key I used to open the door is useless. How did you get in here? No matter. You'll have to take the captain out the way you came in. You must hurry, love. He's very weak."

"All right, it won't be easy, but with your help, we'll manage."

Helena shook her head. "I can't help you, love. My ankle is swollen and I can't walk on it."

Waverley thought a moment. He took off his coat. "You'll have to help me, my sweet." Without waiting for her answer, he removed his shirt. "Sir?"

"*Oui?*" Le Clair's voice trembled.

"I'm going to fashion a sling out of my shirt and tie you onto my back. Can you stand if milady helps you?"

"*Oui,*" the captain repeated in a trembling voice.

"Give me a moment, sir." Waverley lifted Helena and held her tightly. "I love you, my precious raven," he murmured into her ear. "Jess should be waiting outside with my horse. I can't take the chance of bringing the captain into the castle. The Traskers have too many spies. I've a strong suspicion those two have had a hand in the dreadful business of murder and smuggling. Jess will take the captain to the Ship Inn with instructions from me to arrange for Doctor Fenwick to attend him. Then I'll come back for you. Take heart, my love. I'll be as quick as I can." He kissed her hard, a kiss she returned with her heart and soul.

She followed his instructions and the captain was soon secured. "You'll have to hold on to me, sir. I need both my hands to grasp the ledge." He turned to Helena and added, "Be brave, precious raven."

"Come back quickly," she whispered, though she knew he

was out of earshot. All the same, the words gave her courage. She sank down, once again trying to ignore her throbbing ankle, and closed her eyes to rest until Waverley returned for her.

The marquis eased himself into the frigid water. The tide had risen even higher during the few minutes he had been inside. Every muscle urged him to hurry, to go back for Helena without delay. But he forced himself to proceed slowly to protect the captain, dragging his feet through wet sand and stone while his pulse raced.

At last he could make out the walls of the cave leading outside and hurried in spite of his burden. When he crawled out into the light, he squeezed his eyes shut against the sun's harsh glare.

He staggered out of the water, untied his shirt and eased the captain down onto the sand before he collapsed on his hands and knees and panted for breath. He heard someone riding down the ravine and could only hope that it was Jess, for he didn't have the strength to fight off an enemy attack.

"'Ere now, sir. You all right?" the lad asked, holding the reins of the horse. "But where's milady? An' who's this?"

"Where are the others?"

"Out searchin' for milady, like you said, yer lordship."

"Her ladyship is waiting for me to return for her. She's twisted her ankle badly. This is Captain Le Clair, lad. He's very weak and he doesn't speak English. Steady the horse, Jess. I'll lift the captain up behind you and tie him to you with my shirt. Ride hell for leather to the Ship Inn. Tell Tom or Mrs. Wells to feed and bed this man and call Doctor Fenwick to attend him at once. I'll pay all charges. It's important we save his life. Got that?"

"Yes, sir. But what about . . . ?"

"I'm going back for your mistress. He lifted the captain up behind Jess and tied him securely. He slapped the horse's rump and watched them ride off. Then he turned back to rescue

Helena. He splashed back into icy tidewater up to his knees and forced his weary legs to move into the darkness of the cave.

Helena hugged herself to keep the cold from seeping further into her being. Her teeth chattered, but her mind was more at ease now that Waverley had come to the rescue. He would be back for her as soon as he carried the ailing captain to safety. She closed her eyes, rested her head against the damp wall and thought of the man she loved.

The chill she felt turned to heat. She touched her head to test for fever, but she felt cool. Helena put her hands on the floor to shift her weight, astonished to discover that they were covered by an inch of water. She'd been so caught up in her thoughts of Waverley, she hadn't noticed the slowly rising water on the cellar floor.

Why was it taking him so long to return? Helena tried to stand, but her strength failed her. Instead, she crawled on her hands and knees in the direction of the cellar steps as the water began to creep up to her wrists. Her morning gown was drenched, which made it difficult to continue.

Where was Waverley? Perhaps he'd been prevented from returning by the rising tide. She sat up long enough to unfasten the sodden gown, for it was slowing her progress. She wriggled her way out of it, leaving her only remaining garment, the water-soaked chemise, to clothe her body.

When she reached the bottom step, she put her knee on it and tried to pull up to the next one, but the ancient wood cracked beneath her weight. She reached for the third step, grasped it with uncommon strength and hung on with all her might. She pulled hard, tearing the hem of her chemise in the process. As she inched her way up, she tested each new step with the weight of one knee, to make sure it wouldn't collapse under her, like the first one had.

When she reached a higher step, she was above the rancid water. It was then that she noticed the makeshift wrapping on her aching, swollen ankle. It had torn and come undone along the way, leaving only a small piece remaining. She tried to wind it tighter for support, but it too fell away in shreds.

Helena took deep breaths and tried to rest a bit. She could not shut her ears to the sound of water rising as she alternated between shivering from cold and perspiring from heat. A last wave of exhaustion overwhelmed her. She rested her back against the wall and closed her eyes, but they flew open again at an unfamiliar sound. Mice? She couldn't be sure. The scratching sound, at first a mere whisper, grew louder, a quiet rumble. She tried to concentrate, to discover where it came from. Her head swiveled round to search for the source.

Metal on wood! Helena knew that sound. Someone was trying to unlock the cellar door. She turned and scrambled up the last two steps, nearly losing her balance, but she managed to hang on with her hands, by this time full of splinters.

"Waverley!" she cried as the door swung open. "You've come at last."

A faintly familiar voice answered, filled as it were with mockery. "No, Lady Fairchild. I'm here to claim you for my bride, just as I promised I would."

Helena screamed, but the sound was muffled when someone threw a blanket over her. She kicked and struggled all the while she was carried up the back stairs to her chamber. Once there, the sounds of several female voices assaulted her ears.

"Here's the bitch now," a woman said, her voice ominous yet recognizable.

Chapter 22

Later . . .

"Stop strugglin', milady. Won't do you a bit o' good," said Mrs. Trasker, removing the blanket imprisoning Helena. "Hurry up and get the bath ready for milady, Belinda. The earl's impatient to be off with his *bride*." She chuckled at her jest.

"We're doin' our best," said Belinda in a resentful tone. "C'n we help it if she won't stop wrigglin' and be still?"

Mrs. Trasker had enlisted only the maids loyal to her. Nell, Eliza, Rose and Belinda helped prepare Helena for her abduction, but it wasn't easy, for Helena struggled, kicked and fought with all her might. By refusing to cooperate, she hoped to buy enough time for Waverley to reach her.

"Just you let me slap her around some, and she'll stop wrigglin' like a fish soon enough," said Belinda after the maids had managed to put Helena into the tub. They were drenched from the bathwater Helena had splashed all over them. Belinda and the other maids had been trying to wash her dirt-encrusted body, but Helena persisted in frustrating their efforts.

"No rough stuff, mind. His lordship wants her clean, but not beat up. Not even one bruise. He's fixin' to marry her, though why anyone would want a hellion like her is beyond me. She ain't even fit for my Harry when he becomes the marquis."

"Harry fancies her, though," said the saucy Belinda.

"Mind your tongue, girl, and get on with it."

Helena glared at Mrs. Trasker as all four young women pulled her from the tub and began to rub her dry, none too gently. "You'll regret this to the end of your days, Mrs. Trasker. And . . . and, what have you done with the dowager?"

Mrs. Trasker turned her nose up at her. "Never you mind about the dowager."

"May I see her before I go?"

Mrs. Trasker thought for a moment, then shook her head. "No. Don't think the earl would like it."

Helena pressed her when she detected a slight hesitation. "Where's the harm? I just want to say good-bye to her. The earl wouldn't have to know."

Mrs. Trasker saw some advantage in this proposal. "Will you stop yer strugglin' and let my girls finish dressin' you proper?"

"All right," said Helena. A spark of hope eased her heavy heart. "If you give me your word of honor you'll allow me to say good-bye to the dowager, I'll stop struggling and cooperate."

"I can give you only a few minutes with her ladyship. Can't spare any more time than that, else My Lord . . . er . . . his lordship will have my head."

London: Fairchild House

Georgiana crept into his bed and straddled him. "Wake up, you abominable stuffed shirt," she whispered into her brother's ear.

Still wrapped in the fog of sleep, Edward forced one eye

open. "Who's that?" He tried to sit up, but something heavy prevented him. His arms were in captivity, for she held them down over his head.

"Dare you to hit me, you beast. Telling Father on me! How could you do me such a miserable turn?" She burst into a familiar laughter.

"Get off me, you shameless hussy!" Edward said sternly, the corners of his mouth quivering.

"I knew you couldn't stay mad at your favorite sister for long, My Lord Stuffed Shirt. Can't let a stupid pair of boots get in the way of your hopeless adoration of me, now can you? Besides, wasn't it you who taught me all those devious tricks, odious brother of mine?"

Edward put his hands on her hips and lifted her off. "You owe me for those boots, Georgie, and for the clothes you so carelessly ruined."

She crossed her legs as she sat on his bed, for she was wearing pantaloons. "Guilty as charged, love, but I have one small problem. I haven't the blunt to pay you for them. Thanks to you, Father has cut off my allowance, not to mention my riding privileges. He has ordered me to beg your forgiveness. So here I am. Do you have any sackcloth and ashes in your wardrobe? May I borrow them?"

"So that's why you've invaded my chambers, you incorrigible brat," he muttered, trying to climb out of his bed. "Let's see. You've no blunt to spend. You may not ride like the wind in the Park. What next will you do in the way of mischief? I know you can't live without stirring up trouble."

"We can always think of something if we put our heads together, love, can't we? The way we used to when you weren't such a dead bore?"

Edward donned his dressing gown, but before he could knot its belt, Georgie jumped on his back, flung her arms around her brother's neck and wrapped her legs around his waist.

This act was too much for his composure and he burst into a shout of laughter. "Get. Off. My. Back. You detestable monkey."

Waverley Castle

When the marquis returned for Helena, she was nowhere to be found. How was that possible? He called her name yet heard just the hollow echo of his own voice. Unspeakable thoughts invaded his mind as he stood alone in the dark surrounded by nothing but a bleak emptiness.

He raced up to the first cellar, taking care to avoid the rotted steps, but the door was locked. He put his shoulder to it, but he was too weak to budge the door. He bent to peer through the keyhole where a glimmer of light revealed shelves neatly stocked with jars of food. He allowed himself a grim smile. Cook and her staff had lost no time in filling the new shelves Helena had ordered. The sinking feeling in the pit of his stomach would not go away. Was his darling safe? Perhaps someone had already rescued her. If that was so, why did they lock the door again? Something felt wrong.

He made his way back down the steps and found a shred of Helena's petticoat clinging to one of them. The feeling of dread continued to clutch at his heart as he hurried back out the way he came, but the rising tide slowed him down.

Casper was waiting for him. "You look a sight, milord. Where's milady?"

"She's gone, Casper. I don't know where." Waverley was grateful to see Casper holding the reins of two horses in one hand, Waverley's coat and boots in the other. "Let me have those boots, Casper. My feet are bloodied and raw."

"Brought you some dry clothes, milord. A mite big, 'cause they're mine. Dry yourself with this cloth. It's clean if a bit ragged. I carry it with me to wipe my horse down."

Waverley managed a grin. "Give it here, you prince of a fellow, and thanks. I'm soaked to the skin." He stripped bare, dried himself and put on Casper's clothes, grateful for their warmth. When his boots were on, he mounted.

"What's happening? Have you any idea where Lady Helena might be?"

"No, milord. I'm afraid the news isn't good. The castle's under siege by the worst lookin' bunch o' goons I ever seen. What's more, they're armed. Milady must be inside still, for Lemuel hasn't seen any sign of her. He and some of our men are hiding in the woods just outside the front steps of the castle. I've left others watching the kitchen door."

Helena fought back tears as the maids dressed her, but she kept her word and didn't struggle. Belinda combed the tangles from her hair, nearly scalping her in the process, yet Helena refused to cry out. That would give the revengeful maid far too much satisfaction. Mrs. Trasker had chosen one of Helena's ball gowns, the pale blue moiré silk etched with tiny seed pearls.

When the maids helped her into the gown, Mrs. Trasker held up a heavy blue velvet cape lined with sable. "That won't be necessary, Mrs. Trasker. It's May. The weather's too warm for fur."

"The earl 'specially sent this here cloak for you to wear. He said the sea air can be quite chilly. You should thank yer stars you're marryin' such a thoughtful gent, to my way o' thinking."

Helena bit back her tears. She would not let them gloat over the terror she felt. Instead, she forced herself to say, "His lordship is too kind."

Mrs. Trasker examined her prisoner critically. "You'll do, I suppose. Still can't unnerstand why the earl chose you for his lady. Let's go." She held the door open for Helena while

Belinda and the others surrounded her. There was no possibility of escape.

"But the dowager! You promised to let me say good-bye to her," Helena cried as the maids dragged her toward the grand staircase.

"I lied." Mrs. Trasker flung the words over her shoulder as she led the way.

Helena screamed as loud as she could.

"Save yer breath. Won't do you a bit o' good 'cause there's nary a one to hear you. I gave all the new servants you hired a half-day holiday in honor of your wedding. We locked Mrs. Hubley in with the dowager, but we couldn't find Cook and her nieces. They're hidin' somewheres, but no matter. We'll get them later. Help her keep that cloak on her shoulders, girls. Be sure to fasten it tight so she can't wriggle out of it."

When she was satisfied, Mrs. Trasker opened the door and stepped aside. "Farewell, milady. Pleasure to know you."

Keller and Winkle, Mrs. Trasker's ruffians, dressed in full livery, each took one arm and lifted Helena, intending to carry her down the steps to the earl, who waited at the door of his carriage.

"Put me down, you traitors! I can very well walk without your help," she hissed.

They hesitated but stepped back at a signal from the earl. "Good evening, ma'am," he greeted affably. "You look a far sight lovelier than when I first discovered you rooting around that nasty old cellar."

Helena clenched her fists inside the cape. "So. You resort to abduction. Do as you will, but I won't marry you, Glynhaven. It's Waverley I love. Not you."

The earl turned mean at the sound of the hated name on her lips. "Oh, you'll marry me all right, my dear. The captain will do the honors once we're under sail. We're going to France, you see. Lord Saltash—you remember Lord Saltash, don't you? He's invited us to stay at his chateau for our honeymoon. He and his friends—you remember his charming friends? Of course, you do. You met them at my ball. They have all sorts of delightful entertainments planned for us. Have you ever participated in an orgy? No, of course not. A well-bred lady like you would never resort to such forbidden fruits. Harry tells me you are a lusty wench. He informs me that you're no longer a virgin, thanks to the marquis. I regret I wasn't the one to deflower you, but not enough to give you back to my enemy. I promise you that Waverley will never have you again. After I get through with you, my dear, he may never even want you."

Stall for time. Keep him talking. "The marquis will come after you. I'm sure he'll find me and then what will you do?"

Glynhaven laughed, but there was no joy in his eyes. "I think not, my bride. Never mind him. You'll learn to like our particular games. Don't worry your pretty little head too much. Your bruises will heal quickly, I promise."

"It doesn't bother you, my lord, that I despise you and I always will? We Fairchild women have tempers, sir. Best take care once we are married. I'd advise you to stay awake lest I scratch your eyes out."

The earl laughed maliciously. "Fairchild women must be lusty creatures, then. What good news. Be as wild as you like, my dear. I look forward to bedding Waverley's whore."

"So it's revenge you yearn for. Too bad you'll suffer disappointment. Or won't it trouble you that when you bed me, I shall think only of Waverley's caresses? And what of his child growing within me? Won't it be lovely to see him inherit your title and all your worldly goods?"

Glynhaven turned pale. He slapped her face hard enough to leave a mark. "So you're carrying his bastard, are you? If it's a boy, he won't live to inherit, I assure you. If it's a girl, someone else will raise her. I'll see to it. If you persist in disobeying me, milady, once I take a whip to you, you'll change your mind quickly enough." He turned at the sound of horses' hooves, a look of surprise on his face.

When the marquis and Casper reached the men hiding in the woods near the front entrance, Casper asked, "What's to do, Lem?"

"The Earl of Glynhaven's carriage is out front. There are men with guns protectin' him. Best be careful and make your way through the back woods. You can enter through the kitchen door. Tom Wells is guardin' the door there with his lads."

"Lady Helena? Have you seen her?" the marquis asked.

"Not hide nor hair. She may still be inside, I'll wager, for she can't have stepped a foot outside without our notice. My guess? The earl's fixin' to abduct her, but he won't be goin' anywhere, or my name ain't Lemuel. I promise you that."

The marquis and Casper nodded farewell and made their way through the woods to the kitchen. There they met Tom and a group of burly young farmers holding rakes and pitchforks for weapons, all too eager for the excitement of battle.

"Go in through the kitchen, but go quietly. Cook is in there," whispered Tom.

When Sebastian received the marquis' letter, he and Olivia made haste to leave London that same day. They left their baby with the duke and duchess, claiming they had urgent government business elsewhere. They also enlisted the aid of four trained men from the home office and took off on horseback at breakneck speed for Land's End, stopping only long enough to change horses, dine hastily and sleep a mere few hours before starting out again. Thus they reached Land's End in record time.

As they neared their destination, Olivia set her worries about her sister Helena aside to admire the change in their surroundings. The trees had given way to the open sea. The wind kicked up blustery gusts, bringing with it the sharp tang of the sea as seagulls screeched their discordant songs.

"You're frowning, Livy. Don't worry so, my love."

"I can't help it, Sebastian. I'm making an effort, though. Trying to admire the scenery, as it were."

They came to a fork where one branch of the road stopped at the cliffs of Land's End and the second branch continued toward the fishing village of Sennen Cove. Sebastian examined the map he had procured from ordinance at the home office. "We must take the road on the right."

Sebastian gave orders to two of the men to reconnoiter on ahead and report back. The rest turned their horses and were soon treated with their first glimpse of Waverley Castle. It rose above the cliffs, ancient but proud. As they spurred their horses on, Olivia said a silent prayer for her sister's safety.

Chapter 23

Dusk . . .

Waverley and Casper took a circuitous route through the woods. To their relief, no armed enemies were in sight. Instead, Tom Wells and his men were hidden near the stables, within sight of the kitchen.

"No enemies here, your lordship." He said the words with regret, clearly itching for action.

"Is it safe to enter the castle through the kitchen?" Casper asked.

Tom nodded. "Best be careful inside, though. Can't say what you'll find."

"We're prepared, Tom, thanks to Casper." Waverley pulled the two pistols Casper had provided from his leather saddlebag, dismounted and threw the reins to Tom.

Tom grinned at the sight of the weapons. "If we hear shots, we'll come running right quick."

"Best take care, hear?" said Casper.

Waverley and Casper, guns at the ready, stole cautiously across the road and crouched under a small window. Casper raised his eyes above the sill to investigate. He turned and said,

"Emma's peekin' out of the pantry. Cook's there, too, sir. She'd never leave her ladyship alone." Casper entered first, followed by the marquis.

"Casper!" gasped Emma. She curtseyed to Waverley. "Milord. Thank heaven you've come."

Cook began to sob. Casper shot a questioning look at Emma.

In a breath taken without pause, Emma blurted out, "Milady's bein' 'ducted. I heard Harry boastin' to one of the footmen, the brute."

"What of my grandmother?"

"Safe, milord. Trudy and Nurse Hubley were locked in with milady, and Cook and I hid down here when those lyin' Traskers sent everyone else away."

Waverley managed a thin smile. "Thank you for your loyalty. What else did Harry say, lass? Do you recall?"

"He bragged that he and his ma were finally rid of Lady Helena. He said the Earl of Glynhaven took her off to wed her, and good riddance, he said, and . . ."

"Stay here and hide yourselves. We'll find her," the marquis said grimly. "Come on, Casper." He turned and crossed the kitchen into the entry hall leading upstairs to the grand hallway. To his astonishment, Mrs. Trasker and her son, their backs to them, were standing in front of the open front doors.

Waverley crept up and hid behind one door, motioning Casper behind the other. They waited until mother and son turned to come back inside. In one motion, they slammed both doors shut and aimed their weapons, overwhelming the astonished pair.

Casper said quietly, "Move a muscle and you're dead."

"Where has the earl taken my lady? Answer me, you witch!"

Harry took a menacing step toward the marquis, but he stopped when he saw his pistol. "You're surrounded, milord," he blustered. "You'll never get out of here alive. And besides, My Lord promised me I'm to be marquis soon's you're dead."

"Shut it, Harry," warned his mother. She changed her tune to civility. "Nothing out of place here, milord. Lady Fairchild's agreed to wed the Earl of Glynhaven is all. We were just seein' 'em off."

"Where have they gone? Answer me, or else." Casper waved his pistol at Harry.

"Lord Glynhaven's ship is anchored in Sennen Cove, waitin' to take 'em to France. They're to be wed by the cap'n onboard."

When the scouts returned, one of them reported to the group that a coach was swiftly bearing down on them. "There appear to be two people, a man and a woman, within the coach. Two postillions are leading, two more riding alongside the coach, two outriders holding on in back, a coachman and an armed gunman sitting next to him."

"Good work, Samuel," said Sebastian. "We'll ambush them from that bend in the road. You two take the postillions riding alongside. You two remove the outriders in back. Take their places as if nothing is amiss. Leave the coachman and the gunman up front to us."

"What about the two leading postillions?"

"We will do this with precision and stealth. They won't hear a thing until it is too late, Samuel. Take your positions on both sides of the road and watch me. When my fist goes up, we attack. Ready? Good. Take your places." Sebastian took his wife's hand and led her into hiding behind a bramble.

The small group did not have long to wait before the coach appeared. Sebastian let the lead postillions pass and raised his fist. The postillions on either side of the coach were swiftly overcome. Sebastian's men stripped the postillions and donned their coats and caps and took their places, leaving the unconscious men in a ditch on the side of the road. At the same time, his other two men disabled the outriders holding on to the back of the coach and did the same, while Olivia and Sebastian swung over them to the top.

Sebastian pointed to the gunman and nodded to his wife. He was her prey while the coachman was his. She nodded assent, lay flat on her stomach and waited for her husband's signal to attack. When he was sure the others were in control, he crooked a finger, motioned forward and Olivia launched herself on the gunman. A simple chop to his neck with the side of her hand sent him forward. She had to hold the unconscious man until Samuel took him down. But not before she had his long-barreled gun trained on the lead postillions. The entire operation took less than ten minutes, all in silence.

Reins comfortably in hand, Sebastian drew the coach to a halt while Samuel and the others overcame the lead postillions.

"What is this? Why have we stopped? Drive on, I say. We must reach my ship to set sail before the tide turns," shouted the earl from his rolled-down window.

"Good afternoon, Glynhaven," said Sebastian as he wrenched open the earl's door, nearly causing him to topple out.

"Hi, sister," shouted Olivia as she opened the other door. "Going somewhere?"

"Livy!" Helena flung herself into her sister's arms until they both fell in a heap, laughing, sobbing and rolling in the dirt, yet never letting go.

Frantic, Waverley ran down the steps as if he meant to run all the way to the beach, an impossible task. He was halfway up the drive when he was met with a sight he would never forget as long as he lived.

Sebastian Brooks led the bizarre procession, Olivia at his side and Waverley's beloved Helena mounted behind her sister. They were at the head of Glynhaven's carriage, surrounded on all sides by the hastily assembled farmers, a ragtag army led by Lemuel, a mob of young lads, like knights of old, holding pitchforks, long-handled hoes and hastily fashioned clubs as though they were spears and maces, while others similarly armed followed the carriage, prodding the earl's goons ahead of them, all tied securely with strong hemp.

Waverley didn't know whether to laugh or to cry at this preposterous scene. He raced toward Helena, who fell into his outstretched arms. He covered her face with kisses. "Helena, my beautiful black-haired raven. I thought I'd lost you."

"No, my lord. I'm here."

The colorful parade made its haphazard way back to the castle, but all was not well. On the steps of the front door, Casper held Harry by the arm, his pistol trained on the man's head, but he let go and Harry saw his opportunity to escape as the two rolled down the steps in a heap. One of the earl's men leaped out of the bushes, lifted his pistol, took aim and fired at Casper. The bullet grazed his arm just as Tom Wells and his friends came upon them from the direction of the stables. Lemuel got there first with his pitchfork, stabbed the man who shot Casper and rushed to Casper's side.

"Thank you kindly, Lem. Y'saved me life."

The toothy grin of Trudy's beau beamed at Casper. "My pleasure. Lemme have a look-see, Casper." He bent to examine his friend's arm. "Winged ya. Not serious." He ripped off the sleeve of Casper's shirt and wrapped it tightly around the wound to stop the bleeding.

Mrs. Trasker helped her son to his feet, linked her arm through his and, though she had a strong urge to run, began to stroll away with an unhurried air.

"Not so fast," shouted Lemuel. "Tie those two up," he ordered, and two lads jumped to the task with enthusiasm. There hadn't been this much excitement for residents of Sennen

Cove since last New Year's Eve, when the lads celebrated the event by burning down Farmer Hadley's barn.

"Watch out for the men with guns," Casper warned.

Lem grinned. "Those goons ain't got their guns anymore. Whole town's out there trussin' 'em up. There are some folk plannin' on a barbecue tonight, seems like. Them goons might just be the beef."

Waverley handed Helena over to her sister's care. "I've unfinished business, love." He tried to wrench the door of the earl's carriage open, but the earl had locked it. "Open this door, Glynhaven, if you value your worthless life. Do it now or I'll shoot you dead through the window."

To his surprise, the earl opened it at once. "Afternoon, Waverley," he said genially, as if they had met on a country lane. Waverley's pistol remained aimed at the earl's head.

"Game's up, Martin. You're finished."

"On the contrary. You're merely delaying our nuptials. Lady Helena has consented to be my bride, haven't you, my dear?" He nodded to Helena, who stood next to her sister, near enough to witness this melodrama. She raised her head at the sound of a cart lumbering toward them. Captain Le Clair, young Jess and Amy sat on the front seat with the driver of the large open cart. And behind them sat more crusaders come to help slay the dragons.

Lemuel spotted Casper's love and whispered in his ear, "It's Amy, Cas. Here's your chance. Play dead." Casper promptly closed his eyes and rolled his head to one side.

Amy spied Casper at once. She leaped down from the moving wagon and ran to his side. "Casper! Is he . . . ?"

Lem's lips twitched. "Not yet, lass, but he's wounded severe."

Amy fell to her knees, took Casper's large face in her small hands and kissed his eyes, his nose, his mouth. "They've shot you, me darlin', but you ain't killed. Don't you worry, love. Your Amy's here to take care o' you. I love you, Cas. With all my heart." The sight of his bloody shirtsleeve caused her to burst into tears and bury her head on his chest.

Casper lay still, enjoying this triumphant moment. He opened one eye, winked his gratitude to Lemuel, and closed it again.

Helena looked up in surprise. "Desmond! It's Captain Le Clair. But he's not well. Why is he here?"

"He's determined to bear witness, my love. Let us greet him. Come along, Olivia. You're about to meet our fine French friend." The marquis looked around him for someone to stand guard over Glynhaven.

"I'll see he don't move an inch, milord," said Jess, eager to take part in the fray.

Amused, Waverley asked, "Do you know how to shoot?"

"Born to it," the boy bragged.

"Don't, Desmond," protested Helena. "Jess is too young to . . ."

"I ain't, milady. Trust me to do this for the two kindest people I ever met." His soulful brown eyes, too large for such a small face, won the day.

Waverley ruffled his hair and handed him his pistol. "Show me you can cock it, and the task is yours, young soldier."

The boy did so at once and aimed it at the astonished earl.

"Have pity, Waverley. I'm a dead man if you leave that nasty little sod in charge."

Waverley grinned and said to Jess, "Guard the earl well. If you have to shoot him, aim for his leg. I'd rather see him hang, wouldn't you?"

The lad's grin stretched from ear to ear. "It be m'pleasure, milord." He saluted the marquis with one finger, and aimed the pistol at his lordship's leg, with the power of his responsibility writ large on his freckled face. "You heard 'im, mister earl. Move an inch and you'll be limpin' to yer hangin'."

Sebastian joined them as Olivia, Helena and Waverley

hurried to the captain's side. "You shouldn't be here, René. You're not well," Helena said.

"I had to come, my dear. There may never be a better opportunity to find the murderers and bear witness."

"Do you recognize any of the smugglers among these men, sir?"

"I do indeed. That large man standing next to the older woman is the ringleader." He pointed to Harry, sentencing him, in effect, to the gallows. "I saw him murder two of my crew with my own eyes."

The captain's eyes swept over the earl's goons, now disarmed and tied securely. He pointed and said, "That fellow is another murderer and the man next to him. Those six tied up over there as well." Pointing to Belinda, Rose, and Eliza, he said, "Those three young maids dragged cargo to the shore." He continued, "This band of blackguards caused *Le Coq d'Or,* as seaworthy a sailing vessel as you'll ever find, to crash on the rocky shoreline. They silenced the buoy bells and rang a false bell, luring us to disaster in the fog. Determined to go down with my ship, I watched helplessly from the top deck as they murdered my crew and my passengers, women and children among them, for I was the last to leave my beloved vessel." The captain, a devout man, added, "The Good Lord chose to save my life." He nodded to Helena and Waverley. "For good reason. I'm determined to remain in England long enough to bear witness. These men must hang for their terrible deeds," he said bitterly.

"What about that woman next to the ringleader, René?" asked Helena.

"Never saw her before, milady."

The captain turned to the young man supporting him. "Take me back to the wagon, young man. I must rest." But he halted when he heard Harry shout out.

"I ain't the ringleader, Cap'n!" Harry pointed to the Earl of

Glynhaven. "I know I'll hang for it, but he's the ringleader. He done all the plannin' and tol' us what to do. Ain't that right, Ma? Me Ma's right smart. She gets the men we need and we do it, is all. 'My Lord,' we calls him, takes half of what we find. It's him that makes us murder. 'No witnesses,' he allus says. Ain't that right, Ma?"

Mrs. Trasker turned white. "Oh, Harry. You stupid fool," she said softly. "You just signed your ma's death sentence. Now I'll hang, too."

"Take me to the earl, son," the captain said to the lad on whose arm he leaned.

"Well, Captain?" asked Waverley, who followed him. "Do you recognize the earl as one of the smugglers?"

"I'm afraid not, but that doesn't mean he isn't guilty as charged."

"You are mistaken, sir," interrupted the earl. "I never saw that man in my life."

"You planned it," screeched Mrs. Trasker, pointing her finger at the earl. "Yes you did, and you want me and me Harry to hang for it!"

"I don't know who you are, madam. The wages of sin must always end in retribution, they say. My regrets." He turned away from her.

Waverley leaned into the carriage and said, "Glynhaven, you are guilty of attempted abduction and I'll see you hang for that, if for nothing else."

"But I am guilty of no such thing, my good man. Lady Fairchild readily consented to marry me." He looked at her with doleful eyes. "Have you changed your mind again, ma'am? Tsk, tsk. First you spurn Darlington, and now you spurn me. You seem to take pleasure in agreeing to be wed and then jilting your suitors. Unkind in you, ma'am. Most unkind."

"Why, you . . ." Waverley lunged for his throat.

"Let him go, Waverley," Sebastian said, yanking the marquis out of the carriage.

His rage abated, but it turned to puzzlement. "Why did you stop me?" he asked.

"Will you grant me a moment to discuss what's to be done? In private, if you please," said Sebastian.

"As you wish," he said reluctantly.

"We'll join you," Olivia said to her husband. He nodded and offered his arm. Waverley did the same for Helena, but when they mounted the steps, Amy stopped them. "Casper's wounded bad, milady. They're takin' him to town. May I go?"

"Of course, dear. With my blessings," said Helena. Their eyes met and a look of sympathetic understanding passed between them.

Waverley led the way into the library. He shut the door behind him. "What do you have in mind, Brooks?"

"You can't press charges, Waverley."

"But he's guilty. I've no doubt he *is* the ringleader. He certainly needed the money. I know for a fact that his father died leaving him with an estate mortgaged to the hilt."

"That may well be, but his role in this horrid business cannot become known."

Waverley's eyes narrowed. "Why not? We have proof that he is guilty of attempted abduction."

"Be reasonable, Waverley. Do you really want Helena to have to testify against the earl in a London courtroom? It's not a good idea. The publicity would be another disaster for her. She doesn't need any more notoriety, does she?"

Helena was thunderstruck by this. "I hadn't thought of that."

"My sister isn't the only one who would suffer if this gets out. Father holds a lot of power in Parliament. Think what such a scandal would do to him. Think what it would mean for your future as well, my lord. Anyone can see that you're in love with Helena. You cannot begin your lives together under a cloud of scandal."

Waverley recalled his disastrous meeting with the duke, but he said nothing. "What do you suggest? We can't let Glynhaven walk away free from all his dirty deeds."

Sebastian turned to Helena. "Where was it the earl meant to take you?"

"He has a ship waiting to take us to Cherbourg and then to the chateau of his odious friend Lord Saltash. We were to be married at sea by the captain."

"Where is this ship moored?"

"It's moored off the beach in Sennen Cove. It might still be awaiting our arrival, for all I know."

"Very likely," murmured Waverley, his eyes dark with fury.

Olivia and Sebastian exchanged significant glances.

"Are you thinking what I'm thinking, my darling?" Sebastian grinned at his wife.

"You two are too much in love to see the forest for the trees. Sebastian . . . *we* have a better idea," said Olivia.

Waverley looked doubtful. "The villagers may tolerate smuggling, but never murder. They'll want his blood as much as Captain Le Clair does."

"What are you two thinking?" asked Helena.

"Glynhaven's smart enough to know he can make trouble for you," said her sister. "Let Sebastian explain the solution we have in mind."

"Let's offer the earl an alternative. To save his worthless skin, we'll allow him to think he's free to take up permanent residence in France. We'll escort him to his ship and send him off with our blessings."

"What kind of punishment is that?" Waverley asked petulantly.

"You forget the French authorities. They don't take kindly to having their merchant ship destroyed along with passengers and crew, and their cargo stolen as well. Glynhaven will be arrested when the ship lands in Cherbourg, but the French won't bother with a public trial. He'll never leave France alive, I promise you. With Le Clair's testimony, the French will see to it that the Earl of Glynhaven meets his just rewards."

Helena nodded in approval. "A sad, but necessary ending for a vile monster."

"What about the townsfolk?" Waverley objected. "They want his blood. How should I explain your plan, Sebastian?"

"You needn't tell them the whole of it. It's enough to say that our government has stepped in to negotiate a delicate international affair that threatened a crisis. That should satisfy them, don't you think? I leave it to you to deal with the town fathers as you see fit, but swear them to secrecy."

"How do you propose we get the earl on board without creating a stir?"

"I shall send an order to the local militia to detain his ship. It will sail for France only after you and I deliver him to the captain. As for Le Clair, he'll be escorted to London. Someone in the home office will take his deposition and send him home to France. His written statement will be enough to convict the Traskers and their accomplices."

The marquis felt as if Sebastian had taken a heavy burden from him. "I can rest easy now, thanks to your excellent strategies."

Sebastian laughed. "You can't rest easy just yet, my lord. You have a role to play in this drama. Will you come with me and tell Glynhaven that you have agreed to my plan to allow him to travel to France?"

Waverley's eyes lit up. "That would be my greatest pleasure, sir."

"Why don't you see to your sister while we tend to this, Livy? She's been through enough today. She needs to rest. We'll see to the business at hand. Care to join me, Waverley?"

The marquis grinned. "With pleasure." He kissed Helena on the forehead and followed Sebastian out.

Chapter 24

That Evening . . .

Helena shut the door, relieved to be in the privacy of her chamber. "Help me out of this horrid gown, Livy. I'll never wear it again so long as I live."

"Right. We'll burn it to rid the evidence of today's near disaster." She turned Helena around and began to unbutton the offensive garment. "Who would have believed it?" she murmured, warming to her task with such enthusiasm, she tore off some of the buttons.

"Believed what?"

"Father agreed to send you here until the *ton* forgets your broken betrothal to Darlington. And what does my demure sister do, but roil the pot."

Helena stepped out of her gown and turned to Olivia. "What do you mean?"

"If you think news of Glynhaven's disastrous ball did not reach the ears of London gossips, think again. Didn't you guess? It was in all the scandal sheets."

"I hadn't thought. . . . Father knows?"

"Of course, you ninny. The whole family knows." Olivia

reached into her portmanteau and pulled out a letter. "Father asked me to give you this. For your eyes alone, he said."

She tore off the seal with trembling hands, smoothed the single sheet open, and read it.

My Dear Helena,

The Marquis of Waverley paid me a visit to ask my permission to wed you. I regret that I cannot give him my consent, for I am convinced he is not the right man for you. His tainted reputation, I'm afraid, is beyond redemption, especially after the Earl of Glynhaven's ball, when his bordello friends from Paris appeared to renew their acquaintance with him. You have been forced to suffer too much notoriety in your short lifetime, my child. Believe that I have made this decision thinking only of your happiness. I shall give your hand in marriage only to a man worthy of my sweet Helena.

Yours,
Father

The blood in Helena's veins turned to ice. When she finished reading the letter, she handed it to Olivia.

Olivia read it and said, "I'm so sorry, love. Sebastian told me that Waverley came to London to see Father, but I never guessed this would be the outcome."

"So that was why he went to London," Helena said in a flat voice. "'Just business,' he told me, and I thought no more of it. I can't say I'm surprised. Ironic, isn't it? Father turned him down because of his reputation as a rake." Helena's laugh skirted the edge of hysteria.

"The pot calling the kettle black, you mean. Our dear father was no saint, was he?"

"No matter, Livy. I'm in love with Waverley and we'll marry with or without Father's blessing."

About to respond, Olivia changed her mind and kept her thoughts to herself.

"What are you thinking? Don't hold out on me, Livy."

"Father's dug his heels in."

Helena's eyes held the fire of determination. "I'll never give Waverley up. Never."

London

"Come in," said the duke at a knock on his bedchamber door.

"This just came from the home office, your grace. I know it's late, but I thought . . ."

"I'll have it, please." He dismissed Dunston with a wave of his hand and broke the seal. He rose from his chair by the fireside, left his chamber and strode through the connecting door without bothering to knock.

"Your grace! You startled me," said the duchess. With the slightest of nods, she dismissed her abigail, who put the hairbrush down at once and disappeared. "What's the matter?"

He thrust the note at her. "Read this."

The duchess smoothed it on her dressing table and read it quickly, while her husband paced back and forth. "Abduction! Thank God Helena was saved from that fate. We have the Marquis of Waverley to thank for rescuing her."

"Helena fancies herself in love with him but she's wrong. It's nothing but a case of hero worship. She'll get over it."

But the duchess thought otherwise. "I think not, Tony. The marquis saved our daughter's life. Doesn't this change anything for you? I must admit, it gives me food for thought."

"It changes nothing. The whole world knows that this man's an infernal rake, I tell you. I won't allow Helena to marry him. He may have saved her life, but hero worship is not love, my dear. Why can't she fall in love with the right man? First it's Darlington and now it's Waverley. Has she no sense at all?"

The duchess knew better than to interrupt his tirade.

"Two suitors in one year! Our daughter Helena has an uncanny knack for picking the wrong man."

The duchess turned her head to hide her grin.

"Well, Ellen! What ought we to do?"

"You already know the answer, my dear."

He stopped pacing and raised his quizzing glass. "And that is?"

"You must find it in your heart to consent to the marriage. It's not your choice to make, you know."

Land's End

"Walk with me in the garden, Desmond. I want to talk to you."

"Of course, love." He offered his arm and she took it. "How are you feeling?"

Helena didn't speak until they were too far away to be heard. "Bloody angry with you. That's how I feel. Why didn't you tell me you went to London to ask my father for my hand in marriage?"

"He rejected my suit for your hand. I didn't know how to break the news to you."

She couldn't hide her grin. "Coward."

"I suppose I am, but I haven't given up. I'll win you somehow, lovely lady. I promise you that."

The paths had at last been cleared of much of the undergrowth. Spring bulbs poked through, some in full bloom. Daffodils waved their yellow heads at them, but Helena was so lost in thought, she took no notice of their beauty.

When they came to the newly rebuilt gazebo, Waverley said, "Sit with me beloved, and I'll tell all."

When she took her seat, she said, "Go on."

"I did everything but grovel at your father's feet, but an anonymous letter reached him before I did."

"Glynhaven?"

"Without a doubt. The earl made sure the scandal at the ball became known not only to your father, but also to the world. He arranged to have the whole sordid affair made public in the London journals."

"Go on."

He took her hand in his. "There isn't much more to tell. Your father said he would not allow his daughter to suffer a lifetime of humiliation. I argued I was no longer the wild man of my youth. 'Once a rake, always a rake,' he insisted. I could not penetrate that wall of resistance no matter how hard I tried."

"What you may not know is that I am very much my father's daughter." She laughed, but humor was missing. "When we marry, you'll learn just how much my father and I are alike. I was not yet one year old when my father withheld my favorite stuffed bear. I was so much attached to it, I howled loud and long, but my father has a difficult time backing down. When my mother begged him to give it back to me, he said I was too old for such nonsense and refused."

"How cruel. You were a mere infant."

A sly smile curled her lips. "According to my mother, I held my breath until I turned blue. My father was so afraid I would die, he gave me back my bear at once."

Waverley laughed. "Will you hold your breath and turn blue until your father gives in?"

"If nothing else prevails. Shall you hate it?"

"Very likely." He rose and held his arms out. Helena went willingly into what turned out to be a prolonged embrace.

"I want you, Waverley," she said in a rasping voice. Her hands ran down his back.

"My love," he murmured with poignant tenderness.

Just two little words, but they very nearly broke her heart. She made a silent vow. Father or no, she'd have this man come what may. "I need you. Now, my beloved."

"No, my bewitching raven. Not if we're ever to have a chance to win your father's consent. You've already tricked me once into a premature tryst, haven't you? Let's hope you're not with child."

"That might make it easier for us to marry. Father couldn't stand the scandal." She giggled.

"What?"

"I was thinking of the last time I saw you buck naked."

"You thought I was someone else then. What was that poor fellow's name?"

"I've forgotten. Do you remember when I first touched you?"

He smirked in the time-honored way that began with cavemen. "How can I ever forget? It changed my life. Where did you learn such devilish tricks?"

She giggled again. "Oh, I've had worlds of experience in the art of lust."

"Liar. But you do get better all the time." He kissed her.

When he stopped, she said, "Dear me. I see stars."

"I'm that good, am I? Thank you for the tribute, love."

She burst out laughing. "That's not what I meant, my darling. The heavenly stars are out. We'll have to hurry and change or we'll be late for dinner."

Chapter 25

The marquis lost no time in summoning the town fathers to a meeting at Waverley Castle. Among them were Dr. Fenwick and Vicar Swiveley. Robert Nelson, a yeoman and Squire Hawkes, two of Waverley's boyhood friends, had been invited in addition to Sennen Cove's only magistrate, Sir George Wyndham.

"I have asked you here to discuss the case against the Earl of Glynhaven. Undersecretary Sir Sebastian Brooks, Lady Fairchild's brother-in-law, is from the home office. He has authorized me to inform you of the Crown's decision in the matter of the Earl of Glynhaven and the mischief he has caused us all."

"Mischief? No, Waverley. It was more than mischief he brewed," said Nelson. "Ever since we were boys, the earl was envious of you and wanted to best you. We all knew that. Thank God it is at an end now."

"True enough, Robert. I need to remind you that the information I am about to disclose must not leave this room. Do

I have your word?" He looked from one man to the other for agreement.

He explained concisely what was in store for Glynhaven, and why it was necessary. He added, "Captain Le Clair has asked to be taken to London, for he wishes to offer his deposition and return to his home in France as soon as possible. He's a brave man and his testimony will go a long way to putting an end to smuggling here in Land's End. The French government has been kept informed of his role. He shall be welcomed home as a national hero."

When the meeting drew to a close, Waverley said, "If there are no other questions, I bid you good day, gentlemen. Thank you for coming. I need not caution you again as to the secrecy of our meeting."

He shook hands with his guests as each one took his leave. All but one, for Waverley placed a restraining hand on the magistrate's sleeve. "A moment, sir. I must detain you to discuss what's to be done with the Glynhaven estate during the earl's . . . er . . . shall we call it his continued absence?"

Wyndham was an imposing figure, almost as wide as he was tall, but his eyes were kind, especially when he dealt with those less fortunate. To them he administered benign justice, but to others who were intent on malicious mischief, his sentences were indeed harsh.

"What are your thoughts, sir?" asked Waverley.

"Glynhaven has an honest bailiff managing his property. I know the man well. I'll advise him to maintain the estate and to continue to pay the merchants and the servants their wages from the proceeds." The magistrate paused in thought. "I'll request him further to search for contraband. We'll need evidence for His Majesty, if we are to make a case for bestowing the earl's estate on someone more worthy."

"Thank you, sir. Your reputation as a wise man is well deserved."

The magistrate grinned. "You've come a long way from that young mischief maker I once knew, my boy. I'm sorry your father didn't live to see the fine son he raised to take his place. He would have been proud of you."

A flicker of regret crossed Waverley's face. "I'm sorry, too, sir."

Helena labored over the letter she was writing to her father. After several ruined sheets, she turned to her sister for help.

"No, Helena. Cross this word out. You mustn't 'demand' anything from Father. That only serves to raise his hackles. Instead, you must plead for his help in your plight. It's the only way."

Helena rolled her eyes. "Don't I know it! But I'm so angry with him, Livy. How dare he interfere with my happiness. I'm going to marry Waverley with or without his approval, I tell you."

Olivia glanced at the clock on the mantel. "Heavens, it's past four. I'll leave you to finish your letter while I dress for dinner." She blew her sister a kiss and added, "Let me have a look at the letter before you send it off."

"I will," Helena answered and bent to her task. She became so engrossed, she didn't hear the door open.

"What are you writing, my raven?" Waverley kissed the top of her head.

She looked up and touched the hand resting on her shoulder. "A letter to my father."

"Can you hold your breath and turn blue in your letter?"

She laughed. "If only that were possible. I'm done." She sprinkled sand on the ink, folded the single sheet and put it away in her drawer. She rose and wrapped her arms around his neck. "How did your meeting go?"

"Very well. The town fathers were most understanding. We have many good friends here, my love."

"Glad to hear it."

"The vicar was full of news. Banns have been posted by two of our people."

Helena laughed in delight. "Hmm. Shall I guess?"

"Go on."

"Casper has offered for Amy."

"And . . . ?"

"And you have offered for me."

"I have indeed, but we are not the ones he means."

She made a face. "Too bad of you to remind me. Well, then. I can't think who else. You'll have to tell me."

"You surprise me, love. Which of the kitchen maids has been pining over a certain stable boy forever?"

Helena giggled. "You can't mean Trudy and Lemuel?"

He nodded in mock solemnity and led her to the sofa. They sat side by side, one of his hands holding hers and one arm around her shoulder. "Trudy must be thrilled. Let's hope she doesn't torture him the rest of his life for being so tardy. That would be a disaster, wouldn't it?"

"It would, but Trudy means to keep him occupied. She confessed to me she wants a large family. What other news, love?"

"Magistrate Wyndham paid me a compliment. He said my current sobriety would have made my father proud, a refreshing change from my wild youth."

"Perhaps you ought to ask the magistrate to write a letter of recommendation to my father, though I don't think it would do any good."

"I agree. Your father doesn't know our local magistrate well enough to take his word for my reformation."

London

Helena's pleading letter did nothing to soften the duke enough to change his mind. He brought her letter to the duchess to read. "Pretty language, Ellen, but if my daughter thinks to use fine words to get her way, she's wrong."

"She loves the marquis, Tony. Isn't that enough for you?"

"No, my dear. What do you suppose will happen to her the first time he strays from her bed, eh? There will be a second and a third time, I assure you. She is in love with a rake. His behavior may well prove to be too treacherous for her comfort."

"She might marry him without your consent. What then?"

"If she disobeys me, she shall not be welcome in my home," he said bitterly.

"You're forgetting, Tony. It's *our* home." The duchess spoke almost in a whisper, but she knew her husband heard every word.

"You may see your daughter whenever you like, my dear, but you will advise me of her visits in advance, so that I may arrange to be absent at those times."

She folded her arms and tapped one foot. "I'll do no such thing, your grace. Do you mean to banish her from our Christmas celebrations every year? Do you mean to deny yourself the pleasure of dangling Helena's children on your knee? Let me warn you that I will not tolerate such harsh treatment toward our daughter. If she makes a mistake in marrying Waverley, it is quite her own affair. You of all people ought to know better than to behave with such revenge."

"What do you mean?"

"You know very well what I mean. How can you be so hard on your daughter when your own record is so far from spotless?" The duchess whirled around and stalked out of the library, Helena's letter crumpled in her hand.

The duke stared after his wife, his eyes hard and unforgiving. He returned to his desk and wrote a brief answer to his daughter.

Chapter 26

Helena broke the seal on her father's letter and spread the single sheet out on her desk, but the only words that mattered leaped out at her: *You cannot disgrace your family by marrying a rake.* Her eyes blurred with tears as a knock on the door of her library caught her attention.

Without waiting for answer, Waverley strode in, but he stopped, the smile on his face disappearing when he saw her tears. "What's wrong, dear heart?"

Without a word, she held out the letter.

He glanced at it and flung it aside. "Hell and damnation! The sins of my past persist in punishing me. Perhaps I've earned your father's contempt, but you haven't, my love."

"Let me assure you I've no intention of obeying his decree, Desmond dearest. It will have to be an elopement. Shall you mind very much?"

Waverley took her into his arms. She parted her lips for his kiss, a surprisingly light one. There was so much to say, yet neither spoke. They sat on the sofa, mute, like an old married pair who had run out of words. What was there left to say?

"My past haunts me. It always has and it always will. I've

learned to live with it, but I cannot ask it of you as well. If we marry, your family will disown you and the rest of society will ostracize you. I won't allow the woman I love to bear such a burden. We can't marry."

She raised her head from his shoulder. "You don't mean that!"

"I do mean it. You came into my life like a breath of fresh air. I'd do anything to make you happy, my love. But if I marry you, I ruin you. In time, you'd come to despise me for the loneliness and the isolation you shall be forced to endure."

"I don't care for that, Desmond. I care only for you. I'm disappointed with my father's decision, but I refuse to allow it to interfere with our happiness. Besides, it's not only you I love. I've come to love Waverley Castle and the people in Sennen Cove as well. You're a hero in their eyes in spite of your past. You're a hero in my eyes and that's enough for me."

He gave a harsh laugh. "A hero, you say? No, my love, I'm not a hero. This business is tearing me apart, Helena. You see simple solutions where I see endless problems. You were humiliated at Glynhaven's ball. I couldn't bear to see you suffer like that again. And what of our children? Will the sins of their father rain down upon them as well?"

"We love one another. That's all that matters."

"It isn't enough. Your father is a duke. He'll find a way to prevent us from reaching the border. He may even have put such a scheme in motion as we speak. What then?"

Helena's eyes flew open. "I hadn't thought of that, but knowing him as I do, I wouldn't put it past him to stoop to such a low trick. Perhaps, if we leave at once . . ."

"No, my darling. If your father succeeded, he'd drag you back to London, where I might be prevented from seeing you ever again."

"I shan't give you up. I shan't! You may be a rake, but you are *my* rake. You're welcome to hold orgies for all I care, but only *after* we marry."

The door flew open to admit Olivia, who had heard only

the last sentence. "Orgies? Are we to have one? What fun. I've never been to one. May Sebastian and I join you? Delightful notion," she said as she shut the door behind her.

Helena laughed in spite of her tears. "Thank God I have you to lift my battered spirits, Livy." She pointed an accusing finger at Waverley. "This . . . this *beast* refuses to marry me just because Father persists in being a stubborn mule."

Olivia's amused eyes gazed at her host. "As usual. Let me understand you, Waverley. Are you saying that a big man like you is afraid of a little old duke? I find that hard to believe."

Without a word, Waverley retrieved the duke's letter and handed it to Olivia. She read it quickly and stared at him in astonishment. "What has this to do with anything? Do you love my sister?"

"With all my heart."

"Then let us put our heads together and think of a way to change Father's mind. *I* became a spy in spite of his opposition, didn't I?"

Helena brightened. "Oh, Livy, do you think . . . ?"

"I do, indeed. Dry your tears, love. You shall marry your rake, orgies and all."

Lighter of heart for the first time that day, Waverley said, "Sebastian is lucky to have you for his wife, ma'am."

"Certainly. And I never let him forget it, sir," she retorted, her eyes filled with mischief.

Noting the time, Helena said, "Come with me, Livy. Help me change for dinner. The marchioness sent word she's preparing to join us this evening."

Waverley held the door for them, his eyes on Helena until she disappeared from his sight.

The sisters climbed the staircase to Helena's chamber arm in arm. Livy helped her dress, for Amy was still at Ship Inn nursing Casper. "We'll find a way, I promise you. Hand me your hairbrush."

"I waver between hope and despair. Father's dug his heels in, a sign of his stubbornness."

Livy laughed. "Father does not have the advantage of my excellent spy training. The need for a little espionage turns up in the oddest places, don't you think?" She stepped back to admire her work. "There. You look presentable so long as everyone politely ignores your red eyes. Shall we go?"

The sisters found the marquis and his grandmother already in the drawing room when they entered. After they exchanged greetings, the dowager lost no time in getting to the point.

"My grandson informs me that your father has refused his consent once again. What are you prepared to do about it?"

Olivia brightened, understanding that the dowager had an interest in the business. She could very well turn out to be a useful ally. "These two lost souls are wallowing in despair, ma'am."

"Then we must find a way to rescue them!" The dowager's eyes fired up with determination. "There's always a way, you know. What we must do is change that stubborn curmudgeon's mind."

"I couldn't agree more, ma'am," said Olivia cordially.

Helena looked into Waverley's eyes and said, "I won't give you up."

"Why should you, my dear?" The dowager turned to her grandson. "Desmond, come here."

"Yes, Grandmother?" He knelt by her chair and took her hand.

"You must go to London at once and persuade the duke to change his mind."

"He's already turned me down, love."

"No matter. Tell that ridiculous Indian of yours to pack your things. If you leave at first light, you'll reach London in two, three days at the most."

The marchioness reached out for Helena's hand. "Don't worry, my dear. I'm determined to see you wed to my grandson.

Worthless in your father's eyes though he may be, he is certainly not worthless in mine." She turned to Waverley and added, "And when you plead your case, grandson, be sure to remind the duke that your grandmother not only approves, but desires it."

"Do you know my father, ma'am?" asked Helena.

A mysterious smile lit the old woman's face. "Better than you think, my dear."

Hope in his eyes, her grandson kissed her hand. He turned to a footman and said, "Go and tell Rabu to pack my portmanteau. Tell him he is to accompany me to London. And send word to the stable to ready my curricle and my fastest horses. We leave for London at dawn."

Helena allowed herself the luxury of renewed hope. *The dowager knows something she's not telling us. Will it be enough to change Father's mind?* "Will you take a letter to my mother as well, Desmond? I'll write it later tonight."

"If I'm to leave at first light, you must all excuse me, for I need a good night's sleep. I bid you all good night," Waverley said after tea was served.

Waverley was almost asleep when Helena entered his chamber, her letter to her mother in hand. She set the letter down on the table and removed her dressing gown. Desmond's eyes turned smoky as he feasted on the sweet sight before his eyes, for she wore nothing underneath. "Temptress! You're making it impossible for me to wait till our wedding night, you know."

She lifted the covers and climbed in next to him. "Have you forgotten? We've already had our wedding night. It remains only for me to bear our child, but I can't do that without your help. Shall we begin?"

He laughed. "The last time you climbed into my bed, you

wretch, I was asleep and you thought I was someone else. I'm fully awake now."

"So much the better."

Her lips rained soft kisses all over his face, but her hands were by no means idle. His nipples turned hard under her caresses, which brought a smile. "You like that, my rake? And what of this?"

Her hair brushed his chest, a mere whisper as she bent to kiss his navel, but when she moved lower, he stopped her and groaned. "Where did you learn such sinful tricks, vixen?"

"Don't you like it? I rather thought you would." She feathered her fingers across his thighs. "How about this?" She continued to fondle him and he groaned. "Did your French alphabet ladies pleasure you as much as this? Alas, I should have asked them for advice before they were banished from England's shores. No matter. You can advise me. Am I pleasing you properly?"

"You've no need of advice from anyone, my darling. The pleasure's all mine, but you deserve a reward for your . . . er . . . diligence." He rose and turned her on her back.

"Shall I please you thus?" He took her nipple in his mouth and she gasped. "Or thus?" He buried his tongue deep inside her mouth.

His hand spread her legs apart and found her wet with desire. He stopped a moment, his eyes feasting on her, his ears listening to her quickened breathing.

"Don't stop, Desmond," she moaned. To urge him on, she raked his back with her fingernails.

"You are God's work of art, my love. Allow me a moment to admire His creation."

"But only a moment," she pleaded. "I need my reward."

He barked a laugh. "You are a lusty treasure, my love." His lips found the place he knew would drive her wild. "And besides, I never had the urge to do this to any one of my alphabet soup courtesans, I promise you."

Helena arched her back when his tongue teased that most vulnerable spot. "Desmond! Wh . . . what are you d . . . doing?"

He raised his head and grinned at her. "Be quiet, shrew! This is no time for words. Can't you see I'm busy?"

She lost all thought under his merciless assault, writhing and arching her back to meet his attack, wanting more, wanting all he had to give. When waves of ecstasy ripped through her, she shouted for the sheer joy of release.

Desmond lifted himself to reach her lips, his kiss muffling her screams. His body was slick with sweat, mingling, as it were, with hers. Her shudders of release welcomed his entrance, but he slowed deliberately, savoring the extravagance of her response. Her spasms of lust met his every thrust with reckless abandon until he could hold back no longer and his shudders of release met her own. He rolled onto his side at last, his breath pulsating rapidly.

When her heartbeat slowed enough to allow speech, she said, "So this is what it feels like to be made love to by a rake."

"You have it all wrong, my love. A true rake thinks only of his own pleasure when he has a woman in his bed. If you must know, just now my only thought was how best to please my precious raven." He glanced at the clock on the mantel. "I think you'd better return to your room, dear heart. You must allow me a little time to sleep before I leave for London."

"Must I go so soon?" She laid her head on his chest, but her hands were busy. "Oh dear!" Her hand caressed his engorged member. "How can I leave you at a time like this?"

"Good God, Helena! Enough! You'll be the death of me yet!"

London

When his second plea to the duke fell on deaf ears, Waverley returned to Sebastian's home where he was a guest, and ordered Rabu to pack and be ready to start for Land's End in the morning.

"As usual, your father-in-law refused me," Waverley told Sebastian as soon as he returned from the home office that evening. "I leave in the morning."

"Bad luck, Waverley. I'm sorry."

"I can't marry Helena now. The duke will disown her and I can't let that happen no matter how much she protests that it doesn't matter. It bloody well *does* matter, but she refuses to see that. I'm going abroad again just as soon as I can arrange proper care for my grandmother. It's the only way I can think of to make Helena forget she ever knew me."

"Don't bother to rush back to Waverley Park. I've had a letter from my wife. She and Helena have gone to Bodmin Castle. They've arranged for Vicar Cullum's wife to stay with your grandmother until you return."

"A good choice. Grandmother is fond of Mrs. Cullum."

Sebastian eyed the marquis quizzically.

"What's the matter, Brooks?"

"What's all this about orgies? My wife writes that I must ask you."

Waverley laughed. "Your wife's jest. She overheard a chance remark and implored me to arrange an orgy and invite you both. She has a wicked sense of humor, Brooks."

"The wretch! She'd jump at the chance, too. You won't oblige her, will you?"

"Of course not. I left those wild pursuits in Paris."

London: Heatham House

"For the last time, Ellen, I cannot allow that scandalous rake to wed Helena. Such a marriage will be the ruin of her, I tell you. She forgot Darlington quickly enough, didn't she? She'll get over this suitor as well."

"You are making a mistake you will live to regret, your grace," said the duchess icily.

He glared at his wife. "You only call me 'your grace' when you're angry, but you won't change my mind. You must allow me to know what is best for my daughter. Tying herself to a rake for the rest of her life won't do, I tell you. I love her too much to submit her to the censure and the isolation she will have to face."

"Let me remind you that Helena comes of age in August. She won't need your approval then."

"Perhaps not, but if she marries Waverley, she will lose the acceptance of the polite world as well as her family, for I shall disown her."

"You may do as you please, but I can never disown my daughter. It isn't in a mother's power, but I don't expect you to understand that. Good night." She turned the handle to the door of her husband's bedchamber.

He watched in silence as the woman he loved slammed shut the door between their chambers. He heard the click of the lock quite clearly.

When the duke descended the stairs the next morning, his eyes were heavy from lack of sleep, but they flew wide open when they met with an unexpected sight, for the hallway was littered with portmanteaus and trunks. A bevy of servants carried even more belongings from the direction of the back staircase. He sought out his butler. "What's all this, Dunston?"

"Her grace and the children are removing to Bodmin Castle," the butler said, unprepared for his grace's lack of knowledge of this event. He carefully hid his surprise at the question.

The duke's good breeding caused him to show no outward signs of distress at this terrible news. Instead, he asked casually, "Where is her grace?"

"In the breakfast room, your grace."

The duke turned and made his way there without another word. He entered to find his wife in the process of eating her customary breakfast of toast with jam and strong tea.

"Good morning, your grace," she said in an arctic tone of voice.

The duke dismissed the attending footmen with a wave of his hand. "I don't approve of your hasty departure, Ellen. Georgiana's debut ball is only weeks away. You must stay home and attend to the details."

The duchess put her toast down. "Are you forbidding me to go, your grace?"

"No. I'm merely suggesting . . ."

She took a sip of tea, wiped her mouth with her napkin, folded her hands in her lap, and raised eyes filled with fury to her husband. "My daughter Helena is in distress. She needs her mother. Now, if you'll excuse me, I must gather the girls. I'm taking the children with me. I mean to take advantage of daylight travel. We leave within the hour."

His tone did nothing to mask his wretchedness. "Don't punish me like this, Ellen, my love. I'm only doing what I think is right for my daughter."

"And *I'm* only doing what *I* think is right for *my* daughter, your grace. However, you may put your mind at ease on one point. Your daughters and I will return in time for Georgiana's ball."

He attempted to lighten the mood. "At least I'll have my grandson to keep me company."

"No, you won't, your grace. He and his nurse are coming with us. The child needs his mother."

His face fell and he changed the subject. "Will Helena return for the ball, do you think?"

"I have no idea."

Chapter 27

"Lord Fairchild, your grace," announced Dunston, but the duke's younger brother was hard on his heels.

"Come in, Charles. I was never more glad to see you in my life."

The vicar took in the troubled signs writ large on the duke's pale face. "You look like the very devil, Tony. What's the matter?" The duke never sent for him unless he found himself in trouble.

"Ellen has taken the children and gone away," the duke said.

"Why?"

"We've had a terrible row. She's furious with me."

"Your wife has put up with your stormy tantrums for years without so much as raising her voice. What have you done this time to earn her displeasure?"

"It's my daughter Helena. She wants to marry a notorious rake, the Marquis of Waverley, and I refuse to give my consent."

"Helena is in love with the marquis, I take it?"

The duke sighed in exasperation. "You remember Darlington, the lad next door, don't you? Helena hectored me to distraction about her great love for him only to cry off in the end. My foolish child falls in and out of love with disturbing regularity," the duke added bitterly.

"Helena and your wife do not agree with your decision to withhold your blessing, I take it."

"I'm only doing what I think best for my daughter. Am I not her father? It is my duty to see to it that she doesn't ruin her life." His voice cracked on the last word. "She's fallen in love with the wrong man again, Charles. What shall I do?"

The vicar poured brandy into two glasses, measuring out a small amount for himself and filling his brother's glass to the brim. "For a start, you must pull yourself together. Drink this, Tony and let me hear the whole of it."

When he heard the full tale, he said, "Have you sent for me to give my stamp of approval for the position you've taken, Tony?"

"You're my brother. Where else can I turn, if not to you?"

The vicar fell silent for a time, as if searching for a diplomatic way to answer this question. "I'm flattered that you seek my advice, but I can't support you in this, Tony. Not when I have a strong suspicion that you are in the wrong. Are you prepared to listen to some sound advice, or are you just going to wallow in pity and whine like a petulant child?"

"Harsh words from you of all people, dear brother. I had hoped for some solace. A vicar surely knows how to ease the pain of a tortured soul, does he not?"

"A vicar is not required to prevaricate to ease the pain of a tortured soul when he believes him to be in the wrong. If that's all you desire, convert to Catholicism and confess your sins to a priest. He'll absolve you with a recommendation to say a few Hail Marys or something like to cleanse your soul."

The duke glared at him, but he saw something in his younger brother's eyes that melted his heart and he burst out laughing. "Damn you, Charles. You've always been able to coax a laugh out of me. Can you imagine me fumbling with rosary beads?"

"That's better! All that remains is for you to give orders to pack your things."

"Pack my things? Why?"

"You're going to Bodmin to straighten out this whole family mess."

"You'll come with me?"

His brother sighed. "I suppose I have no choice. Seems I can't trust you on your own, big brother. I can't allow you to muck things up with your high-handed ways."

London: The Home Office

"What are you doing here, Hugh?" asked Sebastian.

The spymaster grinned. "Try saying hello before you pepper me with questions, my friend. Classes have ended for this session and the home secretary sent for me to review the plans for graduation next month."

"Sorry, my friend. How are you?"

"Never better. How is your family?"

"Olivia is fine. She's at Bodmin Castle with her sister. And little Tony's on his way there with his grandmother as we speak."

"Bodmin, eh? The scene of your triumph, I recall. That's where you wooed and won Olivia."

"I couldn't have won her hand without your help. I'm taking some time off to . . . how would you like to come with me, Hugh? I'd be glad for the company and Livy would be delighted to see you again. Matter of fact," Sebastian added with a bit of mischief, "the whole family's taken up temporary residence there. Someone else besides my wife would be delighted to renew her acquaintance with you."

"Are you trying your hand at matchmaking?"

Sebastian laughed. "You'd have to catch her first. Georgiana's just turned seventeen, a stunning beauty, Hugh. She asks after you every time we meet. How about joining me?"

"If I won't be in the way?"

"Nonsense. You'd be most welcome."

"Then I'd be delighted. I have some free time. When are we leaving?"

Waverley Castle

"Welcome home, my lord," said the butler taking Waverley's greatcoat.

"How is my grandmother, Paynter?"

"Her ladyship is well, my lord. You will find her resting in her chamber."

Waverley took the stairs two at a time. He opened her door quietly, reluctant to wake her, but she was sitting up in bed, a book in her hand.

"Desmond!" the dowager said in happy surprise. "I missed you. Come here and let me look at you."

He kissed her cheek. "You look radiant, love. I've missed you as well." He took the seat opposite her, still holding her hand.

The dowager searched his face, guessing by the despair she saw that all had not gone as she had hoped in London. She turned to her nurse and dismissed her with a nod. "We are quite alone, my dear. Something tells me you met with resistance from the duke. Tell me the whole of it."

He rose and paced back and forth, deep lines forming on his forehead.

"Take your time, dear. Shall I ring for some brandy?"

"No. I'll do it." He rang and gave the order to a servant. While he waited, he unbuttoned his vest and loosened his neck cloth. He pulled his chair closer to his grandmother and gripped its arms so tight, his knuckles turned white, yet he did not speak until the servant had returned.

"Better?" his grandmother asked when he had downed his first glass.

He smiled at her. "Somewhat, but brandy doesn't do enough to ease the pain I feel. I dread having to tell Helena that her father continues to spurn my suit."

"That hypocrite! What reason did the duke give this time? Be precise, Desmond."

As if to cleanse his soul, his bitter words tumbled out in a rush. "The duke was adamant, Grandmother. Nothing I said would change his mind. 'Once a rake, always a rake,' he said. He's right, you know. The *ton* will treat Helena as an outcast if she marries me. I can't do that to her, Grandmother. She's suffered enough pain from their vicious tongues. There's nothing left for me to do but give up the woman I love." He drew in his breath. "I've decided that it's best, for her sake, to leave the country as soon as I can arrange for a suitable companion to care for you. It's the only way. She'll need time to forget me."

The dowager rolled her eyes in exasperation. "Leave the country? Give Helena time to forget you? What nonsense. Have you lost all your senses?"

He took her hands in his. "No, I haven't. This act is the only unselfish thing I have ever done, dearest. And I do it for love of her. I'm determined not to destroy her life. Her father is right. Can't you see that?"

"Her father is wrong! You'll do no such thing! If you think I'll let you go after all the years I've suffered without you, think again, my dear. Is the duchess in London?"

"The duchess and her children are on their way to Bodmin

Castle to be at Helena's side in her time of need. I'm glad, for it will soften the blow for her."

The dowager rose from her seat. "Ring for a footman and send word to Cook. We dine early tonight."

"Why? Are you not feeling well, Grandmother?"

"Never better. You'll need a decent night's sleep if you are to leave for Bodmin Castle in the morning."

"What purpose would that serve?" he asked wearily.

"If the duchess has left London with her children, I have a strong suspicion that she and his grace do not share the same opinion on the question of your suit for Helena's hand. If I'm any judge of character, the duchess is likely to take your side. Have you forgotten that I am her grace's godmother? We women don't think like men, my dear. We're much more sensible. Humor your grandmother and summon Mrs. Hubley to help me dress for dinner. I have a great deal to reveal to you, my boy. I've never told anyone, for I don't hold with gossiping. Nor do I hold with scandalmongers. They cause too much pain with their vicious tongues."

Waverley was alarmed by the uncharacteristic anger in his grandmother's voice. "Calm yourself, dear. It won't do for you to be upset over this, Grandmother."

"So that charlatan thinks he can turn my grandson's suit for his daughter's hand down, does he? Not if I have anything to do with the matter!"

Mevagissy: Bodmin Castle

Olivia lifted her head, distracted for a moment by a familiar, yet unexpected sound. "I hear a carriage coming."

Helena put down her book and went to the window of the first-floor drawing room, idly wondering who would be coming to visit them this late in the afternoon.

As the sound grew louder, Olivia joined her at the window. The sisters exchanged puzzled glances, their eyes trained on the long driveway. "Sounds like a whole army," Olivia said drily. "Are we under attack, do you think?"

"I see two carriages, Livy."

"There's a third coming round the bend."

"I count four in all, Livy."

They looked at one another as the truth dawned on them. "Can't be anyone else, can it?"

"Mother!" the sisters shouted in unison and raced out the door.

The cacophonous noise of a large family greeting one another after a prolonged absence was like an orchestra tuning its instruments before a concert. Most welcome, but discordant. With a silent nod from the butler, several footmen hurried down the steps to open all carriage doors and assist their inhabitants to descend the steps, others to help in the unloading and transfer of baggage to their proper chambers.

Lord Edward, the last to disembark, reached in for the baby and handed him to his sister. "Take your brat and good riddance, Livy. I have the headache because this popinjay did not shut his mouth for a moment." Before he relinquished his nephew to his sister he whirled him around, to the infant's delighted shouts of laughter.

As for Helena, she dissolved into tears at the sight of her mother and wrapped her arms around her. "You can't know how glad I am to see you, Mother."

"I too, dearest. We must make some time to talk privately."

"I'll come to your chamber after you've had a chance to rest, dearest."

She turned to her sister Georgiana and held her at arm's length to admire her. "I feel like an old crone next to you, Georgie. How is it you grow more beautiful by the day?"

"Georgie primps at her mirror all day long. That's how," said Jane pettishly.

"Have you been spying on your sister again, brat? Try eating less and exercising more and you're bound to grow even prettier than Georgie," Helena said.

Mary looked upon the scene with delight, but her shyness prevented her from joining in the merriment. She was forced to leave London without her tutor, Maestro Bartoli, for he was occupied with his own examinations at the London Philharmonic Society. But he had provided her with enough instruction to keep her at the pianoforte practicing for hours. She couldn't wait to begin.

"Lord Waverley is no longer an irresponsible rake, Mother," Helena said once they were alone. "I'll tell you how good a man he is. When the marquis and I first arrived at Waverley Castle, it was in a terrible state. He's worked very hard to correct the damage done by his traitorous cousins, the Traskers. They're the ones who helped the Earl of Glynhaven try to abduct me. If it weren't for the fact that the marquis sent for Livy and Sebastian, I would be wedded to the earl, an unwilling slave of the cruelest master in creation."

Her mother hugged her. "We must thank God as well, my dear. When shall I meet this paragon of yours?"

"I don't know where he is at the moment. I do know that I won't give the marquis up, Mother. If I did, it would destroy both our lives."

The duchess smiled. "You're as stubborn as your father, my child. Come to think of it, with the exception of gentle Mary, all his children seem to have inherited this unfortunate trait. If only he recognized it. No matter. At any rate, it's not yet time to worry, my pet. Be assured you have my support." The duchess rang for her abigail. "Allow me to dress for dinner. Afterward, you must tell me all about my godmother."

Chapter 28

Wednesday, the Twentieth of May, 1818
Waverley Castle

Waverley barked a laugh with a twinge of bitterness when his grandmother finished speaking. "Short of holding a pistol to his head, I don't quite know what to do with what you've just told me about the duke's past." He had dismissed the footmen after dinner and they were alone.

The dowager reached for a sweetmeat. "Do? There's only one thing you can do, my foolish child. For one, stop acting like a schoolboy mooning over the loss of his first love—especially since you've already had the pleasure of such an experience—and begin behaving like you ought. Remember that you are the Fourth Marquis of Waverley. In short, stop your pouting and start acting like a man."

"I'll do anything you say, Grandmother, but I won't hurt Helena by ruining her reputation. I love her with my very soul and I know she loves me. You see that, don't you? But I'm in despair and my mind is empty of solutions. You must advise me, Grandmother. I'm counting on you." Something in her countenance raised his spirits. "You have a scheme in mind, don't you? I can see it in your eyes. That gives me hope."

The dowager leaned forward and patted his hand. "Are you prepared to follow my advice?" When he nodded, she continued. "You will leave for Bodmin Castle tomorrow morning. If I'm not mistaken, that scoundrel is on his way there already."

"Why? What reason would he have to go to Bodmin?"

"Tony Fairchild cannot face life without his wife at his side. It isn't in his nature, especially after . . . never mind. They've had a row over this business. Depend upon it. The duke will crawl after her with his tail between his legs, so to speak."

"Grandmother!" he said as if shocked. But there was laughter in his eyes.

She grinned. "You are about to meet my godchild. When you do meet her, you will understand. Tonight I shall write a letter to my goddaughter and tomorrow you shall deliver it to her in person. It will be all the ammunition that you'll need to shoot that rogue in the neck, believe me."

Waverley could not contain his elation, for she had lightened his heart of the burden of sadness he'd carried with him all the way home from London. "I'm so blessed to have you on my side, dearest. Not only as a grandmother, but as the very best of friends."

She made as if to rise, and he rose to help her. "Thank you, Desmond." She raised a finger and said, "One more thing before I retire to write my letter to Ellen. The wedding must be performed right here in your ancestral castle. Insist upon it when you enter the lion's den. I know that scoundrel will try to bully you, for he cannot help himself, but you must stand firm in order to earn his respect. If you don't stand up to that tyrant now, you will come to regret it later. He'll ride roughshod over you if you let him. He may be a duke, but you are a marquis, and don't you forget it. There. I've given you enough ammunition in your arsenal to challenge him with."

"Will you not come with me, dearest?"

She patted his arm and smiled. "No. You must fight this battle on your own, my dear. Be brave, be firm, be proud and all will be well, I promise you."

Mevagissy: Bodmin Castle

Helena's spirits rose with the unexpected arrival of the Marquis of Waverley. She had confessed to her mother only the night before her fear that she might be in danger of losing him. He might return to the life he'd lived in Paris. She'd seen firsthand the attention paid him by courtesans only too eager to lavish their brand of love on him.

She had been sitting in the gazebo in the garden when he'd startled her. He touched her shoulder and murmured in her ear, "Hello, my love."

Helena's despair turned to joy. She rose and threw her arms around him. "You've come! How glad I am you're here, my handsome cavalier. Don't leave me again no matter what."

His kiss was one of reassuring tenderness, but he stopped before it turned to passion. "Did you really believe I would give up so easily? Is that what you think of my resolve, foolish woman? I can't, you know. You've crawled under my skin. I forget to breathe when you are not at my side."

"Father isn't here, darling, but he's expected. What can you say to him you haven't already said?"

"Is this your marquis?" Jane asked, interrupting them.

Desmond let go of Helena and turned to examine a full-bodied young girl with a mischievous twinkle in her eyes. "And who might you be, pretty lady?"

"I'm Jane, Helena's sister. Never mind me, though. No one else in this family ever does."

"They don't? How foolish of them, for never have I seen a

more ravishing beauty." He turned to Helena and protested, "How dare you hide this mysterious beauty from me."

Helena checked her laugh at Jane's blush. "Jane's my baby sister. She manages to pop up when you least expect her."

"I'm not snooping. I've been sent," Jane objected in an injured tone. "I came to remind you it's time to change for dinner." She turned as if to leave, but Waverley caught her arm.

He kissed her hand and bowed to her. "I am the Marquis of Waverley, come to court your sister Helena. But she might not have me. If she spurns me, I'll offer for you. Will you have me instead, Lady Jane?"

"Silly!" She giggled and ran away.

Waverley quickly changed into evening clothes, for he had arranged an audience with her grace. She agreed to receive him in her private study fifteen minutes before the rest of the family was to meet for cocktails in the drawing room.

He knocked on the door of her sitting room and entered. "Thank you for agreeing to see me, your grace," murmured Waverley when she rose from her chair and came toward him. He took the hand she offered and put his lips to it.

"We meet at last, my lord. I've so looked forward to it," she said with her customary poise.

"I've a letter for you from my grandmother, your grace." He reached into his vest pocket and withdrew it.

"From my godmother? How kind of her to write. Will you excuse me while I read it?" She sat at her desk and broke the seal. It took her only a few moments to read the dowager's brief note. She turned to Waverley and waved him to a chair.

"Please sit, sir. Let me tell you that your grandmother and I are in full agreement concerning this match. She wants for her grandson precisely what I want for my daughter

Helena, and that is a lifetime of happiness. Don't even think about disappointing us, young man."

"I pledge my life on it, your grace," he said with more cheerfulness than he felt.

"Good! Then it remains for you to follow your grand-mother's advice and petition the duke once more."

"Will he change his mind, do you think, your grace?"

"We'll have to wait and see, son. Won't we?"

Two days of boisterous family sport passed, no one more delighted at the antics of the Fairchild clan than the marquis, who grew up an only child. He rode with Edward in the morning, played card games with Jane in the afternoon, dandled little Tony on his knee and listened raptly to Mary as she played flawlessly in the evening.

On the third afternoon of Waverley's arrival, two more guests on horseback joined them. "Sir Brooks and Mr. Denville have arrived, your grace," announced the butler.

"Show them in at once, Buxton," she said to the Bodmin butler.

Olivia turned in surprise when the door opened. "Sebastian!" she shouted and ran to him. "Hugh? What brings you here, my friend?"

"Just a visit. Your husband begged me to accompany him."

Sebastian wasted no time in picking up his son and cover-ing his face with kisses.

"Dada," said the child.

"He knows me!"

The women laughed, aware that this was the only intelligi-ble word the child spoke, whatever the occasion.

Livy said, "Tony certainly does know his father, my love. He gets smarter by the day."

"And larger. What are you feeding him, wife?"

With the exception of Georgiana, who was occupied with her brother and Lord Waverley in a game of billiards, the women were in the drawing room, for it was raining. Jane sat on the floor playing with her nephew Tony, Mary played the pianoforte softly while Olivia and Helena sorted out the silk colors for their mother's needlework.

"Brooks," greeted Waverley when he, Georgiana and Edward entered the room.

Sebastian shook his hand. "Come and meet my good friend, Hugh Denville." He turned to him. "This is the Marquis of Waverley, Hugh. He was responsible for the capture of the smugglers."

"My compliments . . ." Before Denville could finish, a pair of delicate hands covered his eyes and he grinned. "If I'm forced to guess, these must be the hands of my dear friend Lady Georgiana."

"How did you know, you odious wretch? You haven't seen me in years." She let go and turned him around to face her. "Well? What have you to say to that, Denville?"

"You exaggerate. It's only been one year, milady. My, how you've grown."

"Like what you see?" She turned seductively, shocking her mother.

"Georgiana! Behave yourself!"

Georgie's laugh pierced Denville's heart.

"Denville doesn't mind my banter. He's practically family, Mother."

"Your daughter's full of mischief, isn't she, your grace? I give you my word, I'll not take advantage of her antics." Yet in spite of his promise, her astonishing beauty turned his knees to jelly.

"You won't have to, my friend, for I've met the man of my dreams and I plan to marry him. Care for a game of billiards,

Denville? Come along, then." The saucy minx turned and looked over her shoulder. "I dare you!"

The duchess frowned at Georgiana's shocking flirtation but said nothing. Her daughter's latest paramour, Viscount Willard Ardmore, had the reputation of being as wild as her daughter. She dearly hoped the attraction would not last and that Georgie would move on to someone more suitable. Someone like Hugh Denville, perhaps. He had about him a sober quality. She wondered if he was strong enough to keep her mischievous daughter out of the rakehell pranks she was so fond of pursuing.

The duchess could never get her fill of the joy she felt in her children's boisterous presence, though she suspected that her spouse stubbornly refused to understand a mother's love for her children. How unfortunate for him that he could not share in her joy. All at once the duchess felt alone in spite of a roomful of her children. She wondered how she would manage to survive the rest of her life at the side of such a stubborn mule.

Her grace's worry was to be put to the test the next morning, with the arrival of the duke and his brother Charles.

Chapter 29

Saturday, the Twenty-third of May, 1818

The duke knocked and entered his wife's chamber. She turned to him as if surprised. "Good morning, your grace." Her tone was welcoming, but only for the sake of her abigail's loose tongue. The duchess dismissed the woman with a nod. "What are you doing here?"

"I've missed you, Ellen."

"Why have you come, Tony?"

"Unfinished business, my dear. On the advice of Charles, I wish to settle it. He's come with me."

She gave a short laugh, but there was no humor in it. "Are you such a coward you need your brother along for moral support?"

"You might say that. If it's any solace to you, he doesn't agree with me either, Ellen."

"Remind me to commend him for his good sense, then."

She was not making it easy for him. The duke yearned to loosen his neck cloth but he let it pass. "I understand that the Marquis of Waverley is staying here. How is this?"

"Have you forgotten that his grandmother is my godmother?

He's brought me a letter from her." She added with continued defiance, "The marquis is a guest in my home. What's more, my children have made him feel as one of the family."

The duke winced at being left out of the picture. "*Our* home, Ellen. *Our* children. Need I remind you that I have their best interests at heart?"

"Tell that to Helena why don't you," she snapped.

He hadn't sunk this low in his wife's esteem in years. "I didn't mean . . ."

"It no longer matters to me what you mean. I was about to send for you, in fact. Lord Waverley is anxious to meet with you. He'll welcome your arrival, even if I won't."

The duke proceeded to sink even lower in the quagmire he'd created for himself. "Must I grant him yet another audience?"

"You may do whatever you please, your grace. However, he is a guest in my home and I expect you to treat him as such."

"Your anger wounds me, Ellen. Can you not find it in your heart to forgive me?"

She gave this some thought. "You will have to settle for civility, your grace. The children need not know that their parents are at such odds. Let us join them for breakfast."

He offered his arm, half expecting another rebuff, but she took it. "My godmother was a much-sought-after beauty in her day," she remarked amiably, more for the sake of the servants in the hall. It was well known that servants were the eyes and the ears of a large household and did not hesitate to spread the family gossip. "Did you know that my uncle offered for her? She might have been my aunt, but she chose to marry the Marquis of Waverley instead."

"Yes, I recall thinking her a great beauty. I saw her many times at Almack's and the usual entertainments during the Season, but I was presented to her only once when I was a mere lad. I liked her, you know."

"All the more reason to grant her grandson his request."

When they reached the breakfast room, the boisterous din that greeted them was music to the duke's ears, for he sorely missed his family. Even better was the warm welcome he received from his children.

"Go to him," Waverley urged Helena.

She rose at once and pecked her father on the cheek. "Morning, Father. I'm glad you've come."

This unexpected welcome stunned the duke. He clasped her to him for a moment, swallowed the lump in his throat and demanded, "Where's my grandson?"

"Send for the baby," Olivia said with a smile.

Sebastian grinned at his wife. "Already done, love. Nurse is on her way with Tony."

"Good morning, your grace," the marquis said affably as he rose to offer his hand. "Delighted to see you again."

All eyes turned to the duke. The Fairchild children took family secrets in their stride. Naturally, they knew everything.

Aware he was being watched for signs of his well-known temper, the duke confounded his children by saying pleasantly, "How are you, Waverley? Welcome to Bodmin Castle. Will you join me after breakfast, sir?"

"My pleasure, your grace." The table fell into uncomfortable silence at this exchange, but the duke was saved from further discomfort by the entrance of his beloved grandson.

"Dada!" gurgled the infant with outstretched arms.

The duke's eyes lit up. "He knows my name!" He took the infant from his nurse and nuzzled him, whereupon the seven-month-old's unintelligible conversation replaced the awkward silence.

Waverley took the opportunity to add, "Would you rather we postpone our talk until this afternoon, your grace? I think your grandson takes priority."

"Good of you, Waverley. Join me in the library this afternoon at two." His outward calm did not betray his inner dread of the meeting with the marquis. The duke feared it might not be a pleasant encounter.

That afternoon, like birds falling eerily silent before a hurricane, the servants were hushed. Two under maids polished the library table and dusted the chairs. Footmen carried wood in and lit a roaring fire in the enormous fireplace, for the library was habitually cold due to the doors leading to the terrace. These caused a constant draft despite the duke's best efforts to cure this affliction.

Opposite the fireplace, a wall of books rose the full height of the room, accessible by a ladder that ran smoothly on a track above the balcony. The sturdy ladder had been a favorite glider for the Fairchild children when they were still in the schoolroom, though not a one of them showed interest in reading the books.

"Don't lose your temper, dear brother," warned the vicar. "No matter how much you believe the marquis is trying to provoke you."

"Provoke me? He wouldn't dare do such a thing."

Charles laughed. "Try for some common sense, duke. You've as much as insulted his title by refusing his suit for your daughter's hand. That's enough of a reason for his anger."

"I haven't changed my position, you know."

The vicar threw up his hands. "The more fool you, then. You are swimming against the tide. Can't you see that Waverley and Helena adore one another? I strongly suspect that you'll not win this battle."

"Remains to be seen," he muttered.

"You have my sympathy, but not my respect." His brother rose to leave.

"Where are you going?" the duke asked in alarm. "I begged you to come with me to lend your support."

"I cannot support you when I do not agree with you. I've already told you that. You are on your own in this ordeal, brother duke. I'm off to change into riding clothes. Edward has challenged me to a race across the moors."

"Traitor," he grumbled, stared into the fire and brooded about the difficult task ahead of him, but he did not have long to wait before a knock on the door brought the marquis.

"Welcome," he said with false heartiness.

Waverley paused to admire the room, well known to readers of English guidebooks. The Bodmin library was described as one of the greatest collections in all of England. "An impressive collection, your grace."

The duke motioned him to a seat opposite his own. "I wish I could take credit for my library, but that is far from the truth. My ancestors built this library in the sixteenth century. My only contribution to it is the employment of a dedicated curator who looks after the volumes, catalogs them and arranges for scholars to use the collection for their research."

"Have you read any of your books?" The twinkle in Waverley's eyes gave the mischief away and the duke laughed as Waverley had intended. "That's better, your grace. A laugh or two puts us on easier terms. Shall we get on with it?"

Georgiana was engaged in watching a friendly match between Sebastian and Denville in the billiard room. She awaited the outcome with eagerness, for she had challenged the winner. As she had hoped, it turned out to be Denville. She chalked up her cue, broke the rack and began to hit the balls into the pockets she named.

"You have an excellent eye, Miss Georgiana. Where did you learn to play so well?"

"The Fairchild women are famous for succeeding in all

their endeavors. Everything we do, we do well. Father insists upon it, in fact."

"I shudder to think what he might do should one of his children disappoint him."

She laughed. "Disappoint him? Unthinkable, sir. In our family, one never fails. Olivia didn't fail at your training academy, did she?"

"Far from it. She's a legend, you know. Your sister set such a high standard, the women who follow must work harder than the men to meet her record."

Georgiana's eyes flirted as she said, "You'd be surprised at the power we Fairchild women hold in our lovely little hands, Denville. I'd advise you to avoid our clutches."

In the drawing room, Mary, Olivia, Helena and the duchess kept busy. The only one without a useful occupation was Jane, who managed to irritate her mother and her sisters with incessant complaints of boredom.

"Come turn the pages for me," advised gentle Mary.

"Why should I? You know all the music by heart."

"Find an interesting book to read," suggested the duchess.

"There are no interesting books in this house!"

In lieu of the enormous library collection, Helena and Livy exchanged amused glances, but refrained from laughing, for that room was already in use, as everyone knew.

"What time is it, poppet?" asked Livy.

"It's five minutes later than the last time you asked me," Jane said with the annoyance of a bored child.

Helena said, "Why don't you see whether Georgiana and the men have finished their game of billiards?"

"They threw me out the last time you asked me to see if they were done. Besides, Georgie threatened to beat me with a cue stick if I showed my face again."

"For heaven's sake, Jane! Can't you find anything useful to occupy you?"

Her mother's rebuke brought tears to the child's eyes. Olivia put her silks down, rushed to Jane and wiped her tears away. "There, there, poppet. Don't cry. It's not your fault. We're all a bit on edge."

"Everyone thinks I'm too young to know what's going on, but I know what's bothering all of you all the same! Lord Waverley wants to marry Helena and Father won't permit it. And . . . and Lord Waverley's trying to talk some sense into Father, so there! I'm not so stupid as you all seem to think," she added, her nine-year-old jaw jutting out over her double chin.

"Have you been eavesdropping again, Jane?"

"I didn't have to eavesdrop, Mother. Even the lowliest servant knows what's going on in this family. Am I no better?" Jane's tears turned to bitter sobs.

Consumed with guilt, the duchess put her needlework down and held out her arms. "Come here, my child." She rocked the sobbing girl in her arms as if she were an infant.

Stretched to the limits of her patience as well, Helena burst out, "You're not the only unhappy one, Jane. If Father and the marquis don't conclude soon, I shall go mad. What could possibly be taking them so long?"

Helena's words had a strange effect on Olivia. "Jane?"

"Wha . . . what?" The child blew her nose in the cloth her mother held out for her.

"I've thought of an occupation that only you know how to do well. It may also do a great deal to help us ease our minds."

All eyes turned to Olivia. Even Mary stopped playing in order to listen.

"Can you peek into the library without being seen?"

"Livy!" said her mother, aghast at the thought of encouraging Jane to eavesdrop.

"Don't worry, Mother. Jane won't be able to hear a word. The terrace doors are much too thick." She turned to her little sister and added, "Come back and describe to us what you see. Are they talking? Are they angry? Are they sitting? Are they . . ."

Jane's eyes glowed with eagerness. "I know. You want me to be a spy just like you."

"Exactly so, but you must be sure to remain out of sight. If Father catches you, he will be very angry with the lot of us."

"Be right back," she said and flew out of the room with surprising agility.

Chapter 30

Later . . .

With Jane out of the way, the duchess and her daughters resumed their tasks, but not for long. Jane returned not ten minutes later.

"What have you to report, poppet?" asked Olivia.

"I could not hear a word, and I couldn't see Father's face, but I saw Father waving his arms. He looked very angry to me."

Mary stopped playing. The duchess put her needlework down. Curiosity took the place of her usual calm and she asked, "What was the marquis doing, Jane?"

"I could see him better because he was facing the terrace. He was listening to Father, but he didn't say anything."

Helena voiced her worst fear. "Did the marquis appear to be angry, Jane?"

"That was the odd thing. He didn't seem at all angry. He tilted his head like this." The child illustrated. "If Father were angry with me, I would have been terrified. But the marquis had this little smile on his face even though his lips weren't moving."

"Clever man," murmured Olivia.

Helena, who had the greatest interest in the outcome, said,

"Good work, Jane. Go back again and tell us what's happening now. Do you mind?"

Her young sister beamed, her sense of self-importance elevated in her family's eyes. She ran to the door, turned and said, "Be right back."

"What's wrong with Jane," asked Georgiana upon entering the drawing room. "Where's the brat going in such a hurry? She nearly knocked me down."

Olivia accepted a kiss on the cheek from her husband. "We've sent Jane on an important errand. Who won the billiards match?"

"Your sister did," answered Denville with a grin. He put one hand on Georgiana's shoulder. "I've never seen a more skilled player. I don't know how she does it, but your daughter put me to shame, your grace."

The duchess grinned at this. "The last time they played billiards, she beat her father. Ever since then, he manages to find a host of excuses to avoid a rematch."

Amid much laughter, the door opened to admit Jane. "Oh. You're all here." Unsure, she turned to Olivia, her eyes pleading for direction.

"It's all right, Jane. Everyone knows what you're about. Tell us what you saw."

"Well, I could see only the back of Father's head. He nodded from time to time, so I don't think he was doing the talking. Father was seated with his legs crossed, but his arms weren't waving like they were before."

"What was my . . . the marquis doing, Jane?"

"He looked sort of . . . like my governess when she's teaching me. He was explaining something to Father, but he wasn't waving his hands in the air. He didn't seem at all angry to me."

Hugh Denville raised Jane's hand to his lips. "Well done, Jane. I'll hold a place for you at the spy academy when you come of age."

"Thank you, sir, but I don't want to be a spy when I grow up."

"I agree, poppet. One spy in the family is quite enough," said Olivia. "Though you do seem to have a talent for it, my love. Go back again."

"Make this the last time, Jane," said the duchess, torn between encouraging her daughter to spy, an odious occupation, and her desire to know what was happening in the library.

Helena lost her self-control and said with asperity, "I've had quite enough of awaiting the outcome of this. I cannot allow *my* fate to be decided by my obstinate father." She stormed out of the room, but when she entered the library, her mouth fell open at an astonishing sight. Poor Jane was entangled in an overturned potted palm on the terrace. Waverley looked on in amusement while her father helped Jane extricate herself from the mess of broken stems and fronds.

On the verge of tears Jane said, "I tripped, Helena."

"Indeed you did, dearest. Are you all right?"

"Was it you who put her up to spying on us?"

Helena's face flushed in indignation. "How dare you make such an accusation, Father! I would never stoop to such a low trick."

"Livy said I could," the child said helpfully.

The duke said gently, "I won't scold you, if you promise not to eavesdrop again. Find someone to help you bathe and change." The duke waited for the child to scurry away before he shut the terrace door.

"Helena, his lordship and I . . ." he began.

"Have you decided my fate, then? How kind, Father. How *very* kind. With all due respect, I beg to differ. No matter what you have to say to it, I am determined to marry Lord Waverley. I am well aware of the fact that his reputation is less than sterling, but that is my own affair. If I don't care one whit, why should . . . anyone?"

"I see, but—"

Her eyes blazed. "Rake or no, this man was prepared to die to save me from ruin! Doesn't that mean anything to you?"

"Noble of him, but I'm trying to—"

"*I* might have died when that horrid Harry Trasker locked me in the old cellar. Indeed, I might not be here if the Earl of Glynhaven had had his way. I'd be in France suffering the humiliation of being wed to the worst scoundrel in the world. Lord Waverley risked life and limb to save me."

"So you've said, Helena. However—"

"If you think to throw up in my face once again the fact that the man I love is a rake, you may save your breath, because I know all about his past and I don't care! I love him and I'll never give him up."

Exasperated, her father put his hand up and thundered, "Be silent, daughter! Yes, he is a rake. He's known all over Paris as—"

"*Le roué Anglais!*" She folded her arms in defiance. "What difference can it make to you if it makes none to me?"

Provoked beyond endurance, the duke was roused to anger. "And if you find he hasn't reformed his ways after you marry, what will you do then, daughter?"

"He wouldn't be the first man to do such a thing, would he? Are you not the perfect example of such a case?"

The duke turned beet red. "Don't force me to change my mind, Helena, a thing I can bloody well do even though I've given my word to his lordship!"

"And besides, not only did he save me from the clutches of that blackguard Glynhaven, you owe the marquis thanks for saving us all from scandal by arranging for the transport of the earl to France to face sentencing there." She hesitated. "He saved his worst enemy from losing his bloody life for all our sakes! Wouldn't that have made a pretty picture? How your opponents in Parliament would have gloated! What's more, you have no idea of the good he does at Waverley Park. His people there worship him!"

She turned to Waverley. "Isn't that right, my darling? Tell my father that there isn't a tenant farmer under your wing who would not vouch for you. They respect you for what you've become, not what you once were and furthermore—"

Thunderstruck, she stopped and stared at her father. "*What did you just say?*"

Her tirade at an end, the duke let out a sigh of relief. "I said you have my consent to marry Waverley, you stubborn puss."

"Oh, Father! Why didn't you say so?" She ran into his embrace, tears of happiness streaming down her face.

The duke barked a laugh. "I have been trying to tell you, but you were too busy raking me over the coals to listen. When did you turn into such a hothead, my dear? I give you leave to marry your rake, your . . . er . . . *reformed* rake, that is." He rang for a servant.

"Ask her grace to join us," he said to the footman who answered his ring.

Helena wrapped her arms around Waverley's neck. "You've wrought a miracle today, my love."

"If you must know, his lordship held a gun to my head, so to speak." Though harsh, the duke's words were tinged with humor.

"Did he indeed?" Her grace said, overhearing his remark as she entered the library. "My compliments, your lordship, for . . . er . . . *persuading* his grace to bend to your will when even I could not. How did you do it, sir?"

Waverley's lively eyes spoke volumes. "It wasn't difficult, your grace, once he heard me out."

"What does the duke mean about holding a gun to his head, Lord Waverley?"

"I merely delivered grandmother's message."

Helena beamed. "Wish me happy, Mother. Father has consented to my marriage to Waverley."

"Oh, good! You've come to your senses at last." The duchess squeezed her husband's hand reassuringly. She turned to Waverley and added, "Now I can reveal the contents of your grandmother's letter. The dowager has asked me to help her repair your damaged reputation, sir. It would be best to begin after your wedding takes place, I think."

"They can be wed right here. Charles can perform the ceremony in our chapel and . . ."

"No!" Waverley shouted the word, startling the others.

"No? What on earth do you mean, my love?" Helena stepped away from him, restraining the impulse to keep her arms wrapped around his neck. "Why not here, now that my father no longer objects to our marriage?"

Waverley smiled at her. "We'll be wed as soon as may be, but the wedding must take place at Waverley Castle."

"You are wrong, sir! The wedding must take place here at Bodmin Castle. It's a tradition in our family!" thundered the exasperated duke.

Waverley folded his arms and glared. "No. We shall wed at Waverley Castle or not at all!"

"Bodmin, I say!"

"Waverley it must be!"

In the midst of this shouting match, the duchess took her daughter's hand and led her out of the library, shutting the door behind them. To Helena's bewilderment, her ordinarily dignified mother leaned against the wall and laughed so hard, she cried.

"I fail to see any humor in this situation, Mother," Helena said unhappily.

"Wait till you have your own children, dear," she said, wiping tears of laughter from her eyes. "It may not matter to you who wins this battle, but it matters to the Marquis of

Waverley. If he wins, his future father-in-law will respect him for it and that's what he's after, don't you see?"

"Yes, I think so, but I wanted to marry here, where you and Livy were wed."

"What difference does it make where you tie the knot, you goose? You'll both win. You'll get the husband you desire and the marquis will get the respect he needs from your father if the wedding takes place at Waverley Castle."

The library door opened just then, and Waverley beckoned to them. His lips mouthed the words *I've won!* to the amusement of the duchess and to the relief of Helena.

The duke sat at the head of the long library table, his hands planted firmly like a schoolmaster about to begin a lesson. "Take a seat, please. Waverley has persuaded me that the wedding must take place at his castle, for the sake of strengthening his position in Land's End, you see. That's crucial if the marquis is ever to take a seat in Parliament, which I hope he will consider."

The marquis choked on his brandy at this bald lie, for he had no thought of parliament.

The duke ignored him. "It remains for us to decide how best to redeem his reputation. I won't have my daughter suffer any more scandal. She's been punished enough."

"I'll do anything you say to protect Helena from being shunned by Polite Society. We'll do whatever you suggest, your grace," said Waverley earnestly.

"Good! For a start, we'll announce your betrothal at Georgiana's ball," said the duchess.

"No, Mother," said Helena with firmness. "I won't agree to a betrothal for a second time. I would prefer it if you would announce our *marriage* at my sister's ball."

"Be reasonable, Helena. There's not enough time to arrange a proper wedding before Georgie's debut ball."

"We can be married right away, Mother," Helena replied. "Waverley Park is only a day's journey from here."

"Impossible."

"No it isn't, Ellen," interjected the duke. "With a special license, Charles can marry them whatever day they choose."

"Please say yes, Mother. Waverley Castle has a lovely chapel. Besides, I couldn't agree to marry without the dowager's presence. That dear lady means too much to both of us." She paused and searched Waverley's eyes for confirmation. When he gave her a slight nod, she became emboldened. "Waverley isn't a poet like Byron and I'm not a lady of fashion like Lady Lamb. In fact, neither of us cares if we never see London again."

Her mother smiled at this impassioned speech. "Except for Georgie's debut, of course. You wouldn't want to hurt your sister and miss that occasion, would you?"

Helena saw approval in her mother's eyes. Precisely what she needed. "Except for Georgie's debut," she agreed. "At her ball, Father will announce us to the *ton* as the Marquis and Marchioness of Waverley."

"No bride visits, your grace. My wife and I shall sail for the continent immediately following Georgiana's ball. She's always yearned to travel and I want that to be my wedding gift to her."

Helena's eyes flew open. "Oh yes! That would be wonderful."

"Good notion, Waverley. By the time you return from your honeymoon, you will be well established and the gossip will have disappeared," said the duchess.

The duke exchanged a knowing look with his wife, one of those secret glances between spouses that spoke volumes. "My wife and I are not without influence, you know."

"Thank you both. When we return to England, Bannington House will be ready to receive us. We shall reside there long enough to entertain visitors. Is that to your liking, your grace?"

The duke turned to his wife and took her hand. "Well, ma'am? Have you any objections?"

"A fine time to ask me, after you and Waverley have already agreed." She giggled like a young girl and added, "I dare the doyennes of Almack's or anyone else to snub the daughter of the Duke and Duchess of Heatham and the grandson of the Dowager Marchioness of Waverley."

"It only remains to decide on what day the wedding will take place," said the duke. "What say you?"

"Lady Helena and I shall decide that. But for now, let us all join the family and share the happy news," said Waverley.

"Jane shall have an extra scone for her work as . . . er . . . courier this afternoon," remarked the duke as he offered an arm to his wife.

Waverley attended to his beloved. "I've won, haven't I? It was a hard battle, but you're about to become mine at last."

Before the betrothed couple received the good wishes of the family, word spread among the servants. Under maids and footmen managed to find an excuse to linger in the hallway polishing the already shined brass or dusting spotless tables to wish the couple happy, while the upper servants, many of whom had known Lady Helena since infancy, entered the drawing room to wish her ladyship and the marquis happy.

Jane was not overlooked for her role in the day's affairs, for when tea was served, her sisters urged her to eat as many sweets as she liked. Oddly, this appeared to produce the opposite result. The youngest Fairchild managed to limit her choices to two scones slathered with clotted cream.

Not surprisingly, it was the marquis who received the most praise for the day's events. His eyes glowed at the unaccustomed attention.

"How on earth did you win my father's approval?" asked Olivia.

The marquis laughed. "No use trying to worm my secret

out, milady. I promised your father that my lips would remain sealed."

"When will you two tie the knot?" asked Georgiana, hoping it would not overshadow her debut ball.

"Who's getting married?" interrupted Edward when he and his uncle entered the drawing room. His gaze fell on his father for an answer.

"Your sister Helena is going to marry Lord Waverley." The duke added, "She has my blessing," a challenge in his voice.

"Bravo, Father," said Edward.

"Well done, duke! I'm glad you've come to your senses, big brother."

"How is it everyone claims to have known my mind before I did," grumbled the duke.

"There, there, your grace," his wife soothed after the laughter died down. "It isn't that we knew what was in your mind, so much as the fact that your family counted on you to do the right thing."

When the family dispersed to change for dinner, Waverley held Helena back. "I want a word, my love," he said quietly. "Fancy a stroll in the garden?"

She took his arm and allowed him to lead her to a secluded bench. He held her to him in a tender embrace. "My good fortune overwhelms me, love. I never thought it possible. Shall you really be my wife?"

"Yes. Unless, of course, you decide to cry off," she teased.

"Never."

Helena searched his eyes. "What's troubling you?"

"Too much has been left unsaid. I can't erase them, but I regret my past mistakes bitterly. And I cannot like the fact that your reputation may suffer when you marry me. Perhaps we ought to wait to marry after all. Give people time to forget my past."

"No, darling. We won't postpone our life together a

moment longer than necessary. Leave it to my parents and your grandmother to mend both our reputations."

He grinned. "They'll do it, too."

"Your reputation as a rake is as good as forgotten. Although . . ."

"Have you some objection to the loss of my loathsome past?"

She sighed and leaned her head on his comfortable shoulder. "Only one. Must I forgo the opportunity to experience an orgy?"

"Do you wish to join me in an orgy, dearest?"

"Would it be fun?"

"Oh yes. I'll arrange one for us, but the only two people to take part in it will be the wicked marquis and his disreputable marchioness. Will that do?"

"I suppose I shall have to be content with that." She sighed in mock despair. "On the other hand, I look forward to our wonderful honeymoon on the continent. How clever of you to think of it."

He raised her head and kissed her on the tip of her nose. "What day would you like to wed your rake, my love?"

"Tomorrow?" she asked hopefully.

He barked a laugh of joy. "Too soon, my love. I'll return home tomorrow morning. Give me a week to arrange things. You and your family may join me whenever it suits. We'll marry next Saturday morning, on the thirtieth of May. I'll invite as many of the townspeople as I can fit into the chapel. But the wedding breakfast must include everyone: the townsfolk, our servants and all our tenants. We cannot deprive our own people of that pleasure, can we?"

"No, of course not. We'll celebrate with a grand feast. Tell Cook to begin preparing our wedding breakfast."

Chapter 31

Saturday, the Thirtieth of May, 1818

Weddings celebrate tradition. For Lady Helena Fairchild, dreams of a happy marriage began in her twelfth year of life when she set her sights on the boy next door and wove day-dreams of having his children, of presiding over his house-hold, of celebrating his joys and sharing his sorrows. Like so many females, she had no doubt she would be the perfect wife to Ambassador Christopher Darlington. But she chose the wrong man to lavish her love upon. What had she learned from that grievous error? She was sure she'd learned enough to know her mind this time around.

Tradition. Last night she and her sisters sat in a circle and listened to their mother tell the story of the day Lady Helena was born. Her father had been disappointed, for he had hoped for an heir, but his dismay didn't last long, for he fell in love with this new miracle at once. "Livy needs a sister for a playmate. You'll do, funny face," he'd said as he'd danced around the room holding his second child and crooning nurs-ery rhymes to her.

Tradition. The bride's uncle Charles would perform the

ceremony. Her sister Mary would play the wedding march. Her sisters Olivia and Georgiana would be her attendants. Her brother Edward and her brother-in-law Sebastian would escort the attendants to their seats. Her sister Jane would walk down the aisle strewing rose petals before the bride. The Duke of Heatham would escort his daughter to the altar, where the Marquis of Waverley would be waiting for her.

Tradition. The bride would wear her mother's wedding gown, as her sister Olivia had done before her. The bride's abigail, Amy, had spent hours lengthening the gown, for the bride was taller than both her mother and her sister.

Tradition was altered slightly when the groom insisted upon the marriage taking place at Waverley rather than Bodmin, but in the excitement surrounding the nuptials no one seemed to mind the change.

Amy spread the ivory Belgian lace gown studded with crystals on top of the clean linen on the floor. Two under maids had been summoned to help the bride step into the fragile gown. Helena's heart warmed at the thought that Georgiana, Mary and Jane would also wear her mother's wedding gown one day. She prayed it could be made large enough for her chubby little sister Jane. When Helena was fully dressed, the result was nothing short of astounding. Not surprising, for that is the way it is with brides. She peered in the mirror in wonder at her transformation while Amy and the under maids expressed appreciation for their part in dressing the bride with audible sighs.

Who is this beauty in the mirror? Is this really me? Yes! Who would have thought it? Is this the timid lass, that naïve ninny who once yearned to know the secret of what to do with her arms and her legs during life's intimate moments? The thought tickled her and she laughed out loud for the sheer joy of it.

A knock on the door was followed by a riot of sisters tumbling into her bedchamber.

"What's so funny?"

"Don't ask, Livy," Helena answered, blushing.

"Beware impure thoughts on your wedding day, love," her sister said with a sly grin.

"How do you like my gown?" Jane interrupted, whirling around.

"Lovely, poppet. Pink is your color. The truth is, if we were alone, I'd be bound to confess that you were the prettiest of all my sisters, but I can't say it because they're all here and I don't want to hurt their feelings. Now don't you go falling over potted palms and dirtying yourself on my wedding day." Jane beamed as the bride bent to plant a kiss on the top of her head.

"I'm ready, dear sisters. Shall we go?"

At once, Olivia gathered up her sister's bridal train and Georgiana opened the door only to find the duke waiting in the hallway.

"Go on ahead, girls, if you please. It is a father's right to escort his daughter on the occasion of her marriage." The duke was resplendent in a gray striped silk coat and black morning trousers, accompanied by a meticulous white shirt and neck cloth.

One by one, she kissed each of her sisters. When they were out of earshot, she said, "Thank you, Father, for giving me your blessing."

"I wish you happy, Helena."

The bride could not answer, for fear she would not be able to hold back her tears at her father's unaccustomed tender words.

In spite of such short notice—the marquis sent personal invitations to guests hastily written by his secretary, Rupert, and hand delivered by his own footmen only days before—Waverley Chapel was filled to overflowing. Indeed, the doors had been thrown open to the garden terrace to accommodate additional guests. Land's End folk thought themselves privileged to witness the wedding of the Fourth Marquis of Waverley, a hero in their eyes since the capture of the rogue smugglers. The grand wedding would be talked about for years to come.

When the Duke of Heatham gave his daughter's hand to the Marquis of Waverley at the altar, he hoped to God he had not been mistaken as to his son-in-law's reformed character. Even so, he was relieved when the ceremony was at an end.

A few clouds did nothing to mar the festivities. Wedding guests met the fine weather with a sigh of relief, for it meant their finery—for many wore their nicest clothing—would not suffer.

The lavish wedding breakfast was served on the terrace, with round tables and chairs arranged on the vast lawn around a platform erected for dancing.

While the musicians were tuning up, his grace begged a few words with his new son-in-law. "I mean to hold you to your promise, Waverley. It is up to you to make sure no hint of scandal ever appears to embarrass my daughter or her family. Do I make myself clear?"

"You have every right, your grace, to doubt my reformation, considering my scandalous past, but it is for love of your daughter that I myself have no qualms. I mean to do everything in my power to make the woman I love happy."

"Prove my fears wrong, Waverley, and you will find in me a staunch ally."

"I welcome such an alliance, sir. My hope is that Polite Society agrees with you, for my wife's sake."

The duke chuckled. "They most certainly will, if your grandmother and I have anything to say to the matter. Polite Society tends to ignore our peculiarities because the Fairchild family has already earned the reputation of eccentricity, but they dare not ignore your formidable grandmother."

"In that case, I'll fit right in, won't I?" He turned at a tap on his shoulder from his bride. She had changed into one of her own gowns, so Mother's wedding gown could to be returned without damage to Bodmin Castle for storage. Helena beamed at the two most important men in her life. "Excuse me, but I want to dance with my father. Do you mind, husband?"

Waverley grinned. "Not at all, wife. I shall find my grandmother and see if I can persuade her to dance with me."

The duke offered his daughter his arm and led her onto the hastily built wooden dance floor for the waltz. "In the loss of you, I feel somewhat deprived. My family appears to be diminishing, Helena."

"You haven't lost a daughter, Father. You've gained another son and I mean to see to it he makes us both proud."

He smiled, but the worry in his eyes would not go away. "We need more men in the family, I suppose."

Helena and the duke turned their heads to the terrace, startled by the sound of applause. They saw Waverley resting one foot on the top terrace step and the other on the step below. He held his grandmother's hand, his face registering pride as she smiled and nodded serenely to everyone. A diamond tiara on her head enhanced her queenly stature. She wore a pale lilac gown trimmed with ermine at the wrists and at the hem. The adulation erased the lines of age from her face, which seemed surrounded by a glow very like a halo as her grandson led her to the floor.

Dancers stepped off the platform to give them the stage all to themselves. Heads craned one behind the other to witness the event. The musicians began a slow waltz, her grandson put one hand on her waist, the dowager gathered her train with one hand and gave the other hand to him. They floated across the floor effortlessly, and the eighty-year-old marchioness appeared to become young once more.

The bride and her father broke the spell when they stepped back onto the platform and exchanged partners.

"You bewitch me with your beauty, madam," said the duke. "Dowager, indeed! Come to London for my daughter's debut ball, my girl, and I'll introduce you to a score of suitors guaranteed to fight for your hand."

"Flatterer," she chided, but the look on her face showed joy. "All right, duke. I'll come to your daughter's ball, but I won't be looking for a man to replace my dear departed husband. One marriage was enough for me." She paused as he turned her in the opposite direction, then added slyly, "But if a handsome young man of, say, twenty or so discloses an interest, I might entertain an assignation."

The duke burst out laughing hard enough to cause heads to turn their way. "Why you incorrigible flirt. At your age?"

"At any age, duke. At any age."

"What do you suppose your grandmother said to Father to make him laugh so heartily?"

Waverley's attention was drawn away from his wife's breasts. "Hmm? Sorry, love. My thoughts were otherwise engaged." He pulled her closer and kissed her.

"Desmond! Not in front of all these people!"

"Why not? It's legal now, isn't it?" He tried to kiss her again, but she pushed him away, laughing just the same.

"I asked you a question."

"Question? Oh, yes. I recall. Something about Grandmother, wasn't it?" He thought for a moment. "Whatever Grandmother said, it was bound to be shocking to make him laugh so. She may be old, but her mind is still young. We mustn't interfere with her bit of mischief. She gets such pleasure from it. I say let her have her fun. She retains, I'm happy to say, a wicked sense of humor sometimes bordering on the risqué."

At the steps of the terrace, Waverley and his bride were engaged in bidding farewell to their guests, an exhausting, but necessary duty. Helena's smile hurt her face, in fact. Even so, it would not do to frown this day.

"Bear up, dearest," said Waverley when his weary bride leaned against him. "Our guests will all be gone soon enough."

"A bittersweet moment for me, my love. Half of me doesn't want this wonderful day to end, and the other half can't wait to climb into your bed and ravish you."

"Really? I had a notion you'd be too tired for . . ."

Her eyes blazed with indignation. "For making love? Never! Don't even think such a horrid thought, you beast."

"All packed, my dear?" asked the duchess. "The girls are ready to leave as well."

Her words gladdened the duke for they signified the end of their estrangement. "Yes, of course. I've sent my valet to inform the others to meet us at the front steps." He began to offer her his arm, and when she took it, he surprised her by taking her into his arms and kissing her in a way that deprived her of breath.

"Tony," she said as if shocked, but she did not push him away.

"I'm sorry if I caused you any pain over this affair, my dear heart. I never meant to hurt you. Can you forgive me if I promise that it will never happen again?"

His wife rested her head on his shoulder, to hide the giggles bubbling up within her, unseemly for a duchess. And though she knew he'd once again made an impossible promise he was sure to break, she also knew it to be his Achilles

heel. He could not help himself, yet she loved the poor crea-
ture enough to go on forgiving him for the rest of their lives.

The family carriages were lined up in a row, awaiting their
departure. The first held their grandson, his mother and his
nurse, as well as Jane and Mary, who had already said their
good-byes to the bride and groom.

"Give your grandfather a kiss, you little rascal," said the
duke, reaching for the infant. To his surprise, he got not the kiss
he requested, but a rude sound made by puckering his lips and
blowing out air, a new trick the child had learned from his aunt
Jane. His grandfather laughed at this impertinence, which gave
the child an opportunity to clap his hands in delight.

The second carriage awaited the Duke and Duchess of
Heatham and their daughter Georgiana, who kissed the new-
lyweds quickly, for she had no patience for long farewells.

The duke led his new son-in-law aside for some final cau-
tionary words, which Waverley accepted in good grace, having
heard them several times before ad nauseum.

This gave the duchess the opportunity to speak privately to
her daughter. "Retain your serenity, my child, even in the face
of disaster. And refrain from quarreling with your husband.
There are better ways to skin a cat, as they say."

"What are they, Mother?"

"My advice to you is the same I gave to Olivia when she
married Sebastian. When you disagree with your husband, remember to say, 'Yes, dear.' Then you may do as you please."

Their parental duties dispensed with, the ducal couple took
their leave. Behind them a train of carriages filled with servants
and luggage rolled down the circular drive to the road that
would take them to Bodmin Castle, their first stop on the way
home to London. Lord Edward, Sir Sebastian, Uncle Charles,
and Hugh Denville followed the caravan on horseback.

Waverley and his bride remained standing on the steps
until the last carriage was out of sight. When they turned back

into the castle, they had to run the gauntlet of smiling servants wishing them happy, a ritual they met with grace.

They stopped to see the dowager. "How are you feeling, Grandmother?"

"I've been thinking," she answered in her brusque way. "It's time I moved to the dower house to allow you two to begin your life together without my interference. You don't need an old lady in your way."

"Absolutely not," said Helena. "You belong here with us, ma'am."

Waverley added staunchly, "I insist you remain living with us. We're agreed on this point. Isn't that right, dear?"

"Nonsense. I'll only be in your way."

Waverley grinned at her. "If I have to tie you to your bedpost, you are not removing to the dower house. Your home is with us. Is that understood?"

A smile played on her lips as the dowager leaned back on her pillow and closed her eyes. "Shut the door on your way out, you scamps, before I catch a chill."

In Waverley's chamber, their honeymoon nest, at least until it was time for them to leave for London, Helena slid her hands into her husband's trousers.

"What are you doing, you wretch?" His eyes held mock surprise.

"Isn't it obvious? I want to make love to my husband. You said yourself that it's perfectly legal now. And I have the special license to prove it. I assure you, I'm ready to ravish you."

"Are you? I hadn't noticed." He swooped her up into his arms and carried her to his bed.

"Aren't you going to put me down?"

"Of course." He laid her gently on the bed.

"Where are you going," she asked when he turned toward the door.

"To tell the servants to disappear." He opened the door and looked out, surprised to see no one. He closed it and locked it.

Helena laughed as he came toward her. "There's no one here but me, lover." She reached for his neck cloth with one finger and pulled him toward her. "I'll show you." She teased his lips open and explored him deep with her tongue.

"One kiss and I'm hard. Where did you learn such a trick?"

She looked down, grinned and took his hand. "Let's not waste any more time, my wicked rake. You have a duty to perform."

His lips twitched. "Duty? What do you mean?"

"You must consummate our marriage." She wiggled her eyebrows.

He laughed. "Haven't I already done that?"

"I mean legally, as man and wife. Can we have an orgy?"

"Ordinarily orgies require more than two people, but I'll think of something special for my bride. Are you ready?"

Her breath hitched at the thought. "What do you want me to do?"

"Take off your clothes. Slowly." He took a seat on a chair near the wall, tilted back on two of its legs and folded his arms across his chest.

She loosened the ribbons of her gown and exposed one breast. "Shall I close the drapes first?"

"No. An orgy isn't an orgy unless we think someone is watching. Go on."

She exposed the other breast.

"Try for a bit more lust, if you please."

She licked her lips and moaned.

"Better. Proceed."

Her gown slid to the floor.

"No chemise? Promising. Remove your shoes and stockings one article at a time. Not too fast, mind."

"When does the orgy part begin?" She lay down and kicked off one shoe.

"It's already begun, or haven't you noticed?"

She kicked off the other shoe. "How can I tell?" She rolled down one stocking, arched her foot and slid it off with the toe of her other foot.

"You have only to view my . . . er . . . equipment." His chair fell into place and he rose. "See?"

"Indeed I do." She raised her arms over her head and stretched. "Will you be so good as to remove my other stocking, dear rake?"

"With pleasure, lusty wench." He rolled it down and removed it, covering her leg with tantalizing kisses. She gasped when his tongue licked her toes. He looked up. "Seems you really are ready for me."

She rose to her knees. "No. First you must disrobe for my pleasure. Slowly, my rake."

"You are the very devil of a temptress, my love. I'm so hard, I may not be able to lower my trousers."

"Oh, good! Let me help." She sat on the edge of the bed and pushed his trousers past his knees. Her tongue found his member and he groaned.

"Not. So. Fast."

She grasped his buttocks and took in more of him. He stopped her long enough to remove the rest of his clothing. "Lie down and let the orgy begin!"

He pressed her flat on her back and spread her thighs to examine her treasure.

"For heaven's sake, Desmond. Why have you stopped?"

"It's my orgy, too. I have a mind to admire my new possession." He kissed her thigh and she moaned.

"Make love to me."

"How? Like this?" He kissed her other thigh.

"Oooh! Yes, like that. Do it again."

He laughed and ran his tongue from the inside of one thigh

to the other, stopping where he knew he would elicit a stream of moans from his passionate bride.

"Orgy be damned. I want you now, husband."

"With pleasure, wife." He entered her easily, for he was hard and she was wet.

She arched her back to meet his thrusts, the rhythm steady like music, albeit silent yet thunderous.

He stopped to study her face.

"Why have you stopped?"

"I want to see if you are ready to fly with me."

She raised her head to suck his nipple. "Try me." She grasped his buttocks, and when he resumed, she moved to his rhythm.

Her spasms helped him to climax with her at the same time. He roared like a triumphant lion, rolled over and panted from the exertion.

"That was fun. I'll have another orgy at once, if you please."

"At once? Are you trying to kill me, wife? Another orgy at once may well cripple me for life."

She laughed, as he'd intended. "In that case, I'll let you have a bit of a rest first." She hopped off the bed.

He clasped his hands behind his head. "Where are you going, wife?"

"Fancy some cold chicken?"

"Have we any wine?"

She returned with a platter of fried chicken and a bottle of red wine Rabu had hidden at her request. "I couldn't carry glasses."

"No matter. We'll drink it from the bottle."

She handed him the wine and sat cross-legged on the bed. "Not bad for our first orgy as husband and wife."

"But not the last, my lusty raven." His eyes devoured the dark-eyed beauty who was now his wife. When he leaned toward her and licked her breast, she raised her eyes in surprise.

"What did you do that for?"

A wicked grin stole across his face. "Just removing a piece

of chicken. I refuse to share you with anyone or anything. And certainly not with chicken, my darling."

A slow grin filled with mischief crept across her face. She picked up the wine as if to drink but deliberately missed her mouth and allowed the dark red liquid to trickle down her breasts. The wine collected in a puddle between her thighs. "How clumsy of me. Just look at what I've done. Won't you help me clean it up?"

He removed the bottle of wine from her hand and the plate of chicken and placed them on the bedside table. "I thought I married a prim and proper lady, gentle Helena. Who's the rake now, I wonder?" His tongue lapped up every drop of the wine.

"No longer shall you be known as *le roué Anglais,*" my love." Her hand found his rising member.

"No? I rather liked that name. It set me apart from the ordinary. How do you plan to change it?"

"Easy, wicked marquis. I shall call you *mon roué Anglais.* Never fear. You shan't have to surrender your customary role as a rake, for I mean to keep you enslaved with a lifetime of splendid orgies."

AUTHOR'S NOTE

Le Chabanais, a famous brothel in Paris (1878–1946), took its name from its location not far from the Louvre, at 12 rue Chabanais. Many wealthy investors bought shares in this profitable enterprise. Understandably, these gentlemen insisted upon anonymity.

The entry hall led a client through a bare stone cave and the bedrooms were exotic replicas representing various styles: Louis XVI, Japanese and Moorish, to name just a few.

The Prince of Wales, who became King Edward VII, was the brothel's most famous client. "Bertie" (in an article in 2004, the *Times* referred to him as "Dirty Bertie") preferred a bedroom that carried his coat of arms and contained a tub filled with champagne large enough for the obese prince and his ladies. Guy de Maupassant preferred the Moorish room when he visited.

Toulouse-Lautrec, also a well-known client, painted sixteen tableaus for Le Chabanais. These survive and are now in private hands.

The Nazis appropriated Le Chabanais for use by their officers and Nazi sympathizers during the occupation of France in World War II.

Today, the Museé de l'Erotisme in Pigalle displays a loveseat used by the Prince of Wales in its exhibitions. In 2003, BBC Four produced a documentary (*Storyville—Paris Brothel*) that contains footage of Le Chabanais.

I haven't found any evidence that Le Chabanais rented rooms by the month, but this is a work of fiction and my rake needed a place to live.

—Pearl Wolf

ABOUT THE AUTHOR

Pearl Wolf published her first work of fiction—a short anecdote for *Reader's Digest*—when she was fourteen years old. For this effort, she received the grand sum of $5.00. That was enough to start her on her writing career. Pearl is active in several writers organizations including New Jersey Romance Writers, Florida Romance Writers, NYC Mystery Writers of America and Sisters in Crime, NY–Tristate Chapter (past president). When she isn't writing, she loves to play duplicate bridge and is a life master. She lives in Manhattan, and has two sons and three grandsons. Readers can visit her at www.pearlwolf.com.